SALVATION

SHOLEM ASCH

SALVATION

TRANSLATED BY
WILLA AND EDWIN MUIR

SCHOCKEN BOOKS · NEW YORK

AUTHOR'S FOREWORD

TO SECOND EDITION

I know of no better way to express my sorrow for the tragedy of my people, the Jews of Poland who perished under Hitler, and to comfort myself and others, than to bring to the attention of my readers the everlasting religious values that Polish Jewry left behind. For our ancestors in times past these values were an inspiration to a better moral and ethical way of life; I hope they may provide comfort and uplift for us today.

This is one of the reasons why my publishers and I have decided to bring out my book *Salvation* in a new and revised edition.

Though *Salvation* has been translated into many European languages and has been the subject of much discussion, my impression is that comparatively few of my American readers have actually read it. In 1934, when it was first published in this country, the public was not much inclined to books of a religious nature, and the subject, Jewish spiritual life, was perhaps its chief handicap.

Despite the beautiful and faithful translation into English, from the German edition, by Willa and Edwin Muir (to whom I wish to express my affectionate gratitude), some errors crept in, mostly concerning the customs of Jews in Poland in the early nineteenth century and matters of Jewish ritual and teaching. Also, several chapters that I believe to be essential to the theme were omitted from the first edition, because of a conviction that at that time they would not be understood by the general reader.

In this new edition the errors are corrected, the omitted chapters restored, and some material eliminated that tended to overload the book with details.

It remains to mention the fact that the original title of the book was "The Psalm Jew" and that it bears this title in those languages which possess an equivalent term. In English it would be meaningless, and *Salvation* expresses the character and idea of the book in a word that is common ground for Jew and Christian alike.

SHOLEM ASCH

January, 1951

CONTENTS

BOOK ONE

CHAPTER I

THE SPRINGTIME OF A
JEWISH CHILD

*"I was cast upon thee from the womb; thou art my God from my
mother's belly."*

AN evil time had dawned for the world. The wars of Gog and
Magog had been raging, and the peoples who had been pressed
into Napoleon's armies had just passed through the land. Like
a swarm of locusts they had covered the earth, had slept in every bed,
eaten out of every dish.

Defiled and trampled like a tortured body, the whole land now lay
waste, groaning under the wounds that had been inflicted upon it.
The wars of Gog and Magog were over, but the Messiah was late in
coming and there was no sound of his footsteps.

The young mother lay in her snowy bed, her hand on the head of
her second son. Rivke [the diminutive form of the Biblical name
Rebecca] knew the duties of a daughter in Israel. She was aware that
God had created her to bring many souls from heaven to earth. For
until all heavenly souls have descended to the lower sphere the Messiah
cannot appear. Rivke's pious and learned husband Boruch-Moishe sat
all day in the Talmud school and the synagogue, searched God's Holy
Scripture and thus gathered treasures for himself and his wife that
would benefit them in the next world. So, like a good wife, Rivke saw
to the treasure of this world, and ever since she had felt herself a mother
had laid by each Friday before the lighting of the lamps a few groschen
in a jar specially reserved for the purpose; for she must be able to en-
tertain the guests when they came to greet the newly born and celebrate
his admission into the fellowship of Israel. And thanks to God's help
the table spread for her guests was worth seeing!

In the little chamber the Sabbath already reigned. Rivke's good
neighbor Blimele, the wife of Melech the fisherman and market vendor,
had come to help; the stone floor of the room in which the mother
lay, a living room that served also as a shop, was scoured bright

3

and festively strewn with yellow sand. The oil wicks of the brass lamps that swung from the heavy rafters gave a hospitable light, the candles on the white spread table gleamed brilliantly. The mother lay in her bed, which was decked with white linen. The snowy linen exhaled an exquisite purity, and set a great distance between the mother and the rest of the world. Beside the bed stood a little table on which a Sabbath candle burned, with Rivke's prayer book before it. Blimele, her good neighbor, sat in her Sabbath dress and festal hood beside her to help her in anything that was required. The newly born infant, bedded on a pillow, lay by the side of his mother. At her feet her oldest son slept the sleep of the just with his little Sabbath cap on his head. So everything in the room was prepared for the reception of the guests whom the father was to bring with him from the synagogue. . . .

Boruch-Moishe came back from the house of God, and with great joy saluted the Sabbath in his house, greeting the woman hidden in the white linen, "Good Shabbos, wife! God will help us to bring up our son to study the Torah, to do good deeds, and to come under the canopy."

"Amen, my husband," answered the wife from her bed.

The young father strode up and down the room in his satin caftan and fur-trimmed Sabbath cap, saluting the invisible angels who had entered the house along with him.

"Sholem aleichem, peace be with you, you angelical messengers, you angels of the Most High!"

The long shadows that his lean young body cast on the shop shelves, covered with linen for the Sabbath, followed him softly as he moved. And after him tripped his first-born, velvet Sabbath cap on head, and clapped his hands like his father and murmured along with him the greeting to the Sabbath angels. His father's coming had awakened him.

After the Sabbath blessing had been said the guests began to arrive. First the oldest among the faithful in the town was led in, the gray-bearded Reb Mordecai, a feeble old man. He wore, as was customary for old people on the Sabbath at that time, a white satin caftan and white stockings. For white is the color of grace. Although he was so infirm that his legs were scarcely able to support his weak and tottering body, he was resolved not to omit the duty, pleasing to God, of greeting a newly born child, which he had always regarded as his prerogative. Reb Mordecai was seated at the top of the long white decked table, on which stood glasses for the beer and dishes of apples and boiled peas.

And the neighbors came, men with black or red beards and faces furrowed by wind and rain, market vendors, hand workers, furriers, and hawkers. They led their children by the hand, who had also come to greet the newly born Jew.

They were simple people who sat round the table, who lived at peace with their God, addressed themselves to him in the prescribed prayers and when things went ill with them, in the words of King David, in his psalms. Most of them were members of the Psalm Fellowship, and they greeted the newly born with a beautiful song in cheerful voices, to the tune of a Polish polka brought back from a neighboring village.

"The Lord is my shepherd; I shall not want. He maketh me to lie down in green pastures: he leadeth me beside the still waters. . . ."

The young mother lying in the white bed listened to the pious songs and pressed her newly born lovingly against her heart. Her young face, too soon furrowed by the cares which the support of the family laid on her shoulders, was completely transfigured. A comforting hand seemed to have wiped all sorrow from it. Her eyes had a girlish freshness and her lips arched in a soft bow and showed no trace of the sharp lines cut there by anxiety. She gazed down happily at the little creature lying against her breast, gently passed her hand over its brow and whispered in its ear, "My child, you shall be a pious Jew like these when you grow up."

His name in Israel was Yechiel, that is to say, "the living God." He was now four years old. It was after the Paschal Feast, a spring day; the windows were wide open for the first time, and everything smelt of sunshine and new grass. Boruch-Moishe wrapped his son in a prayer shawl, the mother put a biscuit smeared with honey in his hand, so that the words of the teacher might taste sweet to him, and he was taken to the school. In front of the school was a sunny yard where one could see a patch of clear sky. Inside it was dark, but there were a great number of children, all boys like Yechiel. They sat round the walls on low stools. The teacher had terribly long arms and fingers. He flung open a book and pointed with a long pointer and the tip of his leather strap at a Hebrew A and B.

In a little while the letters A and B in the prayer book were very familiar to Yechiel, as if he had seen and learned them before at some earlier time. He discovered next that this was actually so; he found out that, before a child came to this world, an angel taught him the Torah in Heaven. But before he left Heaven for the earth, the Angel of Forgetfulness removed the heavenly knowledge from his memory. Now, as that vanished memory emerged again, the letters smiled at him like pleasant old acquaintances.

A year later the teacher read through with him the first verse of the Pentateuch: "In the beginning God created the heaven and the earth." The heaven and the earth of the Bible, too, seemed strangely familiar to him. They were not the same heaven and earth that stretched above his head and beneath his feet outside—that heaven and that earth existed, so to speak, only as examples, so that people might see what the real Heaven and earth looked like. The real Heaven and the real earth were to be found only in the Bible, and little Yechiel knew them very well; he had lived there once and would return there again when the Messiah appeared.

So already in Yechiel's earliest childhood his world fell into two worlds. The one was small and temporary and you passed through it as through a corridor. But the other, the true, the great and eternal world was contained in the letters of the Bible. These letters were quite small and yet they held so much. . . .

The childhood of a Jewish boy is not to be found in this world and this life, but among the passages in the Bible which he begins to learn in his tenderest years. On the fields where his first fathers grazed their sheep, by the wells where they drank, he dreams his childish dreams. The beasts and birds of the Bible are the only ones with which he has communication. And it is not the storm that roars outside over the plain that is real to him, but the one that descended when God made his covenant with Abraham.

God showed great consideration for the Jewish boys, for he ordained that the beautiful chapter in Genesis should be taken at a time when outside the snow was whirling through the air and the wind shaking the windowpanes that were stuffed with rags and pasted with paper.

Yechiel sat in the dark schoolroom at a table covered with a layer of tallow, to which surface the boys stuck the candles they brought with them; and in the confused shadows cast by the logs burning on the hearth the boy's great blue eyes saw the entry of the wild and tame beasts into the Ark. They came in pairs, the bull with the cow, the cock with the hen, one species after another. First the smallest, the tiniest creatures, the fly and his female, the dung beetle and his. Then came bigger and still bigger ones, and at last the leviathan and his female knocked with their mighty horns on the door of the Ark. Noah stuck his head out of the skylight, from which later he was to

release the dove, and asked, "What do you want?" And they answered
in human speech, "Take us into the Ark, for we know that God will
send a flood over the earth and drown every living creature."

At dawn, when the frost still smoked on the straw and shingle roofs
of the little town—the father and the eldest son were long since up
and gone—Rivke gently wakened little Yechiel from his sleep.
"Yechiel, wash yourself and be quick. It's late."

The six-year-old boy got up, remembering the words of the Bible,
"fleeter than the eagle and stronger than the lion." He had never yet
seen a real lion except the one in his mother's Bible with whom Samson
fought. But if "the lion rises up at morning in his might to serve God,"
Yechiel could do it too. He tore himself from the arms of sleep and
cast off the comforting lambskin coat which his mother wore when
she went to the market. He hurried over to the water barrel, filled the
pan, and poured the ice-cold water over him. His mother made to put
her wrap over his shoulders, but Yechiel knew already that a boy
mustn't let himself be touched by a woman. And before his mother
knew where she was, he had his Bible and prayer book under his arm,
had seized a burning brand from the fire, and rushed away to school.

There Abraham his forefather and Sarah were already awaiting
him. Father Abraham stood beneath a great tree and entertained the
three angels who were his guests. They ate no flesh, but only "milky"
food. Sarah listened through a chink of the door to hear what they
were saying outside.

But of all the patriarchs Yechiel liked best his forefather Jacob
while he was still a boy at home with his mother Rebecca. She loved
him more than Esau, for Jacob liked to go to school and was always
learning the Holy Scripture, while Esau went hunting. That very week
the passage describing Jacob's election was being taken and Yechiel
read of Jacob's wandering into the land of Haran and how on his way
he felt weary and gathered stones to serve as a pillow. But the stones
quarreled with one another, for each of them wanted the holy man to
rest his head on it alone.

Abraham rather terrified Yechiel; he was a stern old gentleman
and an intimate friend of God. When God commanded him he actually
took his only son Isaac, bound him hand and foot, and prepared to
slay him as a sacrifice to God. Isaac himself, however, did not impress
Yechiel in the least; the only merit that could be allowed him was his
willingness to let himself be sacrificed on the altar in honor of God;
while his hands and feet were being bound he did not even cry.

Yechiel's childish fancy tried to picture himself in the place of Isaac. No, he would never have managed to bring that off! He would have wept and cried for his mother.

He felt very close to his ancestral mother Rebecca. She was like his own mother, and he could see her casting her wrap round Jacob's shoulders and pushing a burning brand into his hand when he went off to school early in the morning. Jacob let his mother Rebecca fasten the wrap round him; Mother Rebecca might be allowed such things, for she was not an ordinary woman like his mother Rivke, but the first mother of Israel, who lay buried in the cave of Machpelah along with Isaac....

The childhood days of a Jewish boy are brief; they scarcely reach to the story of Joseph and his brethren. Yechiel learned about Joseph more through stories that he was told than through Bible instruction. For before he had come to the end of the book of Genesis he was already being instructed in the doctrines of the Talmud concerning divorce.

Before Yechiel began his study of the Talmud he had desired nothing more passionately than to be as far on as his elder brother. He was jealous when he saw Issachar every morning taking up the great folio, which he himself could scarcely hold in both hands, putting it under his arm and setting off to Yochanan the Talmudist. When Issachar was examined by his father on Sabbath afternoons, as happened now and then, or read his lessons over with his father in the evenings, Yechiel always stood behind him, zealously imitated the rocking motions which he made while he was studying, and murmured the sentences after him in the Talmud singsong, though he did not understand a word of them.

But when he had actually to exchange the lovely stories of the Bible for the dry matter-of-fact discussions of the Talmud he found little pleasure in the alteration. He had no wife yet and so had no use for divorce; accordingly the exhaustive debates on divorce did not interest him in the least. Besides, Yechiel was not particularly quick of apprehension. All endeavors by the teacher and his father to supple his mind by the intellectual gymnastics of Talmudist casuistry remained unsuccessful. There neither the teacher's strap nor his father's hard, bony hand were of any use. He had understood the stories in the Bible with ease, but his mind found corresponding difficulty in taking in the Talmud.

"I'm afraid, Rivke, that you must have been thinking of some goy when you were carrying the child. He's such a dunderhead, you would think he was descended from Esau," the father said more than once.

Rivke sighed softly as she bent over her pots and pans, and quietly took the blame to herself. But at night when the boy was sleeping on his sack of straw she bent over his hot brow and whispered with quivering lips, "My poor unhappy child! May God take pity on you and open your mind, so that you may understand His Law."

The summer, which is the happiest time for all the rest of the world, is the saddest for the Jewish boy. Scarcely were the cheesecakes finished that are eaten at the Feast of the Pentecost when the three weeks of expiation began which precede the day of mourning for the destruction of the Temple. And before one knew it the sad days were upon one. Wearily the sunshine crept over the wall outside the window of the schoolroom. Yet quite near the school a hill ran gaily down to the banks of the Vistula, and on each side of the road leading to it were green meadows on which red cows grazed. Some apple and plum trees also grew there and they were "fair game," which was to say that one could pluck their fruit unhindered, as much of it as one liked. Except for the fact that when the lame man who herded the village cattle saw any marauders he chased the "robbers," shouting and swinging his crutch. But before he could get properly under way one was beside the Vistula, and the old man was left standing. The water of the Vistula was pleasantly cool and all day rafts rocked on its waves. But in the schoolroom it was hot and nasty.

Beside the town where Yechiel lived the Vistula wound waywardly through a plain whose sandy soil was covered with willow bushes and reeds. It goes without saying that for Yechiel this stretch of country was "the land of Canaan." Beyond the river lay the green hills of the little sister town, and in the evening tiny lights gleamed out up there from houses snugly imbedded in greenery. For Yechiel these hills were "the land of Haran," and the Vistula was the Jordan. And many a Friday afternoon he set rows of sticks to mark the point in the Jordan where the children of Israel crossed when they entered the Promised Land.

On the highest hill on the opposite bank stood a ruined bastion, which dated from the time of the Polish king Kasimir the Great. It became Mount Ararat, where Noah's Ark once landed when God closed the sluices of Heaven and chained the waters of the deluge. The keel of the Ark had run against the bastion, and thereupon the walls had fallen in. But at the foot of Mount Ararat was, as everybody knew, a cave containing the "nether Paradise." One could recognize the cave by the fact that Sarah, the first mother, always sat in the entrance. She wore her most beautiful Sabbath hood and shook sweet-smelling herbs and flowers from one sieve into another, so that the fragrant odors of the earth should be wafted abroad and bring refreshment to all who diligently studied the Scriptures.

This legend took such a hold of little Yechiel that he resolved to rediscover the place where the "nether Paradise" lay. One Friday afternoon (it had to be a Friday, for one had to be lost in the woods and looking for a place where one could hold the Sabbath), Yechiel made up a plot with one of his playmates, and the two boys set out on a voyage of exploration into the land of Haran to look for Paradise. Unobserved they stole onto the raft of the ferryman Mendel and were taken over the Vistula along with peasants, horses, and cows. Having crossed, they climbed the bastion-crowned hill—of course, at a trackless, impracticable point thickly overgrown with tall grass—and pretended that they had lost themselves in the woods. They prayed that God might lead them to a Jewish house where they could hold the Sabbath, and waited tensely for the moment when the cave would open before their eyes.

But by now Rivke was alarmed that her Yechiel had not returned from school. She learned that he had been seen in the vicinity of the Vistula. That was enough for her, and she roused the whole town. And soon the mother of the other boy, too, came running to the river, wringing her hands. Everybody feared the worst.

The evening was far advanced and Rivke had given up all hope when she was brought the glad news that the two boys had been found on the other bank near the bastion. Although it was already dark a peasant had crossed the river so as to bring Rivke the good news as quickly as possible. The truants could not come with him, for that would have meant violating the Sabbath, and they spent the Saturday in the house of a Jewish family on the other side.

This was not the only time that little Yechiel showed a disposition to test everything for himself. Like every Jewish child he was much troubled in his mind by spirits. He was very afraid of them, and believed that they followed every step he took. There were good and evil spirits. The good ones, who did not torment people, assembled by night in the synagogue, took the Bible rolls from the Ark where they were kept, and encouraged each other to read them out. For the dead did not renounce all contact with the world of the living. Yankel the cobbler, who had lived in the next house, died before his wife brought her youngest child to the world. Yet Blimele had seen him with her own eyes when his wife's hour came. There he stood wrapped in his shroud before the door of his house and would not move from the spot. Only when Boruch-Moishe appeared and cried to him, "She has borne you a son, who will say the death prayer for you," did the spirit of the cobbler vanish.

But there were also evil spirits who because of their sins could find no peace in the grave. At night they went down to the river, hoping to purify themselves by bathing in it. Then it sometimes happened that one of them entered into a living man, for they longed for an earthly lodging in order to be healed and redeemed.

Little Yechiel was afraid of the good spirits as much as of the bad. After he said his prayers at night he never fell asleep without clutching firmly the sacred fringe attached to his shirt, as is laid down in the Bible, for he wanted to have something handy with which to defend himself against the spirits. He suffered from this terror of spirits for a long time, until he overcame it by an effort.

"They can't do me any harm if it's against God's will," he told himself. "So why should I be afraid of them? I've said my prayers and my fringes are kosher."

To convince himself that he had no fear of spirits Yechiel hit upon the plan of having himself locked into the synagogue one night to see the souls of the dead assembling there.

One evening in late summer, shortly before the great feast days, he set about carrying out his plan. The first shadows of dusk were creeping over the garden fences and lay thick in the narrow street where the baths were. Standing on the strip of trodden grass before the baths, Yechiel watched the sky reddening. He knew that this was the hour when the gates of Hell were shut and the dead came to the river to immerse themselves in the water. After that it would not be long before they were at the synagogue.

Now, now they were stealing nearer, the shadows wrapped in their death shrouds; they floated over the garden fences and slipped through the tiny keyhole in the door of the little synagogue. They made themselves invisible, for the evening service was not yet finished, and the candles on the precentor's desk were still burning. So the shadows hid in the darkest corners until the prayer for the dead should be chanted, for that of course concerned themselves. Now the synagogue was emptying. The candles were put out. Only the tiny spark of the perpetual light glimmered through the darkness. Now the whole synagogue was filled with shadows. But in the forecourt, where the little Psalm Room was, Reb Mordecai was still sitting, an old and feeble man.

"He is the only man alive who has no fear of spirits," Yechiel suddenly realized. "Reb Mordecai is a pious and holy man; they can do nothing to him. But they can't do any harm to me either." The boy scrutinized his sacred fringes; they were without blemish. He had no anxiety about his prayers; he knew them by heart.

Everybody had now left the synagogue, except for the attendant, who was busying himself with the Almemor. He had not noticed Yechiel. And now he too was going! He was gone! Alone! ...

"I'm not afraid, they can't do anything to me," the boy kept whispering to himself with trembling lips, firmly clutching his fringes. "God, Who reignest in truth—" With chattering teeth he began to murmur the night prayer.

The whole extent of the synagogue had vanished as if swallowed by a black monster. Even the two glittering shafts that shone through the stained-glass window above the holy ark during divine service (Yechiel called them "the horns of Moses") were quenched. The tiny glow of the perpetual light, whose dark red globe hung by a chain over the precentor's desk, seemed to drown in an ocean of darkness. Yechiel fixed his eyes on the little red light, as if from it and it alone he could expect help. No, he mustn't scream, they couldn't do anything to him, God would not allow them!

In his fear he tried to shut his eyes, but he had not the strength. And suddenly he saw *them;* they were there; in long rows they sat along the walls as if immured there. More and more countless they grew, and taller and taller. Their death shrouds billowed, the spirits were rising, coming nearer and nearer!

"I'm not afraid ... God, Who reignest in truth," Yechiel panted, half choked with tears, and then he screamed through the room, "Mother! Mother! ..."

Old Mordecai heard the scream and came out of the little Psalm Room. Holding a lighted candle in one hand, he shuffled through the darkness. Something white was making toward Yechiel. Reb Mordecai found the boy unconscious on a bench, his hand convulsively clutching his fringes. When after much struggling Yechiel awoke out of his faint, his first words were, "I'm not afraid ... God, who reignest in truth. ..."

CHAPTER II

THE WEEKDAY MOTHER
AND THE SABBATH MOTHER

WHEN Yechiel was reaching his tenth year even his mother
Rivke had to admit what everybody else was already convinced of: her boy was growing up into "a savage." First of
all, he had no pleasure in learning things. It was not merely that he
was a "dunderhead," and that one had a hard job to make him understand the doctrines of the Talmud and their interpretations; he himself had no wish to learn. Very often he played truant from school, and
helped his mother at the market or spent the day in the fields and
woods. In general he displayed very early an inclination to plunge
into everybody's business but his own.

His brother Issachar, who was three years older, was very different;
the "seal of God" was imprinted on his brow, as was but right in a
Jewish boy. His face seemed to consist of nothing but eyes and side
curls. His lathelike little body was lost in a rep caftan which seemed
three times too wide for him. Though only thirteen, he already observed fast days of his own will, and even stuck his nose now and then
in Cabbalistic books. The younger brother was considerably taller and
broader although he was only ten. His arms and legs were as strong as
those of a peasant boy. His face was burned by the sun, roughened and
sprinkled with freckles. His walk was a rush. The long tails of his
caftan, which was always open, fluttered in the wind, his side curls and
his fringes flew out in all directions.

On market days Yechiel would hastily seize the poles and planks
that made up his mother's stand and be away with them before she
could stop him. In a twinkling he had the stand set up by his own
efforts, loaded whole piles of cloth on his back and bore it off to the
market place. He not only helped his mother but the other market
women too, the clothes dealers and hatmakers. When his father heard
of it he rushed out of the House of Study and drove like a whirlwind
into the confusion of peasants' wagons. Among the stamping horses
and screeching fowls suddenly two fluttering side curls and a disheveled

beard bobbed up and a lean body violently drove a way for itself through the crowd.

"This is bad, Rivke! You'll end in Hell if you go on like this, keeping your son from his studies!"

With these words Boruch-Moishe snatched his son away from the stand and with a sudden jerk lifted him on his angular shoulders. Two naked legs and two disheveled curls dangled above his father's shoulders, and Yechiel was borne at quick march to school.

But the mother remained beside her market stand with a bleeding heart. Was not her Boruch-Moishe right? She was keeping her son from the right way by involving him in her profane work!

During the last years Rivke had fallen away sadly. Bearing children had exhausted all her powers, and she was only a shadow of herself. Her skin was lined and seamed, and although she was not yet thirty she looked like an old woman. Her body was nothing but skin and bone, and under her dark headcloth, which sat always askew, a wasted face looked out. Only her figure remained youthful; she was still slender and straight as a tree, with limbs light and graceful as the branches of a water willow.

Of the children that she had borne since Yechiel, three, to her great grief, had not survived. They had had to leave this world prematurely because of sins committed by others. All this grief for her dead children and trouble with her living ones had undermined her health. On top of that there was the worry of her profane traffic in the market. Yet that had to be, she had been created for it; she was a woman and such was her lot. But that was no reason why she should draw her own child into her unhappy fate. Her Yechiel was born for something different; he was a man.

Rivke already saw herself in Hell among serpents and salamanders, damned for eternity. Her Boruch-Moishe sat in Paradise and studied the holy Law, but the footstool at his feet which she strove to deserve by her efforts to earn bread for the family must remain empty. She would not be allowed to set foot in Paradise, for she kept her own child from his studies. So it seemed to Rivke that she had lost both worlds, this world and the next.

When she came home in the evening and with her feeble breath blew to a flame the smoldering fire under the tripod on the hearth, so that she might cook the meager supper, her husband strewed salt on her wounds.

Boruch-Moishe sat at his own table beside the only lamp in the room. Rivke busied herself at the hearth by the light of a burning pine torch. Because of her work at the market the boiled potatoes and cabbage soup were later than usual in coming to table. As Boruch-Moishe had already said the evening prayer, though the supper was not yet served, he was unwilling to begin his evening studies. So as not to sit in idleness he glanced through a little moral book (in which his eldest son immediately followed his example) and employed the opportunity to read his wife a lecture for keeping Yechiel from his lessons. While doing so he rocked in his chair and slowly stroked his thick black beard until every hair was in place. He brought out his rebukes in the Talmud singsong without raising his eyes from the book lying before him, for otherwise his glance might have rested on a woman.

"Our wise men say that there is no more grievous sin than that of keeping children from studying the Law. Any one who keeps children from their studies is to be classed with a man who has committed every sin, or a man who does a murder on Yom Kippur, the Day of Expiation, when it falls on a Sabbath. For it is written: 'It is the voices of children who study the Law that keeps the world in existence. So in holding your child from his lessons you are bringing the world to destruction. . . .' "

Rivke stood at the hearth bending over the pot of potatoes, into which fell tears from her red-lidded eyes inflamed with sun and wind. She softly repeated, "I am bringing the world to destruction—woe is me!"

Yechiel was sitting on the floor going through his Talmud lesson by the light of the torch that burned on his mother's hearth. He had no place reserved for him at the table like his elder brother: that was intended to show the savage that he was not worthy to sit with other people at the table, which served both for study and for eating and in that resembled God's altar.

In spite of his childishness of mind the boy could not reconcile his idea of the divine with evil, punishment, and hellish torments. As he saw it, evil, punishment, and hellish torments had nothing to do with God, but rather with diabolical powers, devils, and all that was bad. What such things were like, his childish imagination could not clearly grasp, but in any case they did not come from God. And whenever he heard something evil ascribed to God he rebelled against the thought in his very soul, as if a personal wrong were being done to him; and he considered it his duty to stick up for God. Without taking time to shut or cover with a cloth the great folio which he held in his hands, he cried across to the table from his place on the floor, "Mother, you won't have to roast in hell! God is a kind Father; he won't let my mother be tortured in Hell!"

"Oh, you're at it next, are you? You dare to disobey me, you dare to contradict me and sin against the commandment to honor your father!"

Boruch-Moishe rose, loosened the leather belt round his waist, seized the savage, and laid him across his knee, "This is what a son gets who doesn't honor his father!"

And Boruch-Moishe laid on with all his might.

But instead of sobbing the savage shouted, "And God *won't* let my mother roast in Hell!"

"Oh, dear, dear, that I should hear such words! Yechiel, you mustn't set yourself against your father!" The mother burst into tears.

"Don't you be afraid, mother! Don't cry! God is good!"

"You see now!" Boruch-Moishe pushed the savage back to his place on the floor and flung a glance at his wife as if to say that she was to blame for everything.

Although a child, Yechiel had already his own ideas of God. Though he could not picture to himself how God looked, he was firmly convinced of one thing: that God was everywhere and whoever wished could find Him at any time. One had only to ask Him, had only to shut one's eyes, pray humbly and earnestly, and tell oneself: Now I am standing before God. Then one actually stood before Him as before, say, a king. One was afraid of a king; one was not only afraid of God, but loved Him too.

Yechiel knew also that God was to be found always with the Jews in the House of Study, but only once a week in his parents' home. He came on Friday evening at sunset, when the Sabbath candles were lit. But in Yechiel's heart God dwelt always; there He had his dwelling place, and He knew everything that happened in Yechiel, all that Yechiel thought and wished. The boy spoke with Him as with a friend about all that moved him, "Forgive me for having eaten this apple without saying the blessing. The evil one had me in his clutches and I forgot. To make up for it I'll say the blessing twice before I eat this pear; once for the apple I have eaten, and once for the pear."

But Yechiel felt the presence of God most clearly of all during divine service in the little synagogue, when the Jews drew their prayer shawls over their heads and intoned the eighteen petitions, and particularly

when the priest pronounced the benediction. During the benediction
one was not allowed to look up. But just because it was forbidden, one
wished to do it, and let oneself be persuaded by one's evil thoughts:
then one could see God hovering over the priest's hands. . . .

The synagogue was stiflingly hot. It was Sabbath, the final prayer
was being said. Densely packed, the worshipers stood side by side,
their heads enveloped in their prayer shawls, and intoned softly the
eighteen petitions. All were sunk in breathless devotion, sighs broke
from their lips, and on their faces was a look of ecstasy. Yechiel stood
behind his father, with his prayer book in his hand. His heart was full,
but he was not praying. This set prayer did not delight him; he
wanted to do something for God that nobody else had ever done. God
would see that it was different. If God were only to ask him to do
something! How gladly he would obey, even if it were to leap into fire!

While he was considering what he could do in God's honor he
thought of the tumblers who came every year to the fair. He could not
turn a somersault as he had seen them doing; it was the one feat of
theirs that he had admired most. But he had learned another trick; he
could stand on his hands and remain there until you counted ten. That
was the longest he could manage. But for God he could hold out until
you counted a hundred, more, two hundred! And he would do it,
"Now, dear God, I will show you what I can do for you."

And at the very moment when the whole congregation was waiting
with bated breath for the Rabbi to take two steps backward, which was
the signal that the prayer was at an end, the savage made a run and
stood on his hands behind his father's back.

He stood so, his legs in the air, and murmured, "Count, dear God,
count. . . . One, two, three. . . ."

One can imagine what shame Yechiel brought on his father by
such and similar exploits. Blows and punishments were of no avail.
The savage went on with his tricks. In the middle of the divine service,
when the congregation were breathless with devotion, he would stand
on his hands or turn a cartwheel; once he actually whistled through
his fingers.

When Rivke heard of this she thought she would sink through the
floor with shame, and despairingly wrung her hands. Her face streaming with tears, she went over to her son, bowed over him, and sobbed
bitterly, "My poor child, why do you bring such shame on me?"

But Yechiel could not tell his mother that he did all this solely for
God. Patiently he endured his father's blows, and bravely he swallowed

his pain when Boruch-Moishe's thin, bony fingers seized his arm like pincers and bored into his flesh until all his limbs trembled. Yechiel did not mind that; the only thing that troubled him was that his mother was so deeply hurt. But he could not spare her that; what he did was for the love of God. And God stood nearer to him than any one else, even his parents; for God, too, knew what Yechiel knew; that he did these strange things not because he himself wished to, but because the evil one goaded him on to do them. He did not want to offend his mother, but to be an obedient son to her; he desired nothing more ardently than to learn diligently and sit perpetually over books like his brother Issachar and be praised by everybody; he did not wish to run off to the market place to help his mother, but he could not look on while she dragged the heavy planks from the shop into the street, he could not endure that she should stand in the market quite by herself.

The father—and the boy knew that—was destined for other things. He had to sit and study in the House of Study. The other life was for his mother; she was a woman and it was her lot. Only a few days before Yechiel had seen his mother compelled to wrestle with a gigantic peasant for a few yards of cloth. Her neck grew tense, her face was dreadful to see, her red-rimmed, bloodshot eyes started out of their sockets. With supernatural strength she shouted for help, "Good people! He's robbing me in broad daylight!" Yechiel could never forget the moment when the peasant gave his mother a blow on the chest, so that she rolled into the middle of the street. Everybody saw it. Yechiel had stood by crying.

Since then his respect for his mother had sunk greatly; it seemed to him as if she had been cast out. She was exempt from most of the precepts of religion. She did not need to study the Word. It sufficed for her to follow a very few commandments; with that all her religious obligations were absolved. But in return she had to stand in the market place, haggle and fight with peasants, and earn the family's bread so that the father, Issachar, and Yechiel might go to the school or the House of Study and devote themselves to learning.

But one day in the week his mother stood so high that no one else approached her, not even his father with all his study of the Law and his treasures laid up in the next world. In a clap Yechiel had a quite different mother, and she was the most important and respectworthy figure in the whole house. All week she was an ordinary, everyday mother. But for a few short hours on Friday evening, from the time when the men went to God's house until the moment when, after the prayer in salutation of the Sabbath, they returned again: in that brief span she was completely changed. No, she was not changed; she was transformed into another mother.

To Yechiel it seemed as though he had two mothers: a weekday and a Sabbath mother. The weekday mother was the one with the shabby old wig, whose black satin band, showing at her brow, was turned green with the sun. His weekday mother stood in the market place, haggled with peasants, screamed, scolded, lied. But when Yechiel returned with his father from the House of Study another mother rose to meet him, his Sabbath mother with a silken shawl on her head and wearing a velvet jacket. Her Sabbath wig was like a crown above her festively gleaming brow. Infinite maternal loveliness shone from her face, from her eyes, from her darkly glowing skin. Her neck looked different; it was soft as down, supple and very very smooth, so that it was a pleasure to gaze at, and he felt a longing to bury his face in it. But the Sabbath shone most gloriously of all on his mother's high and noble brow, which gleamed like a sun.

Yet everything else was altered too, the shelves, the table, the whole room. To Yechiel it was as if, while the men were away, some mysterious change had happened to his mother of which the others knew nothing and were permitted to know nothing. While she was reciting the prayer over the Sabbath candles a holy angel must have visited the house and cast the glory of God over her face, over the table and all the room.

He learned to see his mother with different eyes, because she was connected with the divine beauty of the Sabbath. And now he found the explanation for which hitherto he had sought in vain; in reality his mother was a Sabbath mother; it was only during the worldly turmoil of the week, and because the Jewish people were in exile, that she had to endure being transformed into a weekday mother. But when the Messiah came, then there would only be a Sabbath mother forever and ever....

CHAPTER III

THE LOST SIDE CURL

THE little town lay as forlorn as a cast-off old rag on the sandy bank of the Vistula. On an eminence near the center of the market place stood a white-washed church surrounded by a green fence, to which the peasants fastened their horses when they came to the town for Sunday Mass. The market place extended on every side of the church, and in the middle of it was a little draw well. On all four sides rose little wooden houses, some with shingled, others with thatched roofs. Shops, always open, yawned dark as caves into the square. From it radiated in every direction side streets sparsely dotted with houses and running down to the Vistula. The church with its towers stood in the middle of the Jewish town as if held captive there.

Naturally Yechiel thought at first that all the earth was inhabited by Jews just like his own town. The Gentiles existed simply to put out the lights on the Sabbath and do other menial work not permitted to Jews on their day of rest. But soon Yechiel saw that this opinion was a mistaken one. Fields adjoined the town, and some even extended a little distance into it. They were diligently tilled, plowed, and sown, and always washed clean and bright with the night dews. And on all these fields that stretched away to the next village and far beyond it, there lived people who were not Jews. Hens ran about the field paths, ducks splashed in the runnels beside the low houses, geese waddled in the meadows, and in front of all those huts where Jews did not live, the beast "which ye may not eat" wallowed in filthy puddles.

Twice a week the villagers came to the town with horse and cart and made a halt in the market place. And in a clap the whole town was filled with horses and wagons, cows and pigs, fowls and corn. The peasants took possession of the whole place to the remotest streets down by the Vistula, where the horse and pig markets were held. All day there was dire confusion: pigs squealing, horses neighing, fowls cackling, peasants cursing and guffawing, whips cracking, Jews screaming, women screeching from their market stands, and an eternal bargaining, haggling, buying, swearing. Such was the state of things every Tuesday and Friday, when the market was on.

But on Sunday all these goys came without their beasts, their fowls, their grain; with nothing but their beautifully groomed horses, whose manes and tails were festively decked with plaited bast ribbons. The men too were in their best garb and their top boots smelled of fresh oil. They camped round the church. Thus Yechiel came to learn that the world did not consist solely of Jews.

During this last summer his mind had been greatly occupied by the Gentiles. But hard as he tried to think, he could not come to any clear conclusion about them. It was clear to him that they were needed. God had created them for two purposes: first, so that his mother should sell things to them, cotton, linen, and ribbons, and so earn money for the family. But they were also necessary so that the Jews might endure in their midst all the sorrows of exile that God had imposed on them.

On Friday afternoons, while the Jews were happily bathing in the Vistula, sometimes they were suddenly fallen upon by Christian boys with long whips. Whenever Yechiel had to pass the house of the Christian carpenter who lived on the other side of the street, his heart beat with fear lest the sharp-toothed dog that lay behind the fence might snap its chain and attack him. But the fence exerted an almost magnetic attraction on the boy; for behind it there was a little garden where various kinds of fruit ripened every summer, fruit which were so strange to him that he would have been put to it to decide what blessing to say over them if they had been offered to him. Even while they were ripening these fruits had a lovely scent and were beautiful to look at. The branches of the trees stretched far beyond the fence into the street, and the blossoms and fruit almost touched the ground. One had only to put out one's hand to pluck them. But whenever Yechiel neared the garden the joiner's dog was at the fence with one spring; the boy's heart stood still with terror and without stopping to think he ran away.

One afternoon as he was bathing by himself in the Vistula some Christian boys caught sight of him and flung his clothes into the water. Sometimes they contented themselves with pulling his side curls and shouting, "Little Jew, why did you crucify Christ?"

Yechiel could not remember ever having "crucified Christ." So he accepted such things as visitations, since like all other Jews he lived in exile and would have to endure the sufferings of exile until the Messiah came. He knew that God had created Gentiles for these two purposes; but in the next world they would be judged. When the Messiah came the Gentiles would cross a bridge of iron and still fall through, while the Jews would pass safely over a bridge of paper. Surely the Gentiles would not rise from the dead. But why had God created Gentiles? He might himself, God forbid, have been born a Gentile!

The thought was unbearable, and he found an opportunity to ask Boruch-Moishe, "Father, have Gentiles too a share in the Hereafter?"

"You should know the answer, Yechiel. It is written: 'The righteous among the Gentiles have a share in the world to come.'"

Yechiel was pleased that he had got something for his Gentiles.

"And when the Messiah comes, will they also rise from the dead?"

"Those who have become Jews."

"And the others?"

"Why should they rise from the dead? They are not Jews!"

"But, father, it is not their fault. Is it not written that a man is not to be blamed for what he does unknowing? They do not know it is a sin to be born Gentiles."

"Dunderhead! They can become Jews, for all are given the choice. It is written that when God offered the Torah to all the peoples of the world, only the Jews would take it. Therefore the Gentiles are perverse, because they would not accept the Torah. Can't you understand?"

"But the Gentiles today, it is not their fault that they were born Gentiles! It might have happened to us, God forbid!"

"What do you mean, you stupid boy? When our souls stood at Mount Sinai and the Torah was given to us, we cried, 'We hear and we obey.' How then could we have been born Gentiles?"

"But when a Gentile becomes a Jew," Yechiel persisted, "he is the same as if he had been born a Jew. Isn't that so, father? Though he did not stand on Mount Sinai?"

"Because God takes pity on him. When a Gentile becomes a Jew he passes through a great temptation."

Delighted that he won from his father the admission that Gentiles might become Jews and rise, like all Jews, from the dead, Yechiel did something that summer that might have been serious for him and for the whole Jewish population of the town. Luckily the Gentiles did not understand what Yechiel said to them. There was only a flurry of excitement, and Yechiel lost one of his side curls.

This is how it happened:

On Corpus Christi there was every year a procession through the square and the streets where the Christians lived. It always stopped in front of the burgomaster's, the Christian baker's, the butcher's, who all erected altars at the ends of their houses, which they decked with sacred pictures and greenery, and before which they spread carpets. The burgomaster, the baker, and the butcher lived in the Christian part of the market place, close by the Town Hall. In the Jewish streets all the doors were shut, and the people stayed in their houses all day. The Jews who lived in the market place spent Corpus Christi in fear and trembling.

The dwellers in the Jewish streets had been "spared" the procession thus far. But this year the Christian joiner who lived opposite Rivke, obviously resolved not to be outdone by the baker and the butcher, set up an altar in front of his fence, too, and decorated it with greenery and holy pictures. This became the source of much worry for Rivke.

Yechiel, who was always eager to know about everything new, would have given anything to peep across at the joiner's to see what was happening there. He knew, nevertheless, that as a Jew he was not permitted to gaze on such things.

From early morning, ever since the altar on the opposite side of the street had been decked with leaves, flowers, and ribbons, ever since the first peasant girls in their white, frilled dresses and the lads with white bands wound round their hats and sleeves had appeared in the street, Rivke had been in fear of her life. The church bells rang without stopping as if there were a fire, and their sound filled Rivke's heart with terror. The leathern skin of her emaciated face changed color perpetually, was now white, now green. She kept wringing her hands and sighing, "Woe is me! This bower of the joiner's will be the death of me!"

She gathered her brood round her and stuck rags in their ears so that they might not hear the bells. Then she shut herself in her room with them, closed the shop door and pushed in the bolt, groaning, "Father in Heaven, let this day pass without harm to us!"

Yechiel had not gone to the school, for no Jewish boy could venture into the streets on a Christian festival except at the risk of his life. His father and his elder brother had left for the House of Study early in the morning, so as to spend their time there until the procession was over. Yechiel stole to the shop door and tried to peep through a chink at what was happening in the street. His mother kept reminding him that he might, God preserve her, be struck blind at the sight or go stupid in his head. The latter threat did not alarm Yechiel much, for he heard his father telling him every day that he was a dunderhead. He knew well enough that it was a great sin to look at the Cross; yet that was not what was troubling him, but something quite different.

Standing behind the door, he kept on murmuring, while outside the endless procession went past. "Turn quickly to us before the Messiah comes, so that you too may arise from the dead!"

"Yechiel! Do you want to be the ruin of me? Come away from that door at once! You'll be the death of us all!"

His mother seized him with one hand (her other held her youngest to her breast), and dragged him away from the door.

But Yechiel could no more be constrained than the wind. Scarcely had his mother dragged him from the door than he was there again peeping through the chink. He saw still more crowds of people passing. Men and women pressed round the altar. Yechiel had never imagined that there were so many Gentiles in the world. Peasant girls in white dresses and bridal veils were carrying fluttering long ribbons attached to something. Candle flames leapt up and were quenched. Yechiel could not see the Cross, nor did he wish to. But one could surely look at the people! Again girls in white dresses were passing; they were carrying flowers and great candles. Then for a long time he could see nothing but peasants' top boots, an endless succession of peasants' top boots. He had an uncanny, constricted feeling, a feeling such as one has in a room packed full of people. . . . Now a song arose, mingled with shouts. Suddenly all was still. Something must have happened, for everybody was crowding round one point, from which long ribbons radiated out to the white-clad girls with the candles and flowers.

"Turn quickly before the Messiah comes; then you'll be like the Jews! Turn before it is too late!"

"Yechiel, do you want to kill us all and destroy the whole town? Get away from that door! Why, they'll hear you!"

"They don't hear me, I'm speaking quite softly," Yechiel reassured his agitated mother.

Suddenly everything was still as death outside. Then a few scattered drumbeats. Every sound echoed menacingly. Rivke trembled in every limb, and her fear was caught by her children, who crouched at the stove beside her in the dark room. But Yechiel's eyes were fixed as by a spell to the chink of the door. For he had suddenly caught sight of something which shocked him deeply and made his whole nature rise in revolt. No, he was resolved not to look on the Cross, and what he had seen was not the Cross. His eye had fallen on something black—yes, right enough, it was a human body, naked, fettered, stained with blood, but above the naked body Yechiel could clearly make out Hebrew letters! He looked harder than ever.

"O God, Hebrew letters, our holy letters!" cried the boy in a ringing voice, without paying any attention to his mother's warnings. Absorbed in the spectacle, he did not notice that the door against which he was leaning had suddenly given way. With flying side curls he hurtled straight into the crowd.

Through the open door dull and muffled noises penetrated into the room, somewhat like the sound that is made when one lets a stone fall into a deep well: one involuntarily holds one's breath and waits tensely until the stone strikes the water. So Rivke waited for something to reach her ears; she was so terrified that she forgot even to scream. And it was quite a long time before she heard anything. Scattered shouts arose, a woman's voice screamed something or other. Thereupon a sudden hubbub, which quickly died down. Then silence again.

Only then did Rivke realize what had happened, and she managed to bring out, "We are lost!" With a wild scream she rushed to the door.

"Yechiel!"

Like lightning her glance took in the picture: Yechiel, barefoot, coatless, high above the heads of the crowd of peasants and white-clad girls! Then some one gave her a push, so that she fell back into the room, and the door was banged to behind her.

"Murderers of Christ—" she was still able to hear.

Now everything was finished, her child was lost!

Hastily she gathered herself together and reeled across to the door. Behind her the children began to wail piteously. She did not know what to do. Yechiel was lost, and presently it would be the turn of herself and the other children. Scarcely conscious, she remained standing with crossed arms in the room. Her feet were like lead. She would collapse in another moment—she felt it. No, she mustn't break down! Her teeth chattered as if she were in a fever.

"We're lost now! We're all lost now!"

Suddenly she pulled herself erect, flung open the door, and cried to the rigid wall of people, "Kind, good people, have pity on him! He's only a child, he meant no harm!"

Then a familiar wailing voice reached her ears. To her it sounded like glad news. And thereupon Yechiel, sobbing, white as death, his shirt torn to rags, appeared above the heads of the crowd and flew in a wide arch toward the door. Rivke received a violent shove in the chest and at the same time some one pushed the boy into her arms. Then mother and son were bundled into the shop and the door slammed after them.

Rivke could hear an angry murmur from outside; it dashed like the roaring of a river against the house: "Murderers of Christ! Blasphemers of God!"

She felt as if she were environed by flames. In her deadly fear she thought of nothing but how to save her son. The flames were leaping nearer—quickly she pushed the boy under the bed, and flung some old rags over him to hide him.

The mother did not know in what state her Yechiel had been returned to her, nor did she trouble about it. For another fear completely mastered her mind: the river whose waves were beating against her house might burst in the door at any moment, pour into the room and destroy everything. . . .

Several moments of terror passed by. Then the procession turned into another street. Nobody came to murder Rivke and her children. Now at last she ventured to examine her boy. Thank God! He had come off with nothing more than a fright. They hadn't made him into a cripple. Only one side curl was missing, partly torn out, partly cut through with a knife; and a peasant girl had struck him in the face with her necklace. The marks of it remained for a long time afterward.

The leading Jews of the town begged the priest's pardon for the occurrence. Next Sabbath the Rabbi publicly said the prayer of thanks for rescue from deadly peril. Yechiel was indemnified for the loss of his curl by innumerable cuffs and blows dealt out by his father, his teacher, and all the God-fearing people he encountered.

But far more painfully than all these blows he felt the shame of having lost one of his side curls. . . . His father was ashamed of being seen in the street or in the House of Study with him.

When on the following Friday Rivke saw the boy sitting at the supper table without his curl, it sent a pang to her heart. Filled with love and pity, she laid her hand on his head and murmured sadly, "Oh, my child, what is to become of you?"

CHAPTER IV

A FRIEND IN HEAVEN

YECHIEL was obsessed with curiosity about Heaven. In his childish fancy he often yearned to go there. But how was one to get up to Heaven? He could think of no way, except by the ladder whose feet are set upon the earth and the top reaches to Heaven, the ladder that Jacob saw in his dream. For this, one must be a patriarch like Jacob and spend the night in the holy place, in Beth-El, where the ladder stands. So it was no good, and Yechiel could not get up to Heaven.

But one night when he was lying beside his brother on their straw pallet, puzzling about the Messiah and feeling very sad, it seemed to him that he was beside the ladder of Jacob's dream. And without wasting a moment, Yechiel started to climb, skimming lightly up the rungs, before he could be caught and hurled down again. Suddenly, there he was in Heaven, where he could see nothing but heavens and heavens, long, broad expanses, bright gleaming fields which were constantly moving. And he ran swiftly from one heaven into the next. He saw no angel, no soul at all, no one, only one heaven after another. Beginning to feel frightened, lest he should lose his way among all the heavens, he thought of turning back to the ladder, when he saw an angel in the distance, a boy of his own age, in a lovely white satin caftan, and a cap, and beautiful, curled side curls, the like of which he had never seen. Yechiel, ashamed of his own lost side curl, tried to hide the place with his hand so that the boy angel would not notice it. In a twinkling the boy angel was at his side—he lifted his wings, and there he was. He did not give his hand to Yechiel in greeting, but spoke to him angrily.

"Son of man, what are you doing here? Don't you know what it says in the Scriptures: The heavens are the Lord's and the earth is for the sons of men? This place is for angels."

"If that is so, why do angels come down to earth? If you may come down to earth, men may come up to Heaven," said Yechiel stoutly.

For a moment the angel was disconcerted by this answer. Then he

said to Yechiel, "That has nothing to do with me. You must get out
of here at once, before I call the custodian angel. Don't you know that
no living man may come up to Heaven, except only one, the Prophet
Elijah?"

"What of the saints who ascend to Heaven every night, bearing with
them the prayers of the Jews?"

"But you are not a saint," said the angel.

"Yet God is good," Yechiel answered, without fear. "And let me
tell you that I have as much right to be here as you have. I am a Jew,
Father Abraham's grandchild, and my soul stood at Mount Sinai and
received the Torah. And I keep all the commandments, not like you,
who are absolved of all those duties because you are an angel. Do you
wear fringes? Show me! Look! See! I wear fringes!"

The angel realized that he had got hold of a tough son of man. He
stood for a minute lost in thought. Then he said to Yechiel, "Tell me,
son of man, whom are you looking for?"

"First of all, you have forgotten to give me your hand, and to say
sholem aleichem. That's what *we* always do with visitors."

"I can't give you my hand. If I were to touch you, you would be
burned up."

Yechiel pulled back his outstretched hand.

"Very well! I came up to Heaven because I want to see 'The Bird's
Nest' where the Messiah dwells."

"What do you want of the Messiah?"

"I have something to ask him."

"Are you good at your studies? The Messiah will see only great
scholars."

"Not very good," said Yechiel, hanging his head. "But I know a
little."

"Are you a good, pious little son of man? Because the Messiah will
see only the pious."

"I want to be a good and pious Jew. But I have an evil inclination
which won't let me be," said Yechiel. "You're lucky. You have no evil
inclination to lead you astray; it is easy to be a good, pious angel."

"No, you are better off! Because when you overcome your evil
inclination your reward is exceedingly great. I wish I had an evil inclination," said the little angel to Yechiel, not without envy.

So Yechiel felt sorry for the little angel, and comforted him. "You
are ever so much better off, being an angel, instead of a sinful human
being like me. You can be as good and pious as you like."

"But what do I gain, if I can't keep the commandments like you? And therefore I shall have no share in the next world, as you will."

"I'll tell you," said Yechiel, excitedly, "I'll keep a commandment for you each day!"

The angel smiled happily, and he said to Yechiel, "Now I see that you are a good little son of man! I shall leave you to go wherever you wish."

And the angel moved away.

Then Yechiel remembered Jacob, how he wrestled with the angel all night, and would not let him go until he blessed him. So Yechiel said, "I shall not let you go until you have blessed me."

"Good," said the angel. "How shall I bless you?"

Yechiel had to think what he should say. Then he exclaimed, "I know! Let us be friends!"

"On one condition. That no child of woman may know about it."

"Very well," said Yechiel. "But how shall we meet? You live in Heaven, and I live on the sinful earth."

"We shall meet. One day I shall come down to you. Another day you will come up to me."

"Good!" said Yechiel. "Then it's settled. And we are friends!"

"Now let me go! They will soon sound the shofar for the song of praise, and I must be back to the hosts," said the boy angel, and he began to hop away from Yechiel, on his two legs, like a bird. Suddenly he stopped and called to Yechiel from the distance, "We have forgotten something important! What is your name?"

"Yechiel ben Rivke. And what is your name?"

"What does it matter?"

"How shall I call you when I want you?"

"Call me Friend! And I shall come to you!"

"Remember!" said Yechiel, running quickly to the ladder, for it was already beginning to dawn, and he was afraid the ladder might be taken away. And as he ran he fell. And he woke up.

Pleased as he was with this lovely dream, he was annoyed because in his talk with the angel he forgot what was most important, the Messiah, whom he had gone to look for. But he had one consolation. He now had a friend in Heaven.

CHAPTER V

BY THE WATERS OF BABYLON

AFTER the day of mourning for the destruction of the Temple followed the "Sabbath of Consolation." And on that day, while all Jewry comforted itself for the passing of its holy shrine, Yechiel consoled himself for the loss of his side curl.

During the three weeks of mourning no one was permitted to cut his hair; and meantime Yechiel's thatch had grown so thick that when the days of mourning were over Rivke decided to sacrifice a few pennies and send her son to Yarmiel the barber. Usually she cut his hair herself with her scissors, and it did not worry her if after this proceeding her son's topknot showed several levels of differing heights. But this time she nourished a faint hope in her heart; perhaps God had taken pity on her and Yechiel's lost curl had grown on again! She devoted a whole groschen to the work and handed over her son to the great artist Yarmiel, a master of his craft, whom even the great people in the neighborhood occasionally sent for, so as to entrust their noble heads to his treatment. Perhaps God would show favor to her through the barber's ministrations and remove from the boy the shame of his lost side curl.

And sure enough Yarmiel's scissors worked the longed-for miracle. He arranged the hair round the temple so skillfully that the loss could scarcely be remarked. When Yarmiel had brought off this masterpiece he could not but admire his own cleverness. He pinched Yechiel's cheek affectionately and said, "There! Now you have 'the seal of God' again!"

Yechiel ran in great elation to his mother's market stand (it was Friday afternoon), and shouted to her while he was still quite far away, "Mother! Mother! There isn't even a sign of it now!"

And full of pride he showed her the rewon side curl, which he held firmly in his fist like a precious jewel, as if he feared he might be robbed of it again.

Rivke was so deeply moved by the thought that her child no longer need bear the mark of Cain, that in the excess of her happiness she embraced the little Talmud scholar in the middle of the market place and kissed him. And to indemnify him in some measure for all the jeers he had to bear through the loss of the curl, she sent him to the hatter Nachman; there Yechiel was given a new silk cap, in which he would be able to greet the Sabbath of Consolation with credit; the price to be paid off in installments of two groschen weekly.

It can be imagined what joy the mother felt when shortly afterward Yechiel strutted back from the stand of the hatter, the new cap on his head, and exalted by the consciousness that he once more possessed "the seal of God" by virtue of his new, correctly cut side curl. Nevertheless Rivke did not allow him to wear the cap yet for a while. He was not to put it on till later, when he returned from the baths with his father and had on a clean shirt; then he could go to the House of Study and there recite the blessing on his new cap.

It was not long before his father arrived; he was in a great hurry, for the preparations for the Sabbath had still to be made.

"Well, why aren't we making a start? It's high time to prepare for the Shabbos."

Yechiel patted his rewon side curl to draw his father's attention to it. But Boruch-Moishe did not notice him, but hastened to gather together the wares and carry them back to the shop—the afternoon was already advanced, soon the Temple servant would announce by three hammer blows that it was time for divine service, and Boruch-Moishe wanted to go to the baths first.

Yechiel kept turning his head so that his father might see the curl, but Boruch-Moishe still noticed nothing.

"Look here, father!" Yechiel could no longer hold out; he showed his father the curl won back with such pains. "It's quite whole again!"

The father threw a glance at the boy and saw the new curl. A smile —a rare guest on Boruch-Moishe's face—creased his lips. He affectionately stroked Yechiel's cheek. "Now you have 'the seal of God' again; it's high time for you to become a good Jew."

Yechiel gravely nodded his agreement and firmly resolved to become a good Jew from that moment. . . .

When he returned with his father from the bath he was already wearing the new cap, over which he had recited the blessing. In possession once more of two side curls he marched proudly beside his brother, as a full and rightful member of the family into which he had been newly reinstated.

It was already growing dark. The synagogue servant knocked with his wooden hammer on the shop doors, and hastily one closed after another. The market place was quickly empty. Only a few drunken peasants were reeling toward the inn. The landlord pushed them violently from his doors, swept his last guests out with the broom and kept on shouting, "Sobota! Sobota!"

Then he hastily shut the door. The drunken peasants slipped and slid on the heaps of dung which the cattle had left behind them.

The wind blew across the market place and swept dust, straw, feathers, and horse's hair before it. The weekday still reigned in the streets, but in the Jewish houses the Sabbath had already begun. Candles gleamed from the small windows. The sun sank in the west in splendor. Nowhere in the world can evening silver the clouds so delicately or stretch such a celestially beautiful light over the heavens as it does on Friday evening in a little Jewish town. Sabbath veils of vapor shimmer, bathed in that strange and unearthly light which God seems to keep among His heavenly treasures exclusively for Friday evenings in little Jewish towns.

The gates of Hell were today already shut, for in honor of the Sabbath the damned had been released earlier than usual, and they would not return to Hell on the morrow, the day of rest. Accordingly the sky itself was not so red as usual, but silvery blue, and shone as if newly washed just as Yechiel was.

The boy walked on air. All his limbs were filled with the Sabbath. From his side curls, still damp from the bath, drops fell on his white Sabbath shirt. And today he had a new cap, and the lost curl had grown on again! He felt very light, as if he could ride straight into Heaven on the bright gleaming clouds. Clearly he saw the heavenly Paradise before him with all its golden and diamond halls, its tables decked with white cloths, its gleaming candles in their jeweled candlesticks; the holy first mothers in their rich Sabbath hoods blessed the candles which shone over the world; their blessings sank down from Paradise, hovered like the transparent filmy clouds in the celestial blue, sank down and down until, lightly and tenderly, they wrapped the Friday evening. Such was the festal robe of Heaven, put on to welcome the Princess Sabbath, who now with soft step made her entry into the town.

Only the market place still belonged to the week. Cheerfully intoxicated peasants reeled toward their horses and wagons. Noisy shouts flew from side to side. Several peasant lads were rolling in a drunken knot on the ground, and were forcibly dragged into the wagons by their friends. Horses neighed farewells to one another. Foals importunately ran round their mothers.

A little later the wagons set off. Yechiel gazed after them. The thought tormented him: How can they do such things on the Sabbath? It was incomprehensible to him how the Gentiles could possibly be unaware that this day was different from all the other days of the week. Can't they feel the Sabbath, that like a pure and tender bride makes its entry into the town? Why does nothing tell them that this is the hour when they should go to the bath, wash off all the dirt of the week and put on clean raiment? Don't they see the shimmering veils that hang in the sky? O God, why don't You take pity on them?

Apart from the Gentiles, there were other things too which Yechiel could not quite come to terms with.

In the town lived a woman before whom all the other women trembled. She was called "The Pious Wig," and was, so to speak, the Rabbi of the women; for she strictly saw to it that they kept all the commandments concerning cleanliness, supervised their way of life, and watched lest they departed from the right way. The Pious Wig had the habit of leading the younger women to "the waters of Babylon" and there giving them a course in morals.

"The waters of Babylon" was another name for the banks of the Vistula. Countless felled tree trunks with the bark peeled off lay there; whole woodland cemeteries waiting to be rafted downstream. On these trunks the women rested from their daily work in the summer evenings.

One evening the Pious Wig led Yechiel's mother there and described to her all the torments of Hell. For she had come to know that Rivke had kept her son from his lessons, and she overwhelmed the unfortunate mother with reproaches.

"Rivke, mark this well. A wife must joyfully take upon her the duty of earning the family's bread, so that her husband may be able to study the Law. The husband must be the real lord and master in the eyes of his wife; so you must bear everything in love and humility."

Rivke was quite bowed down under her load of reproach and did not answer a word. She squatted in silence beside the Pious Wig and seemed to become still smaller. She dumbly bowed her head like a dove that is to be slaughtered, prepared to bear all in love and humility.

As Yechiel showed no bent for his studies, he was punished in this way, that he was made to go with the women on the summer evenings, instead of remaining with the men. So now, outstretched on a tree trunk, he was lying with his head against his mother's side. Rivke kept wiping the tears from her eyes with the end of her head-cloth. Without intending it she brushed the boy's mouth with her hand, and he felt on his lips the tears with which it was wet. They had a bittersweet taste unlike ordinary tears. But his mother's hand was softer than any other in the whole world.

Yechiel felt very sorry for his mother. He had no longer any wish to go and hear the frogs in the "Sea of Rushes," where their evening concert was just beginning. The Sea of Rushes was the name given to a backwater which the Vistula had worn in the sand. There little boys and girls were now paddling along with the town ducks. Yechiel would have given anything to go and look at the frogs, for in reality they were wicked men whose souls had been imprisoned in frogs as a punishment. To set them free one had only to say the blessing over a scrap of bread or fruit and fling it into the water. If a frog snapped at it and devoured it he was redeemed. . . .

Although Yechiel would very gladly have carried on this good work of redeeming sinful souls, he did not go to the Sea of Rushes, for he felt an infinite pity for his mother. He swore a sacred oath to himself, and confirmed it by striking himself with his fist, that he would help his mother as soon as he was older and bigger. Then he would stand in the market place and sell things to the peasants. He hated the Pious Wig for tormenting his mother with moral saws.

While he was thinking all this, his eyes remained fixed as by a spell on the heavens. Whether it was allowed or forbidden to gaze on the heavens Yechiel did not know with certainty; but the sight took him completely captive, for the horizon was now quite bathed in red. A burning stream of light irradiated the whole sky and poured over the blue cloud islets which emerged out of one and the same dark ocean. The red fire at the verge of the sky was the gigantic maw of Hell, which opened at this hour in the evening to let out the damned. Now they were permitted to rest from the torments that all day long they had had to endure in the boiling caldrons down there; they could bathe from the blue islands and tend their wounds. Some, it might be, would flutter down to earth and bathe in the familiar streams of their home or visit the House of Study by night. But at the first sign of dawn, as soon as the morning star appeared in the sky, they must all return to Hell again.

"Why is there a Hell?" the boy asked himself. "Why are there damned spirits? Why doesn't God arrange it so that all men are good and pious?"

The thought gave him no peace: he had to find a justification for God. It was no fault of poor God for He wanted to forgive sinners. Yet there were many Pious Wigs, and they demanded justice from Him. And as God was just, He had to yield to them and keep to the Law.

As violently as he hated the Pious Wig, he began to hate all self-complacent religious people who demanded justice from God. These Pious Wigs seemed to him to have a secret connection with the angel of the underworld, that dreadful angel who was the first to meet men's souls after death and ask them their names. For after death all these Pious Wigs would become "angels of destruction"—of that Yechiel was firmly persuaded—and they would stoke the fire under the boiling caldrons of Hell in which the sinners were scalded. But their reward was certain.

"When the Messiah comes he will set free all sinners, shut the gates of Hell forever, and drive away the angels of destruction."

While he was painting the just fate of the Pious Wigs in his mind, he felt his mother's hand touching his. He softly passed his mother's fingers over his cheeks. He knew that it was a sin to touch a woman, even if she were his own mother—but he could not help himself. There were so many sins that did one good it was impossible to withstand temptation—but God would forgive.

Yet soon the Pious Wig caught him playing with his mother's hand.

"Here's a fine sight—a Talmud scholar fondling his mother! Is that permitted? Don't you know that a boy must not touch any woman, even his mother? Why are you here with the women, anyway? Away with you to your lessons!"

"Let him stay, Muhme, he's only a child, after all!" the mother said in defense of her son.

"Ho, think of that, a child! Other boys of his age are at the high school, and betrothed too—and he hangs on to his mother's apron strings! Do you know, Rivke, what is written in the holy books on 'The Conduct of Women?' It says: 'A woman may not take pity on her son and keep him from his studies, for otherwise—that's what the holy book says—'she shall not escape Hell!' "

Rivke hastily took her hand from Yechiel's head. To make good her obligations toward the Law and God she began peevishly complaining of Yechiel.

"I have nothing but worry from him! His father gets nothing but shame from him!"

He lay forlornly on the logs and thought how wicked he was; he brought his mother worry and his father shame. But Yechiel had not much time to give himself up to his grief. The fiery river on the horizon was vanishing; now all sinners were already free and bathing their tortured bodies in the cool, murmuring, lustral waters between the blue islands. Soon all of them would be healed again and enter into everlasting rest.

Hell had completely sunk. On the edge of the horizon blue veils had formed, hiding the heavens from human eyes. A pale gleam lay on the river; away in the distance the sky met the plain where the long waves of dark grass broke. The lights on the rafts gleamed out, songs floated across, voices and long drawn out cries echoed through the stillness. The frogs croaked in the swamps—the captive souls crying to be set free.... And on the other side of the "Jordan," wrapped in dark greenery, rose "Mount Ararat." Noah's Ark had put in there, and all the beasts and birds that it contained were already asleep. Only a few lights glimmered from the windows of the Ark; they sank and were drowned in an ocean of dark greenery and blue veils.

Yechiel too slept—not in his mother's arms, but in God's bosom....

THE PILGRIMAGE

B RIEF is the springtime of a Jewish child. Before Yechiel knew where he was, heavy responsibilities were resting on him. It happened in this way.

To the town, small though it was, came tidings of Rabbi Mendele, the new light that had risen in Israel. The Chassidic community in Przysucha (to which Yechiel's father had also belonged) had chosen him as their leader after the decease of their Rabbi, the celebrated Reb Bunem. He was smitten with a longing to renew the glory of the Law and the holy service of God which the founder of the community, he who was called "The Holy Jew," had initiated. Rabbi Mendele gathered round him only a few chosen men, who completely renounced the joys of this world and dedicated their life to one aim—the bringing nearer of the Messiah. "Give me fifty pious men who are of the same mind as myself, and I will bring nearer the day of the Messiah's coming!" was one of his sayings which was repeated among the faithful Chassidim. In Tomashov, which Rabbi Mendele had chosen as his seat, the essential thing—so it was said among the faithful—was not to find and possess God, but to search for Him and long for Him, and feel the pangs of love which that longing and that search brought with them; for life did not find its end in the satisfaction of desire, but must be a continual intense thirst after justice and truth and the love of God. "The Rabbi does not exist"—so ran another saying of Rabbi Mendele—"in order to divide the scraps of this world among his followers, but to bind together the souls of the faithful and to raise and sanctify life." Consequently no one was admitted to the community who was incapable of dedicating his life to that aim, and in Tomashov lies and flattery were hated, for there truth was a primary object. To realize these precepts the Rabbi had made a rule that his followers must earn their bread by the work of their hands. A number of them hired themselves as daily laborers and thus supported the others. So they were dependent on nobody, for the community of Tomashov held firmly to the principles of the holy life, through thick and thin.

These tidings, everywhere they went, were like a fresh spring on arid ground. Boruch-Moishe and all the other young men longed ardently to see the new light that had risen in Israel. In the last few years there had been little joy in Boruch-Moishe's life. Since his master the Holy Jew had died an all too early death he had sat at no Rabbi's table, for he could not make up his mind to pilgrimage to another. At his supper table on Sabbath Eve, where the Chassidim of the place congregated, the old melodies of the holy Rabbi were certainly sung and the company told one another marvelous stories connected with him; but that was like talking about wine instead of drinking. Boruch-Moishe longed to go to the fountainhead and refresh himself with the new gospel that had arisen in Tomashov. Consequently he was resolved, whatever happened, to make a pilgrimage to the new light in Israel for the next New Year's Feast. The journey there was a long one, for Tomashov lay beyond the Vistula deep in the heart of the country.

Boruch-Moishe had the intention that his eldest son should accompany him. Issachar was almost thirteen now, and it was time to think of finding him a wife and a father-in-law. The boy had a good head, picked up things easily, and was already a skilled swimmer in the sea of the Talmud. So the father decided that the time had come to initiate his eldest born into the mysteries of the sect.

In the one room which served both as shop and living room for the whole family, while the shadows gradually darkened during the lengthening summer evenings, Boruch-Moishe told his son Issachar of the day of the Messiah, as it is described in the Cabbalistic book, "The Zohar." The mother stood by the hearth preparing supper by the light of a burning pine torch. And at the table, which, according to the holy books, resembles an altar, father and son rocked over the mysterious book and their grave, singing voices filled the room.

Yechiel knew that the book which his father was reading with Issachar was full of deep mysteries, and he felt an uncontrollable desire to be present at these lessons and listen to them. When his father and his brother sat at the long table rocking to and fro in pious ardor as they read, the boy would steal nearer without being observed, rock his body too behind his brother, and listen intently to the deep sentences.

For the book that his father was studying with Issachar was holy and filled with mysteries.

"From every word of this book that is uttered there is born a flaming angel, who flies straight into Heaven," his father had said to Issachar, adding, "For that reason every word must also be well pondered."

In the semidarkness of the room Yechiel imagined he could see the angels fluttering up at every word of his father and his brother. In the warm and sweet summer night they glimmered like glow-worms, and Yechiel saw them literally flying up to heaven. His father was just translating the passage in the book describing how the advent of the Messiah would come about. . . .

"And the Messiah shall descend to earth on a pillar of fire and subdue it completely to himself. Then darkness will reign on the earth and in the darkness all the wicked among the Jews will perish. But then the light will return again, deep mysteries will be revealed, and the glory of God will be enthroned amidst the Jews. Father Abraham will stand on the right hand of the Messiah, Father Isaac on the left, Father Jacob before him and our teacher Moses before Jacob. They will lead the Messiah into a hall, which is called The Bird's Nest. There he will be permitted to look at the place of the ruined shrine and at all the faithful and just, whose blood was spilt like water. And our King the Messiah will put on the robes of vengeance. . . . And he will be crowned, and his reign will begin. And God will discern him in his robes of vengeance with his sword girded round him, and will kiss him with His kiss. Then all the worlds will tremble in fear. . . . But afterwards he will go into another hall. There are assembled all those who mourn for Zion, and they will also give him a robe of vengeance. . . . And the holy hosts will draw near him and gather about him. . . . Then the Messiah will journey to Jericho and there his kingdom will be revealed to the world. . . ."

Young Yechiel drank in these burning words with all the ardor of his soul. Carried away, he ventured to leave his station behind his brother. Now he stood beside Issachar and rocked gravely and devoutly to his father's words, keeping time with his brother.

In vain Issachar tried to indicate by a silent jerk of his elbow that he should go away; Yechiel stayed where he was. Then Issachar silently gave him a buffet and pushed him away from the book. Yechiel accepted the buffet gladly, but would not let himself be pushed from his place, until at last his brother lost patience.

"You aren't worthy to listen to the Zohar!" With that he violently flung his brother from him.

This was too much for Yechiel's overbrimming heart. He burst out in loud weeping.

Rivke was at that moment racking her head, as she did every evening, over how she was to arrange the sacks of straw so as to bed the numerous members of the family (for two other children had followed on Issachar and Yechiel). In the middle of this occupation her ear was caught by Yechiel's sobs.

Rivke was always touched by the boy's sorrows. Probably it was because he had much to suffer through his slowness of understanding which was perpetually held up against him, and so she loved him the more, the more he was cold-shouldered by the men of the house. So this evening she could not bear to hear her Yechiel crying.

"Don't cry, Yechiel, don't cry! Your father will teach the book to you too!" Thus she tried to comfort the boy, and she added, addressing the men, "What harm can it do you to let the child listen to the holy words, seeing that he's so eager to do it?"

The mother knew that in asking this she was guilty of interfering with things on which, because of her feminine weakness, she had no right to any say. She was herself alarmed by her daring and hastily tried to make good her offense, but her words only made it worse.

"The child is so eager to hear—perhaps he'll actually understand things like these better!"

Boruch-Moishe, who never addressed his wife directly but always spoke to her as across a wall, this time departed from his custom.

"There's no sense in trying to explain such things to a woman. And one can't even get peace in this house!"

That was a severe reprimand for Rivke. She saw what an error she had committed, and now vented all her annoyance and embitterment on Yechiel's head.

"Of course, when a boy has nothing in his head but wicked tricks, he must be set on studying the holy book!"

The father got up, closed the book, and reverently kissed it. Then he put it back in the little bookcase, and drew the green curtain. He sighed heavily and said, "Yechiel, come here! Stop crying!"

The father dried his son's tears, wiping them away with his sacred fringe, rocked piously to and fro, and then gave the boy, who was trembling like a leaf, a long lecture.

"You know, Yechiel, that the High Feast days will soon be coming. But do you know what the High Feast days mean? Even the fishes in the water tremble before the Judgment that awaits them, not to speak of man, the chosen among all creation, as the Scripture calls him. You're already ten, Yechiel, and our wise men say: 'A boy of ten years shall serve the Law.' But you don't learn, Yechiel. Our wise men say too: 'An ignorant man cannot be one of the faithful.' But you want to belong to the community of the faithful and pilgrimage to the Rabbi, don't you, Yechiel?"

Yechiel nodded.

"But how will you become a Chassid if you don't pay any attention to your lessons, and spend your time in follies? And quite apart from the fact that you won't learn, you are heavily burdened with sins, your soul is perforated with them like a sieve. You have looked on things that a Jew is not allowed to look on—just cast your mind back and ask yourself what has become of that side curl. You have broken the commandment that you should reverence your father, you wound your mother by the shame and reproach you bring on her; and you have many other sins of the same kind, more than you have hairs on your head. Who could count them all? And now the High Feast days are coming, Yechiel. And our wise men say: 'Repent one day before your death.' But as no man knows when—God forbid—he is going to die, you should tell yourself: 'Perhaps I shall die—God forbid—tomorrow!' Repent today, Yechiel, for tomorrow—God forbid —it may be too late. . . ."

All the time that Boruch-Moishe was giving his son this lecture the mother was occupied in laying out the sacks of straw on the floor and expressing her agreement with her husband by subdued sighs. In one way the father's words gave her pleasure, for she was proud to be the wife of such a pious man, who held his children to the path of God. But nevertheless her heart bled for her child at every sentence and she thought: That's surely enough now. But she could not bring herself to say so.

Yechiel stood trembling between his father's knees. Full of sadness, he thought of his sins, which could not be counted and in part were not even known.

"Have you heard my words, Yechiel?"

"Yes, father."

The father once more employed his fringe to dry the boy's tear-stained face, and combed his side curls, which had become disheveled.

This was Yechiel's sole consolation for all the humiliations he had had to endure in the course of the evening.

"Go now, say your prayers and go to sleep."

The mother would have given anything to caress her son and assure him that he was not yet quite lost and with God's help could still grow up to be a good man. But she feared lest she might profane her husband's pious rebuke by her foolish woman's words, and so decided to content herself with silently patting as smooth as possible the straw sack on which Yechiel slept along with his father and his elder brother, so that he might be quite comfortable.

Never had Yechiel recited his prayers so devoutly and amid so many tears as that night. Now he lay beside Issachar wide awake, and stared into the darkness. He saw a brilliant light there, saw the strange hall called The Bird's Nest, and there sat the Messiah along with the patriarchs; they clothed him in the robe of vengeance, girded a sword on him, and set a crown on his head.

Actually the boy had had quite a different picture of King Messiah from that which his father's reading from the holy book had just given him. He could not picture clearly the Messiah of his fancy, but one thing was certain: his Messiah was very far from being the one he had learned about that evening. A Messiah with a sword, and clothed in a robe of vengeance! The robe of vengeance seemed most dreadful of all to Yechiel; it must burn like fire and send out flames that must destroy every living thing! All this had no resemblance to the Messiah he bore in his heart. This troubled him so deeply that he awoke his elder brother.

"Issachar!"

"What is it?"

"Will the Messiah really wear a sword and wage wars?"

"But you heard it yourself—greater wars than Napoleon's, the wars of Gog and Magog."

Yechiel thought for a little; then he asked, "Will he wage wars with soldiers?"

"Dunderhead! By the help of the Divine Spirit, of course!"

That put everything right and, reassured, Yechiel fell asleep.

On the evening before father and son set out on their pilgrimage to the Rabbi, Rivke cried a great deal. Boruch-Moishe took pity on his wife and tried to comfort her.

"When Isaac sent Jacob to Padan-aram that he might get him a wife, Rebecca herself persuaded her son to go. For it is said: 'And

Jacob obeyed his father and his mother, and was gone to Padan-aram.' It follows, according to the holy Scripture, that Rebecca *re-joiced* because the favor was granted her of rearing her son for the Law, for marriage, and good works. But you cry."

"How can I help crying? I don't know whether my eyes will ever see him again."

"Why shouldn't you see him again, silly woman? If God wills, at his marriage. . . ." Thus Boruch-Moishe sought to encourage his wife.

"But perhaps the marriage will take place far away and I won't have any money for the journey."

"No, no. I'll make it one of the conditions of my agreement with the father-in-law that he must provide money for the bridegroom's mother, so that she can be present at the wedding. And I'll insist not only on the travel money, but on new clothes for you as well, so that you won't need to feel ashamed before the other people."

"You won't forget?"

"Why should I forget? Am I a woman, God forbid? Women have a short memory, says the Talmud. . . ." Boruch-Moishe actually condescended to jest with his wife before his departure.

"And when will you come back? I'm so afraid. . . ."

"If God wills, I shall be back soon."

Reassured and comforted, Rivke wiped the tears from her eyes with the end of the traveling pack.

When next morning the little band of pilgrims boarded the ferry to be taken across the Vistula, where the wagon was waiting, there rose a weeping and wailing such as is heard on the day of mourning for the destruction of the Temple. The wives and children of the pilgrims, as well as their fathers and mothers, were assembled on the banks. Their hearts were heavy—the journey to the Rabbi might be fateful for them. The new center of the community was famed far and wide. Often young men who went there forgot wife and family and had to be dragged back to their homes again by prayers and threats.

Dumbly Rivke strode behind her husband through the streets. She had not managed to utter all her thoughts to him. One could not say everything to a man.

Boruch-Moishe held Yechiel, his younger son, by the hand, and gave him instructions on his future behavior.

"You're the oldest in the house now. So you'll have to say the blessing on the bread and the wine on Sabbath and holidays."

Yechiel listened in silence.

"A boy of ten is of an age to understand and to bear responsibility like a grown man. Do you understand?"

"Yes."

"And will you do your best to learn well?"

"Yes."

"And not offend your mother?"

"Yes."

"Rivke, see to it that he goes to school. And don't keep him off his lessons—do you hear? That is a great sin!"

Boruch-Moishe turned his head and spoke these words over his shoulder in the direction where he presumed his wife was.

When the pilgrims were sitting in the boat and the signal to leave was given, Rivke took heart and shouted across at the departing ferry.

"Boruch-Moishe! Boruch-Moishe! Don't forget that you have young children, who expect you to show them the right way! Do you hear, Boruch-Moishe?"

Boruch-Moishe heard, but he was ashamed to show before the others that he attended to the words of a woman. So he gave a movement of his thin, high shoulders and cried back, not to his wife, but to his son.

"Yechiel, if God wills, I'll mention you to the Rabbi, so that you may become a pious Jew and take more pleasure in your lessons."

Then Rivke knew that these words were intended for her.

As the boat got under way all the women broke out in loud weeping. The pilgrims, on the other hand, were in festive, almost wild spirits. And one of them turned jokingly to Boruch-Moishe.

"Boruch-Moishe, have you ever heard how the Rabbi interprets the text of the Talmud: 'He who goes to war for the House of David must leave his wife behind'? The Chassidic community of Tomashov signifies war against the powers of evil, and any one who goes to Tomashov must leave woman behind him...."

Yechiel went home with his mother. He knew that he was ten, and was therefore of an age to understand and to bear responsibility.

His childhood was at an end.

CHAPTER VII

EXPELLED FROM SCHOOL

RIVKE fought heroically to keep the promise she had given her husband. She did her best to save up the school fees for Fishel, the Talmud teacher with whom Boruch-Moishe had arranged before his departure to look after Yechiel's education. In rain and shine Rivke stood in the market. She went hawking her wares in the villages; streams of sweat poured down her, for her pack was heavy; she tramped in her torn shoes through knee-deep mud; she traveled all night in rickety peasant wagons to the most distant fairs: but she did not take her son away from school. She scrimped and spared every bite she could of her own and her children's food to save up the school fees. For the school fees are the first and foremost care in a Jewish house. . . .

But there came a time when necessity fell on Rivke like a savage beast and brought her down. Even the torments of Hell which she held up before herself were of no avail; she was forced to drag her son into "misfortune" and set him to earn.

As she had foreseen, Boruch-Moishe remained buried in Tomashov and never sent her a word. Winter was approaching with all its discomforts, snow, and frost. The peasants came but seldom to the town, so she had to go to them in their villages on frequent fairs in distant towns to earn some money. Her powers began to decline. She had never been very strong; but lately she had been visibly growing weaker. Some time before she had got "water-on-the-ribs" on her way back from a fair, and she had never recovered.

Nevertheless she exerted all her strength to keep the boy at school. But gradually, in spite of herself, the "evil one" drew her into his net. At first she begged leave of absence for her boy only for half days, and even then only on the weekly market days, so that he might help her with her stand. But when custom fell off she sent Yechiel with "packages" to peasants she knew in the nearest lying villages, at first only for afternoons; but sometimes—and that happened more and more frequently—the whole day was lost in this way.

The mother reproached herself bitterly, but she could see no other way out. To expiate her sins she devoted a candle to the synagogue or fasted for half a day. The Pious Wig plagued the life out of her, evening after evening. But what else could she do? There was no help; the children needed food.

But Rivke punctually paid the school fees, for she was resolved to keep the boy at school whatever happened; he must have the feeling that he was having regular tuition with the Talmud teacher.

What was bound to happen happened: Yechiel fell behind in his studies. When, after a half or a whole day's work in the market or a wearisome trudge through the villages, he hastily rushed to school, his cheeks reddened with wind and snow, his hands swollen with cold, his comrades jeered at him. The teacher told him he had little of a Jew left about him and looked more like a goy. As his schoolmates had gone on with their studies during his absence, he presently found that he could not catch them up, or take part in the lessons. He could not make out what the day's reading was about, and all his efforts to find his way through it were vain.

So very soon Yechiel sat in the school as if he were a stranger, forlorn, an outlaw. When he could not answer some question, the teacher did not even punish him, but simply said, "This is labor lost, I'm afraid, Yechiel. It would be much better for you to go to the market and help your mother!"

Finally the teacher ceased to ask him any questions, and no longer troubled whether he came to school or not. If he was away for two or three days he was not asked the reason for his absence. Out of pity the teacher let him take part in the lessons, and he gazed like the others at the Talmud folio lying before him, but without understanding what was being discussed. The other boys never spoke to him. When school was over they ran off in a hurry, so as not to have his company on their way home.

When at the beginning of next month he brought the school fees, which his mother had wrapped up in a piece of paper, the teacher put out his hand for the money, turned it over, looked at it, but then gave it back with the words, "Yechiel, your mother has to work very hard to earn this money. I'm sorry about this hard-earned money of hers. You can come to school and listen as often as you like. But I can't take any fees for it—why, you know quite well yourself."

He did not dare to go home. He could not bear to cause his mother such terrible suffering, and tell her that the teacher would not take any fees for him. He wandered aimlessly through the market, where he sank to his knees in mud, and then turned down toward the Vistula. The river was not yet frozen. Countless little ice blocks were floating down the stream. The land of Haran on the opposite bank was covered in places with watery snow, which oozed into the sopping ground. Only Mount Ararat, where the Ark stood, wore a snow cap on its summit; the slopes were wet and dirty gray. The bare trees with their damp twigs reminded him of plucked hens that had fallen into the water. A misty sky, which seemed to have come lower, held the earth as imprisoned and poor and sad as Yechiel himself. It almost seemed as if God had shut Himself in up there and allowed nobody to approach Him. The whole world, sky and earth, was expelled from school and no longer allowed to study the holy Law. . . .

At last the boy plucked up the courage to go home. In the room all was already dark. Nobody could be seen; the place was filled with dense smoke, for the funnel of the stove was choked. The children were crying. Rivke was again feeling very weak and lying in bed so as "to have a little rest," as she put it. When she heard her son entering she cried to him in a feeble voice, "Yechiel, take the feather duster and drive the smoke out, or else I'll choke."

Yechiel obeyed. While he was driving out the smoke he began hesitatingly, "Mother, the teacher has sent me away from school."

"What for?"

Suddenly his mother had got her strength back and sat up with a jerk.

"The teacher thinks—that I'll never become much of a scholar in any case. He says it's a waste of the school fees."

"Well, there's a limit to everything."

Apparently the mother had cheered up and was resolved to resign herself to the inevitable.

But that lasted only a moment. All at once came the clear knowledge of what had happened: her child could no longer study the Holy Scripture! In despair she buried her face in her hands. "Yechiel, what are we to do now?"

Helpless, crushed to the ground by the greatness of her despair, Yechiel stood before her and could not find a single word.

"I only hope God will take pity on you, so that you may remain a good Jew at least! Go to the House of Study now, my child."

Yechiel went slowly through the streets to the House of Study. The tears streamed without stopping from his eyes. The raw wind whipped

his face and tugged at his tattered cap. With one hand he held together
the tails of his light linen caftan so as to hide the rents of his trousers,
through which his naked skin showed. With his other hand he kept on
his cap. So he struggled on, muttering ceaselessly to himself without
moving his lips.

"O God, help me to remain good at least!"

It was still early in the evening and in the House of Study blind
Reb Leibush was sitting at the so-called "hand workers' table" going
through the legends of the Talmud with the workmen. Quite at the
back, near the washing basins, some ten men were sitting on low
benches: furriers, hatters, tailors, and cobblers, who practiced their
trades only in winter, and in summer cultivated vegetables or fruit.
Their faces were furrowed by rain and snow, their hair disheveled,
their beards unkempt, their bodies bent by the winds. They sat with
simple, credulous faces at the table and gazed dumbly at the torn,
thumbed books that lay before them. At the top of the table, where
blind Reb Leibush sat, a dripping wax candle burned in a cast-iron
candlestick; it was, of course, superfluous, for the blind man knew
his lesson by heart.

Reb Leibush was a strange character, such as is only to be found
in the bygone Jewish communities shut off from the rest of the world.
He was in a manner of speaking the "Rabbi" of the Psalm Fellowship
which the small hand workers and market vendors of the town had
formed. Every Friday and before every feast day they sent to the
Street of the Synagogue, where he lived, a few coins wrapped in paper.
For the most part, his payment was in kind and consisted of food. Every
Friday the fisherman Melech gave the blind man's wife a small fish
for the Sabbath, and Selig the butcher often flung into her lap a bone
to which a little meat still clung. When necessary the cobblers of the
place finished at their own expense a pair of boots for the blind man
or his wife. In return Reb Leibush translated for the hand workers the
Psalms and other parts of the Holy Scripture.

There were no regular attenders at the table where he taught, and
accordingly it had been named "the table of free study." All day the
blind man sat at this table and read out aloud without stopping,
whether there was any one to listen to him or not. Whenever a hand
worker had the time or inclination, he threw up his work and went
to the House of Study, sat down at the table, and listened to what the
blind man was reciting.

Reb Leibush was not a great scholar. He could only translate the Scripture word by word and explain it to his humble scholars as best he could. Yechiel listened at first from a distance. He had a great wish to go nearer, but it would have been unpleasant for him to be seen at the hand workers' table by one of his schoolmates. For those who learned from the blind man were regarded as ignorant and despised by the educated. Yechiel feared also that if he sat at the hand workers' table that it might become known that he had been shut out of school and was no longer a scholar, but had been relegated instead to the class of the ordinary hand workers. So he made himself as small as he could between a water carrier and a hatter, that he might not be observed. But the reading of the blind man attracted him more and more strongly, for the literal translation made the text far more comprehensible to him than it had ever been before.

Reb Leibush was just reading how God sat lonely on His throne and cried in His lion voice: "Woe is me, that I have destroyed the Temple and driven my children from their father's table!" The boy felt a deep pity for God, Who suffered so deeply for having burned His house and sent the Jews into exile. God's sorrow brought tears to Yechiel's eyes. He wanted to comfort God; unutterable love flamed up in his heart. His fancy transformed God into a broken old Jew supported on a long stick, with a beggar's scrip hanging at His side, wandering from town to town and from house to house; but nobody recognized Him, nobody knew that it was God. The boys flung stones at Him, the grown-up people hardened their hearts against Him and drove Him from their doors. He, Yechiel, was the only one who knew that the wanderer was God; through a rent in His beggar's rags he had seen the kingly robes gleaming. And he, Yechiel, was God's servant, who kept watch while God slept at night in the House of Study beside the Ark where the Torah was kept. Then he heard God suddenly starting out of His sleep and crying in His lion voice: "Woe is me, that I have destroyed my holy place. . . ."

Now Yechiel had no longer any fear of being seen at the hand-workers' table. They could laugh at him if they liked—what did it matter? God was in exile. God had disguised Himself as a beggar. Could He have been the wandering beggar who had slept all night in the House of Study the week before? And the boy resolved from now on to seek God among the poor. Now he understood why it was a religious commandment to take guests into one's house. For God was to be found among the poor and the homeless. . . .

Occupied by these thoughts, Yechiel sat quite small and humble

between the two hand workers and listened devoutly to Reb Leibush's
words. Suddenly the blind man stopped, stared apprehensively out of
his vacant eye sockets as if he had seen an apparition, and asked his
listeners, "Who has come to the table?"

Perhaps it was Yechiel's young voice rising above the older dulled
voices of the men that had betrayed to the blind man that some new
visitor was at the table, but it may have been an inner vision—for
the old man's dead eyes strayed, apprehensively searching on every
side, and he asked again in an astonished voice, "Tell me who it is!"

"Nobody. Only a boy," they answered.

"A boy . . . a boy . . . bring him to me."

Amazed and fearful, Yechiel went nearer. The old man stretched
out his nervous, fleshless hands, slowly felt Yechiel's face, brow, and
side curls, as if trying to establish by his finger tips who this boy
was, and muttered without stopping with his toothless mouth.

"A boy . . . a boy . . . who are you, boy?"

"Yechiel, the son of Boruch-Moishe, the Chassid. The teacher has
sent me away from school."

"Why?"

"My mother is ill; I have to help her in the market."

"Whenever you have time in the evening come to me, my child.
I shall read with you."

So the blind old man became Yechiel's teacher. The boy went
every evening to the House of Study. His former comrades jeered
at him and called him an ignoramus. But Yechiel no longer cared
about that.

CHAPTER VIII

THE PROPHET ELIJAH
AT THE FAIR

REB BERCHYE was the town banker.
He did not lend cash, but goods. He credited the women dealers with the woolen cloths and other commodities which they sold to earn a livelihood for their husbands. He provided the hand workers with the raw material which they needed to sell their products at the annual fairs. But although Reb Berchye was very pious, and studied and prayed all day, and painfully observed every precept of religion, his piety did not hinder him from fleecing and browbeating all the poor women and hand workers; and, thanks to his learning, he perfectly understood the art of squaring his usury with his piety, so that both his pocket and the Law were satisfied.

Reb Berchye was the nightmare of the small tradespeople and the poor hand workers. Every morning, having zealously prayed and studied, he took his stick, put on his glasses, stuck his purse in his pocket, and set out for the poor quarter of the town to "supervise" his debtors.

He was quite small, almost dwarfish, and in walking stepped as softly as a cat. Thus he could appear quite unexpectedly and noiselessly, like a specter, in shops and workrooms. Once there, he spied into every corner, and looked into every pot to see what was being cooked for supper.

All the market vendors of the town were on his books. After every market day the hand workers had to account to him for their takings, pay off part of their debt with interest, and sign a new promissory note. In his ledger all the entries were written with painful exactitude in beautiful Hebraic script, and all the figures were expressed in Hebraic numerals.

When Reb Berchye, stick in hand, stole through the town, the people in the poor quarters were filled with mortal fear. The children hastily ran home and shouted from afar the fateful words: "Father, Berchye is coming!" Then the cobbler occupied himself more busily with his thread and awl, the tailor bowed his head more diligently over the

peasant jacket he was making, and the market women competed still
more loudly for the custom of the peasant men and women who were
examining their stalls: the pawnbroker should see that they weren't
idling! If one did not pay, Reb Berchye took one's goods away, and
that was an end of one's business.

Rivke had a particular terror of the pawnbroker. She was firmly
persuaded that he tormented and persecuted her more than any of the
others. And in reality Reb Berchye, a bitter enemy of the Chassidim,
thought ill of their wives, since they nourished their husbands by their
small buying and selling. For him the Chassidim were idlers and
boozers. He regarded their pilgrimages to their Rabbi not only as an
unnecessary interruption of study, but as actually impious. So Reb
Berchye's accumulated wrath was poured out over the wives of the
Chassidim; for by earning the family's livelihood they made it possible
for their husbands to pilgrimage to the Rabbi.

"Where is your husband? Is he still leading his loose life with the
Rabbi?" was Reb Berchye's usual greeting when he entered Rivke's
house.

She herself deeply blamed her Boruch-Moishe for having forsaken
her, but nevertheless she could not allow a strange man, and an enemy
of the communion of the faithful at that, to speak slightingly of her
husband and his Rabbi. She was only a sinful woman, it was true, but
through her husband she felt closely bound up with the communion of
the Chassidim. She too belonged to the faithful, and any blow at them
struck her. She could not and would not endure such words from a
stranger! And in spite of her deep terror of the pawnbroker in whose
power she found herself, she retorted, "He's not staying with the
Rabbi at your expense, Reb Berchye!"

"Very well. If you don't mind his staying with the Rabbi drinking
from year's end to year's end, it's all the same to me. But what will
become of my goods? I don't see that you've been selling anything.
And you aren't able to travel to the fairs."

Rivke became as pale as death. A forced smile twisted her lips,
"Who isn't able to travel to the fairs? What are you talking about,
Reb Berchye? I don't need Boruch-Moishe's help to travel to the
fairs!"

But since Rivke had suffered from water-on-the-ribs, the pawnbroker had been tormenting her almost to death. He kept a perpetual
watch to see that she went to the annual fairs in the neighborhood and
traveled round the villages with her goods. And woe to her if she

missed a fair! Immediately Reb Berchye appeared in her shop like an angel of death, tapped violently with his little thin fingers on the lid of the snuffbox which he always carried with him, and ceremoniously took a pinch. Then he would begin.

"What good are my wares to you, Rivke? You're ill and can't see to the selling of them. I'll have my few scraps of things taken away."

"What are you talking of, Reb Berchye?—long may you live! Who is ill, God help us? It's my enemies that say so!" Rivke raised her hands imploringly. "My enemies—I ill? If God wills I'll set out first thing tomorrow morning."

She sprang out of bed with one leap to show Reb Berchye that there was nothing wrong with her.

Day after day she had to beg the pawnbroker with tears to let her keep the few things that remained in her shop. But now the date of the great annual fair in Ilsza was approaching nearer and nearer. It was the last great fair before the coming of winter. Rivke knew that everything was at stake. If she did not go Reb Berchye would take away her few things; her shelves would be empty and all would be over.

When Yechiel returned from the House of Study in the evening he found his mother putting on her clothes.

"What have you got up for? Why, you can scarcely stand on your feet!"

"Berchye has been here."

Yechiel saw everything. He sat without speaking in a corner of the dark, smoky room and considered how he could help his mother. A sudden inspiration came to him; yes, it seemed the best solution. He could surely go to the fair himself? He saw clearly that if he once began to go to the annual fairs everything was finished; with that he severed himself completely from the class of Scripture scholars and sank to a lower class, that of the hand workers and market vendors. But didn't he belong to them already? As it was he was one of those who sat at the hand workers' table!

"Don't you worry, mother," he began resolutely. *"I'll* go to the fair at Ilsza."

"You—what are you thinking of? You would be a fine one to sell things! How are you to travel to the fair? You would never manage it by yourself!"

"I'll ask our neighbor Reb Melech to give me his advice. I'll go to him at once—yes, mother?"

After supper Yechiel went to his good neighbor and begged him to speak to Rivke.

Reb Melech was always happy and in good spirits. No worry or care could daunt him. He was always good tempered and had a gay greeting for everybody. His standing sentiment was: "The only wish I have is to survive the day; God can look after tomorrow. For"—so he would philosophize further—"man is like a beast in the stall. Its master must throw down fresh fodder before it every morning, otherwise it would forget that it had a master. Just in the same way God helps man day by day." So he was commonly called "Reb Melech Day-by-Day."

Reb Melech's shoulders were always ready to shove when the axle of a wagon broke, and his hand gave help wherever it was required. But Rivke was his particular care, and since Boruch-Moishe had gone to the Rabbi he had redoubled his solicitude for the forsaken woman. So he entered now with a friendly smiling greeting. On his small face, whose skin was like freshly tanned shoe leather, there was always a somewhat fixed, reassuring, and at the same time confident smile, which seemed to say that its wearer's little scrap of blessedness in the next world—he did not ask very much—was certain and assured. From the door, Reb Melech shouted a long drawn friendly "good evening" into the room, and then turned to Rivke, "Why, what's the matter with you, Rivke? You're lying in bed!"

Thereupon he sneezed ceremoniously into his huge red peasant handkerchief and began, "The fair of Ilsza's going to begin in a little, Rivke. What will Reb Berchye say if you don't go?"

"That's why I've asked you to come, Reb Melech. What am I to do? The pawnbroker has been here. He gives me no peace; he wants to take my few things away from me."

"Whether it's Reb Berchye or somebody else is all one. God sends a whip for every nag. But God is our father too, so don't you worry! Tell me, Rivke, why shouldn't Yechiel travel with us? He's a grown lad, after all. At his age I was betrothed. I'll make a place for him in our wagon. Yechiel, take the boards and poles for the stand and come along with me!"

"But what will become of his studies? Am I, God pity me, to make a market hawker of him like us? That's what I was born for; it's God's will. But *he*"—she pointed at Yechiel—"he's a man; he was intended for something else; he was intended to study the Law."

"I'm a man too and yet I'm a market hawker," Melech struck himself on the chest, "and I'm just as much a Jew as the others are. I recite my prayers every day and say over my psalms. God is our father, so what have I to fear? Yechiel"—he turned to the boy— "don't you mind them, you just be a market hawker like us! I'll get you into the Psalm Fellowship, you'll have to get up early every morning, say the morning prayer as quick as you can and a chapter of the Psalms, not forgetting to take a glass of brandy with them, and you'll be a Jew like all the rest of us. And sometimes you'll meet the prophet Elijah at the fairs, upon my word, Yechiel!" He seized the boy's right hand in his own wealed, thick-veined ones. "Will you come to the Psalm Fellowship?"

"Reb Melech, have you ever actually met him?"

"Met who?"

"The prophet Elijah."

"You don't believe me? More than once! You'll see him too if you go to the fairs. But come—no more talk! Pack up the goods and bind the poles together. We'll load up everything this very day. Tomorrow morning we set out. Yechiel, I'll take you with me. God grant that the roads may be passable!" Melech ran to the window and wiped the glass with his sleeve. "Thank God, it's freezing! That will turn the mud hard."

Dumb and full of anxiety for her son's future, Rivke carried the pieces of cloth from the presses where they were lying and tied them up in linen sheets in large and small bundles. Yechiel helped, and was meanwhile initiated by his mother into the mysteries of the business. The most important of these was that the cloth marked with the word "Tov" in Hebrew script was "first class," and must not be sold under three gulden a piece. Although Yechiel knew all about the business by past experience, he listened attentively. He was filled with importance and considered himself of more account than all the town boys who attended the school, for he was intrusted with a whole shopful of goods for the annual fair! Like a magical island the fair rose in the ocean of the next few days, which might conceal yet more surprise. And the fact that such a marvelous figure as the prophet Elijah dwelt on that magical island, that there existed a possibility, however faint, of seeing him in the flesh, transformed the annual fair into a great feast day which Yechiel awaited with impatience.

Next morning—it was still dark and the stars shone palely in the low sky that brooded over the town—Reb Melech knocked at the door

to waken Yechiel. He had not to knock long, for the boy had been
waiting all night for the signal.

"Are you ready, Yechiel? Hand me the bundles; I've left a place
for them."

From the surrounding houses came other hand workers: a cobbler
bore countless boots suspended on two poles, a hatter dragged a chest
filled with peasant hats. By the light of lanterns and flickering pine
torches the wagon was loaded high.

"Thank God, the road will be hard. It has been freezing all night."

Reb Melech was in the best of spirits; he loved a light frost above
everything, and flapped his arms in the peasant fashion to warm them.
The women, who wore coats of all colors lined with wadding, and
were enveloped in heavy wraps, shivered with cold and blew on
their frozen hands. Rime lay like pure white linen on the low shingled
roofs and sparkled in the starlight like a fabric woven of innumerable
jewels.

When all was ready the women kept guard beside the wagon with
their lanterns; but the men took their much worn prayer shawls under
their arms and hastened to the gray, cold Psalm Room for morning
prayer. A warm fume that came from the burning candles and the
praying hand workers comfortably enveloped the newcomers. They
stood on no particular ceremony with God. In this circle the comings
and goings with Him were very fraternal. He knew that these Jews
had no time to worship Him ceremoniously on weekdays; now they
had to set off for the fair. So they finished their morning prayer
hastily and hurried back to the wagon.

During the journey Yechiel wondered constantly whether it would
be granted him to see the prophet Elijah. That Elijah could be found
wherever Jews lived was known to him, and also that the prophet
possessed the ability to appear in the strangest way to people; one time
he would drop a purse of money in the way of a poor man, another
time he would send, by the hands of a child, a true remedy to an
invalid or the true interpretation of a difficult Scriptural passage to a
scholar, or again sell, disguised as a peasant, a whole sack of oats
to a Jew for a mere song. The beautiful verses which told how Elijah
let himself be sold as a slave to help a poor man with the money,
Yechiel had sung with his father at the close of every Sabbath. And
that the prophet would be present at the fair the boy was firmly convinced. Would he appear as a peasant with a red belt, or as a wandering juggler with blue birds who extracted people's "fortunes" from a

box? The boy's thoughts returned again and again to the same point: whether he, Yechiel, would be granted the favor of beholding the prophet. Surely not! He was only a sinful little boy. . . .

All day Yechiel stood in the fair. Many peasant men and women bought from him, but he had not yet encountered the prophet Elijah. He was in despair, and the good business he had done no longer gave him joy.

In the evening—the fair was ended and the bundles already loaded— Reb Melech told Yechiel to keep watch on the wagon, and went to the little synagogue for the evening service.

As he sat alone in the wagon, Yechiel was overcome with deep sadness. He remembered that all day he had not had a book in his hand, nor even prayed; and now he was sitting here while all the Jews were gathered for evening service in the synagogue. Whether it was permitted to recite his prayers in the wagon he did not know; but for all eventualities he prayed to himself, and his heart was heavy.

When he came to the passage in the prayer which says: "Lead me back, O God, to Thy Law," he stopped and thought of his situation— flung out of school, cut off from study, cast out in the street! Never would he learn, never become a pious man like his father and his brother, but instead remain always an ignorant, uneducated village hawker! Sobbing bitterly, Yechiel ardently repeated several times the passage in the prayer: "Lead me back, O God, to Thy Law, draw my heart to Thee that I may serve Thee!" And he added, "I beg you, God, let me learn!"

Suddenly he saw through the tears that blinded his eyes a little old manikin. It was a Jew who bore on his back a cage filled with blue birds. Yechiel had been struck by his appearance during the day; there he had stood in the market place and sold to the peasants "stars" which his birds extracted with their beaks from a little box. The queer looking man had a short white beard and childlike blue eyes with sagging lids.

The old man stopped by the wagon, touched Yechiel's hands, and said, "Sholem aleichem, my boy! Why are you crying?"

Yechiel looked at the stranger in astonishment, and did not know whether to reply or not. But the old man's face seemed strangely familiar to him, as though he had already seen it somewhere, and that gave him courage.

"I'm crying because I can't study."

"Such tears are good ones, my little man. If you can't study, then say psalms like all the other Jews."

"Psalms?"

"Yes. Everything is contained in the Psalms."

The old man gave Yechiel his soft hand and said, "Don't cry, little man! God will help you, and you'll study yet."

Only when the stranger was gone did it occur to Yechiel that it might have been the prophet Elijah himself. He was filled with doubt.

"No, it couldn't have been the prophet Elijah, for he wears a red belt, and the old man had a bast belt round his coat."

Nevertheless he followed the old man's advice and thenceforth said psalms like all the other Jews.

CHAPTER IX

THE DISCOVERY OF THE PSALMS

EVERY evening Yechiel went to blind Reb Leibush in the House of Study for instruction. The old man taught him what he could: the oral traditions of the Mishna, the proverbial wisdom of the Haggadah, which expressed the Law in parables, sometimes a moral scripture. But the main part of the lesson consisted of translations of the Psalms. Yechiel had a particular affection for the Psalms; he understood every word of the text and knew certain chapters by heart. For that reason he was ironically called among the Talmudic students the "psalm scholar."

Apart from these evening lessons, Yechiel also went to school whenever he had a free hour during the day, and studied alone or begged some of the pupils to go over a few pages of the Talmud with him. In return he ran messages, fetched water or honey cakes for them. Sometimes too he paid a few groschen, which he had himself earned, for these lessons. And now that he had to pay in such ways for every page of the Talmud, every legend, every chapter of the Psalms, he found much more pleasure in his study and understood what he read far better than formerly. For the fear of remaining an uneducated boy was with him perpetually.

Comical as it may sound, Yechiel had, in spite of his youth, the bearing of an old man. He read psalms like the old people, and like the old he occupied himself more with the legends and the moral scriptures than with Talmudic disputations. The fact that he was a pupil of the blind man, and often sat with the hand workers, also put him in an unusual position. He was no longer on the same footing as his former schoolmates, who passed their days in study. People called him a "dunce" or an "ignoramus." But Yechiel had a secret which he kept hidden: it was his joy in God. . . .

This joy in God which he had felt from his earliest childhood was often spoiled for him by care. His bargaining in the market brought him in contact with all sorts of men, and he soon recognized that life was a hard master, who pitilessly drove people to the wall and finally flung them into the dark gulf that is called death. Yechiel's heart bled a hundred times daily on account of the need and misery which he was forced to see among people known and unknown to him, among the Jews of the town and the peasants he had come to know during his rounds of the villages. The population of the villages where he hawked his wares consisted for the most part of serfs and semifree peasants. But both the free and the enslaved were subject to the same king and judge, who could at his whim grant them life or death; and that was the landlord. More than once Yechiel had had to look on in some village while the landlord's agent had a peasant dragged into his master's courtyard to undergo a whipping.

For the need and misery that men had to suffer Yechiel could not and would not hold God responsible, for his conception of the nature of God was one which recognized no connection between the Lord of the universe and evil. He was firmly convinced that God suffered from the "Evil One" just as the poor town people and the peasants did. But —he would argue—God could surely help Himself by putting an end to the Evil One! God no doubt had that power; but the meddlers, the "just" would not allow Him to use it because the day of the Messiah had not yet come. For that reason the world had still to be governed according to the "Law," and just as in the next world there was a hell with angels of destruction, so here on earth there was a life with "evil." And the Messiah could not come because men were not yet prepared for him.

Rivke's eyes lay so deep in their sockets that it seemed as if they must completely sink there. Her pinched nose grew longer, and her cheekbones showed sharp and angular beneath the thin skin. When Yechiel looked at her face he had the feeling that it was fading away gradually and irrevocably.

And it was. Ever since Rivke had returned with water-on-the-ribs she had been on her way to her last unknown destination. She could hardly stand now; her legs gave way as if they were made of soft putty. The barber prescribed his most effectual remedies, wormwood, quinine, calomel, cloves in spirits of camphor; they were of no more use than the rubbings with all sorts of salves. With many groans Rivke tried to get up every morning, but her legs would not support her and soon she had to lie down again. Blimele, her good neighbor, nursed her like a mother. She neglected her husband and took on Rivke's duties, cooked for the children, and when necessary helped the household over its difficulties with a bundle of firewood or a loaf of bread. Sometimes too she brought herbs or salves, which she had got from a village "witch," or a parchment amulet inscribed by a celebrated Rabbi and containing the mysterious names of various angels—this was counted the most effectual remedy for all illnesses. But nothing was of avail—Rivke continued inexorably on her way into the unknown.

The burden of earning food pressed heavily on Yechiel's shoulders; he had to summon all his strength to bear up against it.

Day after day a leaden gray sky brooded over the little town. A fall of snow or even a blizzard made an almost festive change in the monotony of winter. The whole earth seemed imprisoned and held captive beneath the thick white blanket which covered everything to the remotest distance. The town was cut off from the world and looked out despairingly like a desert island from the ocean of winter, which assailed it on every side with tempests and cruel frosts. Not a single peasant was to be seen. The inhabitants lived like ants on the stores they had gathered in summer: pickled cabbage, potatoes, barley flour were their only food.

Rivke had nothing in the house. So it was a matter of living from hand to mouth and fighting every day for the family's food. Twice a week Yechiel went in wind and snow to a peasant's wife in the nearest village who had always been Rivke's patron and protectress. He took a heavy pack on his young shoulders and brought back a small sack of potatoes, a few cabbage heads, sometimes a few eggs, and when God was particularly gracious, even a few groschen.

In the room it was bitterly cold, for there was no fuel. The frost held the room as within iron bands; on the broken windowpanes, whose holes were stuffed with rags, bloomed the flowers of the poor. Icicles clung to the door; the water in the butt was frozen. The two youngest children lay all day in bed with their mother, so as to keep moderately warm. Rivke was fully dressed and wore her outdoor jacket lined with wadding in which she went to the annual fairs.

In his rounds of the villages Yechiel had nothing to protect him from the cold but his summer caftan; his trousers were in tatters. His mother vainly implored him to put on her fur vest under his caftan, and to bind a wrap round his ears. Immediately after his morning prayers he set out over the hard frozen snow to the surrounding villages; the only warmth he had came from the pack that he carried on his back; his food for the day consisted of a chunk of bread and an onion.

The wind struck to his marrow, cut countless rents in his caftan, and nipped his flesh where it showed through his tattered trousers as with burning pincers. The storms carried his cap into the clouds, tugged at his side curls, and flung themselves so boisterously on him that they almost lifted him off his feet. He defended himself as best he could, firmly digging the hobnailed soles of his worn boots into the frozen snow. Because of the pack on his shoulders he had only one hand with which to hold onto his cap and his caftan. His lean young body rocked like a ship in rough weather.

Sometimes he returned comparatively early; sometimes he had to say his evening prayers under the open sky: that depended on whether God was particularly gracious to him and sent him a kindhearted peasant who drove him home in a sledge.

But no hardship could disturb Yechiel's joy in God. The things that he read in the moral scriptures about the holy men of Jewish legend early became an example to him. So even in his working week he chose out certain days which he dedicated to God. As soon as he opened his eyes in the morning he would resolve to devote the coming day to God. On ordinary days he said his prayers as quickly as he could and thought of his mother's illness, hoping that God would cure it, or prayed to God for good business sales. When he returned he would wash hastily, eat, and hastily recite the grace after food. He never attempted to open a book. But God's days were quite different. No sooner had Yechiel decided to dedicate the coming day to God than it became a feast day. Whatever he did, whatever happened to him, he was able to transform everything and give it a higher meaning.

On such a day the bare Psalm Room, with its poorly clad workmen, looked quite different. A boundless joy filled him at the thought that he, too, was one of the children of Israel and was permitted to live in their midst. The little Psalm Room was God's dwelling. On such days he asked for no favor from God. He prayed only in honor of God, and the words of the prayers took on deeper meaning—he could read into them whatever he liked. Suddenly they revealed themselves to him, and a casket locked until now stood open before him. Yechiel gave the words his own meaning; he had the power to fill them with content and substance.

And while he stood in the faint dawn beside the poor people, whose cries for help and desperate petitions beat against the cold walls of the low-walled House of Study, he was in a different world. The room with its four walls and its roof vanished and Yechiel hovered in a sea of clouds. God was no longer an abstract conception to him, but a living being in whose presence he stood and with whom he spoke. He asked nothing of Him, but only rejoiced in Him. He was happy to be allowed to come so near God and tell Him how greatly he rejoiced in Him, how ardently he loved Him.

This sense was with him not only during the hour of prayer, but afterward as well. When he returned from his prayers he did not hastily wash and sit down to breakfast as usual, that he might set off for the villages at once. On such days he told himself, "Now I am going home to eat to your glory, God." With this thought he sat down at the wretched table, wiped it carefully so that no speck of dirt remained, spread the cloth on it, and laid out everything—the rolls, the onions, the saltcellar—methodically, as if it were a Sabbath. Then he washed, recited the blessing, dipped his slice of bread in the salt, and began slowly and devoutly to eat. While he did so he pictured to himself that God was sitting opposite him and seeing that he was eating in His honor.

But Yechiel was able to turn, not only his breakfast, but the business of the day and all that happened during it into a holy service of God. When he set out he would say, "Now, God, I am going in your honor to the villages." How different did the cold mornings seem then! Even on the most cheerless winter morning he consoled himself with the thought that Heaven was there behind the leaden clouds, though it was hidden for the moment. And he no longer felt the heavy pack pressing on his shoulders, no longer felt the wet slush that soaked through his tattered boots. He felt as though he had wings. The snow fields sparkled and glittered like fragments of Heaven that had fallen to the earth. Yes, they were like splinters of the gates of Heaven which, burst by the prayers of the faithful, had tumbled crashing to the earth. Now they lay smashed to fragments on the fields strewn over the white covering of snow. And the gates of mercy stood wide open. Every man's prayer soared straight through the wide open blue sky to the throne of God, and was heard at once.

So Yechiel wandered on singing psalms that came to his mind, and some that he himself invented on the spur of the moment, without sense or meaning. Presently his words ceased and he merely sang—it was a joyful noise and nothing more. At last he would burst into tears and shame would seal his lips. . . .

One day when he returned happy and elated, for he had brought with him from his round food for almost a week, he found the scourge of all the women of the town, the Pious Wig, sitting by his mother's bed. The old dame usually made her sick visits to Rivke in the late afternoon, when it was getting dark and Rivke was alone. The Pious Wig seemed to grow from year to year; she was almost supernaturally tall, her arms and legs grew longer and longer, not to speak of her head, which resembled more and more that of a horse. Her whole face was horselike. Great, yellow horse teeth protruded between her lips; she had a long chin; her nose was small and flat.

As a protection against the cold the old woman had bound round her ears a cloth with a huge bow which was balanced on her ancient wig, green with age. The two ends of the bow stood out against the wall in the falling darkness like the shadows of two gigantic birds. The Pious Wig sat over Rivke in the half-dark room and spoke seriously and urgently. She accompanied her words with gestures of her long, bony fingers, whose joints she kept on cracking. The gesticulating hands too looked like uncanny shadows against the wall.

At Yechiel's entrance she interrupted herself, heaved a deep sigh, turned her eyes on the boy, and shook her head for a long time. Then she said pityingly, "So that's what you've become—a village hawker!"

Yechiel gave no answer.

While he shook the snow from his coat and put down the sack of potatoes, he threw a glance at the bed. In the leaden gray twilight his mother's yellowish-brown face gleamed against the pillows like old amber. Yechiel saw that her face was bathed in sweat, as if, lying there in the black shadow of the Pious Wig, she felt a heavy load upon her.

As it was already late he took his prayer book and went to evening service.

When he returned the pitch-black room was filled with sounds of lamentation. His mother was weeping loudly in bed and the younger children sat crying on the floor.

"What has happened?" asked Yechiel in alarm.

After he had hastily lit a pine torch at the hearth, a sad scene met his eyes: his mother was sitting up in bed striking her withered breast with her fists and crying despairingly.

"I know I'll go to Hell, to the place of fire! I know that I'll be spared no torment there! For I've kept my own son away from studying the Law. I know that Hell is the least I can expect!"

The children accompanied her laments with loud weeping.

Yechiel stood before her in helpless despair. After a while he remembered his sole friend, his good neighbor Melech, and hurried to him.

"Fling her out, Yechiel! Whenever that dirty Wig puts her foot across your doorway take a stick and drive her out! It's she that's been frightening your mother with Hell!" declared Reb Melech, who at once grasped what had happened. Then he went over to Rivke's bed and spoke encouragingly to her.

"Why should you go to Hell, Rivke, of all people? Why, one would need to have a heart of stone to send you to Hell! Have you had such a good time in this world? Have you attended balls every week? Have you eaten chickens roasted in butter? In what way have you deserved Hell? God isn't so cruel as that! In the next world we'll be judged fairly and rightly. They'll only have to call me as a witness! I'll tell them how you've worried and worked yourself to death since your man left you. And you did everything you could to let your son study the holy books. How could you help it if you fell sick? I ask you again—in what way have you deserved Hell? Don't you believe that old witch. The Wig will roast in Hell herself for saying that God is unjust and tormenting her fellow creatures. But you'll go to the finest Paradise of all, yes, I tell you you will! Yechiel, you fling that woman out! Drive her out with the broom—take my advice, Yechiel!"

Reb Melech's words reassured Rivke a little. She agreed with him that she had not enjoyed much pleasure in this world. Her despairing moans faded into a faint sobbing. But when her good neighbor had gone her terrible fears came back again.

"Yechiel, I'm afraid of the torments of Hell, for I've kept you from your lessons."

"Don't believe her, mother! God is good."

"But your father was always saying it too. Yechiel, I'm terribly afraid of the road I must walk now. Oh, I know all that awaits me there! The old woman told me all about it."

Rivke was calm for a moment when Blimele appeared with a pot of food for the family.

"All my troubles on her head!" exclaimed the good neighbor. "That old Wig! Look how she's frightened the poor woman. Get a plate, Yechiel, and a spoon, and give your mother some of this. I must go back to lay the table for my old man."

Yechiel handed a plate of food to his mother in bed. But no sooner

had she lifted the spoon to her mouth than she was again caught in the
net of terror that the Wig had cast over her. She shrieked as she
pushed the plate away. Her eyes, dimmed with fever and dread, saw
terrifying pictures.

The Pious Wig had been telling her about a Book of Emmanuel and
its story of a man, Daniel, who visited Hell and saw flaming serpents
and scorpions endlessly devouring human beings and lakes of filth in
which human bodies drowned. And about a miracle worker, Reb Isaac
Chayes, who had also been accorded the privilege of visiting Hell. He
had seen a woman and child bound by their breasts to a chariot of
fiends and demons. That had been the woman's punishment for having
kept her child from his studies. The same thing, the Wig pointed out,
would happen to Rivke.

Yechiel was in despair. His comforting words had no effect.

His mother was no longer crying. Her eyes stared rigidly out of
their sockets. A look of helpless terror was on her face. She seemed
to be gazing into the abyss that would open to swallow her as soon
as her life ended. Yechiel could see the terror in her face and cast
about in his mind for help. It was clear to him that here even his neighbor Melech would be able to do nothing. He sought for some other
help. "O God, whence cometh my help?" he asked himself in the
words of the Psalmist. And he answered himself with another verse
of the Psalms: "In the day of my trouble I will call upon God." And
since he knew of no other help, he sat down on the firewood beside
the hearth, took up his psalm book and began in a broken voice to read
the page at which he chanced to open.

What the words meant that he was reading no longer mattered to
him. He poured all his own wretchedness, his own grief into them.
And strangely enough the words took on a quite different meaning;
they uttered what he, Yechiel, was feeling now. They uttered it to
One who knew all and could do all that could be done, One who had
the power to make everything right again. And Yechiel saw that One
before him now, stood before Him and made his complaint to Him.

His mother still stared before her; her eyes were fixed immovably
on the terrifying pictures which her feverish phantasy conjured up.
Suddenly she heard the words of her son. Her glance strayed to the
hearth: Yechiel was sitting on a stool there praying for his mother.
Once more the tears poured from Rivke's eyes, and they loosened the
freezing terror of death that confined her heart. Through the mist that
covered her eyes she thought she could see, in the corner where Yechiel

sat with his psalter on his knee, a strange light. But she was too tired to look, and her mind was not clear enough to take in what she saw. Exhausted by the fears and terrors that environed her, she fell into a light sleep in which she still sobbed a little, breathing uneasily. Gradually that passed over into a convulsive fit of childish weeping. At last she was sleeping calmly and deeply: her dreams had transported her into another world.

She found herself in a dark wood, which was full of lizards, toads, and other loathsome creatures. But at the very end of the wood some one was waiting for her. There opened a valley, which lay in an unearthly beautiful light, and in the middle a House of Study gleamed in the homely light of countless Sabbath candles. Inside men in prayer shawls sat before holy psalters and read in a loud voice. But she herself was standing outside looking in through the window. Then she saw her Yechiel: he was sitting among the men piously rocking over his psalter. . . .

When Yechiel paused in his reading he saw that his mother's face was lighted with a peaceful, childish smile. He softly stole to the door on tiptoe, meaning to go to the House of Study. Then his mother awoke and looked at him with astonishment.

"Was it really you, my son?" she asked.

"Who, mother?"

"Nothing."

Rivke sank into dreamy thought.

"What is it, mother? Are you in pain?"

"No—not now." Comforted, Rivke wiped the tears from her cheeks. "Go to the House of Study, my boy, and warm yourself. It's cold here."

"I'm afraid if I leave you you'll cry again."

"I won't cry any more. Go to the House of Study, my son."

CHAPTER X

YECHIEL GOES TO FETCH
HIS FATHER

THE winter is long in little Jewish towns. It is like a bottomless vessel into which the days and weeks fall, but without visibly filling it up. Once the gates of heaven are barred with leaden gray clouds they remain shut until shortly before the Passover. Nor does one expect anything else.

For Rivke the weeks followed one another without a glimmer of hope. Each day was the same as the last—all began and ended in misery.

Boruch-Moishe sent no word. Since he had gone to the Rabbi he had been as good as buried. Now and then a wandering Chassid, passing through the town, brought Rivke a greeting from her husband, but if she asked when Boruch-Moishe was coming home again the stranger would reply that she could not count on his returning soon, for he had found with the Rabbi what his soul desired and was at peace. Rivke submitted humbly to her fate. At home with her, she knew, her Boruch-Moishe would never have come to anything, so why drag him into her misfortunes? It was enough for one to be burdened with misery. And she told herself that if he stayed on with the Rabbi he no doubt knew what he was doing.

In the last months, however, Rivke's condition had grown so much worse that it became necessary to think of sending for her husband, for she was very ill. Her neighbor Melech said to Yechiel, "Yechiel, things aren't looking too good. We must find some way of sending for your father."

But how was that to be set about?

One day when Yechiel went to the House of Study he found there Mayer the Jewess, the traveling colporteur, who every spring appeared with his books in the town, for he regularly made a round of the whole neighborhood with his little book cart. The neat little man was nicknamed "the Jewess" because the ornament and pride of every Jew worthy of the name, a beard, had been denied to him.

68

Mayer the Jewess's headquarters, naturally, was the House of Study. There on two tables he piled up his books.

Beside big brand new volumes of the Babylonian and Jerusalem Talmud, of Maimonides, Schulchan-Aruch, and other learned authorities, lay innumerable little booklets which had been printed in the most various places, in Zamosc and Cracow, Zolkiev and Berditchev, Petrikau and Vilna, even in Salzbach and Frankfort-on-the-Main. Every Jewish boy longed in his heart for these little volumes. They consisted of moral and edifying tracts, tales from the Cabbalah and Chassid histories, sayings of Jewish martyrs, and other wonderful legends: everything was to be found in them. If one was ingenious enough one could actually deduce from them the exact date of the advent of the Messiah. That date was precisely given in Genesis, but in such circumstantial terms that only holy men, perfect in righteousness, could calculate it.

Naturally, Yechiel longed with all his heart to possess such books. Like all the other boys he could not be dragged away from the Jewess's bookstand. He fingered the little volumes, turned over the pages, and could not tear himself away from such a wealth of glorious things. His eyes rested longingly on the booklets which told of miracle workers, famous Rabbis and great Cabbalists, and of the founders of the Chassid sect. He gazed just as enviously on the little volume describing the journeys of Rabbi Pessachya, who had traveled round the whole world and actually visited the lost ten tribes, the red Jews, who dwelt beyond the fabulous river Sambatyan. With wide, greedy eyes Yechiel contemplated these marvels.

Mayer watched the boy for a while; then he asked, "Would you like a book? I'll let you have one, and you can pay later."

"But I don't know whether I would be able to pay," replied Yechiel.

"You're an honest lad, anyway. Now, I'll make you another proposal —you can pay your debt by work. Have you strong arms? Can you carry parcels?"

"Yes, I'm used to that; I carry packs of cloth for my mother to the villages."

Mayer, who was a feeble little man, regarded Yechiel's powerful arms and broad shoulders with pleasure.

"Listen, lad. Would you like to become my assistant? I need a strong lad to help me to carry packages of books to addresses in the different towns."

"I must help my mother. She's sick."

"Where is your father?"

"My father is with the Rabbi in Tomashov."

"In Tomashov? Why, I'm going straight there! Listen, my lad. Come with me! I'll take you there at my own cost, and in return you'll help me with my books."

Yechiel first consulted with Melech; then they put the plan before Rivke. Knowing that she had not much longer to live, and wishing to intrust her brood to Boruch-Moishe, she readily agreed. Her good neighbor Blimele guaranteed to look after her and the children, and Reb Melech said, "You, Yechiel, go to Tomashov and bring your father home by the nose—you can rely on me for everything else."

So Yechiel journeyed with the colporteur in his book wagon to Tomashov.

The boy was used to carrying packs at the annual fairs. So Mayer the Jewess loaded Yechiel's back with as many books as could find a place on it. Yechiel carried them to the House of Study at all the places where the wagon halted, piled them up on a table, and acted as Mayer's assistant. The shop was always the House of Study, but all day packets of books had to be borne to the various houses. Mayer and Yechiel spent their nights in cheap hostels, in some little room filled with men and women.

Outside business, Mayer also employed the boy for personal service. The colporteur's greatest pleasure in life was to have his back scratched at night before going to bed. That was for him an ecstatic joy, and he would groan with rapture.

"Oy, me! Just a little more! ... Yechiel, just a little more!"

Mayer the Jewess's second passion was tea drinking. Safely ensconced among his piles of books lay a little wooden box furnished with many locks, which he guarded like the apple of his eye. It was filled with the most diverse kinds of tea derived from all sorts of herbs, roots, leaves, blossoms, and grasses. These were well-proved specifics against every kind of sickness. And as Mayer, God be thanked, suffered from every conceivable malady, he employed his teas against all his pains, aches, and sores. The little manikin could drink whole rivers of tea. It was incomprehensible where all these boiling and scalding torrents found room for themselves; considering the amount of tea he drank he should have been as huge as a leviathan.

For the preparation of his tea he had a curiously shaped can and a cup that he always carried about with him. As soon as he wakened in the morning he first of all sent Yechiel with the can for hot water.

"Put in some of the lime-flower tea this time—no, the wormwood tea would be better: it's good for pains in the stomach and bowels."

So it went on all day, and every now and then the old man would say, "Yechiel, could you get a little hot water from some one?"

And the boy took the can, went into strange houses, and was given boiling water by good souls who took pity on him. A few moments later it had vanished into the little belly of Mayer the Jewess, and nobody could have guessed where it had gone.

But Yechiel was quite happy. Without complaint he bore the heavy packages of books from house to house, carried them from the inn to the House of Study and back again, scratched Mayer's back before he went to bed, went into strange kitchens to ask for hot water, hungered by day and froze by night, had not a whole rag on his back, and always an empty stomach. But in return he had books in abundance; he almost swam in books. Only he had very little time, unfortunately, for reading them. So he turned night into day. In this way he managed to read this or that volume, or at least to glance over it. And soon he was able to distinguish a rabbinical booklet from a Chassidic one, a Cabbalistic tome from a volume of sermons, and to recognize which books were easy reading and which required a good knowledge of religious literature. During his tour with Mayer he became acquainted with countless stories about Wonder Rabbis and holy men. And when, after weeks of traveling from town to town, Yechiel at last reached Tomashov and said farewell to Mayer, he had in his traveling kit, apart from the second shirt that he had brought with him from home, a little prayer book, a little collection of the Psalms, a few booklets containing wonderful stories about great Rabbis, and a Cabbalistic scripture in which were described the ten spheres. These he had earned by his faithful service to Mayer the Jewess, by carrying books and fetching water.

In Tomashov Yechiel found his father in the overcrowded House of Study among a group of men who had just come from their work and looked like masons, for they were covered with lime and brick dust.

The boy could scarcely trust his eyes. He hardly recognized his father. Boruch-Moishe looked like a poor, starving day laborer. His cap was without a peak. Round his torn caftan, defiled with chalk and lime, he wore a thick rope such as hod bearers use. His clothes flapped round his meager body, which was all skin and bone. In the two years since Yechiel had last seen him he had become an old man. The thin muscles of his neck seemed hardly able to support his head; he looked as if every moment it must fall, so thin had his neck grown. But the most painful thought of all for Yechiel was that his father, whom his mother had guarded at home like the apple of her eye, so that he might study the holy books in peace, had become here at the Rabbi's a day laborer. What had happened?

"Sholem aleichem, father!" said Yechiel, pushing his way through the crowd of men.

"Yechiel! You here!"

"Father, mother is very ill. I've come to fetch you."

"Let's sit down in a corner."

Father and son withdrew to a quiet corner of the House of Study.

"What is wrong with your mother?"

"I don't know. She got water-on-her-ribs when she returned from the fair."

"And who is looking after the upkeep of the family?"

"I am," replied Yechiel timidly and awkwardly.

"You? And what about your studies?"

"Father, the teacher told me not to come back again. I had to go with a pack round the villages. Mother is very ill. . . ."

"A village packman!" groaned the father. "And you've done nothing about your lessons?"

"I've been sitting at the hand workers' table in the House of Study in the evenings listening to Reb Leibush."

"O God, sitting with the hand workers!" After the first shock, pity began to awaken in Boruch-Moishe. "But after all what could you do? You had nobody to guide you."

"Father, mother is very ill. Ask the Rabbi to pray for her recovery. She's so low, it breaks my heart—"

"What can I do? I wouldn't dare to mention her to the Rabbi. Our Rabbi has no time for such things. . . ."

"We've been waiting all this time for you to come back. It's been such a long time. . . ."

"The Rabbi wouldn't allow it. . . . And after all, what could I do at home, God help me? Carry a pack round? Become a hawker? What use would that be to any one? At most, that would only be one peddler the more."

"But what good are you getting here?" Yechiel ventured to ask.

"Just think how you have changed, father! And you carry bricks and mortar. . . ." The boy burst into tears.

"Be silent! You don't understand. Here great things are being done. To carry bricks and mortar here isn't the same as carrying a pack at home. It's a holy work. Your brother Issachar would understand that. I carry bricks and mortar so that we should need nobody's help, so that we should all be free from care. *I* do it today, another will do it tomorrow, whatever one the lot falls to. We do that so as to earn a bare livelihood. But in return we can devote ourselves to our mission with all our mind, we have obligations to nobody, we are free men and live as men should live: we are bound to our Rabbi in a holy fellowship. 'The just man is the foundation of the world,' it is said. And through the just we are bound to the service of God. You won't understand that; there's a deeper meaning in it. . . . At any rate, you must understand that great things are being accomplished here. This isn't busy idleness, as work is at home. . . ."

"No doubt you know what you're doing, father."

"I'll see . . . perhaps I'll manage to get the Rabbi to see you. Usually he drives away visitors. But with God's help perhaps I'll find a favorable moment. May God grant it!"

"And what is to happen to mother?" asked Yechiel urgently.

"What can I do? How can I help?" Boruch-Moishe despairingly raised his hands to heaven. "God knows, I can't say anything about it to the Rabbi. I daren't trouble him with such things—God help her. . . ."

Yechiel was greatly downcast by this answer, but he did not dare to contradict his father—it must be as he said. Two sensations—pity for his mother and unutterable joy at seeing his father again—filled him simultaneously. All at once he felt himself a child again; it seemed as though the burden of age which had grown upon him during his father's absence had suddenly slipped from his shoulders. He had found his childhood again, and claimed the right to be a child. He held his father's hand in his own, and wanted never to let it go. He already forgave his father everything; for his sake he even forgot about his mother. And although his father was in rags and had a rope tied round his waist like a peasant, although his toes showed through the holes of his shoes, Yechiel was proud of him.

Now he saw his father in a truer light. This man who was his father had dedicated himself to God, not for a day merely as he himself was accustomed to do, but for his whole lifetime. He had sacrificed everything, he possessed nothing now, neither home, nor wife, nor children: he belonged solely to God.... And suddenly in Yechiel's eyes his father's tattered clothes became priestly robes, his meager, emaciated body the body of a saint. What right had one to burden this man with a sick wife, with children and a home? Yechiel's sympathy at that moment was more for his father than his mother. Mingled pity, pride, and happiness made his eyes smart with tears.

"Father!... Father!... Father!" he stammered, tenderly pressing his head against Boruch-Moishe.

"You're not a child, Yechiel, you're grown up now."

"Father, I want to ask you for something. . . ."

"What is it?"

"Teach me. . . ."

"What do you want to learn?"

"The holy books."

"All books are holy."

"You know what I mean—the one you taught Issachar at home, the holy Zohar."

"Issachar!" The father's weary face lighted up. "Issachar, he's become something! If I had only brought you as far forward as Issachar—oh, that God had granted it!"

"Yes, father—how is Issachar? We've heard nothing from him."

"He is in Lublin studying to prepare himself to be a Rabbi. If it's God's will, he'll get his certificate, and after that he'll marry."

"Oh, mother will be so glad of that!"

Father and son sat down at a table and began their lesson.

But Yechiel did not feel really at one with his father until later on, when he lay with him in the garret, where sacks of straw were spread for the community of the faithful who surrounded the Rabbi. Lying among the sleepers the boy had the feeling of being accepted into the holy fellowship. And beside his father he felt the deep meaning of the Biblical phrase, "as a father pitieth his children."

CHAPTER XI

THE RABBI

THE town of Tomashov looked askance at the strange way in which Rabbi Mendele held his court. All were repelled by it, for they could not understand such behavior in a Rabbi.

When Rabbi Mendele was chosen from the celebrated fellowship that had gathered round the great Rabbis of Przysucha, there was great rejoicing in Tomashov. Rabbi Mendele had married a Tomashov woman, and was therefore in a sense a townsman; his wife and children lived in the town. And now he had made Tomashov his actual residence! Apart from this distinction, which the town was never tired of boasting about, there was also the prospect of good business. People expected the place to flourish and already saw a river of gold flowing into it: for the whole land would come on pilgrimage to Tomashov. Every Jew in the town set up a hostel and set about sewing a new purse.

But behold—Rabbi Mendele used his prestige quite differently from the common run of Wonder Rabbis. He actually repulsed the crowd. He drove away the rich leaseholders who came to him for help and advice. The merchants and manufacturers fared no better, though they always brought the richest presents; nor did even the women. In vain they stayed for whole weeks in the town, attended all day in the Rabbi's antechamber, watched his doors and windows, despairing and humbled, so that it was painful to see them. The Rabbi surrounded himself with a crowd of young people—sponging wretches and starving scarecrows who had run away from their wives and had not a whole shirt to their backs; he kept them beside him for months, for years, and would not give them permission to return to their homes. And this group led a strictly secluded life. Every day Chassidim came down into the town to earn a few coins. They undertook the roughest work, and built a House of Study with their own hands. The money they made they gave to their fellows; then spirits were bought and they all drank together. Not even the prayers were said properly in this fellowship. The Rabbi himself seldom appeared at divine service. Certainly they all occupied themselves—and very zealously—with study, but that was mostly esoteric. They buried themselves in the Zohar, bathed at un-usual hours; in a word, the whole behavior of these people pointed to the conclusion that they were devoting all their energies to bring on the advent of the Messiah!

The Rabbi's wife was just as ill-pleased. She had waited and hoped so long for the fulfillment of her ambitious desires: to hold a brilliant court as the other Wonder Rabbis did. Of that she was disappointed. Wasted were the cares and anxieties of the past years in which she had taken upon herself the whole burden of bringing up the children and earning the family's livelihood, while her husband sat with the great ones of Przysucha. How she had longed for the moment when her Mendele, whose name sounded so well, would at last become a Rabbi! And now all her ambitious hopes were buried.... The poor, hungry, young men who lived at the Rabbi's court ate everything bare as a swarm of locusts and carried the last sack of straw out of the house.

From scores of towns there appeared every now and then indig-nant fathers furnished with stout cudgels, and accompanied by weep-ing young women who had been deserted by their husbands. And the fathers-in-law too made themselves heard: "The Rabbi is hindering the salvation of the people, for he is keeping the young men from fulfilling the commandment to multiply and replenish the earth...."

The man round whom, as round a sun, revolved the whole life of the court, who was the object of the love and hate of a world, locked himself in as if he were a mysterious being behind seven doors. While in his court every mind was occupied with him, he sat in his cold room with the bare whitewashed walls, from which the damp mortar was peeling. In reality he had been shuffling about the room in his down-at-heel slippers ever since midnight. Now and then he would suddenly rush across to the warped armchair, from whose upholstery the springs protruded. Nervously he would snatch up one of the Cabbalistic, ethical, or legal works that lay, some of them open, some shut, on the great table.

The Rabbi's hair and beard were as wild as if he had not left the room for months. His whitish-gray beard covered his face like a jungle; his long, thick brows almost concealed his eyes. As a protection against the cold he wore a wadded caftan such as only hand workers usually own. Over his caftan hung his prayer shawl with its long fringes; it almost covered him. The fringes trailed on the floor behind him.

Sunk in deep reflection, the Rabbi walked up and down the room chewing at his beard. Impatiently he kept snatching with nervous, hairy fingers at some volume on the table, threw a glance at it, flung it away again, and began to shuffle about the room once more. Without stopping he took a pinch of snuff, scattering most of it on his beard. Still sunk in thought, he opened the door and stepped into the House of Study, which adjoined his room.

The Rabbi did not see that his appearance had a chastening, indeed almost dismaying, effect on all the worshipers, who reverently rose from their seats at his entrance.

Some gave way before him, afraid of his rebuke or displeasure. But others approached him, stretching out their hands in greeting. The leaseholders, the poor men and women who had been waiting to see the Rabbi and lay their petitions before him, made ready to seize the favorable opportunity. They pressed toward him and cried beseechingly, "Holy Rabbi!" But he impatiently pushed them away.

The thoughts that occupied him so deeply revolved round nothing less than the position of the children of Israel. He was resolved to establish what place Israel occupied in the kingdom of God.

In thought, Rabbi Mendele was a rationalist, an adherent of Aristotle and Maimonides. He wished—what so many before him had wished in vain—to unite fire and water, Aristotle and Plato. But here he was brought up by two still more salient antitheses, between which he wished to find a bridge: the rationalist philosophy of Maimonides, and the mystical teaching of the Zohar.

Like Maimonides, Rabbi Mendele believed that the way to God led solely and entirely through the reason, not through the heart, and that the "governing reason" was the only mediator between man and God; for of the four sciences that man possessed, the material, the physical, the moral, and the rational, the highest and indeed only true one was the rational. Through his understanding man was united with the efficient reason which ruled all spiritual substance, and through it alone was the highest plane to be reached; only he who possessed reason was worthy of the name of man; all the rest were on the plane of the animals, and their souls were lost. Not all Israel had a part in the next world, but only the man who employed his reason; the others were mere worms.

If that was so, and the man of reason was the only man of deeds, who had a soul in him and who was bound to the Active Reason, to God, what place did the individual Jew hold as one of Israel? Only a

few individuals, the elect, could be called men of reason. All the rest—
what were they? Like straw, over which each day must be said the
blessing: "He has not made me an ignorant, unlearned man." And
reason was not an attribute God had given only to Jews. Many belonging to other peoples had reached the Active Reason—Aristotle, for
example. It must be admitted that a non-Jew who was a man of
reason had a share in the world to come. On the other hand, a Jew
who kept all the Laws and possessed a good Jewish heart but was not
a man of reason would have no share in the world to come, and his
soul would be lost.

But now arose the torturing question: What place was to be found
for the children of Israel as a totality? Every Jew was a descendant
of the patriarch Abraham and of the higher Adam, an image of God,
formed after the divine pattern. . . . Man was God's channel through
which the divine, through which grace and the ideal attributes of the
ten spheres were brought down to the earth. Every soul had its pre-
destined place in the world order. How could one dare, therefore, to
rob the simple, ordinary man of the possibility of a glorification, of a
next life?

In his need, Rabbi Mendele summoned to his aid the great ones.
He remembered the author of the "Kuzari," the great poet, Rabbi
Yehuda Halevy, who maintained that the Jews, through the seed of
Abraham from which they came, held an exceptional place, different
from all other peoples. Therefore they were the heart of the world,
suffering like the heart in a man's body for all the world's ills. He
turned to the author of "The Duties of the Heart": because they
kept the Torah, the Torah which is from Heaven, every Jew was
cleansed, elevated, and set in a special place. And so would man be
cured and cleansed. He even invoked "the Jewess," as he called the
author of the "Book of Chassidim," Rabbi Yehuda Hachassid, through
the love of God the Jews had bound themselves to God. He summoned
all the lovers of Israel. But Maimonides stood above them all, like a
cold steel sword that cut mercilessly: only those who attached themselves to the Active Reason were of value. The rest were lost and, like
the beasts, would have no share in the world to come. He finally called
on his own master, the Holy Jew. He saw before him the little man
with the ascetic frame standing sunk in prayer amid his fellowship.
His ecstasy suspended even the laws of his physical existence, and he
swooned away and only came to himself when Rabbi Reb Bunem
played on his violin the psalm, "The dead praise not the Lord." But

this was no help either; for the Holy Jew had held the axiom: "Only those thirsting for it attain holiness."

A ray of light in the darkness: Rabbi Mendele reminded himself of what had happened when God brought the Law down to Sinai. He had wished to impose the Torah on all the peoples of the world, but none of them would accept it save the children of Israel. Through that Israel became a holy people, and every single child of Israel....

While the Rabbi was fighting this hard battle with Maimonides, the door, which he had forgotten to lock, softly opened. A bent old man unobtrusively appeared. The old man was a familiar figure in the Rabbi's court, and was among the oldest supporters of the fellowship. Pale and trembling, he remained standing in the doorway. His beard quivered, and he stretched out his hands toward the Rabbi, raising his eyes imploringly. His glance was blind with fear, and with trembling lips he stammered a few incomprehensible words.

"What do you want? What do you all want of me?" cried the Rabbi, yet less as if he were angry than as if he were pleading for mercy. "Why do you all hang on to me? What do you want of me?"

"Holy Rabbi! I want nothing for myself—really nothing!... I have a grown-up daughter at home, she's over twenty, nebbich.... It's a great grief to me.... My heart bleeds, I can't bear to think of it.... She never says a word... she's as gentle as a dove.... But her eyes speak! Holy Rabbi, I want nothing for myself...."

The old man got no further, for Rabbi Mendele shouted at him, "Am I a marriage broker? Do you come to me to marry off an old maid?"

"I thought... if the Rabbi, long may he live, would only wish me well... perhaps the Lord of the universe would send me His help then."

"Who are you and what are you that the Lord of the universe should concern Himself with your affairs? Do you expect Him to send a husband for your daughter down from Heaven, along with a sackful of money? The ideas these people have!" The Rabbi's voice broke, and in his agitation he kept pushing his velvet cap backward and forward on his head. "I fancied my fellowship thought of nothing but the Messiah, who sits before the gates of Rome and waits for the great summons; and this man thinks of nothing but his grown-up daughter! Is she too wretched to wash and cook? Out of my sight! Maimonides was right: 'They have the souls of brute beasts and they deserve no part in the next life.' I have no use for brute beasts! Get out! Get out!"

Without noticing what he was doing the Rabbi rushed after the terrified old man, into the House of Study. There was great agitation there when the people saw the Rabbi storming after the white-faced old man and shouting, "Maimonides was right!" From every side people rushed in and asked in terror, "What has happened? What has happened?"

When they grasped at last the cause of the Rabbi's discomposure, they were all deeply troubled and cast down and sunk their heads. Round the Rabbi there was an icy silence. He noticed it, raised his powerful head and glanced round him. Everybody became rigid. Rabbi Mendele's eyes flashed. The fear and grief of his disciples mounted.

"Oxen! What are you staring at me for? The words, 'with my whole heart I long for Him,' signify that every personal will must be annihilated before the one great will. All desire must end in *one* desire, all longing flow into *one* longing—the longing for Him. You must not pray for something from Him, but for everything for Him! So that His glory may be revealed to the world."

The Chassidim trembled at the words of the Rabbi and reeled like a wall that is about to fall. Only one man out of his immediate circle, a man thin and slender as a birch, replied with a sigh, and his side curls swayed like willow branches.

"Oh, Holy Rabbi, if one only could do that!"

"If you can't, what use are you to me? Out of my sight, you beggars in this world and in the next!" The Rabbi was pale with fury, his beard and eyebrows quivered, he began to stammer in his agitation, "We're afraid of the pettiest estate owner, the stupidest peasant, but not of God! We're small and humble in this world, spat upon by everybody—but surely there must be *some* place where we are masters? I thought that at least in Heaven we should be great lords; in that case it would be worth while to lead our wretched life on earth and bow to every peasant here so as to be free men there, in the next world! But if we are to be beggars in the next world too, what is the use of such a life?"

The pale, thin man ventured to reply again.

"Rabbi of Tomashov—you say we should be lords before God? And what about humility of heart? It is said: 'Out of the depths have I cried unto thee, O Lord.'"

"But it says also in the Song of Songs: 'My beloved is mine, and

I am his,' and that means: If I am a friend of God's, God is my friend. Beggars can't be friends! All of you who want to be beggars, go with him!" The Rabbi pointed at the thin man. "Take them and go; I have no use for beggars! The fellowship of the faithful should be the armed hosts of God. The timid of heart can remain in their homes for all I care."

With that the Rabbi turned and hastily shuffled into his room.

The men hung their heads like offenders taken in the act.

"They're lucky, the ones that reach such a high plane," said one of them with a sigh. "What fire!"

"He won't manage it, all the same; the people can't do without their daily bread."

CHAPTER XII

LAW

EVERY night on his hard pallet Boruch-Moishe had to fight a difficult inner battle alone with himself, without help. Since Yechiel had brought the news that Rivke was dangerously ill, the father had kept asking himself whether he really had a right to draw a line between himself and his family duties and think only of the salvation of his soul. Hitherto he had silenced every argument that rose within him when he thought of his dependents at home with the argument: "The obligations I have taken on me by becoming a member of the fellowship of Tomashov take precedence over all others." And he had worked upon himself so well that at last he actually felt that he was justified in leaving his family, and casting all his former life behind him. He had done this too with his sensual life. Whenever evil impulses awoke in him during the night he told himself that he was already an old man and had no need of a wife, and at last he became aware that, thanks to God's help, his hair was growing gray.

So Boruch-Moishe rose to a plane where he despised sensual things, and his evil impulses left him in peace. That, it was true, was not much to boast of, for the Rabbi taught that one could achieve nothing by merely despising sensual things; one must begin to feel the awakening of the other state, which lies beyond the sensual. Yet Boruch-Moishe was on the right road. And now he was expected to destroy the work of months and years, to leave this place and sink once more in the slough of life, give himself away in little bits—his prayer would no longer be real prayer, his study no longer real study! What was he to do? A hundred times he had made a resolution to remain deaf to the tumult of the world, to defend himself against the claws stretched out for him, seeking to fling him back into the abyss from which he had laboriously climbed.

But evil can take many shapes. This time it came in the cloak of piety and appeared at his bedside in the night with tormenting reproaches: "Boruch-Moishe! You've left your sick wife to God's mercy

at home there; your children are hungry and forsaken and there is
nobody to care for them. And you stay here with the Rabbi, and fling
the burden off your shoulders. Do you think that is serving God?"

And the Evil One, who can use learned arguments when needful,
supported them with quotations from the holy books: "As you take
pity on my creatures, so will I take pity on you." ... "The Lord of
the Universe prays every day. What is the Holy One praying for?
'May it be granted me to take pity on my creatures.'" ... In his zeal
to seduce man the Evil One employs countless such quotations, and
actually he succeeded in making Boruch-Moishe's heart more and
more open to the sufferings of his wife and children.

"O God, help me!" he groaned on his bed.

But what was he to do, since the Rabbi would not allow him to
go? Every day he begged Hirsh, the attendant, to go to the Rabbi
and remind him that Boruch-Moishe wished to go home.

"But listen to me. It's a matter of life and death; my wife is dying,
the children have nobody to look after them; there's nobody there.
It's breaking my heart...."

"Go to him yourself. Why do you ask me? You've seen yourself
what the old man got for his pains. Why should I get myself into
trouble? Do it yourself."

Boruch-Moishe took up his post outside the Rabbi's door. He
resolved to stake everything on one throw, come what might. There
was nothing but to wait for a favorable opportunity—perhaps the
Rabbi would consent to see him. So Boruch-Moishe stood outside
the door hour after hour. Behind it he could hear shuffling footsteps
padding to and fro, to and fro, like a lion in a cage. Now and then
he could hear a voice talking. He became rigid with awe. He was
convinced that the Rabbi was an angel from Heaven, and so behind
the door great things must be happening now: the angels of the higher
spheres must certainly be gathered with the Rabbi.

Yechiel followed his father's example. He also stood at the Rabbi's
door, rocking piously like Boruch-Moishe, and his heart beat loud
with reverent awe. His fancy painted daring pictures of the things
that must be happening behind the door. The roof was open and
there stretched from Heaven to the room a fiery ladder on which, as
in the Bible, angels ascended and descended. They bore the Rabbi's
prayers up to Heaven and brought back help and fulfillment. Yechiel
wondered to himself whether he would be granted the favor of seeing

the ladder: No, that's impossible, for one would need to be one of the really righteous to do that!

But far more powerfully than by these pictures he was moved by certain other ones in his mind, they were vague, only half-realized shapes, most of them resembling azure islets, and on them dwelt the patriarchs, along with holy men and Rabbis. These imaginations awoke in Yechiel a strange mixture of fear and pious curiosity.

Then father and son could hear the Rabbi's shuffling footsteps quite near the door. Their hearts pounded. The door opened, the Rabbi appeared and threw an astonished glance at Boruch-Moishe as if he had never in his life seen him before. But before the father could pluck up courage to state his request Rabbi Mendele, sunk in thought, had vanished into the House of Study.

The Rabbi was not always so violent as he had been the day before with the old man. He had gracious moments; then he emerged smiling from his room, paused beside some group of his trusted disciples and even made witty remarks. At night, when everybody slept and the whole House of Study lay in darkness, a light still shone from the Rabbi's window, where he sat sunk in thought over his "worlds." Now and then, too, he would recite the midnight prayer. On such nights—so it was said—beggars who had arrived late in the town sometimes made in the darkness toward that solitary light and ended by finding themselves in the Rabbi's room. He welcomed them kindly, gave them his bed to sleep on, and tenderly covered them up. Only next morning did they discover in whose bed they had been sleeping.

The Rabbi allowed himself one hour of recreation. Every day about noon he left his room and amused himself with an old musical clock, which played an ancient air. He said that this was the only impulse which he allowed the Evil One to gratify in him, in order to bribe him as it were. At such an auspicious moment he noticed Boruch-Moishe standing at the door and recognized him.

"You're Boruch-Moishe, if I'm not mistaken, yes? What are you doing here? I know you from the time when I was in Przysucha with the Holy Jew. Come in."

Boruch-Moishe was drunk with joy.

Yechiel, his eyes gaping with awe and his side curls swinging, followed, holding firmly to his father's caftan.

Boruch-Moishe had made up what he was to say during the night. But before he had time to pull himself together the Rabbi began to pour out his heart instead. His words seemed a continuation of the thoughts that occupied him.

"In Przysucha we set ourselves to build up again what the old men had destroyed: to lead the Chassid teaching back from the market place to the altar. And what do these people here want to do? To drag us back to the market place again! Our daily bread—I hear of nothing else! Here, just look at this!" He excitedly rummaged among a heap of petitions that lay on a plate on the table; they were pleas for help by needy people. "The whole place is rotten! These men have nothing in their heads but business; they want husbands for their daughters, education for their sons, remedies for illness, and such base matters. They haven't a single sigh to spare for the glory of God, exiled in this world, no burning desire for the Messiah, who waits in chains at the gates of Rome for us to give him strength for his work! Nothing, nothing at all but bread, marriage, and medicine! It cries to Heaven!"

Without deigning to give Boruch-Moishe a glance he began to pace up and down the room, his fringes trailing after him on the floor. He spoke to himself, as if nobody were there.

"What can I do? I can't be a righteous man at God's expense! And I don't want to interfere in God's affairs! God hasn't set me up as an apothecary, to sell medicines in His name. I am Rabbi of a holy community which wants to achieve something, not of a herd of cattle that low for their fodder!"

Suddenly he stepped up to Boruch-Moishe and seized him by the caftan.

"In the holy Zohar it is said: 'In the beginning God created Heaven and earth,' and that He did so by thinking first of the word 'heaven' and so creating the heaven and then of the word 'earth' and so creating the earth. For the Word is the soul, the kernel of all things. Every word is a world in itself. It consists of its letters, and when one lies one robs the word and destroys its letters. More, one kills it and thus breaks the commandment: 'Thou shalt not kill.' For a word has life in it, just like a human being, and just as one must not offend against a human being, so one must not wrong a word by lying. Rabbi Pinchas said: 'I would rather my soul deserted my body, than that a lie escape my mouth.'"

Boruch-Moishe trembled like a leaf. He was resolved to pocket again the petition which he held convulsively clinched in his fingers, and to say not a word of what he had come to say. But the Rabbi himself reminded him of it. After he had walked about the room for a while in silence he suddenly stopped in front of the terrified Boruch-Moishe, who retreated defensively toward the door.

"Well, what is it that you want? Since you've come to me, you must certainly want something."

"Holy Rabbi!" Boruch-Moishe brought out with difficulty.

The Rabbi did not wait, but snatched the crumpled letter from Boruch-Moishe's hand, unfolded it, and cast a brief glance at it.

"Aha! You're troubled about your son! Is it *he?*" He pointed at Yechiel who, hidden behind his father's caftan, was gazing at the ceiling with wide eyes to find the opening through which the angels descended into the room.

"Yes, Rabbi. He has come to fetch me. My wife is very ill, the children have nobody to look after them." Boruch-Moishe plucked up courage.

"So you want to go home? My best people are leaving me. Who will be left with me?" the Rabbi sighed deeply. "The red noses and the long pipes that sit by the wall and talk against me because I drive away the brokers and the bargainers. Can I achieve anything with them, bring about our salvation with them?"

Rabbi Mendele grew very sad. Boruch-Moishe was seized with deep pity. His heart overflowed with love and devotion. He saw the Rabbi in all his loneliness; quite by himself the Rabbi was climbing an impregnable wall, and nobody, nobody offered him a shoulder or tried to help him. Boruch-Moishe rued his words and tried to take them back, "Rabbi of Tomashov! I won't go home, I shall stay here."

"No, no—as you've made up your mind to go home, go, and a happy journey! Your mind wouldn't be with our cause, your thoughts would be elsewhere, with your sick wife and your children. What use would you be to me in that state?"

Boruch-Moishe stood by the door like an outcast. Yet he still did not go, but glanced apprehensively after the Rabbi, who was shuffling toward his chair.

"Why are you standing there? What more do you want?"

"Holy Rabbi!" began Boruch-Moishe hesitatingly.

"Oh, yes—you're worried about your children!" The Rabbi remembered the letter. "The things a Rabbi has to do, he must actually be an elementary teacher—" he smiled ironically.

Nevertheless he turned, stepped up to the trembling Yechiel, and took him by the chin.

"Is this he?"

"Yes. My eldest one, thank God, has got far on in his studies; but this one, God help me, has a slow mind."

"Tell me, boy; what do you want to become?" Without paying attention to the father's words the Rabbi turned to Yechiel.

Yechiel had stood trembling with dread beside his father, but when the Rabbi took him under the chin an inexplicable sense of security fell on him. He did not look into the Rabbi's face; his great blue eyes were fixed on the ceiling, through which the angels had floated down; and in a clear, firm voice he replied, "I want to be a pious Jew."

"A pious Jew? A good answer. Here's a cake in reward for it." The Rabbi took a cake from the plate on the table and handed it to Yechiel.

"What should I do with him? Study comes hard to him."

"To be a pious Jew he doesn't need to study. He only needs to fear God. Buy him a psalm book! Many get farther by saying the Psalms than by much study."

Boruch-Moishe still lingered by the door.

"What are you waiting for now? Begone!" The Rabbi was growing impatient.

"I wanted...I would like to ask the holy Rabbi...my wife Rivke, daughter of Genendel, asks to be healed...."

"What do you want of me? I don't interfere in God's affairs, I have no pity to give away, for there is a Law...."

Father and son hoped to be with Rivke on the day before Passover. They arrived just in time for her funeral.

Rivke was lying on the floor covered with a black cloth. A lighted candle stood at her head. Beside her sat the Pious Wig; the two ends of her headcloth cast sinister shadows on the wall. The sobbing of the children could be heard from Blimele's house, where they had found a refuge.

"The poor thing kept expecting you up to the last minute. It's a pity you've come too late." Thus Reb Melech greeted the returning father and son.

"What is a wife after all? She's nothing in herself. If she leaves good, studious sons behind her things will be all right with her in the next world. But as it is—God help us!..." the Pious Wig cast a rebuking glance at Yechiel and sighed.

While the corpse was lying on the floor the pawnbroker Reb Berchye appeared, his silver snuffbox as ever in his hand, his clerk behind him. Reb Berchye tapped his snuffbox and sighed.

"Sad, very sad, nebbich!"

Thereupon he hastily snatched one piece of cloth after another from the shelves and handed them to his clerk.

After he had cleared the shelves he went up to the women who were sewing Rivke's shroud, felt the linen, and held it close to his shortsighted eyes.

"Dear, oh, dear, such fine linen for a woman's shroud!" Thereupon he seized the piece, which was already stitched, and flung a remnant of coarse peasant linen to the women. "That's good enough for the worms! And she was only a woman, God pity her!"

While the father stood beside his wife's dead body he remembered the words of the Rabbi, and now he understood what the Rabbi had meant when he said that he had no pity to give away, since there was a Law.

But Yechiel thought of a verse in the Psalms, and repeated it now to himself: "When my father and my mother forsake me, then the Lord will take me up."

Blimele, their good neighbor, had undertaken to bring up the younger children. So Boruch-Moishe, released from all responsibility, returned to his Rabbi.

Yechiel was left to his own fate.

BOOK TWO

CHAPTER 1

THE VILLAGE

BEYOND the immeasurable forests which drained all the life out of the soil, leaving nothing but sand, begin the black, fertile meadows of the valley of Topolye. The domains stretch away for miles to the horizon, a moist peaty soil intersected with swamps and dark pools. In the dawn of time the whole valley, which lies like a flat basin between the oak and pine forests and the steep sandy banks of the Vistula, must have been quite covered with water, forming a single swamp which later dried up. Even now one finds rotten trunks of oak and other species of trees in the soil, which must have sunk there at that far distant time. Today the valley is dry and forms a fertile green pasture which is much enjoyed by horses and cattle, yet the ground is not yet quite firm, indeed in parts dangerous. The sunk forests of an earlier time have been transformed into peat which the peasants of the whole neighborhood steal and use as fuel or manure. And in places the ground sometimes gives way beneath one's feet. Quite often a cow or a horse vanishes without notice; the swamp draws it down into its depths. Sometimes even a peasant disappears and is no more to be found. In the middle of a field a deep peaty hole suddenly yawns, water rises in it, containing all sorts of curious reptiles. Strange looking frogs also hopped about the meadows; they had a curiously green hue, such as could be seen nowhere else, and at night their croaking was heard far and wide.

Not far from the great pond rose a white house. It stood in the midst of a neglected park, and was cut off by wrought-iron gates covered with green rust. Long before one reached the village one could see the white tower of the house rising high above the tops of the chestnuts and birches. There lived the lord of the manor, Pan Wydawski, Count of Topolye. He was hardly ever to be seen outside his castle, for Pan Wydawski was an old bachelor and an eccentric. Cut off from the whole world he lived in his castle, never received visitors, and paid no visits. Only rarely did he go beyond the gate of his garden. According to the people in the villages on his estate he slept all day, for at night he entertained evil spirits and held wild orgies with them. In reality Count Wydawski was merely lazy and careless, and an enemy of new fashions in clothes. Day after day he went on wearing, as if they were a second skin, his shabby, spoiled trousers, and his long, frayed frock coat, whose lapels were already turning green. And not all the riches of this world and the next would have induced him to change his wide-legged trousers. When his chamberlain one morning reached him another pair, he was given a good dressing down.

The chin and cheeks of the tall, lean count were covered with a fortnight-old stubble. His mustache reached from ear to ear. From early morning till late at night the Pan would sit along with his gigantic bulldog Titus in the dilapidated veranda with the broken windows, that looked out on the castle pond, and wait with his blunderbuss for any wild fowl that ventured into the water. Often a half or even a whole day would pass without a bird showing itself. For the birds knew what was what and kept on the opposite bank, so as not to come within range. Pan Wydawski was too lazy to leave his veranda and beat up the birds, although at the other side of the pond, which was quite easy to reach, the water swarmed with wild fowl in the shooting season.

The only representative of the outer world whom the Count admitted was his tenant Shloime-Wolf Pokrzyvy (he had been given the last name, which is that of a poison thistle, by his master in place of his honest father's surname, and had to wear it without complaint). Wydawski consulted with his tenant on questions concerning the working of his estates, also on personal matters. He even divulged to him, though he was a Jew, his troubles with his army of relatives, male and female, who were all waiting for his death. Through Shloime-Wolf he received news of all that was happening outside his castle, and he paid more attention to what Shloime-Wolf had to say about the condition of his estates than he did to the reports of his steward. Shloime-Wolf was, so to speak, the liaison officer between him and the outer world. But that did not prevent him from cursing the Jew heartily during their most confidential talks, and even setting his dog upon him. . . .

Shloime-Wolf would have given his life for his landlord. The "Poritz" (so the Jews call a noble land proprietor) was the pride of his heart and a constant source of vanity to him. The Jew took it very much to heart that the Poritz should neglect his appearance so grievously. When he was with his acquaintances, the tenants or cotters of other land proprietors, they made fun of him and called him jestingly "The innkeeper of the king of the shnorrers."

But Shloime-Wolf knew that his Poritz was richer than all the others, although they wore gray frock coats in the latest fashion and lived all the year around in Warsaw or abroad on borrowed money. The Pan neglected his appearance out of pure laziness. One day Shloime-Wolf resolved to take a decisive step—he went to the town, bought the finest cloth he could get, and ordered Feivel the tailor, a master in his trade, to make a pair of trousers for the Poritz. And when the Count once more summoned him to the castle, Shloime-Wolf cast himself at his feet and passionately kissed his hands. At the same time he held up to him the trousers, which were in the latest fashion, and said imploringly:

"Poritz dear, change your trousers for the dear Lord's sake! You're a great Pan, the lands of the other lords aren't worth two of your stables—I can't bear to see them better dressed than you; it breaks my heart! I'm ashamed before the other tenants. Poritz dear, do me a great favor, change your trousers!"

If the Count was in a good mood, Shloime-Wolf was let off for such impertinence with the ejaculation "Filthy Jew!" and the threat of having Titus set upon him, which alone was enough to make his hair stand on end. But if the Count was in a bad mood, he had his tenant whipped and threatened to lock him in the piggery if he ever presumed in such a manner again. But Shloime-Wolf refused to be beaten; his grief was too great that his Poritz should wear ragged trousers and his neighbors make fun of him. Accordingly, whenever he came to see the Count, he always had the new trousers tucked under his caftan, though he did not always dare to offer them again.

For although the Pan was on very familiar terms with his house-Jew and summoned him to the castle every time he was in trouble, Shloime-Wolf's lot was not to be envied. Every time he was sent for his heart stopped with terror and sweat started from every pore of his skin. For one could never say beforehand how such a visit would end. During the whole way to the castle Shloime-Wolf sighed and groaned and prayed to God. And all through his absence his wife sat trembling in the darkest room of the house with the children, praying to God to preserve her husband. Even the youngest member of the family knew that father was in deadly peril, and went about on tiptoe. And in reality the danger was considerable, for though the Pan might greet his Jew ever so affably, be familiar with him, even summon him in the middle of the night, when his lordship felt sleepless, and divulge his most intimate cares to him, one could never prophesy how these flattering relations might end. Sometimes after one of these "interviews" Shloime-Wolf would return streaming with blood caused by Titus's teeth. And he knew just as little how he had come to lose his master's confidence as how he had gained it.

The Count treated his estates exactly as he did his favorite Jew. For months he completely neglected them. Then he would lie on his veranda waiting for wild fowl, or would stroll in his dirty cloak through the overgrown alleys of his park, muttering incomprehensible words into his enormous mustache. At such times the steward dared neither to report to him nor to ask him for money, and the estate went to ruin. So the steward ran it as he thought best and mainly for his own advantage. The peasants did not render their usual compulsory service. The estate was a picture of complete dilapidation —the buildings were roofless, many of the fields lay fallow, the horses and cattle, coated with dirt, never groomed, trampled wherever they liked; the paths were covered with weeds, the bridges were half falling down, and frequently horses had to be fetched from the castle to drag a peasant's wagon or a rich man's carriage out of the stream. Thus the manor of Topolye was like a ship without a rudder.

But then the Count would suddenly remember his duties as a landlord. He would summon the steward, demand an account of everything for months back, and require an explanation of his finances. And everybody knew beforehand how such interviews would end. Either both the steward and the innkeeper would be carried out of the castle streaming with blood caused by Titus's teeth, or the Count, who was also the chief magistrate of the district, would send for the village constable and a few peasants. In that case the steward was the sole scapegoat; his trousers were torn off him and he was given as many cudgel blows as he could stand.

The most grievously oppressed and neglected dwellers on the estate were the peasants. True, they had only to work a few days in the week for the lord of the manor, but the other duties they had to fulfill in return for their houses and plots of land were endless. In reality, they and their wives and children existed in lifelong slavery. The Count could, if it pleased him, command any of his peasants, through his agent, the steward, to do all sorts of things for him; he could choose from their families the neatest girls, the most capable boys, and use them for his personal service in the castle. Every peasant was liable to be awakened in the middle of the night and sent off with his horse and wagon on some distant errand of his landlord. As district magistrate the Count was entitled by right and precedent to punish disobedience with a public whipping. He had delegated this right to his steward, and the steward usually himself executed punishment with the hunting whip or cudgel which, like his master, he always carried about with him. The whipping followed on the offense, and without regard to age or sex.

Nevertheless the peasants on the manor of Topolye were not really badly off. They had enough ground and pasture to suit their needs and were allowed to keep as many cattle as they pleased. When there was a lack of fodder the remedy was an easy one—they stole it from the Count's barns, which, owing to the general dilapidation, were easy to get into, or drove their cattle at night to the Count's pastures. So it came about that the peasants of Topolye were famed in the whole district for possessing the finest and best horses. When they went to the annual fair in the town or to some festival at a neighboring village, Jews and Christians alike assembled to admire the Topolye horses, which were not in the least like the usual small Polish nags. The fertile pastures produced a good breed. The peasants were very fond of animals and proud of their beautiful cattle. The Jewish butchers of the whole district competed keenly for the Topolye oxen.

Thus the peasants of Topolye led a far pleasanter existence than those on other estates. Their wives were just as plump and well nourished as their cattle, and were fond of ribbons and gay dresses. They knew the art of dyeing their wool and linen in bright colors. The peasants from the other villages regarded them enviously, and the Jews called them "the spoiled children of Topolye." Yet a Topolye peasant could no more escape the whip than any living creature can escape death, no matter how diligent he might be, nor how hard he might try to fulfill his obligations to his landlord. For in spite of his laziness, and although he sometimes did not see his steward for months, the Count remained resolutely true to the axiom which was general at the time in Poland, and which ran: "A peasant can only be ruled with the cudgel." The steward knew quite well that the first article of his report had to consist of complaints about the laziness of the peasants, accompanied by a list of those who should be whipped. True, Topolye was in a state of such complete neglect that both the live and dead stock on the steadings were covered with dirt; but one thing was done with punctilious precision—the whippings. And one was not whipped at Topolye for mistakes or transgressions, but, in accordance with the universal governing system in Poland at that time, at the pleasure and whim of the master.

On a hill close by the wide entrance to the village stood a long, white-washed house, on which like a heavy nightcap was planted a moss-grown thatched roof. The house was divided in two by a great red entrance door. On both sides of it long benches ran along little windows with green sashes, whose ledges almost reached the ground. On the benches newly washed wooden milk basins and buckets were set out to dry, the brightly polished handles glittering in the sun. The entrance to the village and the square before the inn were crammed full of wagons and vehicles of all kinds, some yoked, some unyoked. The wind whirled dust, mingled with wisps of straw from the loaded wagons, high into the air in miniature dust spouts. Hens stopped scratching the ground to steal corn from the horses. The slumbering wagon drivers, Jews and peasants, who in spite of the pleasantly warm sunshine were wrapped in heavy coats of lambskin, snored on the ground beside their wagons. The hens hopped round them and picked kernels of corn from their beards and clothes. But that did not disturb the sleepers. They did not waken to life until their impatient companions roused them with their own whips.

In the inn there seemed to be a great coming and going. A confusion of voices, mingled with other sounds, floated through the open windows and the wide open door. Into the haggling and quarreling of Jews broke the rumbling voices of drunken peasants. From time to time the great door spat out along with the noise some unwanted peasant, who rolled down the steps, quite drunk, bawling a song. A group of short burly Jews with long coats under their caftans and wild tangled beards emerged from the inn gesticulating violently and awoke the sleepy afternoon landscape with their lively disputations.

Otherwise everything round about was completely still. The wide blue sky sent down great waves of light and warmth. The air was scorching. Field, tree, bush, and grass slept motionless in the rigid heat. The square lay on a slight eminence. From there one could see as from a roof the valley which opened on all sides for miles beneath one. The pale-blue firmament, sown with little silvery white clouds, arched itself over green, well-watered fields, intersected with a network of water courses, brooks, and pools. The meadows were bordered with tall green poplars and white birches; in pairs or in groups the trees climbed here and there the exquisite green slopes of the little hills. White, red, or dark dots could be seen moving against that background; these were herds of lazily grazing cows or cantering horses. No sign of man's handiwork disturbed the harmony of the green valley; it swept like a smooth sea to the horizon, where it was bounded by an endless dark-blue line of enormous forests.

From behind the white inn emerged a flock of snow-white geese and peaceably cackling ducks, guided by a wand which a young girl held in her hand. The girl could not be much over twelve, but she looked much older. The cause of this was a long cotton dress picked out with red flowers which reached past her bare feet and trailed after her on the ground. It made her look unusually tall and slender. On her long girlish neck was perched a small proud head covered with pitch-black curling hair like the wool of a black ram. Beneath her tangled locks two restless black eyes looked out of her little sunburned face.

With energetic waves of her wand she drove her flock before her, at the same time munching a slice of bread and butter that she held in her hand. She guided her charges downward over a well-trodden meadow path toward a thicket of willows and burdocks, behind which in the lush grass a clear brook lay hidden. The geese and ducks vanished with much excited cackling into the running stream. Without troubling to see whether there was any one in sight the girl flung off her dress with a single movement, shook her hair to loosen the plaits in which it was bound, and holding her wand, jumped in after her flock. Naked in the water she kept her geese together as strictly as she had done clothed and on dry land.

For a long time she gamboled with her geese, the twig in her hand. Nobody saw her nakedness except a strayed cow which, driven by thirst, forced a way to the brook through the willow bushes and now greedily stretched her long neck to get at the water. Occasionally a lonely hawk described a slow circle in the air, to plunge down like a stone to the surface of the stream, snatch a fish in its beak, and vanish again. The naked girl threatened it from afar with her willow wand. During the afternoon the village stork paid a short visit to the brook in the course of his rounds, to bring his young ones a worm or two.

When toward evening the girl was driving her washed and full flock homeward, she caught sight of a cloud of dust near the end of the village. She knew what was the cause of it and stopped with her flock to await the comer. Presently a high wagon drawn by two powerful white-flecked gray horses detached itself from the cloud; they brought Shloime-Wolf, the girl's father, back from the town. In her joy she forgot to get out of the way, and as if resolved to have a good-humored jest the horses cantered straight in among the wildly cackling geese, who scattered on all sides with indignant squawks and a rain of feathers.

The arrival of the wagon brought the landlady of the inn to her door. On the steps appeared a tall, fair woman, whose ample bosom stuck out like a bastion. Her sleeves were rolled up; at her waist hung a bunch of rattling keys fastened to a piece of flat wood. A swarm of children, boys and girls, with disheveled side curls, and hair powdered with dust, surrounded their mother. With a noisy jerk the wagon stopped before the door of the inn. A big man covered from head to foot with dust jumped down; he had a thick broad beard, which seemed white at first, but after violent shaking turned out to be black.

"Father, father, what have you brought me?"

In a second the children were clinging to him and searching the pockets of his big coat.

"I've brought you a teacher with a big strap to whip you! Out of my way, you baggage. Notte, Antek, unload this wagon!"

The order was unnecessary. Already two big lads in topboots, their hair shining with sweat, their sleeves rolled up, had begun to lift from the wagon casks of brandy and beer, sacks of salt, bales of cloth, tuns of herring, bunches of candles hanging from long poles. And from among the casks and bales a crumpled and apprehensive figure crept out—Yechiel. His lips trembled and his side curls waved wildly.

"Oh, is that all there is of the teacher?" asked the ample woman, standing in the door of the inn and bursting into uproarious laughter. Her pregnant body heaved so violently in time with her laughter that the bunch of keys at her waist began to rattle loudly.

"What have you against the teacher?" Shloime-Wolf contemplated Yechiel searchingly and turned him around so as to see him better. Could it be that he had not chosen the right one after all?

"You call that a teacher? He's all very well to herd the geese! But these little mice," she pointed to her offspring who had gathered around her, "they need a cat, not a gooseherd."

Reisel—such was the name of the goosegirl—had meanwhile crept into the wagon and was searching every corner in which her father could have hidden a present. The inquisitive geese followed. Now she stuck her woolly head out of the wagon and her astonished glance fell on the terrified Yechiel.

"Well, Reisel, now you won't have to herd the geese any longer. Your father has brought a gooseherd back with him!" her mother shouted at her.

Reisel's black eyes attentively scrutinized the timid boy. Then with a violent movement she flung her head back and said, "I don't need him. I can look after the geese myself."

The innkeeper was still examining Yechiel from every side. At last he laid his great hand on the boy's shoulder and turned to his wife.

"Is he too small for you? Give him lots to eat, and he'll grow all right! And remember that he's an orphan; he's lost his mother; so you must treat him kindly."

"An orphan, that's a different matter!" The woman drew Yechiel to her, as if she wished to shelter him under her ample apron, and led him gently into the house.

CHAPTER II

THE INN

THE walls just beneath the low ceiling were a grayish black from tobacco smoke and the fumes of the stove, which always drew badly. In the fog of smoke and alcoholic vapor that constantly filled the room, human beings and things could be dimly descried, appearing and vanishing again. The fume of smoke made everything look unreal and gave it a vague dreamlike character. Bands of intoxicated peasants reeled about as if they were floating on rafts; they held on to each other by the neck or the lapels of their jackets and filled the room with their loud brawling. In a corner there suddenly loomed out of the fog a group of eagerly haggling Jews; they disputed hotly and finally came to an agreement, at which they began to rock to and fro as if praying. It was stiflingly hot and sweat ran down the drinkers' excited faces, flushed with their potations. Caftans and coats were flung off and left lying where they fell. Several drunk peasants were lying about the floor; the others stumbled over them every now and then and they got many a knock. Then they were pushed aside with a foot as if they were inanimate objects. The drunkards made no resistance and remained lying as they were. In a corner a wandering beggar slept with his sack under his head. Imagining that he was a package, one or two peasants sat down on him and there emptied their glasses. The beggar made no sign.

The ruler of this kingdom was Malke, the innkeeper's wife. She stood behind the counter, on which were set out brandy and piles of the homemade honey cakes which were beloved by the Jews and the peasants alike. Behind her rose shelves filled with dry goods, and from a leather string hung long bundles of wax candles. The landlady wore an indefinable dress in gay colors that reminded one of a gypsy costume and set off her voluptuous contours. On her shorn head was a wig and a hood which in shape was somewhat like a soldier's cap; it was worn at a slant and coquettishly pushed back from her brow. Several jewels of questionable value, as well as brooches of the same kind, glittered in her false hair and on her bosom, although it was a weekday. Though her hair was cut according to the Jewish regulation, a few ringlets shyly peeped from beneath her richly ornamented hood. Stout and well nourished, she stood there in her broad apron, with her powerful neck, in defiance of the ruling fashion, pretty amply exposed, and her sleeves rolled up over her round white arms, keeping her eye on everything. She supervised her assistants, the maid Yadviga and the inn-boy Notte, who unceasingly replenished the tin and pewter tankards with brandy.

"That peasant over there has had a whole quart and paid nothing yet! Fling out that man by the door; he's blind drunk and making too much row. . . . There's a man wanting a pound of salt."

She noticed everything and at the same time followed intently the bargaining of the Jewish dealers who were negotiating in a corner over grain.

"Reb Joshua, we get five gulden when you dispose of the Topolye wheat! We're entitled to get a commission on everything that is sold from Topolye!" she shouted across to the corner where the Jews were haggling.

"Your husband did not put the business my way: how should he be entitled to a commission?"

"Whether he put it your way or not, Topolye is our affair."

Although she was talking like this she found time to put a cross and two strokes in chalk on the board under the name "Chmielnik," which signified that the peasant Chmielnik had had a quart of schnapps and a pound of candles on credit.

And during all these activities Malke had not once ignored the door which led into the adjacent alcove, where her husband was negotiating with the great cattle dealer Reb Shaye over the purchase of a drove of oxen from Topolye. Though for the time being the oxen still belonged to the lord of the manor, at this moment the innkeeper and the cattle dealer were sitting with the pock-marked steward and trying to persuade him to sell the oxen on his own responsibility. For the Count was once more leading his hermit existence, saw nobody, and had no taste or leisure for business affairs. It was urgently necessary that the oxen should be sold, for the season was already over, and if one waited for the autumn one would have to feed them over the winter. The steward's skin prickled when he thought of the results which such a piece of presumption might have for him. On the other hand he was greatly tempted by the considerable sum of money he would be able to pocket if he accepted the proposal.

Malke decided to intervene. She knew very well that nothing helped
more in carrying through a business deal than a glass of brandy and a
woman; not without reason did the proverb run: "A beautiful woman
is half a man's livelihood." Accordingly she had a carafe filled with
brandy, not forgetting a little bottle of oil for Reb Shaye, who was
delicate and could only drink his brandy mixed with oil on account of
his weak heart. She herself filled a second carafe with sweet mead from
a hidden cask, which she exclusively reserved for the rich land proprietors. As she was filling it a drop fell on her plump finger; she licked
it off with relish. She ordered the inn-boy to carry the brandy into the
next room; she herself followed with the mead, not without first cock-
ing her coquettish hood at the right angle, and cleverly arranging her
gypsy dress so that her neck should be displayed to the best advantage.
For she knew that, though Reb Shaye was a Chassid and one of the
intimates of his Rabbi, he was not averse to seeing a beautiful neck
displayed to his gaze; whenever he saw her ringlets peeping from underneath her hood, and her bare arms, he always gave a deep sigh and
a piously shocked "Oy, oy!" but his eyes spoke a different language. . . .
Malke seized the carafe and followed the boy. When the thirsty peasants and hungry Jews sitting on the low benches smoking their pipes
saw the handsome landlady in full war paint haughtily bearing a carafe
of mead into the alcove, they knew at once for whom it was intended,
and envied the cattle dealer that choice draught and its lovely giver.

"What about it? Isn't the business settled yet?" Malke asked, turning to the steward as she entered. "What is there to be afraid of? He
won't eat you alive."

"If the Count comes to know of it, it's my backside that will know
it, not yours!" The sly little eyes of the steward came to rest com-
placently on the posterior of the landlady.

Reb Shaye, short, but broad and burly, wore his woolen wrap round
his neck though he was sitting indoors; it was midsummer, but Reb
Shaye thought that it did no harm to be prudent. He blew a thin puff
from his pipe and cast a short glance at the voluptuous figure of his
hostess, which was only too clearly revealed by the gay gypsy dress.
Then he covered his eyes with his hand, peeped through his fingers
and sighed.

"Woe to the eyes that must see such things!"

Obviously in order to lead Reb Shaye into still greater temptation,
Malke beat her ample breast with her hand and began, "I'm only a
woman, but I tell you I wouldn't be afraid of the old fool! He thinks,

no doubt, that while he sleeps the world can go to ruin! And you call yourselves men?..."

"Malke, what are you saying? The 'Urel'"—that meant, the uncircumcised—"understands everything you say. Do you want to bring misery upon me?" cried the innkeeper to his wife, pale with terror.

Certain of her success, Malke left the room with a haughty bearing. But before she reached her place behind the counter again she shrank as if she had been stabbed to the heart and began to tremble in all her limbs. For in the doorway of the inn stood in person the "Angel of Death."

The Angel of Death wore a red livery which might have been the very symbol of the dilapidation of the estate of Topolye. A greasy red coat with two rows of silver buttons, most of which were missing, hung loosely round the thin, narrow shoulders of Anton Chmiel, body servant of Count Wydawski, who had been christened the Angel of Death by the village. The former wearer of the coat, to whose measure it had once been made, must clearly have had a pot belly. For round Chmiel's belly the coat was so wide that it looked like a blown-up balloon. The lackey's face had that gray-bluish color which is produced by long imprisonment or sleepless nights. In his case it was the latter. As the Count sat up for whole nights Anton had to remain awake in the next room and be prepared whenever his master called him. Accordingly, during the day he could scarcely keep his eyes open, and he blinked perpetually, for the light pained them. His long potato nose drooped over his mouth. He always kept his head bent, so that his eyes could scarcely be seen. He avoided people's glances, as if he had something to conceal. And he was suspected of that. The peasants firmly believed that the Count was in the toils of a female devil who during the day took the form of the bulldog Titus; all night witches' carnivals were held in the castle, and that was why its windows were always lighted. Anton had signed his soul away to the evil spirits and was already in their power; the Count had given him a witch as a wife, and that was why he could look nobody in the face and was like a drowned corpse....

"The Pan wants the innkeeper. He is to come to the castle!" said Anton in his graveyard voice, without lifting his head.

This message created an immense sensation not only among the innkeeper's dependents but all the customers, Jewish no less than Christian. At the words "the Pan wants" everybody involuntarily jumped up from their seats. Glasses fell from some of their hands, they

all sobered up in a moment, and rushed to the door of the alcove to
bring Shloime-Wolf the terrible news:

"The Pan wants you!"

Shloime-Wolf did not need the warning. Somewhere in his mind the
magical apparatus which we call terror had already signaled approaching danger. He stepped to the door.

"Malke, my Sabbath caftan!"

The steward had vanished. Reb Shaye remembered his piety, and
began to rock his body gravely and devoutly, murmuring as if he were
standing by the bedside of a sick man: "God shall send help! God will
send help! God must send help!" Malke helped the pale and trembling innkeeper into his Sabbath caftan, stroked his side curls smooth,
and combed his thick beard with her fingers, so as to remove the
crumbs. While Shloime-Wolf put on his Sabbath kalpak, he heaved
a humble sigh, "May God send me His help!"

"May God grant it—lucky foot foremost!" said his wife, wiping a
tear from her eye.

All the customers, both Jew and Christian, looked grave as they
watched the innkeeper leaving with the lackey, as if he were setting
out on a dangerous journey whose outcome was uncertain.

The man whose name caused such terror—the rich, high-born Pan
Wydawski—was meanwhile striding restlessly in his fur-topped boots
through the huge ballroom of his castle. Tall doors led from the ballroom to the glass veranda, where the Count loved to lie in wait for
wild duck. Great beams of light fell through the high dust-covered
windowpanes. When the Count could not sleep at night he would often
see as in a dream-vision dozens of couples floating through the ballroom in the brilliant radiance of the crystal chandelier to the music of
a polonaise. Now the crystal chandeliers were dark, covered with dust
and cobwebs, spotted with drops of wax. The whole room was in no
better case. The once white varnish of the walls was a dirty gray; from
the wooden paneling the gold paint was peeling away. Here and there
in solitary state stood a half-decayed beautifully ornamented Louis XV
commode or a genuine Renaissance chest. Once, in the time of the
Count's grandfather, these pieces of furniture had been conveyed from
Paris to Topolye by the castle's own wagons. The beautiful handworked
Regency furniture with the rich Gobelin upholstery—a rosebud pattern
on a cream-white background—was covered with dust and moth-eaten.
The chairs were springless, some of them broken, the sofa coverings
in tatters. Here and there shone out from the dust and dilapidation a

Gobelin rose on some chair, pathetically beautiful in its vivid color and noble form.

Its master resembled the room. Wrapped in a shabby spotted dressing gown, which lacked the greater number of its buttons, the tall, lean Don Quixote figure wandered up and down. His eyes were deeply sunk behind their swollen, almost lashless lids, which were covered with brownish-yellow spots, the relics of a gall-bladder attack. The stubble, several days old, on his flabby cheeks emphasized their ashen-gray hue. The only part of his face which had kept its salient shape was the nose; sharply bent like the beak of an eagle it rose with self-conscious aristocratic pride from a face wasted with illness, forming its last undamaged outpost. The impressive effect of the nose was enhanced by the huge gray mustache, whose carefully curled ends reached to his ears. Two deep hollows ran at either side of his grave, lofty parchment-hued brow into thick hair only faintly tinged with gray and glistening with pomade. The open neck of his nightshirt, which showed over his partly buttoned dressing gown, gave a grace to the line of his long neck on which the veins stood out. So the Count strode up and down, nervously crumpling a letter in his bony hand, which he held at his back.

Underneath the family coat of arms, which was woven into a screen standing before the fire, lay stretched out the magnificent light-brown bulldog Titus, whom the peasants accused of being a transformed witch, and with quivering wet muzzle and liquid eyes he followed every movement of his master.

The Count of Topolye was a freethinker, or, in the ecclesiastical phraseology of his time, a heretic, a follower of Voltaire, filled with enthusiasm for the French Revolution and its motto of "Liberty, Equality, and Fraternity," and with unshakable faith in the great Napoleon, whom he worshiped almost idolatrously. He allowed no priests near him and never visited the church. That was the mainspring of the rumors of his relations with witches and evil spirits, whose dissemination among the ignorant people was encouraged by the Church. But all these ideals: Voltaire, Liberty, Equality, Fraternity, the French Revolution, the Great Emperor, had not the slightest reference to his country or his inferiors, to the peasants and Jews whom he ruled with whip and rod. His own property he regarded as a sort of cattle stall, in which lived filthy animals on whom French methods could not be employed, and his neighbors were ignorant inferior creatures not yet ripe for liberty with whom nothing could be done. To the Jews he did grant some value: in his eyes they were useful tools without which one could not manage; they were also interesting puppets whose slyness amused one at least, to set one's dog on such and such an animal now and then was an enjoyable recreation. The peasant, on the other hand, was for the Count a two-legged beast that could only be ruled with the cudgel. Wydawski was an ardent Polish patriot, had fought for Poland in several wars and been wounded at the battle of Leipzig. For Poland he was prepared to give his life; his isolation too was a consequence of his love for his country. Yet he was incapable of widening the idea of "country" to embrace more than his own caste. Poland for him meant exclusively the aristocracy. The peasants and the Jews had no part in it.

In the great Corsican he saw the incarnation of his ideal. For him Napoleon was the savior of Europe, the redeemer of mankind. His wars were wars of liberation from the tyranny of the small states and principalities and in support of the privileges of the nobility. In the Emperor's victories he saw the realization of his dream of the fraternal union of all peoples in one fatherland, a free France under one scepter, that of Napoleon. The Emperor's "glory" fell also on him, on his age and his view of the world. For him Napoleon was not only a political idea, but in a sense a personal matter. He felt closely bound up with all the Emperor's deeds; every victory of Napoleon was *his* victory. When the great army entered Poland in its March against Russia, the Count joined it. He was not a combatant, himself, it is true; but he had the strongest lads in his villages lined up, stuck them in uniform, and put rifles in their hands. But to explain to them for whom and for what they were fighting he did not consider worth his while; the peasants were, after all, his property, with whom he could do what he pleased.

After Napoleon's defeat and the entry of the Russians into Warsaw the Count withdrew to his castle, since he could not bear to witness the nobility of his country making submission to the Czar Alexander. He waited confidently for the return of the Emperor. Even after Waterloo was lost he still went on hoping that the "Marseillaise" would resound yet once more in Poland's forests. Sometimes he even sent out couriers with the order to tell him at once when the dust cloud heralding the approach of the Emperor's battalions was to be seen.

Then came a day when all hope for the return of the Emperor vanished. The Count withdrew more and more from the world. He was wounded and embittered. When he encountered his neighbors there were always quarrels about the peace signed with the Czar. Wydawski gradually lost all contact with his fellow men and buried himself in contemptuous indifference. He had neither wife nor child. The nephews and cousins to whom the property would fall after his death belonged to the *jeunesse dorée* of Warsaw and amused themselves at the balls which the Russian Governor gave at the Belvedere to dazzle the Polish youth. So the Count finally broke with his relations too. He remained invisible for weeks, for months, and admitted nobody to see him. Life had lost all meaning for him. For whom and for what did he live? He thought of suicide, and thought of destroying himself and the castle by fire. At night he was tormented by bad dreams, so that he grew afraid of sleep. Finally he came to a stage where he no longer slept and kept the lights burning in the castle all night.

Wydawski's strange way of life evoked wonder and many head-shakings among his neighbors. And among the ignorant peasants in his village arose the legend of his relations with witches and evil spirits —cleverly assisted by the Church, which could not forgive the Count his freethinking ideas.

The real pretext for this stupid rumor was provided by the Count's strange behavior. Loneliness had driven him into the arms of the Cabbalists and alchemists. The castle had contained the whole apparatus of a laboratory ever since the time of one of his ancestors who had studied in Padua and brought the various instruments back with him so as to devote himself to alchemy and astrology; among them was an ancient telescope which had once been imported from Holland. The Count frequently made use of it. The castle library also contained a great number of Latin books with strange figures, astronomical tables, representations of cycles and epicycles, Cabbalistic signs, among them that of the ten spheres and other symbols. In his many idle moments, especially at night, the Count buried himself in these works and took up again the alchemical experiments of his ancestor, in particular that of making gold. Thus he hoped to gain the means to wage war against Russia and set Poland free.

In the eyes of his peasants the Count was an unhappy man ruined by black arts and held captive in his castle by witches, devils, and other evil spirits. When his fury burst forth and he had all the peasants in the village whipped, they were convinced that he did not do this of his own volition; for they looked upon him as at bottom a good man. They put the blame for these outbreaks on the devil who "gripped" their master, and prayed to God that He might free the Count from the evil spirits who had him in their power. They also ascribed to their master all the misfortunes that befell themselves, their children or their cattle. When the cow yielded no milk the peasants would exchange silent glances and point significantly at the slack udders; they were convinced that the Count's witches had sucked the cow's milk dry.

Wydawski naturally knew what people said about him, yet did nothing to dissipate the legend, but rather contributed by his behavior to make it grow fantastically. He regarded the gossip about him as an insult to his caste and his honor and considered it beneath his dignity to reply to it or seek an understanding with his peasants. So he persevered stubbornly in his contempt and rage and soon was at feud with the whole village.

Deeply disappointed in his ambition, deeply wounded in his pride as an aristocrat, slandered by his enemies, avoided by his relations, who longed for his death, at odds with the world, a terror to his inferiors— the Count perversely withdrew more and more from the world until he fell into the state already described and sent for his favorite Jew, a thing which had not happened for a long time. For in the last few months Wydawski had admitted no one to his presence.

CHAPTER III

PAN WYDAWSKI RESOLVES TO GET INTO TOUCH WITH THE PEOPLE

WHEN he reached the gates of the castle park, the innkeeper stopped and drew a deep breath. With a devout and heavy sigh he pressed the latch of the little garden door. When he was in the avenue he once more slowed his steps. His skin suddenly began to prickle, fear of the approaching peril set all his muscles and nerves jumping, and his lips kept on murmuring, "Father in Heaven, help me!" He had the feeling that thousands of dogs with wet, sniffing muzzles and sharp white teeth were crouching in every corner of the great house, prepared to spring on him. He scrutinized with particular intentness the white marble steps that led up to the glass-paned door: for there the angel of death in the shape of Titus might appear at any moment. All the thousand eyes which, according to legend, the angel of death possesses stared out of the house on the square space in front of the bright glass door, which glittered cheerfully in the sun. But the Jew standing there had a thousand and one eyes and ears to do him service, and they were all directed on the glass door.

Yet Shloime-Wolf's apprehensions were superfluous. This time no danger awaited him, but the friendliest of receptions. For the Count had summoned him so as to take counsel how he could get into touch with the people.

Count Wydawski had decided to get into touch with the people. For in the last few weeks something important had happened. By secret channels he had received a letter from an old comrade of the Napoleonic era with the request to hold himself in readiness. The letter ran: "Countless arrests are being made in Warsaw. The Polish people are at last wakening out of their long sleep. . . . The July Revolution in Paris has roused new powers of resistance in the youth of Poland. At last they have ceased their dilly-dallying and their attacks on the Jews. The students are uniting—all classes are uniting to drive the Russians from the country. . . . Napoleon's old guards," the letter ended, "must be in the forefront this time too, as they have always been. They must show that the spirit of the Emperor still lives. The nobility have resolved unanimously to unite with the people, to fraternize with the peasants and the Jews. Yes, the Jews too must be brought in. The nobility have at last recognized that they have committed a grievous sin against the fatherland in neglecting the people. Consequently the word has gone out to get into touch with the people, to educate them so that the peasant no less than the Jew might be worthy of becoming a citizen."

In Wydawski the old Napoleonic spirit reawoke. Voltaire, the herald of the new ideas of liberty, equality, and fraternity, those clarion notes of the Revolution, lived to him again. The letter made the lord of Topolye shake off the dust that had accumulated upon him during his years of isolation. The glory of Napoleon's empire flamed up again in him, and for the last time; and he was even prepared to get into touch with the people. For years he had lived in error! Now it was his duty to acknowledge it, to give his hand to the people, and teach them to be citizens. But how was he to begin? The only language he could talk to the peasants was that of the whip. The Jew was really nearer to him. So he decided to send for the Jew and discuss the matter with him. "The idea is a good one," he told himself. "The Jews must help me. If the Jews stand by me the peasants will have to follow— they always take their step from the Jews; if the Jews come in, then they'll feel that it's all right."

The Count was firmly resolved to receive the Jew kindly, and not set the dog on him even once. He would do his very best to greet him graciously and get in touch with him. For the fatherland he was prepared to do anything!

But at the very sight of the Jew standing hesitatingly at the door of the room, his fur cap in his hand, bowing without ceasing, the noble blood in the Count's veins rose, and Titus's eyes gleamed.

The dog turned his head toward his master and waited for orders.

"Down, Titus!" shouted the Count, sinking into an armchair beside the stove. From there he stared at his favorite Jew.

At last Shloime-Wolf's bowings and scrapings glutted the Count's noble appetite for abject submission, and satisfied his sense of his importance. His heart overflowed with graciousness and in a paternal voice he called to the innkeeper.

"Come nearer, Shlomko."

More crawling than walking, the innkeeper, with many further

obeisances, reached at last the Count's feet. There he cast himself down
and tried to seize his master's hand and kiss it.

"Enough, enough!" The Count affably clapped his tenant on the
shoulder. "Stand up!"

Shloime-Wolf rose with a triumphant glance at the disappointed
Titus, who, obviously to express his regret at the improper behavior
of his master, laid his nose between his front paws. The Count wanted
to give the Jew a proof of particular favor.

"Shlomko, now you can make a new pair of trousers for me, and
a coat as well! The days of mourning are over, Shlomko!"

Shloime-Wolf once more flung himself on the ground, and tried to
seize the Count's hand. Not succeeding in this he clasped his feet
instead. "Poritz dear, you make me so happy! I'm ashamed before the
other tenants to see my Poritz going about in such clothes."

"What? You're ashamed of your master before the other tenants?
Do you fancy I haven't a second pair of trousers?"

"But, Poritz dear, who says that? God forbid!" The innkeeper
became white as chalk. "Why, don't I know that my Poritz has whole
chests full of ducats?"

But the Count no longer heard his protestations. His noble blood
was boiling. He violently pushed Shloime-Wolf away and shouted.
"Titus!"

With a leap the dog was at his master's feet, panting with eager-
ness and excitement.

"O God, help me—" began Shloime-Wolf, his face pale as death.

"Don't be afraid; as long as you don't move he won't touch you.
Titus!" the Count turned to the panting dog. "The Jew is not to
move from the spot until I return!" With that he turned to go.

His tongue hanging out with excitement, Titus took up his position
in front of the kneeling innkeeper.

"Poritz dear, for God's sake don't leave me—he'll tear me to pieces
—have pity on my wife and children!"

"Don't be afraid! I've told you already, he won't do anything to
you. But don't stir from the spot, or else he'll eat you up like a juicy
Jewish dumpling!" The Count went, leaving Shloime-Wolf behind
with the dog.

Shloime-Wolf did not know how much time had passed, nor was
he conscious that his limbs were in danger of failing him. He only
felt that the shirt and the Sabbath caftan that he had put on in honor
of the Count were growing wet with sweat and sticking to his body.

Without warning the Count appeared before him in the uniform of an officer of the Uhlans, with a clean white leather belt, gold braid, shining top boots, and a tall black kepi, on which glittered a white eagle, the emblem of Poland. Shloime-Wolf heard a curt military command.

"Get up!"

The innkeeper helplessly glanced from the Count to the dog and back again. Then with an imploring gesture he stretched out his hands toward his master, but without taking his eyes off the dog.

"Poritz dear, I'm afraid!"

"I command you to stand up!"

"Poritz dear . . ."

Shloime-Wolf wiped the sweat from his hair and neck with his sleeve, putting on simultaneously a glad expression to evince his joy at the transformation in the Count's appearance, and said in a flattering tone, though there was still terror in his eyes and sweat on his brow, "Oy, oy, how grand the master looks!"

As if nothing had happened the Count turned to his tenant, who still had not overcome his fears.

"Listen, Shlomko, I want to have a talk with you. It's about a very grave matter and you, my little Jew, are a clever fellow. All Jews have good heads." The Count pointed to his brow. "They aren't like our peasants."

The innkeeper made a deep bow.

"I'm listening, master."

"Well, then, Shlomko, a grave time is dawning for our land, a time when it will need all its children. And we are all its children; yes, everybody, without distinction of race or class. It's high time we rid ourselves of all those class distinctions. Every man of good will who is prepared to accept responsibility must be freed from the medieval bonds that confine him today. Yes, it's high time to proclaim the equality of all classes in our land too. Equal duties and equal rights for all!" The Count became more and more enthusiastic as he went on. "We too must get rid of our medieval ways and train all our sons to be citizens!"

Shloime-Wolf stood as on needles. His terror of Titus had not yet died down. He was not at all clear what the Poritz wanted of him, but he felt instinctively that he wished him well, and he was infinitely grateful to him for speaking so affably. The Count's kindness was balsam for his terror and humiliation. He forgot everything; he forgave the Count the cruel trick he had played on him. Now Pan Wydawski was once more his Poritz, for whom he was prepared to go through fire and water.

"Golden words, master, golden words—they should be written down in a golden book. Truly it is high time, has been for a long time. . . ."

The Count flared up. He remembered to whom he was speaking. The Jew was too familiar; presently he would forget whose presence he was in. Wydawski's sense of his own rank awoke. His mustaches curled and he went on in a sarcastic voice.

"Naturally the privilege of being an equal member of the community must first be earned. One must first of all pass the test, and show that one possesses the necessary *qualifications*"—he underlined the word—"such as honesty, conscientiousness, and a sense of one's duty, before one can be regarded as worthy of fighting for one's country or of sharing the rights and obligations of a citizen. Unfortunately the vast majority of the people in our country do not possess these qualifications. We have neglected them too long. We must awaken proper feelings in them, must make the peasants conscious of their duties, the Jews conscious of their duties to themselves. Both must first of all be made worthy of being citizens. And to do that is the duty of the privileged classes, the higher classes in the country. In that respect we have unfortunately sinned grievously against the people. . . ."

The innkeeper did not understand a word of this long harangue, but his sensitive instinct warned him that the Poritz's mood was in danger of changing and the interview of coming to a disastrous end. Shloime-Wolf had only one desire: to escape as soon as possible from this cat and mouse game. For although the Poritz was in a good mood—the Jew felt that the words he had just said were well meant —one could never foretell how such conversations might develop. All this time he had the feeling of walking on a tightrope which at one point—though which he could not tell—was half cut through and must break some time or other: consequently he watched his steps with the utmost caution. He did not know how he should respond to the Count's words so as to hit the right note. All that he knew was that he *must* respond in some way, for the Poritz had taken him into his confidence. Shloime-Wolf felt his way in darkness. But when the sentence, "We have sinned grievously against the people," fell on his ear, he imagined that he was in duty bound to agree.

"Very true—golden words—they should be written down in a golden book."

The Count flung the Jew a glance whose significance was at once grasped by Titus.

"Hold your tongue, Jew—else Titus will teach you how you should demean yourself before your master!"

"Ach, Poritz dear, I didn't know what I was saying! I didn't mean anything!"

"Silence!"

"Yes, Poritz dear."

"Of course we must bring about the equality of all classes—equal rights and equal duties for all. Do you agree, Jew?" the Count shouted furiously at his tenant.

"If the master says so, how can I, a poor Jew, say no?"

"Equality of all classes, I said, as in France! We must prepare the people to rule themselves. That's why I've sent for you, Jew. I can't talk with the peasants; they're stupider than cattle, my horse understands me better. There's only one language you can talk with peasants—the stick. But you Jews have good heads and if you stick by me the peasants will come in too. So you must talk with the peasants in your inn, and explain to them that all classes must be equal. Do you understand?"

"Who am I not to understand?"

"Your God is a god of vengeance. You are descendants of the Maccabees; as they rose once on a time, so must you. Yes, Shlomko, a new era is dawning for Poland. . . . But now leave me. The whole room is stinking with garlic already; it'll have to be thoroughly aired."

"Thanks, thanks, Poritz dear! Topolye has the best master in the world, long may he live in health and happiness!" Shloime-Wolf flung himself on his knees and clasped his master's boots.

"That isn't necessary! That isn't necessary!" Wydawski suddenly remembered the new era, and would not suffer his Jew to kiss his boots. "From today you mustn't kneel at my feet any longer. You understand? Only kiss my hand," the Count stretched out his hand to be kissed. "We must become like the rest of Europe."

"What kind of world will it be when one can't kneel at one's master's feet? No, Poritz dear, I can't obey you; a man must kneel before his master, it's only right!"

"Jew, shall I ask Titus to teach you proper respect? I tell you

you're to kiss my hand—and that's what you'll do! No more kneeling! All classes must be equal! Do you understand?"

To these arguments, but above all to Titus's eyes, which sparkled malignantly, Shloime-Wolf had to submit, and he seized the moment of hand kissing to take his leave.

Overjoyed that his balancing on the tightrope was over, he retired thankfully toward the door, walking backward. This crabwalk served two ends simultaneously—he could both show his respect for the Count and keep his eye on Titus, and thus protect himself from an attack from the rear. When he reached the door he turned with a deep sigh of relief and began, "I thank thee, God . . ."

But instead of finishing the sentence, he let out a heartrending cry. "Oy, God of Israel . . . !"

His terror was superfluous. Titus, who had been instructed by his master not to bite, did Shloime-Wolf no real harm. He only tore off part of his caftan and trousers with an adroit leap and pranced, his booty in his jaws, back to the Count, who rolled in his armchair with laughter.

"Shlomko, that is your reward for offering your master a pair of trousers!" cried the Count to the chalk-white Jew, who tried to cover his nakedness with the rest of his caftan. "Titus hasn't hurt you really, has he? I gave him strict orders only to go after your caftan, nothing more."

"No, Poritz dear. . . ."

"Fine, Titus, well done!" The Count patted the panting dog on the back and turned again to the Jew.

"Shlomko, Shlomko, I'll let you off your next quarter's rent!"

Laboriously holding the rest of his clothes together, Shloime-Wolf made a deep bow.

"I thank you, Poritz dear! Topolye has the best master in the world. We shall pray for your health. . . ."

Quite out of breath and bathed in sweat, the half-naked innkeeper sank into his wife's arms before the inn; she was pale and had been watching for his return for a long time.

"What did he want? What a sight you are, God help us!"

"Praise be to God, I've returned alive!" gasped Shloime-Wolf.

CHAPTER IV

POOR THADDEUS

YECHIEL had not very much to do in his new job. The inn-keeper's children were still small; accordingly he had only to instruct them in the Hebrew alphabet and reading, and trans-late with the older ones the passages from the Bible that were usually taken at school. The rest of the day he was free and could do what he liked.

Actually Yechiel could not have been more fortunate. The inn-keeper's wife, who ruled the inn like an absolute monarch, treated him very well, first because she was afraid of offending God by neg-lecting an orphan, and secondly because Yechiel soon showed himself to be very handy. Because of the skill that he had acquired in dealing with peasants at the annual fairs, he was able to help in the inn. Being a bright boy, he took an interest in everything, made a place for him-self in his new surroundings and did his best to be useful. And soon he was treated like one of the family. He was given as much food as he could eat, always had a whole shirt to his back, and found time also for study. So he taught himself as best he could.

Yechiel did not own many books; his library consisted of the few volumes Mayer the Jewess had given him and a few from his father as a farewell present, but he studied them as deeply and often as he was able. And there was always some Jewish customer at the inn whom he could ask about obscure passages.

But Yechiel was far more interested in the life round him than in his studies. In his first few weeks in the village he had come to know life far better, acquired more experience of the world and seen more human suffering, than in all the years that he had spent in his native town. Poverty and hard work had robbed him there of his childhood and kept him constantly under their yoke. Destitution had blinded him to the world that lay around him. Now, assisted by his untiring gift of observation, he drank greedily of the river of life that flowed round him. He became conscious of a great and mighty world which he had never known before—the world of human joy and sorrow.

Jewish merchants met in the tavern to conclude business deals, to arrange marriages, and to exchange stories about their troubles at the hands of one Poritz or another. Yechiel was everywhere, listening to everything, discovering how Jews live, and marveling at the miracles God worked for each one of them, day in, day out. Otherwise, he concluded, it would be impossible to understand how they managed to survive.

One of the innkeeper's duties was to keep in repair the road running through Topolye and the bridge across the river Topolyevka, close by the mill. Though the bridge was always broken, always giving trouble, the innkeeper could not bring himself to erect a solid bridge; he preferred a thrashing from the Count rather than to keep it in order. The horses feared to set their feet on the rotting planks, wheels stuck in the cracks, and all too often a Poritz, with an overloaded carriage, had to be pulled out from the muddy stream. The Poritz vented his wrath on the innkeeper, who had to watch his brandy casks being smashed while his family fled to the woods.

Sometimes the long road leading from the outside world brought to the inn a coach filled with Chassidim on a journey to their Rabbi. If they encountered other Chassidim of a different Rabbi, a discussion was soon started. In the midst of drunken peasants, with the place reeking of brandy and cart grease and thick with smoke from many pipes and a leaky stove, they argued on weighty matters, about Cabbalah and the different schools of thought, of the Holy Ari and of Reb Moishe Cardovero. The greatness of their respective Rabbis came in for hot discussion, and they tossed out texts from the Talmud and passages from the Zohar with a hidden meaning. Holy names were mentioned and heavenly interests invoked. Between one learned discussion and another a business deal might be concluded—timber or brandy, oxen or corn, or a marriage arranged between two fathers; and then they would all join in the evening service. In the kitchen Malke would be busy cooking borsht for their supper—well peppered, so that the crowd would call for plenty of brandy. After drinking together they would betake themselves to the straw pallets for the night.

The most interesting among the visitors to the inn, and those by whom Yechiel was most attracted, were the poor vagrants who were housed for nothing. One never knew what secret might be concealed beneath the rags of such people. For Yechiel they were enveloped in mystery. Among them were men who refused to sleep on a straw sack, and insisted instead on lying on the hard floor. One of them who visited the inn regularly always carried in his bundle a great heavy stone which he used for a pillow at night. It was said that this was his gravestone, and that his name was already engraved on it. Another never opened his mouth. Originally he had been taken to be dumb, but once he cried aloud as he silently prayed: "Hear, Israel!" People said of him that he was a very rich man from a distant city; but because of a grievous sin he had taken upon himself the penance of forsaking his home and wandering through the country. In order not to betray who he was he never spoke.

Many such stories of penances and vows were related by passing vagrants. In Yechiel's eyes these wanderers were not ordinary men, but mysterious figures who concealed their real nature. He was certain that among them were saints, who belonged to the band of Thirty-six Righteous Men on whom, according to the Jewish legend, the existence of the world depended, and wandering souls who could find no rest in the next world and had been sent back to the earth to retrieve their errors. These vagrants spread stories and legends about known and unknown wonder-workers, just men who had the power to ban evil spirits, cure the sick, save sinners by imposing penances, redeem unhappy souls from their wanderings through the world, and give them admission to eternal peace, and to accomplish many other mysterious things.

Yechiel never left the side of these vagrants, but served them and looked after them to the best of his power. Often he surreptitiously put his own pillow under the head of a sick, wandering beggar, or stuck his dish of meat or bread into a man's scrip to eat on the way. At other times he would steal from his bed in the alcove so as to sleep on a straw sack beside the vagrants, and listen to their stories and observe their ways at first hand.

Soon he had acquaintances of his own in the village. One of the first villagers that he made friends with was a peasant who was universally known as "Father Care" or, after his Christian name, "Poor Thaddeus."

Actually Father Care had nothing about him worthy of particular notice. His house was the last one in the village; it was a good distance away from the inn, almost outside the village bounds altogether, a decayed hut in perpetual danger of falling. The thatched roof was supported by worm-eaten beams, between which were half-rotting boards held in place by rank creepers. Poor Thaddeus's all consisted of a few acres of meager ground which lay on the very verge of the sandy forest zone. Stumps of felled trees still protruded from it. Father Care had great trouble pulling out oak roots before he could plow his little scrap of land at all.

From the window of his room Yechiel could see Father Care already at his work when the morning mists lifted. Wrapped in his tattered sheepskin coat, the little man would be standing in his fields pulling out of the ground with his fork the deep stretching many-branched roots. The verse of the psalm: "Man goes to his work and his labor does not cease till evening," seemed to Yechiel to fit Father Care particularly, for the little man was work incarnate. From early morning until nightfall Poor Thaddeus stood in his fields. Rain, hail, and snow made no difference to him; with a wet sack round his shoulders, he stood beside his horse in the worst downpours, and never tried to seek shelter. He seemed to be a part of the soil like the trees and the cattle in the pastures.

Yechiel saw the man's endless patience. Not without reason was he called Poor Thaddeus. For he was the poorest of the poor; he possessed nothing but his wretched horse, which was just as lean and overworked as its master. Man and beast were inseparable. As Poor Thaddeus was the poorest man in the village and the most patient, he got far more kicks than all the others together. Everybody jeered at him and tormented him. In return for his few acres of sandy ground and his ruined hut, the steward imposed harder burdens on him than on the better off peasants, who grew fat and prosperous. Poor Thaddeus never ventured to protest. In the middle of his work the steward ordered him off with his lean horse to do forced labor for the Count, wakened him in the night and sent him miles away to bring something or other. Poor Thaddeus always obeyed. He did not seem to know that disobedience was possible. Just as his shoulders were framed to bear injustice, his hands to guide the plow, so his ears served merely to receive commands. And so everybody, the steward, the farmers, even the farm servants, ordered about Poor Thaddeus; and so did the innkeeper, for whom the little man worked now and then to earn a few pennies to buy his dry bread.

But who knows the thoughts of a poor peasant as he stands barefoot in the rain with his horse, a sack round his shoulders? What torrents of bitterness must gather within him at such moments? In Father

Care's bright, peat-brown eyes, which never ventured to look any human being in the face, a curious fire started up sometimes when he entered the inn and saw the rich farmers sitting comfortably over their brandy, and the buxom landlady with her fine white skin. Although he was obedient to the verge of slavishness, sometimes he would shoot a glance under his low, furrowed brow at the innkeeper, which gave Shloime-Wolf a very uncomfortable feeling. A second later the little man would make an obsequious bow and seize the Jew's sleeve, so as to kiss it humbly—but his glance remained sticking like a thorn in his patron's hide. When, whip under arm, Poor Thaddeus stopped in the doorway of the inn, he sometimes contemplated the landlady in the strangest way, and a hateful smile would flit over his open, toothless mouth, hid in his tangled beard. Beneath that glance the landlady's hands trembled so violently that she spilled the glass she was carrying, and she would shout to her assistants.

"Fling that man out! His eyes bore through me like steel so that I can't hold anything in my hand!"

In spite of his servility the poor man sometimes became as savage as a mule. Then he would thrash his consumptive wife and send his sickly children to beg in the village. He himself would go to the inn, kiss the landlady's hands and feet, implore her to give him a quart of brandy and assure that he would pay for it by extra work. Malke always refused to give him it. Then he would pull out of his breast pocket a last few coins which he had saved up for salt to last him through the winter. The landlady did not want to take the money.

"You would do better to keep it for hard times."

But now the little man demanded the brandy with the right which the possession of money gave him.

"It's always hard times with me! And a poor man's money doesn't stink!"

Truly Father Care had a forcible way of expressing himself when it came to the scratch.

But the landlady knew her business and would not let herself be browbeaten. She retorted, "Now, Poor Thaddeus, you keep quiet, or else I'll have you flung out on your neck."

Presently, however, the little man's prayers became so beseeching and his eyes so doglike in their yearning, that the other customers intervened and Malke magnanimously drew off a pint of brandy.

But as soon as Poor Thaddeus began to get drunk he said such things about God, the Count, the steward, the priest, the assessor, in short about every authority in heaven and earth, that Shloime-Wolf put his hands to his ears in horror and ran about the room lamenting.

"Oy, oy, the goy will be the death of me yet! You're my witness, good people—I've heard nothing!"

The landlady was more energetic; she went up to Father Care, held her clenched fist under his nose, and screamed, "Will you be quiet, you dolt? If you don't, I'll set about you!"

"Then do it, for all I care! I'm afraid of nobody now, neither the Count nor the steward. You can set the dogs on me, but what I have to say I'll say. All they can do is to trample on the poor people—that's their whole bag of tricks! The Count, the steward, the Emperor, yes, God Himself—they can only trample on the poor people, that's all they can do!"

He only stopped when some one poured a bucket of dirty water over his head and flung him out of the room.

But as soon as he had slept out his drunken fit on some dunghill, he returned to the yoke as patiently as his horse and submitted himself to his fate as if nothing had happened. When any one reminded him of the things he had said while he was drunk he would retort with a hateful smile. "Good people, when a stupid peasant gets drunk and lets his tongue wag, you should just give him one on the jaw."

With that he would fall on his knees, clasp his questioner round the legs, and beg for forgiveness.

Then he would go about his work and humbly accept the blows that the steward dealt out to him for his insolent words as if they were a just punishment. From such chastisements he was borne pale as death and streaming with blood, for the rods were steeped in vinegar and the blows correspondingly sharp. His consumptive wife came running to the shed where the execution was taking place, beat her head with her fists and kept on screaming. "Have pity on him, for God's sake!"

Weeping, she took her husband's head into her hands. He stared at her in astonishment with his bright eyes and usually said nothing at all. But sometimes he would gasp in a weak voice.

"There's nothing to be done! If one wags one's tongue against the great, one is made to repent it."

But the jeering smile did not fade from his lips.

Father Care had a particular way of greeting people—he bent his knee and doffed his hat to everybody. Before the great he flung himself on the ground, contenting himself with kissing the hands of the less exalted. He made obeisance to all the villagers and saluted them with almost touching humility. Yet during all these bows, prostrations, and hand kissings the uncanny smile, which contradicted so strangely the rest of his bearing, never vanished from his hard, slightly twisted, and almost toothless mouth. And any one who was greeted with such exaggerated submissiveness never quite knew whether Poor Thaddeus was according him a mark of honor or making fun of him. Such humility verged on the ludicrous and the grotesque. Accordingly people always put up a defense against it—"That's enough!"—they would say—but they had to tear their hands away from his lips almost with violence.

Yechiel's acquaintance with Poor Thaddeus arose from the little man's peculiar mode of greeting.

Yechiel noticed with amazement that Father Care took off his hat respectfully and made a deep bow whenever he met him. At first he could not think that the greeting was intended for himself and did not respond to it. But the little man obstinately continued to greet him with an exaggerated bow until his eyes were opened.

Painfully moved by such politeness in an elderly man, he did his best to avoid Poor Thaddeus. And when one day the man greeted him again by bowing deeply and taking off his hat, Yechiel replied in the same fashion and with a still deeper bow.

The little man stared at him in astonishment. Never before had anybody bowed and taken off his hat to Poor Thaddeus.

"You mustn't bow to me, sir; I'm only Father Care, the poor peasant," said Thaddeus with his peculiar jeering smile.

"And you mustn't bow to me either; I'm only the teacher of the innkeeper's children," replied Yechiel, who had picked up some Polish at the annual fairs.

"Better than a poor peasant, all the same.... Everybody in Topolye is better than Poor Thaddeus," replied Father Care glibly.

"And better than I am too," Yechiel retorted.

When Poor Thaddeus was convinced that Yechiel had really no standing in the village, he stopped bowing to him and instead put on a contemptuous smile whenever they met. Yechiel greeted the little man as before with great gravity. And gradually the boy's honest glance drove the embitterment out of the little man's heart. Yechiel was the first human being whom Poor Thaddeus met on terms of equality. Thus with time they became friends.

CHAPTER V

MORNING SERVICE

THE village of Topolye had no House of Study and no Psalm
Fellowship, but it had fields and skies. So the great wide
world became God's house for Yechiel.

He had read in a holy book: "It is good to be in the field in the
early morning, when the newborn day is still young and free from sin,
to pray among the pious grasses, and sing with all creatures songs of
praise."

The boy loved to wash in the morning dew and see creation renew-
ing itself day after day. From the hill beside the inn he watched the
young day leaping from the womb of night.

The wide meadows were wrapped in a milky white mist. It was
rent by strong arms. Hilltops rose through it. As the tree trunks
could not be seen, it was as if the branches floated in the air. Then
the sun arose in the sky, reminding one of the words of the psalm:
"Who coverest thyself with light as with a garment: who stretchest
out the heavens like a curtain. . . ." Streams of light poured over the
firmament and dried the moist earth like a cow licking her new-born
calf. And soon there was full day in heaven and earth. Silver fringed
cloud islets floated in the azure sea; one thought of the sentence:
"God rides upon the clouds. . . ." And with the coming of God the
earth flung off her veils. Out of the thick mist appeared suddenly
the verdant green pasture land, stretching away for miles to the dark-
blue line of forest. The lush green of the meadows made Yechiel
think of the psalm: "He sendeth the springs into the valleys, which
run among the hills. They give drink to every beast of the field. . . ."
Soon too, the little pools and brooks appeared from beneath the
blanket of white mist. It lifted and the smooth waters gleamed like
mirrors fallen from the sky, and framed in green. Bit by bit the long
narrow strips of field emerged from the varicolored prospect, some
of them covered with green, bearded corn, others with golden wheat,
others again with blossoming broom, round which since early morning
bees had been humming: "He causeth the grass to grow for the cattle,

and herbs for the service of man: that he may bring forth food out of the earth. ..."

The birds had already been awake for a long time. With noisy twitterings they flew from field to field, and yet all the world seemed still. ... In the pastures the cattle had begun their day. Red and spotted cows suddenly appeared in the meadows, lowered their heads and lazily cropped the grass. Horses bowed their graceful necks; foals leapt round them on quivering limbs. Heavily burdened with their load of wool and guarded by a watchful sheepdog, a herd of sheep grazed peaceably among the white-flecked birches. An endless line of snow-white geese made a great clatter. "He watereth the hills from his chambers; the earth is satisfied with the fruit of thy works." In the words of the Psalmist, God's grace was spread over the earth like a garment, spread over the thatched roofs, fallen in with age and rain, where the poor dwelt.

Yechiel's heart was filled with a thousand blessings and good wishes for the world. Tears of joy started to his eyes. He could not believe that this world was the fleeting world of everyday, a corridor which only served as a way to another one. It seemed to him the world of the future, the Messianic world. In his heart ripened a prayer; he stretched out his arms: "O God, take up *this* world in Thy eternal protecting grace!"

"Heaven is God's dwelling; the earth is man's." The poor earth once fell from Heaven because of man's sin. But when the Messiah comes the earth too will be redeemed and become a part of the eternal, heavenly life, as it is said: "Jerusalem will stretch until it covers the whole world." Then the earth will again be filled with the blessing that rested on it before Adam ate of the tree of knowledge. ...

Yechiel could never resist bathing whenever he saw a stream or pool. From the hill he could see the Topolye brook after which the village was named. Like a silver ribbon it wound through the green meadows, then vanished behind thick undergrowth and did not show itself again. With a leap Yechiel dashed down the slope and forced his way through the tall grass, still wet with dew, and the dense bushes behind which the stream lay hidden. Soon he was jumping over the boulders and driftwood which it had carried down along with it. Flinging off his clothes he plunged like a trout into the water. The fish scattered in terror; the frogs, croaking apprehensively, hopped on to the bank. Yechiel was borne downstream, and could not get back to the point where he had started. He tried to battle against the current, but in vain. Like a drenched poodle he scrambled ashore. It was some time before he found his clothes again, which he had hidden among the bushes.

Water purifies not only the body, but the soul, while the coolness of water laves one's body no evil can come. After his swim Yechiel felt cleansed and capable of reciting his prayers to God. For always after a bathe he was overcome by a peculiar feeling of devotion, and an irresistible desire to speak to God. For this rite he had found a special place—the little green hill with its sparse covering of white birches. In their slender, thick-leaved branches dwelt all the birds of the field. There was a perpetual twittering and piping and fluting, as if a birds' annual fair were taking place. In the early morning the father and mother stork were also there; they had made a nest for their young ones on the gable of the inn. Not far from the hill there was a lush meadow where countless worms were to be found; it was an excellent feeding ground for the storks and the other birds. Yechiel was convinced that the stork joined the other birds simply in order to take part in divine service with them and sing praises to God. The boy stole very softly to the hill so as not to frighten the birds, stepped under a tree, and recited his prayers. In his fancy he was just one of God's birds praising his creator along with his fellows. His imagination changed the birds into the pure souls of holy men, and his prayer mingled with their song.

In the early morning Poor Thaddeus often secretly led his lean horse to the Count's pastures to give it a taste of the fresh juicy grass before it started on its heavy day's work. Hidden in the bushes he observed all Yechiel's doings. He saw the boy standing for a long time under the tree, praying piously to the twitterings of the birds. Poor Thaddeus scratched his head and muttered, "A pious soul, that lad— a pity he isn't a Catholic!"

After his morning prayers Yechiel returned to the inn to teach his master's children. His class consisted of a few little boys and girls of different ages; in addition to Shloime-Wolf's children he taught those of a Jewish neighbor, who worked the water mill.

First of all Yechiel took the youngest children, those of four and five, and taught them the Hebrew alphabet. He took his vocation very seriously. He remembered what his father had so often told him when he explained the meaning of the letters to him.

In every letter of the alphabet the whole Law was contained. With any one letter one could evoke whole worlds. The letters were the bricks out of which the edifice of the Law was built, and when a Jew merely said over the alphabet, it was as if he read the whole Law. Besides, every letter had, in addition to its actual meaning, a hidden, higher meaning as well. And as man was an image of God, so every earthly letter was an exact counterpart of that fiery script which God possessed in Heaven and had once revealed to Moses, the master and teacher, on Mount Sinai. A letter uttered by the lips of a sinless child was perfect, without a flaw, and could create a holy angel. God had great joy in a child's voice, when it uttered a letter; for as children are pure it comes from their mouths complete, with all the worlds it bears within it, just as God formed it at the beginning. And it was a good work, more, a great act of piety, to teach children the alphabet, for it was their song of praise to God.

So Yechiel practiced his vocation with zeal and love. His teaching of the children became a holy work. And to himself the true meaning of the alphabet now revealed itself in all its fullness. . . .

But things were not always so clear and comprehensible to him. Sometimes Satan assailed him with violence and he was tormented with all kinds of doubts.

The first man who put evil thoughts into his mind was Poor Thaddeus.

On his way home from morning prayers Yechiel often passed him on the sandy field. There stood Father Care and contemplated with resignation the consumptive, half-empty ears growing on his scrap of soil; they waged a desperate battle with the dry winds which periodically scattered loose sand over them. Involuntarily his glance strayed to the rich green fields of the Count, which lay in the lush valley, and his eyes compared them with his own sparse crops.

Poor Thaddeus and his horse worked hard on the poor farm. But their labor was in vain. Except for what his horse earned by outside service, and what he himself stole in the night from the rich fields of the Count, Poor Thaddeus possessed nothing.

Nevertheless he stuck to his wretched croft with wonderful stubbornness, nursed and tended it as if it were a sick child. He shoveled together the horse dung before the inn and carted it to his "sick wife" (as the village jestingly called his farm). But everything turned into a curse with him. When rain fell it swept away the black soil which he had dunged with his labor, and bore it down into the valley to the Count's fields. So Poor Thaddeus was left again with his bare, sandy soil. And yet he did not give up. He stuck to his bit of land and guarded it like a treasure. It was his only possession; he had nothing else.

One day Yechiel met him again. Bathed in sweat, Father Care was standing in his field shoveling dung. It was a beautiful morning and one of the great Catholic holidays. Since dawn the church bell had been calling the faithful to worship. But for Poor Thaddeus there were no Sundays or holidays. Whenever he took the notion, the steward would order the little man to do the most menial work even on the Lord's day. Things which in others would have been counted grievous sin were permitted to him; it was as if everything were permitted to him, as if for him there existed no God and no holy day.... The village street was filled with festively attired peasant women and girls, carrying prayer books under their arms and candles in their hands. The men, clad in their Sunday best, were hastening to take their places in the Corpus Christi procession. And there Poor Thaddeus was standing beside his cart of dung, plastered breast high with filth.

When he caught sight of Yechiel he said, apparently to justify himself, "What can I do? I'm allowed to spread the Count's dung on Sunday, so I can surely be allowed to spread my own! The master claims all my weekdays for himself, so there's no time for my own field except the holidays."

"Oh, don't you worry, Thaddeus! God never forsakes a man, not even when he's shoveling dung."

"God?" asked the man in astonishment. "What need has God of Poor Thaddeus? God has the fine Count and the well-fed villagers, who all pray to Him—what can Poor Thaddeus give Him?"

"Don't talk like that! God listens to the poor more willingly than to the rich; He loves the poor."

"Oh, I can feel that in my own flesh! I know His love for the poor! He loves to bring vengeance on them, to play with them as a hawk plays with a poor hen that he catches among the corn."

"It is a great sin to say things like that, Thaddeus."

"The good Lord doesn't even know that there's anyone called Poor Thaddeus in Topolye. If He did know, He would look after His own people!"

Yechiel was terrified.

"Have you no fear of God?" he asked.

The uncanny smile appeared on Thaddeus's mouth, and he pointed toward the sky.

"He is so high, and Poor Thaddeus is so low," he held his hand just over the ground. "How can He trouble whether a poor peasant fears Him or not?"

"Don't talk like that! God is our Father, He sees our deeds and knows all our thoughts."

"Even if He does see them and know them—what does it matter? Do you fancy that He bothers very much whether we poor wretched worms think this or that? Whether we love one another, as the priest commands us, or eat one another alive? If it really troubled Him he wouldn't allow one to own everything," and he pointed toward the green valley, "and another to slave himself to death here...."

Yes, the little man could fairly talk!

Yechiel was unable to find a reply, for he too was tormented by the question that had given him so much worry ever since his childhood: Why do the righteous suffer poverty and the evil prosper? Now it rose again like an impregnable wall before him.

Misery early revealed its dreadful countenance to him, and did not spare him.

The inn had a garret, and it was a veritable hell. Occasionally a vagrant fell ill and could not go any farther. Then he was carried up to the garret and bedded on certain half-rotten sacks of straw, which always lay there. Fearing that the village might come to know that a sick man was lying in the inn, Shloime-Wolf would keep the man in the garret until he was able to drag himself to the next town, or ended his wanderings for good, forsaken and alone. In the latter case he was conveyed by night to the nearest town and clandestinely buried there.

The garret was spacious and well removed from the public room, and the groans and death rattles that filled it were not heard outside. Yechiel was often in it. When a sick man was carried up to it he remained with him, tended him, brought him a jug of warm milk, covered him with an old coat. And there he heard many a sad story.

The verse in the Psalms: "I am forgotten as a dead man out of mind: I am like a broken vessel," seemed written for these men. In Yechiel's eyes there was no creature on earth more wretched than a human being who could not go on. A man who stays in the same spot begins to rot. No argument, such as that it is a joy to be released from this world, or that the soul has to wander about as a punishment for the sins of a former existence: nothing could drive away the worm that gnawed at Yechiel's heart when he beheld human misery: Why must man pay to the uttermost groschen? Where was God's grace and compassion?

No, that question could be answered by no logical argument, but simply and solely by blind, trusting, absolute faith, and the confidence that all that God did was done for the good of man.

And Yechiel found that answer in the morning on the little hill beside the inn, from which one could look down into the valley and watch the world being created anew. There one could see God's grace visibly descending upon it. At such hours all his questions were answered and he was cleansed of all the torments of doubt. His heart had room for nothing but the perfection of the world, and blind trust in its Creator.

CHAPTER VI

THE GOOSEGIRL

THE Sabbath is the one day on which Hell is at peace—so quiet ruled in the inn too. The sale of spirits, it is true, went on, for the maid Yadviga stood behind the bar and supplied the peasants. But the innkeeper's family were invisible; they were sitting in the little alcove where during the week Yechiel held his classes. There on Friday evening the landlady recited the prayer over the candles and set the Sabbath table; there the family took their meals, and there too was held the Sabbath service.

After Yechiel came to the village it quickly became his task to give to the innkeeper's household a religious tinge. Previously there had been few religious observances in the inn. Shloime-Wolf hadn't worried about it, even though the Jews in the town condemned him and especially his worldly wife; it was said that they cared nothing for the things that are important to Jews. But with Yechiel's coming, he suddenly became ashamed and tried humbly to learn from the boy, even asking him questions about Jewish customs and Jewish religious law. On Friday nights he pulled Yechiel to the table.

"You say Kiddush!"

The innkeeper lifted the cup of wine in his hand and repeated the words of the Sanctification after Yechiel, his eyes intent on him, afraid that he might mispronounce a word.

In spite of her love for money, the innkeeper's wife was touched by Yechiel's piety, nor did it fail to impress the simple village Jews; so they not only greeted the boy with respect but regarded his devoutness as an asset which God had granted them that happiness and abundance might be their portion. They regarded Yechiel as a sort of talisman and guarded him jealously lest they might lose him.

Malke set herself to feed him up properly. At table she put the juiciest portions on his plate and made him eat them all up.

Whenever Reisel appeared in the "schoolroom," Yechiel felt the burning gaze of two wide, astonished eyes fixed on him.

Accustomed from childhood to avoid the sight of women he lowered his eyes. But the girl stubbornly followed him with her glance.

All week Reisel ran about in her gypsy dress, her hair disheveled. Her mother did what she could to keep her away from the inn. The young landowners, the other Christians who stopped at it must not notice that the landlady had a beautiful daughter. Malke herself had to suffer all sorts of caresses and evade all sorts of dangers, and that was bad enough. For herself she feared nothing; she knew how to deal even with drunk country squires, and had shown herself equal to the most ticklish situations. But life at an inn was dangerous for a pretty young girl. Consequently, so that Reisel might not attract attention, her mother refrained from dressing her hair and clad her in all sorts of impossible clothes. Girls were not obliged to study the Law; so to keep her away from the inn Reisel was sent into the fields as a goosegirl, dressed in her shapeless garment. In this way her mother hoped to conceal her charms, which were already noticeable.

Reisel passed the whole week with her geese and ducks. But on Friday evening, before lighting the Sabbath candles, her mother carefully locked the door of the alcove, washed her daughter from head to foot, braided her hair in two plaits and bound them with gay ribbons, and made her put on the flowered cotton dress which had been bought for her in the spring. And wild Reisel was changed beyond recognition.

Once as Yechiel piously recited the Sabbath blessing, she stepped to the table and gazed at him fixedly. She contemplated the dark lashes of his closed eyes, his longish face with its spiritual expression, and a strange feeling woke in her heart. The landlady had fitted Yechiel out with a new Sabbath caftan and saw to it that he was supplied with clean shirts. Reisel stood opposite him and almost devoured him with her glances. The idea that a girl should be shy was quite unknown to her. She drew nearer; her fresh lips opened, revealing two rows of white teeth. Knowing nothing of feminine diffidence, she leant her chin on her hands and stared into Yechiel's face; her eyes pored on his moving lips and his long thin neck; her ears burned. Malke saw, and rebuked her daughter.

"What are you standing there for, gaping at him? You should be ashamed of yourself, a big girl like you!"

"But I want to!" replied the girl, breaking into tears and rushing away from the table.

"Come back at once—else I'll take the strap to you!" shouted the father.

"I won't!" cried Reisel, running out through the door.

The mother went to look for her and found her in tears before the house.

"What are you crying for, you silly child?" she said, laughing to reassure the girl.

"Because I want to!"

"Come, it's silly to cry. If you cry you'll never get a husband."

"I don't want a husband!" cried Reisel.

"Oh, yes, you do." Malke dried the girl's tears in her apron and softly pushed her into the house.

Reisel was lying in the grass beside the stream. A curious unrest had come over her lately. Hitherto the companionship of the geese and the ducks had satisfied her. Every day she drove them into the dense undergrowth. She loved to hide herself with them behind the thick bushes beside the stream. For her the geese were friends. She swam about with them naked, hunted them, mimicked their indignant cackling, played tricks on them, and ducked them under the water. She sported for hours at a time in the meadows with the sheepdog Burek, who was her constant escort. She played like a boy. She had no girl friends; Malke had forbidden her to have anything to do with the peasant girls in the village. She was not allowed to loiter about the inn; whenever she entered, her mother roughly ordered her out again. So there was nothing to do but bathe with the geese and play with the dog.

Up till now she had felt very content with this way of spending her time. But in the last few weeks a change had taken place within her which she could not understand. The geese bored her, Burek the dog interested her no longer. Often she would lie for hours, almost concealed by the tall grass, in her nook among the bushes, or wander aimlessly about the meadows. She felt so sad, so dejected! And often she found tears in her eyes without knowing why.

If only Yechiel the teacher would come out and play with her! But he always sat in the alcove over his books. And when he did go out for once in a time, he always rushed away over the fields alone or made for the woods. He would do better to come here! She would show him how to dive, and frighten the geese by swimming under the water. They flapped their wings so funnily then, beating the water until drops were scattered on every side.

He was so strange and severe: one daren't even look at him! And yet she was so fond of looking at him; he had such lovely ring-leted curls; they made you want to wind them round your finger. And his eyes were so bright, his eyelids so lovely, like rose petals moist with dew. When he closed his eyes in prayer his eyelids arched, and it was as if two big cherries were hidden behind them—it gave one such a longing to touch them with one's fingers. . . . Why did he never come out to see her? Why did he never play with her? Why did he never speak to her? When Reisel thought such things her heart became quite heavy.

"White Yendrich," an insolent gander who tyrannized all the geese and kept them in strict order, pensively waddled past, conscious of his might and dignity. He saw that his guardian was sad, and think-ing she needed him approached to comfort her. But to his great surprise she seized her willow wand and drove him away.

"Get out, you white devil! I'll set Burek on you in a minute! . . . Burek!"

Deeply offended, the gander turned tail and cackled something or other in a most impertinent fashion.

Burek, who was following the scent of a field mouse and was far away by now, heard his mistress's summons and obediently came to heel. He saw that the gander had fallen into disfavor, and took the opportunity to pay off old scores with his enemy. There rose a battle in which the other geese soon joined. Amid a furious din a white cloud of feathers rose into the air. White Yendrich lost half his plumage, but Burek also emerged with bloody wounds, which he at once proceeded to lick. The combat did not stop until Reisel separated the opponents, and with her wand dispatched the dog to hunt field mice again and the gander to bully his wives. . . .

Bored with everything, Reisel flung off her clothes—and they were not many—and noisily plunged in among the geese swimming about in the stream. As she waded in the water, which came up to her breast, she suddenly heard footsteps in the distance. Holding her breath, while her heart pounded loudly, she stopped and looked round her. To one side, where the meadow sloped up to the green hill, the teacher was walking along speaking to himself and gesticulating with his arms. The sight amused Reisel so much that she broke out into shrill laughter.

With a plunge she was in the water, swam powerfully to the bank nearest to Yechiel, and cried, "Yechiel! Yechiel!"

The boy glanced over the meadow in surprise and peered through the tall grass, but could see nobody, for the willow bushes along the bank of the stream hid the girl from him. Reisel rose out of the water and waved, "Yechiel, here! Here!"

The boy went in the direction of the voice. He tried to fight his way through the willow bushes and lost his direction.

"I'm here! I'm here!"

Yechiel pushed the branches aside and reached the stream. There he saw Reisel standing in the water, naked, to the hips.

"Take off your clothes quick and come in!" she cried.

The fact that Reisel was naked made little impression on Yechiel. He had been used to the sight of nakedness ever since his childhood, both at the baths and swimming in the Vistula. It was simply an inner instinct that told him that Reisel was a woman. He had never before seen a woman naked. He knew, of course, that there was a physical difference between a woman and a man, but Reisel looked just like a boy. She was tall and athletic. So Yechiel never thought that here was a woman standing before him and replied quite without embarrassment.

"I can't swim with you. You're a woman and I'm a man."

"Oh, yes, you can! I'm not a woman. Mother says that until you're thirteen you're nothing."

"Oh, yes, you're a woman," Yechiel suddenly shut his eyes. "You have the two hills that the Song of Songs speaks about, and they signify Moses and Aaron...."

"I have no Moses and Aaron. You don't believe me? Here—look there!"

Thereupon Reisel ran out of the water toward Yechiel. He remembered that a man must not look at a naked woman, and he held his hands before his eyes so as not to see.

Reisel commanded him to sit down on the grass beside her. He obeyed, but he kept his eyes firmly shut. Then he remembered again that he was sitting beside a woman, and a naked one at that, and started to spring up.

"Don't go, Yechiel!" Reisel implored him, holding tight to his caftan, and she threw her arms about his neck.

He jumped up and broke away, like another Joseph, and called back, without turning round, "We mustn't do this, Reisel! It's a great sin!"

But when he was out of sight he sat down beside the stream. A feeling of strange sadness fell upon him. Now he understood what had happened, and he was astonished at himself for having actually sat down beside a naked woman. A stream of tears poured from his eyes. He felt very wicked. There was no longer any hope of higher things for him. This came of his having given up his studies, and spending his days here at the inn with peasants, and never hearing a word of the Law. Oh, God, how was it all to end?

Yet strangely enough, in spite of his annoyance at the trick that Reisel had played upon him, he never blamed her even in his thoughts; on the contrary, he found within himself quite a new feeling for her. It was compounded of pity and something else which he could not define. He felt strangely drawn toward the girl. This caused him great worry, but he could not help it. At night thoughts came to him that he had never had before. When Reisel brought him food he deliberately avoided her eyes, for he was ashamed of looking her in the face.

The same thing was happening within Reisel—all at once she had become shy and shamefaced.

When he prayed Yechiel beat his breast and recited with particular emphasis the words of the prayer: "Lead us back, Heavenly Father, to thy law, and yoke us again in thy service!"

CHAPTER VII

THE PITCH JEW

A N UNUSUAL stranger had come to Topolye not long before. He looked like any other wayfarer, but he behaved quite differently. He did not leave the village like the rest, but prowled about through the fields and forests.

He did not go to any houses and, though he was Jewish, he avoided Jews. Somehow he had obtained authority from the Count—no one could understand how; and it set malicious tongues wagging—to settle on the edge of the forest and draw off the resin from the pine trees, the kind that are called Californias, to distill pitch from them. He had brought a cart with him, with all sorts of vessels for boiling the resin, and a big box of books. With the steward's permission he moved into a hut in the forest made out of planks and boards. After covering the hut tightly with bark from the trees, the "Pitch Jew" settled down to his work of distilling pitch and tar oil, which he supplied to the squire.

At first the innkeeper, the miller, and the butcher were glad that the village was to have another Jew, since it would be easier on the Sabbath to get a minyan [quorum]. But the stranger answered no questions and kept strictly aloof. He did not join the minyan on the Sabbath. He astonished the villagers by not buying kosher meat; it turned out that he ate no meat, but lived on herbs and vegetables, which he boiled in his own pot. Only to buy food from a peasant did he ever come to the village; and he never went to the town.

From the peasants it was learned that there were lights in his hut all night and that, early each morning, he bathed in the pool in the forest and spent his mornings in prayer. The hut was full of Hebrew books, which he studied even when he was burning resin. The peasants reported that he swayed and shook himself to and fro all the time he was reading and studying. Though they respected him, they feared him too. In the village it was said that he was a holy man, one of the hidden Thirty-six Righteous Men, who had come to the forest to hide from the world. They respectfully got out of his way, not to disturb him in his holy separation. Indeed, they felt enriched and happy because he was among them, that a holy man had chosen to dwell in their midst.

But a stranger passing through the village and staying at the inn, having heard so much about the holy man, went into the forest to try to see the recluse and recognized him. "Would you believe it?" he exclaimed. "This man is a believer in the False Messiah, Sabbatai Zvi, curse him!"

And the stranger told an extraordinary story about the Pitch Jew. He came from a town far away on the other side of the Vistula, in the Plotzk region, where he had lived in a forest, engaged in the same work, distilling tar and pitch, and had lived in the same strange isolated way. People thought he was a hidden saint, a miracle worker, and women and ordinary, unlettered Jews came to him for medicines and cures. He provided them with herbs and gave them amulets which he wrote himself. When the Rabbis and scholars opened the amulets they found the name of the accursed False Messiah there, disguised, of course.

"When the Rabbis saw that," the traveler continued, "they sent the butcher boys to bring him to the town. After examination in the synagogue vestibule, they tortured him so long that he confessed he was indeed a believer in the False Messiah. The Messiah has already come, he said. Woe to the ears that hear this! He was on familiar terms with the Catholic priest of the town and used to visit him secretly at night. The Rabbi and the Dayanim and the scholars tore their garments in mourning, because he was a great Talmudic scholar and well versed in Cabbalah, and if he had kept to the right path he would have accomplished great deeds. He was placed under ban, excommunicated, in the synagogue, with black candles.

"They would have killed him if the Catholic priest and the local Poritz had not protected him and allowed no harm to come to him. A few weeks later he repented and came on the Sabbath to the synagogue. Standing by the door, he prayed Jews to trample on him. The common folk, the carters and the butchers, had already taken off their belts, but the Rabbi would not let them harm him, even though they did not accept his repentance. They only wanted him to leave the town quickly, the sooner the better. Because of him, they were afraid things might go badly for the Jews. Soon afterward, he disappeared. They all thought he had long ago been baptized and had become a big man with the Pope in Rome. For he was a scholar, and learned in Cabbalah, and such a man can go far. And now look, here he is, here in the forest!"

There was great excitement in Shloime-Wolf's inn when they heard this story. Jews wanted to run at once to the forest and burn down the hut with the Cabbalist inside. But they were afraid of what the Count would do if they should harm him. After all, he was there under the Count's protection!

That was the beginning of the talk of a secret compact between the Count and the Pitch Jew. Peasants whispered that the Poritz often went to the Jew's hut in the forest or had him called to his castle at night. Sometimes the Poritz was seen going to the forest to the Pitch Jew. Thus people, being afraid, avoided him, and the Pitch Jew became another of those abnormal, frightening creatures of whom Topolye had several. The peasants, like the Jews, steered clear of him and saw to it that they did not pass his hut in the forest. In time the Pitch Jew was forgotten and remained in their minds only as a distant, uneasy fear.

One day when Yechiel was in the forest, he heard the plaintive Talmudic singsong chant among the trees in the distance. Following the chant, he came upon the Pitch Jew's hut. He stole behind a tree to listen. The Pitch Jew, in his prayer shawl, with his high-domed forehead and long, thin beard, was poring over a Talmud volume.

Though Yechiel had heard the stories about the Pitch Jew and had kept away from him, he was greatly interested in his study of the Talmud. His singsong was so sad, so heartfelt, and he shook and swayed so devoutly, that Yechiel found himself feeling sorry for the outcast, living his lonely life in the forest. There was something here, he felt sure, out of the ordinary, something not easy to understand. Perhaps he was a hidden saint, who did not wish to be revealed. He imagined that unseen souls were hovering about the Pitch Jew and was suddenly fearful. But the Pitch Jew had seen him. He shut his book and called out:

"Is there anything you want here, boy?"

"I came to ask you to teach me Torah."

"Aren't you afraid of me?"

"No, I am not afraid."

"You had better go. You know what they say about me."

"I don't believe what they say about you! I know that you are a hidden saint, and do not wish it known. That is why you took the sin upon yourself."

"How do you know that, boy?"

"I have seen you studying and praying devoutly."

The Pitch Jew thought for a while.

"And what do you want me to do?"

"I want you to teach me Torah."

"I warn you again to leave me. You are running into danger."

"I shall not leave you till you will teach me," Yechiel said in a firm, assured voice.

The Pitch Jew took the long end of his beard in his hand and began to sway.

"The Torah, my son, you must know, as the holy Zohar says, is like a beloved. When her lover encircles her house with longing for her, she grants him a glance through the crack in the door. That is Halacha, the Law. Many are content with that. But when the lover is consumed with passion for her and will not go away from her house, but stands behind her door in longing and love, she grants him a higher favor—that is Aggadah, the Legends. There are those who are still not content, or, rather, the favors which the beloved has bestowed upon them have inflamed their heart with a great frenzy of love. They are not like the indolent who lie down at night to sleep, but they rise up in the middle of the night athirst for her, for the Torah, the daughter of heaven. As the text says: 'By night on my bed I sought her whom my soul loveth.' That means the wise men who rise at night to learn Torah. Then the beloved, the holy Torah, comes and bestows upon those who thirst a greater favor. She takes them behind the curtain and kisses them and reveals herself to them, and hands over to them the deep mysteries of the Torah. . . . Which do you want to learn, my son, the revealed things, or the hidden?"

"I know neither the one nor the other. I only know that I long to know God's ways."

"Why do you want to know God's ways?"

"Because I love God and I want to know how to serve Him."

"Love is a high grace, my son. It is the sign of the tefilin, 'the frontlets between thine eyes.' If you love the Lord of the World, you must wear His tefilin a long time, both in prayer and in study. For tefilin, that is love between the Creator of the World and the Jews. When you bind the four texts upon your hand and put them on like a seal between your eyes, you are then united with the Lord of the World in love."

Yechiel pleaded, "You know so much. I beg you to teach me! I shall serve you. I shall do everything for you, only teach me! Be my Rabbi! Your knowledge is so great!"

"I see from your great thirst for the Torah that your soul is able to receive the hidden things. 'By night on my bed I sought her whom my soul loveth.' It means: Get up early, with great longing, come out here to me when the morning star is rising, when the day is still young and clean, without sin. Your coming to me must be concealed. You must guard against touching any unclean thing. All the way here you must step carefully, not to tread any living thing underfoot. For who knows whom you tread upon? And your walk must be slow and graceful. And you must have the fear of God in your mind. Not because He may do you any harm, or because you want something from Him, but out of holy awe. The text says: 'The first sign of wisdom is the fear of the Lord.' God is not closed away. He is like a tap that pours out holiness and godliness into His vessels. The vessels of God are the saints. And now go, and let no child of woman know that you have been with me."

That night Yechiel was in a trance, his heart full of fear because of the step he was taking. He remembered what they had said in the inn about the Pitch Jew. Perhaps it was true. And here he was going to do something which might, God forbid, be against the Jewish faith. No, it could not be true! The man's appearance, his piety, his sad singsong all proved him worthy. Yechiel weighed and considered over and over again the words which he had spoken. They were all such holy and pious words about the hidden Torah and the fear of God, and not one word of Sabbatai Zvi, God forbid, or any other. The Pitch Jew must be a hidden saint, who for some good cause had taken this penance upon himself.

When the dawn began to filter through the shutters Yechiel was already sure of himself and no longer afraid of offending God. For he had decided, should the Pitch Jew say anything to him that was against the Jewish faith he would run away from him at once.

He crept quietly into his clothes and out into the street as quickly as possible. The morning dew was gently falling, though the stars were still shining faintly. After he had washed at the well in the yard he felt purified and fit to receive God's Torah.

He recalled the words of the Pitch Jew in the forest, that he should take upon himself the holy fear of God. Going through the meadows toward the forest he thought he was being carried on wings. There was so much tenderness in his heart that he had no fear of treading upon any worm. It seemed to him that his feet skimmed along above the ground, that they did not touch the earth. When Yechiel reached the hut at the edge of the forest the door was closed, but through the crack he saw the light of a candle. His heart beat fast and the frightening thoughts that came to him at night returned. Too terrified to knock, he almost ran away, but suddenly his faith grew strong in him, and he knocked firmly at the door of the hut.

"Who is it that knocks at my door?" a voice within asked him.

"I, Yechiel."

When the Pitch Jew appeared at the door Yechiel did not recognize him in the gray dawn. The Jew seemed to have grown taller, his beard longer. His eyes were red, as though he had been awake all night. Instead of the clothes he had worn at his work, he was wearing a long white garment, the kittel, his shroud.

Yechiel started to speak, but the Pitch Jew put a finger to his lips, and led the way into the forest. As they reached a hidden pool in the forest, concealed by branches and leaves, they startled some deer who fled away in alarm. Yechiel felt sure the frightened creatures were hidden souls. The Pitch Jew motioned him to be quiet. And Yechiel did not speak.

The Pitch Jew flung off his garment and waded far out into the water, till it reached his neck, and he immersed himself three times. He beckoned to Yechiel to do the same. When Yechiel, up to his neck in the cold water, stood at his side, the Pitch Jew whispered in his ear strange hidden names of angels, that Yechiel could not even repeat, to keep them in his mind.

Having bathed, both, though still wet, dressed quickly. On their way back they again ran into a herd of deer coming into the field to graze, and again the Pitch Jew signed to Yechiel to be quiet. Arriving at the hut, he entered first, wrapped himself in his prayer shawl, put on his tefilin, and by the lighted candle, though it was already day, sat down with Yechiel to teach him the mysteries of the holy Cabbalah.

The Pitch Jew's face was long and pear-shaped, his brow broad and domed, and his side curls flowed into his beard over the field of his sunken yellow cheeks. His side curls finished in the long end of his yellowish-white beard, which extended to a narrow point, growing thinner and thinner until at the end it consisted only of single long hairs. All the rains of the centuries seemed to have poured over that face. The fact that his beard and side curls were half yellow and half gray was witness of the troubles and persecutions he had endured. It was as though the gray had not come naturally, with age, but that a robber had fallen upon him half way along the road of his life, and had stayed, hanging on till the grave.

Like a poplar tree torn out from its roots, with a tousled, ruffled head of yellow-gray hair, he went through the forest with a sharp tool, collecting the resin from the pine trees into a bucket. Yechiel followed with a second bucket, and listened diligently to what he was saying, for more than from any book he imparted the Torah to his pupil by word of mouth.

"You must know, my son, that man's life on earth consists not of bits and pieces; here you add, there you subtract, here you snatch, there you grab. Man's life is something whole, complete, rounded off, from his first day till his last. One day of life, one hour, one minute is not superfluous; it is like a brick in a building. Since that is so, you must do something new every moment of your life. For man's life is his world, which he creates, to which he afterward returns, because of which we say after a man's death, 'Sheholoch le-Olomi,' 'he has gone to his world.' That means the world which the man has created through his life, for man is the 'Yotzeir,' the creator, and his life is the 'Yetzirah,' the creation. Do you understand, my son?"

Yechiel had been listening attentively. The Pitch Jew continued collecting the resin from the pine trees, and went on, "There are those who gather riches in order to enjoy all the pleasures of the world. And there are those who gather Torah, gorge themselves with good deeds, to have a share of the world to come. But both those who gather riches and those who gather Torah and good deeds are alike. They lose by what they gain. For just like those who stuff their bellies with food, so are those others who devour Torah and guzzle good deeds. They have accomplished nothing with their learning. Their learning turns to stones that will lie as stumbling blocks on their way to the higher worlds. Their good deeds are transformed into rivers that will not let them cross to the other side, to the heavens."

Yechiel gravely nodded his head, at the same time helping in the work.

"But what should one do? What is the way of life? The goal of life is that which leads to union with God, the Creator. Man has three stages of union with God. The first is simple—to imitate His ways. God is just. Let man strive to be just. God is merciful. Let man also be merciful. And so with everything a man has to do, he must consider

himself God's messenger, and he must render an account to himself—
how would God have acted in his place?

"That is the simple way. But the Lord of the World has in His
Grace left to man a higher stage—to cleave to Him. Therefore He
has chosen man to be His companion, His partner in Creation, in the
work of the six days of creation. Previously, before Adam's sin, man
was like unto the angels. He had no needs, because the world was
perfect. Man found everything prepared. Through Adam's sin the
world fell, but man rose. Why did he rise because of the sin? Because
man showed that he has the choice, freedom of will. God desires that
man should cleave to Him, seek union with Him, not because he has
no other choice, like the angels, but of his own free will. God has left it
to man to improve the path, to repair that which was spoiled after the
first sin. Man's work in this world is to make better the bad, and thus
he cleaves to God and becomes His partner in the creation of the
world.

"But there is still a third stage. God is holy and pure. You can
achieve union with Him only through holiness and purity. The road to
God is thin and fine.

"Therefore it is dangerous. It may break. Man may never know that
his road to God has been broken. It is easy to fall into pride. Therefore
it is better that man should be united to God through all three ways—
by his good deeds, by putting right something that is wrong in the
world, and by a pure and holy life, so that he can always look back to
see whether the cords that bind him to God are strong and unbroken."

These and similar teachings the Pitch Jew transmitted to Yechiel,
his secret pupil. The lad felt that each day he grew in understanding
because of this teaching.

CHAPTER VIII

JACOB AND RACHEL

ONE evening the innkeeper and his wife were mixing spirits in the alcove or, to be more exact, Shloime-Wolf simply poured a pailful of water into the brandy cask and his wife, her sleeves rolled up, kept stirring the mixture. Yechiel was sitting over a book at his table in the corner, rocking himself violently and reading in the singing drone of the Talmud student. Malke nudged her husband.

"I tell you what, Shloime-Wolf, it seems to me it's high time to think about a husband for Reisel."

"Why so early?" asked the father.

"She's been stung; I've noticed it."

"Goodness gracious, what notions you take into your head!"

"I know what I'm talking about."

Shloime-Wolf cautiously poured the water into the cask and winked at his wife.

"Take a look at that boy over there. If he studied properly for a year or two, he might become a Rabbi."

"That's what I say! I've had an eye on the lad for a long time."

"I took a fancy to him the first time I saw him."

"Well, why are you shilly-shallying? You're her father. Do you want to wait until he slips through your fingers?"

"Slip through my fingers—what are you thinking about? He belongs to me! I would give my head for him! Have you any idea what could be made out of a lad like that?"

"Shloime-Wolf, you frighten me with the things you say!" Hastily Malke turned down her sleeves over her arms and piously lowered her eyes. "If it were only settled, dear God! What are you waiting for? You're the father!"

The innkeeper left his work, tugged at the sleeves of his caftan, and went up to Yechiel.

"What are you doing, Yechiel, studying the holy Torah?"

"I am trying," said Yechiel, shyly. "I know so little."

"Would you like to know more?"

"If I had the opportunity to sit at the feet of a teacher—"

"Well—if you'll become my son-in-law I'll send you at my own expense to a Yeshivah. What do you say to that?"

Yechiel, confused, grew red in the face. After a short silence he replied, "I will write to my father. It may be the will of God."

"Malke, where are you? Why don't you come? Yechiel is to be our son-in-law!" cried Shloime-Wolf joyfully.

The landlady let the ladle fall into the cask, rushed across to Yechiel, and made to embrace him. The pious youth instinctively raised his hand to repulse her. The happy mother gave vent to her tenderness in words instead.

"My child, you're always praying and have no thought for anything else. I'm sure you're hungry! Have you had anything solid to eat today? Reisel! Reisel! Bring a plate of cream from the cupboard and some cheese for Yechiel!"

"He'll have to say his evening prayer first; I'll wager he won't eat before he does that," said the innkeeper, nodding to Yechiel as if to say that he too understood something of such matters.

He was puzzled about how to approach Reisel after her parents' proposal of marriage. The two had not spoken since their encounter by the stream, when he told her that they had both sinned against God. She resented him, and he had avoided even looking at her. No longer did he consider her an agent of the Evil One, who had plotted to lead him into temptation. But he must comfort her. So next morning, after he had made sure that no one was watching him, Yechiel proceeded to the stream where Reisel herded her geese.

The girl was lying in the meadow, her head hidden in the tall grass, and cooling her face, which still glowed with some shame and resentment, on the dewy blades. At the first glimmer of dawn she had gone with her geese to the stream and had stayed there, without returning as usual for breakfast. Her parents had much to do in the inn, and nobody thought of the girl. Reisel was much surprised to find tears on her hand. In her shame and rage she stamped her naked foot on the ground and flung herself down. Then she heard a sound in the bushes. Who could be creeping about there? Reisel, who was not fainthearted, commanded Burek to go and see. Immediately the dog greeted with a loud barking—Yechiel.

When Reisel saw him she jumped up and ran. Yechiel could only see a flock of geese with Burek driving them before him, and far in front a head of flying black hair.

"Reisel! Reisel! Reisel, I want to speak to you."

"I won't, so there!" Reisel stopped in the middle of her flock.

So Yechiel stood at one side, Reisel at the other, and the puzzled Burek halfway between them.

"But do listen, Reisel. I want to tell you that our souls were united in Heaven—before we were born."

"No, our souls weren't united in Heaven—before we were born," she retorted defiantly.

"I tell you we are destined for each other!"

"No, we aren't destined for each other!"

Reisel sank to the ground and sobbed into the grass.

Yechiel softly went nearer, sat down at a fitting distance from her, and spoke comfortingly to her.

"God has helped me, and I have found favor in your father's eyes. He wants me to be his son-in-law: he has spoken to me about it. And he's going to send me to a Yeshivah to study. Reisel—forty days before we were born it was announced in Heaven that we were meant for each other, and so you are my chosen for all eternity."

"I'm not your chosen!" Reisel sobbed. "I'm nobody; I'm only a goosegirl. I'm with the geese all the time, and nobody teaches me anything."

"You are a daughter in Israel and God has granted you great loveliness, just as He did to our mother Rachel," Yechiel replied tenderly.

"God has not granted me great loveliness," cried Reisel.

"God has put a great love for you in my heart."

"Then why do you run away from me? Why don't you let me play with you?"

With her ice-cold trembling hand she softly stroked Yechiel's curls. But he started back as if touched by a red-hot iron.

"We should not," he replied with closed eyes, "for we are not yet married to each other after the law of Moses and Israel. But if God helps me, and I achieve anything in my studies, the half of it all will belong to you, for you are my mate and my soul is bound to yours as Jacob's was to Rachel."

Thus he spoke to Reisel and won her heart.

CHAPTER IX

FACES

THE sun was rising in the forest but had not yet reached the sky, which was obscured by a web of red leaves that the autumnal treetops had woven out of their intertwining branches. The loud twittering of the birds announced the sunrise; it was seen in the tracks left by the beasts of the forest in the dew-soaked, moss-covered earth over which they had just passed, and most of all in the flecked sunlight which was beginning to play among the crowding tree trunks. There was a festive morning freshness in the forest, yet with all the loud twittering of the birds and the patches of sunlight it seemed enveloped in a strange silence.

Yechiel was standing by the Pitch Jew's hut. The door was closed, and from inside a lighted candle was shining out, despite the morning brightness. Sometimes the Pitch Jew locked himself in his hut and would not show himself to Yechiel. This time Yechiel heard a movement through the cracks, as though there were someone else inside with the Pitch Jew. He heard whispering in low voices. Fear and trembling fell upon Yechiel, and for all his curiosity he dared not look in through the chinks in the door. He moved carefully away and stood behind a tree waiting for his teacher.

Presently the Pitch Jew appeared. He was wearing not as at other times only his white linen garment, his kittel, in which he went to the hidden pool for his ritual bath, but also his prayer shawl, his tallith, and his tefilin. His face was flushed, as with a high fever, and his eyes wild and disturbed, as though he did not see. He staggered about, in his tallith and tefilin, stumbling against the spreading roots, seeming about to fall. As he lurched among the trees, he talked to himself continuously, like one possessed. Clearly the Pitch Jew could not see and was not aware what he was doing.

Yechiel followed him at a distance, in great fear. He heard him talking to himself, incomprehensible words, half texts, invoking names, the names of angels, lifting up his hands to heaven and shaking them as if he were shaking the palm branch at the Feast of the Tents. And all the time he was bending and bowing, as if to someone who was with him. Finally he fell to his knees, stretched his arms to someone in front of him, and called out incomprehensible words.

Yechiel hurried to help his Rabbi. As he came near, he heard him stammering, with trembling lips and glazed eyes, "Blest be the Lord and His Messiah, the Anointed of Jacob!"

His pupils stood rigid for a moment in their white fields. Then the lids dropped down, and he fell into Yechiel's arms.

Yechiel, terrified, tried to rouse him from his trance.

"Reb Nathan! Reb Nathan! What has happened to you? Reb Nathan!"

The Pitch Jew opened his eyes, and looked at Yechiel in surprise.

"Did you see him?" he cried fearfully, with bloodless lips.

"Whom?"

"King Messiah!"

"Where?" Yechiel looked round, amazed.

"He was here a moment ago, in his royal robes, with the crown on his head that God wore when the Israelites crossed the Red Sea. Round him stood Hannah's seven sons who were all martyred. He knocked at night at my door. He revealed to me secrets. We sleep, but Messiah is awake. As the text says: 'I sleep, but my heart waketh.' The heart means Messiah. For Messiah is the heart of the universe."

"Reb Nathan! In God's name, what are you saying! King Messiah has been in your room?"

"Yes, my son. Whole nights I have been preparing. I went to the sacred pool. I dipped six-and-twenty times, according to the numerical value of God's name. I prayed with great devoutness. I wept long till my prayer was answered. I asked for a sign, that there is an eye that watches over our night, that our weeping and our cries reach the Throne of Glory. I demanded a sign! I insisted, I stormed, till they yielded to me. With the first ray, light filled my room. The whole host of ministering angels who accompanied him, with Hannah's seven sons—they all stood aside, and he, with great favor, approached me. I pronounced the blessing: 'Faithful Shepherd!' And I prostrated myself on my face before him. But he told me to stand up, and he said to me: 'See, I am girded with the sword which the mourners of Zion have girded upon me, and with the graciousness of the kiss which Mother Rachel bestowed upon my brow, crowned with the Crown of God. And I stand in the night behind your door and wait for you to open to me. Your tears are being counted, your groans collected. The measure is almost full; the fruit is nearly ripe.' Then I asked: 'Shepherd, Shepherd, when will you come to your sheep?' And he answered me: 'I am always with you, but I shall reveal myself when you will want me.'"

Yechiel led his Rabbi to the hut. He picked up the tefilin which had fallen from his head, and brought them along. Seating his Rabbi on the bench outside, that the sun, which had now come out from between the trees, might warm him, he went into the hut and found a little goat milk and a pan and brought it out.

The Pitch Jew held the pan for a long time in his bony fingers, and his eyes, sunk deep behind his brow, stared out upon the world with great yearning and not without pride. With a victorious smile he said, "I knew that with the Song of Songs I could bring him down! Prayers did not help, only the Song of Songs did it!"

He had hardly finished these words when the pan of milk fell from his hand. His eyes again glazed, and he began to slip off the bench.

Yechiel with great effort held him up, and as he led him into the hut, he noticed that the Rabbi was bathed in sweat. After Yechiel had laid him on his straw bed, his eyes closed; for a moment he seemed to be in a deep sleep. His face was still flushed and burning, his eye sockets sunk deeper into his skull, and his breast heaved, lifting the hair of his beard. But soon he was talking to himself again, stretching out his thin arms, and calling out the names of angels, names that Yechiel could not understand. He burst out singing in a strange chant the joyful words: "A beloved son is Ephraim unto us, a child of joy." Then came other passages relating to the Messiah: "Unto us a child is born, unto us a son is given." and now he was singing a song about the Prophet Elijah and King Messiah.

Yechiel trembled, fearing for his soul. He remembered now the stories that were told about this Jew, that he was a believer in the False Messiah. Till now he had never betrayed himself by one word, carefully avoiding any talk about the Messiah. Now Yechiel was hearing phrases from his Rabbi which might be interpreted to mean that he was connected with that terrible sect which had deviated from the Jewish road, the road that leads to baptism. But he shook off the dread suspicion. He was convinced that the Pitch Jew was a hidden saint. If so, then the Messiah had really been with him in the night, and had transmitted to him great secrets. Perhaps he had revealed to him the eternal secret, when he would come and redeem the world.

God! He was in the room where the Messiah had been this night! The room indeed looked dreadful, like the place where Jacob spent the night and saw the ladder with the angels. The table was littered with open books and parchment scrolls and amulets.

"These are sacred, secret writings," Yechiel told himself, " in which the time of the Messiah is revealed, and other wonderful things, that no man knows. God, where am I?"

His heart beat like a hammer, not with fear, but with awe, that he was privileged to be here where the holy things were happening.

He felt the imminence of mysterious events, that he was among angels and seraphs, now being brought forth by the names which this sleeping Jew was stammering with his parched lips out of his sleep, and that soon the whole room would begin to ignite and whirl him away to Heaven knows where.

As he sat beside the slumbering Jew, full of anxiety and wonderment, the Pitch Jew suddenly awoke from his sleep and looked round astonished, as though he had arrived from far-off realms, into a strange and unknown world.

He jumped from his bed, rushed to the table where the books and amulets were lying, and covered them with his hands.

"The tallith! Quickly, give me the tallith!" he cried.

Yechiel gave him the prayer shawl, which was lying on the bed, and the Pitch Jew covered the books and writings with it.

"You haven't, God forbid, looked into them?" he asked Yechiel, pale and frightened.

"No!"

"Thank God!" he sighed with relief. "You might, God forbid, have been hurt, or even worse. Go outside. I shall come to you soon."

"Rabbi, I shall not go out until you tell me who you are!" said Yechiel firmly.

The Pitch Jew went quite white.

"Did you see what happened here?"

"Yes, I saw everything."

"Forget it. And tell no son of woman about it."

"Rabbi, I shall not move until you tell me who you are!"

"Who I am? Who I am?"

He suddenly went to Yechiel, and looked straight in his face with his great eyes.

"Will you be able to grasp it? Will you comprehend?"

"Yes."

The Pitch Jew again looked searchingly into his face, and tried to fix Yechiel's eyes with his eyes. He pressed his heated brow against

Yechiel's forehead, placed his thin hands on Yechiel's head, and said piously, "Your soul is my sister. They both come from one place, from the chamber of love. I see the image of God on your brow. Listen, my son. I shall now reveal great secrets to you. Because you had the privilege today to see what happened in this place."

His eyes glazed, and he shook and swayed as he chanted piously.

"It is written: 'If you find a nest in the field, you shall send away the mother, and take the children.' You must know that it does not mean an ordinary nest of birds. The 'mother'—that means the First Cause. The children—that means Messiah. It is written: 'A beloved son unto me is Ephraim.' 'The son of the fruit of Joseph.' For in Messiah God repaired the sin of Adam, and through him the world attains perfection. Therefore when Messiah comes we shall be released from all the commandments. For the commandments are here only to put right what went wrong through the first sin. But through Messiah our souls attain eternal perfection. Thus we no longer need the commandments. For God is united with us not through our keeping the commandments, which are only the outward garb, but by contact through the pipe in which runs the holiness—through King Messiah."

Yechiel listened with bated breath. He would have liked to ask something, but the Pitch Jew motioned to him not to interrupt, and he continued, in a singsong voice, as if he were reading aloud:

"You must know further that Messiah is one, like God, the Lord of the Universe, but in many shapes. And like the grass which breaks through the hard snow as soon as the sun begins to shine, so Messiah breaks through to us. He comes to us in each generation, and seeks to redeem us, only we fail to recognize him and we drive him away. Messiah comes not only to us, but to the whole world, to all peoples, and assumes their shape and speaks their language and adopts their customs and ways. For just as Abraham took Hagar, and Ishmael was born, and Jacob took his concubines and the tribes were born, so Messiah comes to the nations of the world, to lift the uncleanness and to lead their souls to Mount Sinai, that they should thus find redemption. For it is written: 'The world will not be redeemed till the whole world will come to know God.' But they do not know that it is Messiah. And they repulse him and drive him away, with insults and indignity, and cause him great pain. Messiah never goes away from us. He stands like a beggar behind our door and pleads that we should let him in. We should admit his holiness into our hearts, so that we should speed the redemption. For if Messiah were not with us, we could not live for a moment. We should be like the animals and the beasts. Messiah links our life with all the eternities, with the source of goodness, and with the great hope. Even in shame and disgrace, in poverty and despair he is with us. If he were, God forbid, to leave us for a moment, we would lose our contact with the source, and the world could not go on. For only through him does our life acquire meaning and our souls exist."

Yechiel stood with head bowed, his heart and his brain beating as with hammers. What terrible things were being said he did not quite comprehend, but his conviction grew that they were against the Jewish faith. The pit had opened before him, and he had one foot already in it.

"Alas, alas! What things I hear! How has Messiah already come if we are still in exile? Is it not written that when Messiah comes all evil will cease upon earth? How can Messiah have come when the world is still full of evil? Alas, alas!"

He put both hands over his ears, so as not to hear more.

"It is because we drive him away that we are handed back to the Law. But for the chosen he is here!" the Pitch Jew cried with an unnatural voice. "Messiah, Anointed of Jacob, is always here! He comes to us in each generation, and we drive him away. But he is the same Messiah. As the holy Ari says: 'The first redeemer and the last are one. For both their souls are hewn from one place.' That is Messiah in many forms. The Messiah who revealed himself to me today is in the image of my lord the King, the Anointed of Jacob, Sabbatai Zvi!"

"Sabbatai Zvi, the accursed! His name should be blotted out!" Yechiel cried in a voice of terror. "Sabbatai Zvi, the apostate! Oh! Oh!"

And Yechiel rushed from the room and, with all the strength he could summon, across the fields to the village.

The Pitch Jew went to the door, and watched with an ashen, anguished face as Yechiel ran from him. He said nothing, and shut the door behind him.

CHAPTER X

YECHIEL'S PENANCE

W HO and what am I that I dared do such a thing? I am an ignoramus, an unlettered blockhead! How could I have done it!"

But Yechiel was not one to remain in despair for long. Always spinning and weaving in him was his faith in God, who had helped him out of all his troubles. When he had finished weeping, he calmed himself with the confidence that God knew his heart and was aware of his intentions. And God would forgive him and help him to remain a good, honest Jew.

Nor had he any resentment against the Pitch Jew. On the contrary, he pitied him, sure that the poor Jew had lost his way. He had plunged so deeply into his studies that he had strayed from the true path. Yechiel prayed to God that He should open the man's eyes.

He felt a need to go to his father, so that his father should give him a thrashing. But as his father, Boruch-Moishe, was not there, Yechiel went home, took the tefilin his father had given him, caressed them, and tried to defend himself.

"Father, I am not guilty. I wanted only to learn."

Having made up his mind to keep away from "those things," he felt a sturdy skepticism about scholars. They seemed to him like peddlers who went into the villages, setting out in a blizzard through unknown fields, never knowing where they might end. They might find themselves plunged into a pit and buried in the snow. Nothing seemed so good as a warm hearth, sheltered under a roof, behind firm walls, secure with his psaltery, which he had lately been neglecting. There he understood each word. There he knew that the word of the psalm he uttered was a sure road, on which he could not go astray.

He wanted to be a simple Jew like Reb Melech and say his psalms every day. What more does a Jew need?

But there was a different destiny in store for him. As though an unseen hand were pushing him, he was being forced to choose a road, seemingly foreordained, toward a dark and unknown destination.

And soon something happened that frightened him and made others marvel.

A feast was being held in the tavern, at which plates were broken for luck, for Yechiel's betrothal. Reisel's hair had been washed; her mother had tied her plaits with red ribbon, put her into a new calico apron, and even bought her a pair of shoes. She was not to be recognized! She had changed into a different girl. Though her beauty was always there and had shone out even from the gypsy dress she wore among the geese, now she looked like a princess! Her mother could not take her eyes from her lovely Reisel.

They had tied into her stocking a little bag with a piece of bread and some salt—against the evil eye. For brides are in great danger of the evil eye.

The innkeeper had had a new suit made for Yechiel and bought him a pair of high boots and a new hat. And the betrothal agreement was signed.

As it happened, there were many strangers staying in the inn, traders on their journeys, and a little Rabbi with a group of Chassidim on their way to the Rabbi of Kotzk. Shloime-Wolf, wanting to show off his son-in-law, had had the Shochet kill a couple of Reisel's geese; a table was laid for the Chassidim, a cask of brandy was opened, and was served not only to his own guests, but also to the peasants of the village, who had gathered in large numbers in the tavern, in the not-unjustified hope of getting a share of the good things. Of course, Poor Thaddeus was among the first.

This peasant, Father Care, was lurking in a corner with evil thoughts about the innkeeper's wife. He had been warming himself, on his rotten straw sack, with the image of her white buxom body, of her bosom showing over her dress, as she stood behind the bar. In his imagination he laid his ugly pock-marked face on her breasts, dragging the thought of her back to his corner like a dog with a bone. Not for nothing had she been complaining for some time that he was piercing her with his gaze, so that she spilled the brandy she was measuring out for the customers. He stood all day hidden in a corner of the tavern watching her, drinking in her womanliness with his eyes. And having saturated himself he crawled home with it to his hole. Now he was obsessed with horrible desires, over which he growled and snarled in his dark corner. They were as dark and black as the night.

Yechiel, sitting at the table in his new caftan, at the side of the Rabbi, saw from the distance how Poor Thaddeus in his everlasting dirty sheepskin had fixed his wicked gaze on Reisel's mother. There was an evil gleam in his eyes, which followed her every movement like two unclean worms, and an ugly, greasy smile on his twisted chin, on his fleshy snub nose, on his half-parted lips.

"Man was created in the image of God. When man is at peace with God there rests on his face the glow of the divine light. But when a man is going about with evil thoughts, the image of God on his face is distorted, and the glow is extinguished. There is a bad smell coming from that Poor Thaddeus, from his evil thoughts," Yechiel thought to himself. It disturbed him and spoiled his joy.

The innkeeper's wife bearing the bottle of brandy went about among the peasants and peasant women, filling their glasses. Suddenly Yechiel felt terribly uneasy. He had seen the peasant looking at Malke with so malevolent a gaze that he was reminded of wriggling snakes.

Then suddenly the face disappeared. He looked for the peasant, all his senses aroused. He could see something black and unhappy standing in the corridor, behind the door of the tavern, watching someone. Yechiel looked for his mother-in-law. She must not go out there! He followed her with his eyes and suddenly saw her about to go into the alcove, the Sabbath room, where she kept her treasures. He must not let her go! He rose from the table and stole away, toward the door.

"Please don't go in there, I beg of you!" he pleaded with Malke.

"Why not?" she asked, surprised, one foot already at the door.

Yechiel opened the door, stepped into the dark corridor, and went up to Father Care, who was crouching there, hidden behind the door.

"Thaddeus! I know all you want to do! Think of God! Do not give way to sin!"

The peasant was terrified.

"How do you know?"

"I know you have evil in mind," said Yechiel, seizing his hand. "What have you there?"

"Olia boga! O God!" Thaddeus cried out, rushing past Yechiel, screaming, and dropping a knife with a clatter on the floor.

Yechiel returned to the tavern, his heart pounding with fear because of what had happened—and because of himself. For the first time he had sensed the power that was in him. And he was afraid.

"Where have you been? What has happened?" Malke asked him.

"Nothing has happened."

And Yechiel, dead pale, returned to his place at the table.

Poor Thaddeus was rushing across the fields, as though the fiends were after him. And he kept crossing himself. The boy had seemed to rise over him like a giant and had driven him out with red-hot rods. He was chasing him now, and would hunt him down to the pit, if he didn't go back to the tavern now, fall on his knees in front of everybody, and beg for forgiveness for what he had done.

"Who is he? Olia boga! In the name of God! What is he?" Poor Thaddeus kept muttering.

CHAPTER XI

YECHIEL'S WEDDING

PAN WYDAWSKI was prepared to sacrifice everything at once on the altar of his country; his riches, even his life. There was only one thing that his ardent love for Poland could not overcome: his unbending pride. He was incapable of getting into touch with the people, for "one can't talk to animals except with a stick."

Still, so as to give money support at least to the Polish noblemen who were preparing for the rebellion of 1831, he sold the huge woodlands that lay outside the village. Through this the Jews in Topolye received an accession to their number, for the great timber dealer Reb Danziger installed himself with his innumerable family of sons, daughters, and sons-in-law, in the castle in the woods which he had bought from the Count, along with the timber.

So a real House of Study presently rose in the woods. Reb Danziger had a ritual bath set up for his own use, and together with his sons, sons-in-law, and Jewish employees, held divine service on the Sabbath and the feast days, to which the Jews in the surrounding villages also found their way. When Yechiel appeared there one Sabbath he saw to his great joy a room crammed with books and parchments, just like a complete House of Study.

Reb Danziger was a very rich man, of distinguished ancestry and unutterable arrogance. In his house he ruled with a heavy hand, and everybody trembled before him as before a monarch. Never before had Yechiel seen such riches and splendor, such great splendid rooms, so many silver candlesticks, such huge, crammed bookcases. He was almost afraid and felt quite small before such grandeur; here the joys of the Law and the pleasures of earthly riches were united!

Naturally the study of the Talmud was diligently pursued in the timber dealer's house. All day there were disputations; one son-in-law tried to outdo the next in keen dialectic. In the other rooms, where the daughters and daughters-in-law lived, children were born with great rapidity, and one circumcision followed another.

The master of the house was very pampered. He had a room to

himself, where he studied almost all day. Yechiel saw him only on the Sabbath, at divine service. There Reb Danziger was always enveloped in a heavy silken Turkish prayer shawl with a broad gold fringe. From beneath it peered a pale, bloodless, pimply face to which was attached a red beard. That face looked as if it had never felt a breath of fresh air, but had been wrapped in cotton wool ever since birth. The long hooked nose was of the same unhealthy yellow hue.

In his room Reb Danziger was perpetually surrounded by myriad silver boxes decorated with filigree work and containing snuff and herbs which he was always conveying to his nose. For he was extremely taken up with himself, and all his life his hands had waited on nothing but his own body. They had a spongy look, as if morbid juices flowed in them, and so thin-skinned that when Yechiel saw them he was always afraid lest one of the veins might burst and all the blood flow away. On the Sabbath, before divine service, Reb Danziger appeared along with all sons and sons-in-law in his House of Study and went over with them a section of the Talmud. When Yechiel saw them from afar in their gleaming silk caftans and costly fur caps outrivaling each other in the dialectical art, he gazed with envy at the great beautiful tomes and felt like a poor man at a rich man's table.

One day the innkeeper said to him, "My son, I think it would be a good idea for you to go to the House of Study. You could study there for the time being. Why should you waste your time on the children? That isn't work for you; you should be studying higher things."

"It is a pious deed to teach children," replied Yechiel.

"I'll soon get a teacher for them; you should look after your own studies."

So it came about that Yechiel often visited the House of Study in the woods, even during the week. He would take some book down from the shelves and glance over it or read it. One day he was noticed by no one less than Reb Danziger himself. The rich merchant asked in his faint voice, without looking at Yechiel, "Do you like studying?"

"Yes."

"Do you know much?"

"Very little."

"Modesty is a rare quality," Reb Danziger said, and, without ceasing to rock over his book, turned to his sons and sons-in-law.

"It is a very good deed to instruct a poor young lad in the Law."

After this all the sons and sons-in-law competed for Yechiel, and stuffed him with wisdom. But that did not last for very long; soon they had forgotten him again, and he was left to his own devices. Actually he preferred that—the tenants of the castle were not people after his heart. They seemed to him living examples of what a wise teacher had meant when he spoke of misers who heaped up riches in the next world.

And once more his father came to his aid. Reb Feivush, who instructed the merchant's family, was known to Boruch-Moishe, who had met him at Rabbi Mendele's. They had met frequently at Kotzk, where Rabbi Mendele had since moved from his former residence. When Reb Feivush heard that Yechiel was a son of his friend Boruch-Moishe he looked after him as if he were a child of his own. He gave him regular instruction in the Talmud and the commentaries, and exerted himself to make him understand everything. And Yechiel became the pupil of the great scholar Reb Feivush in the rich merchant's House of Study.

Shloime-Wolf was inexpressibly glad that God had found him worthy of acquiring a son-in-law versed in the Law. Although he and his wife had minds fit only for business—or perhaps for that very reason—they sunned themselves in Yechiel's spirituality. He was for them the Sabbath of their very prosaic life; he made good all their sins. Through him their life with all its trials, all the humiliations from the Count and his dog, suddenly acquired meaning and value.

Now that Yechiel had in such an unexpected way found his road open to the study of the Law, Shloime-Wolf resolved to proceed with the marriage and keep the young couple with him until Yechiel had achieved something palpable. For to the innkeeper Yechiel was a precious jewel; consequently he did not want to send him far away before he was married, for he feared lest a richer man might snap him up.

"I don't yoke a horse so that another man may drive off with him!" said Shloime-Wolf to himself. "Let his father come here, and we shall arrange the marriage—and then to the Yeshivah!"

Thanks to Yechiel, Reisel's estimation also rose in the house. They regarded her now as a being destined for higher things. Obviously she could no longer be allowed to herd the geese. To brush her up and make her worthy of being the spouse of such a pious young man, she was sent to an aunt of hers in the town. There she was taught to read the women's Bible, and instructed in the few religious commandments which women are supposed to obey. When her education was finished she was brought back from the town and a date fixed for the wedding.

Although the Count possessed a dog called Titus who was a scourge to the children of Israel, Shloime-Wolf acknowledged only one God and one temporal master. Whatever happened he always said, "After God the Poritz!" So, as he wished to marry off his daughter, he put on his Sabbath caftan and in defiance of Titus went to the castle to invite his master to the wedding.

He could do nothing without the assent of the lord of the manor, such being the law at the time. Accordingly the Count made known that he desired the wedding to be celebrated in his tenant's house in a manner befitting the consequence of the Topolye estate and the dignity of its owner. The Count's vehicles brought a small townful of Jews to the village, including a number of Rabbis and their assistants, a band, and a master of ceremonies. The steward saw to it that there was no lack of food and drink.

It was late autumn. In the mornings the stream was covered with a thin sheet of ice, which later melted in the sun. Although Reb Danziger had a ritual bath Reisel was led to the stream in the early morning to take the prescribed bath—she had to put up with the substitute, since there was no other alternative. Two proved and pious women accompanied her this time instead of the geese to see that she immersed herself according to the law, right over her head. Then they clothed Reisel in her new wedding dress and made her sit down on a chair. With that she was ready for the ceremony of "veiling the bride."

Some Jewish musicians whom Shloime-Wolf had sent for from the town scraped on their fiddles; the master of ceremonies mounted on a chair and sang the bride's praises in moving strains. Then two men led Yechiel out of the adjoining room. He held a silken wrap in his hand and laid it over Reisel's head.

The public room was crammed, members of the family from the town, uncles and brothers-in-law, with iron-shod top boots and wide fringed garments bulging from their open caftans, and women and girls in flowered cotton dresses and colored ribbons. Of course Reb Melech was present with his wife Blimele, high on the list of honored guests. Melech and Blimele, with Rivke's two children whom they had brought up, felt they had a special right. Hadn't Melech carried Yechiel in his arms when he was a baby?

"Didn't I tell you, Yechiel, that you would find a wife in the village?"

Blimele burst into tears. She was thinking of his mother, Rivke. "If she had lived to be here! Poor woman, she never had any luck."

The inn was stiflingly hot. For besides the invited guests, the fiddlers had drawn to the inn all the peasant folk of the village.

There were guests even from Reb Notte Danziger's palace. Not he himself, of course, nor his menfolk; but to avoid snubbing the poor people he had sent along the women. Naturally Yechiel's teacher, Reb Feivush, was present in his threadbare caftan. He was eager above all to meet Boruch-Moishe again.

The innkeeper had kept his word. He had fitted out his son-in-law's father with a brand new set of clothes and at the same time had had a new satin caftan made for himself, so that the Chassid should not feel ashamed to stand under the canopy with a simple innkeeper.

Yechiel could scarcely recognize his father. In the few years of separation Boruch-Moishe had become an old man with a faded gray beard.

Before the nuptial ceremony, the master of ceremonies recalled to the bridegroom in well-turned verses adorned with Biblical quotations the memory of his dead mother Rivke, who now was gazing from a window of the heavenly Paradise on her child. At this picture the women sobbed bitterly; in accordance with the tradition they were all sitting together at one side of the room. Yechiel did not cry. Shutting his eyes, he could see quite clearly his mother Rivke sitting in an upper hall of the women's Paradise where Miriam, Moses' sister, ruled. ... Since his mother died he had not spent a moment in regretting her. He felt sure that she must be much better off in the next world than she had ever been in this one. The period of correction after death must long since have passed; now she was certainly sitting in the beautiful lofty hall along with countless holy women, and resting after the many years of suffering that had been her lot in life, and waiting for the arrival of her husband, that she might take her place on the golden footstool at his feet.

Since his wife's death Boruch-Moishe had gone on leading his monkish life in the Rabbi's fellowship and had refused to marry again. His companions in Kotzk took this ill of him, for in acting as he did he offended against the commandment: "Be fruitful and multiply." The verses of the master of ceremonies left him quite unmoved. More, they almost seemed blasphemy to him. He was persuaded that Rivke dwelt in the highest Heaven; by her pious life on earth she had certainly earned a great reward, and here was this fool lamenting for her!

With the contempt of a Chassid from Kotzk Boruch-Moishe made a sign to the master of ceremonies and cried, "Enough! Enough! No more idle words!"

When Reisel, veiled in richly hued silks, stood with Yechiel beneath the marriage canopy, he told himself that now he was taking her as his wife, and that she would be the same to him as Rachel was to Jacob. His love for her grew deeper. He had reached the stage of the sacrifice of self. He had read in a Cabbalistic book that it is good to stand for a long time under the canopy. Because the canopy of the bride and bridegroom is a token of the great Canopy of Peace. He felt purified and exalted. This girl standing beside him in her silks, her slender head covered with a veil, was no longer Reisel the goose girl, but the eternal bride of whom the Song of Songs and many other holy books spoke with such yearning. Yechiel could hear the rustling of wings over his head. A sacred loveliness, the loveliness of the Sabbath, rested on his beloved's veiled head. Now he understood why the Sabbath was likened to a bride; for it seemed to him that beneath Reisel's veil the Princess Sabbath was concealed.

When the "golden soup" was served, when they were both seated side by side, he did not speak to her. He had not spoken to her since he went to her in the field. Now it was permitted, yet he was silent. And she was silent too. For wild Reisel had been tamed in the time that she stayed with her aunt in the town. She seemed not to know where to hide her eyes. Yechiel could hear her loudly beating heart. And not only were her eyes ashamed to look, but it seemed to her that her very skin was ashamed, even the tips of her fingers, and she tried to hide completely behind her veil. He could feel her shyness through his caftan, and he would have liked to say a kind word to her, comfort her heart, but he too was shy. So they both sat there silent.

The wedding was a long one, a merry one, and full of abundance. The inn shook under the hopping and jumping of iron-shod boots. Brandy flowed like water, and the crowd was enjoying itself. Malke, in her best clothes but with sleeves rolled up, went about among the guests and peasants with a big bottle of brandy, filling everyone's glass. Poor Thaddeus was also there, but the sign of Cain had been wiped from his brow. Yechiel saw that it was gone. He was laughing and joining in the fun and footing it with the dancers. A man with sinful thoughts could not be so carefree.

But it was getting late now. Bride and bridegroom must be led to their room. The crowd pulled the bride into the middle of the ring and tied her in a knot among all the dancers. Everyone wanted to dance with her separately, until poor Reisel was almost danced off her feet. Shloime-Wolf nodded to his wife. "Hurry up!"

And Malke managed with much difficulty to snatch the bride out of the ring. She whispered in her ear, "Don't shame me, daughter! Be a good Jewish wife to your husband."

And to Yechiel his father whispered, "A Chassid behaves like a Chassid even under the bedclothes."

They were led into their room and the door locked behind them, so that they should never run away from each other.

In the Sabbath room, the alcove, which had been prepared for the occasion, well heated and piled with many pillows and covers for the beds (so as to provide for the children who would come out of this union), the bride stood in a corner, her head hidden in her veil. Now she was permitted to him. Therefore Yechiel went to her, and spoke to her heart.

"Reisel," he said, swaying piously as in prayer. "Now you are permitted to me according to the law of Moses and of Israel. Why do you turn away from me?"

"Because I feel ashamed in your presence," Reisel answered, sobbing into her veil.

"Why do you feel ashamed? You are my wife now. I have married you and sanctified you."

"I am not ashamed because of now. I am ashamed because of the other time. You know!"

"I don't know!" Yechiel exclaimed.

"Because I committed a great sin before I was married."

"What sin did you commit?" Yechiel asked, frightened.

"I know. The bathwoman told me. Because I came near to you when I was not yet permitted to you."

"Is that what you mean?" Yechiel said, turning red. "Nonsense! We turned that sin into a virtue. And God has forgiven us."

On the second day wild Reisel's hair was shorn off like a sheep's. She put on a cap, and she was a wife.

It was essential that Yechiel should be introduced to the Count and Titus. Custom demanded that the lord of the manor should be thanked; besides, he had to be asked permission that the young couple should live in the village. So Shloime-Wolf and Yechiel put on their Sabbath caftans and, while the women wrung their hands and prayed to God that everything might go well, betook themselves to the castle.

Before they set foot on such dangerous ground Shloime-Wolf instructed his son-in-law how he should comport himself toward the Poritz and Titus.

"Do nothing and say nothing—have you got that? Keep your eye on me, and whatever I do you do the same. When I throw myself at the Poritz's feet, you do it too. When I kiss his right hand, you take his left hand. And if he should, God guard and preserve us," the inn-keeper grew pale at the thought, "if he should set that savage dog on you, you mustn't think of defending yourself, but fall on your knees, stretch out your hands to the Poritz and beg him, 'Poritz dear, have pity on me and my children!' That's the only thing you can do, we're in his hands. . . ."

The Count received his visitors very ungraciously. He was in a bad mood or—rather to use the expressive language of his peasants and Jews—"the worm was gnawing him."

Humbly Shloime-Wolf brought out his petition that the Poritz would graciously permit his son-in-law to live in the village and pursue his study of the Holy Scriptures, while his young wife sold dry goods.

The Count burst out, "You want to pollute the whole village with your race. There will be nothing to me soon but to smoke out all Topolye—the Jews will have ruined it completely with their onions and garlic."

The Count talked himself into a higher and higher rage, and at last commanded Titus to sniff the new Jew.

Titus, who had been waiting for a long time for such a sweet morsel, sprang out at Yechiel with a powerful leap.

Pale as death, Shloime-Wolf flung himself down and begged with clasped hands, "Pity, Poritz dear, pity!" Yechiel did not follow the advice his father-in-law had given him, but remained quietly standing where he was, and steadfastly fixed the dog with his eye. Titus barked at him, true enough, but did not venture to touch him.

Ever since the time when he had carried his pack through the villages, Yechiel had been accustomed to dealing with dogs. But that was not the reason why Titus remained quiet. In Yechiel's glance was that confidence and assurance which once, in the early age of the world, subdued the first animal to man. His face was pale, his lips trembled slightly, but his posture expressed such human dignity that Titus was forced to sink his head. The dog contented himself with sniffing Yechiel from every side. He recognized in him the familiar odor of the village and noticed that this man's legs did not tremble, but were firmly planted and tense with energetic resistance. Titus good-humoredly recognized Yechiel's power and quietly trotted back to his place behind the family coat of arms.

A Jew who was not afraid of a dog was something quite new to the Count. Instead of giving the visitor a sign to approach, as he usually did, he rose from his chair and went up to Yechiel, his whip held behind his back. This Jew must be brought to reason! The Count was pleased, true, that the young man was not afraid of the dog, but at the same time he felt vexed, for he saw in that something resembling a lack of respect for his own person. He stepped close up to Yechiel and mustered him curiously from head to foot. Yechiel met the Count's gaze calmly and impressed him too, as formerly the dog, by the assured look in his eyes. Wydawski's rage was immediately over; more, the calm, curiously frank look in Yechiel's great eyes pleased him.

"I like this young Jew! He has a clear look in his eyes," said the Count to himself, a little taken off his guard, and then turned to Yechiel.

"What's your name, little Jew?"

"Yechiel."

"What do you want to do in my village?" The Count had found his usual tone again.

"I want to study God's teaching and work for my living," replied Yechiel dauntlessly.

"Will you work honestly?"

"I will work as God has commanded in his Law."

"You have an honest face."

The Count regarded Yechiel gravely.

"But, Poritz dear—is he really to be supposed to work?" the innkeeper interrupted exultantly. "His wife will work, and he will study to be a Rabbi."

Among other ambitions pertaining more to his rank, the Count had also an ambition that his tenants should acquire learned sons-in-law. That was a distinction, like the possession of a beautiful prize horse. The landowners when they met reckoned up with something like pride the number of Rabbis that lived in their villages. So the Count became affable.

"Shlomko, I like your son-in-law. Tell the steward to bring him a few cartloads of firewood for the winter. I am very pleased that a tenant of mine should have a scholar instead of an innkeeper for a son-in-law!"

When Shloime-Wolf left the castle with Yechiel, he gazed at his son-in-law with almost reverential shy admiration and asked, "How was it that you weren't afraid of the dog? And the way you talked to the Poritz—he could play a fine game with you if he liked!"

"That isn't in his power. He's only a tool in God's hands. If God does not wish it, what harm can he do me?"

"Yes, my son, you are right! I had never thought of that."

Shloime-Wolf sighed heavily; he was thinking of the slavish submissiveness of his whole life. . . .

Happy that he was leaving his son in good hands, Boruch-Moishe returned to his Rabbi. And Yechiel devoted himself properly to his studies. For weeks at a time he stayed out in the forest at Reb Notte Danziger's House of Study. Under the guidance of his father's friend, Reb Feivush, he set out to swim the great ocean of the Talmud.

BOOK THREE

BOOK THREE

CHAPTER I

THE LAND OF THE JEWISH SOUL

FOR five years Yechiel sat at the foot of his teacher, Reb Feivush. To spare himself a daily journey of several versts he lived in the rich merchant's house. He appeared in the village only on the Sabbath, and in winter, when the snow lay deep, he remained for weeks and once for a whole winter in the woods. He slept with Reb Feivush in a little attic room and ate with him at a table reserved for themselves; for since Reb Danziger lived in great style, he did not like to see strange faces at his table. Yechiel and his teacher were not displeased that this should be so, for the women of the family sat at Reb Danziger's table.... Although the rich merchant would not let Yechiel pay for his board and lodging, for he regarded such charity as a good work, Reisel's geese wandered one by one from the cool stream that prattled so cheerfully between the willow bushes into Reb Danziger's basting pans. Reisel's geese and ducks paid for Yechiel's knowledge of the Law. And in gratitude for Yechiel's upkeep Shloime-Wolf was perpetually bringing butter, eggs, and milk; for the rich man's pots and pans were insatiable....

In the Scripture the Jewish law is compared to an ocean. But it resembles more a land of fantasy given by God to the Jews in return for their lost home.

During his years of study Yechiel came to know a good part of that land. To be quite frank, he did not scale the highest peaks, where the eternal snow, the absolute "endlessness" of the Cabbalah lies; nor did he plunge to the bottom of the deep waters of Talmudic exegesis; nor did he penetrate into the dark, primitive jungle, thick with roots and undergrowth, of casuistical theology. On the stony paths of tradition he progressed but slowly and painfully, but on the other hand he loved to loiter by the bright islands of legend and the refreshing streams of Jewish devotion.

The life in that land was not real; it was full of a thousand complicated happenings and surprises, of unexpected and extraordinary situations such as could hardly be imagined. Yechiel took part in

disputes which more than two thousand years before had been conducted with fiery Oriental passion and the obstinacy of an Essene in
the sun-scorched courts of the Temple in Jerusalem, and later on
in the Houses of Study of Yabne and Pumbeditha in Babylonia.
Yechiel learned the countless safeguards with which the Diaspora had
surrounded every generation of Jewish life, so that the Jewish
soul might be preserved unsullied in the melting pot of world his-
tory. Like a refreshing draught he drank the wise proverbs which
had defied the avid action of time and lost not a jot of their value and
meaning. Not only the Law itself, but also the exalted lives of the
great teachers became his model. These men were to him living
examples of true piety, real guides not only in their teaching, but also
in the self-sacrificing spirit which raised them to heroism and made
them go to death for their convictions. Like torches they lit the dark
nights of the Diaspora.

In accordance with the saying, "He who teaches you the Law
should be regarded as your father," Reb Feivush became a second
father to Yechiel. He was very fond of his pupil. Yechiel's love of
the mystical part of the Torah was entirely after his teacher's heart.
Reb Feivush saw in Yechiel a reflection of himself and wished his
pupil to fulfill all the hopes that he himself had failed to realize.

Reb Feivush, too, had at one time possessed wings and aspired
toward the heights. . . . In his youth he had observed extraordinary
fast days, taken cold baths, and even rolled himself in the snow, as a
particular act of penance, so as to achieve great things. But life had
taken him by the throat and flung him down from his dreamed-of
heights. One child followed another, his parents-in-law grew weary
of feeding him and his family and requested him to begin an occupation that would keep a man alive, and become a teacher and a Rabbi
in Israel.

So Reb Feivush had to give up mysticism and apply himself
seriously to his studies to secure his diploma as Rabbi. He never
achieved his aim, for to do so one required an influential father-in-law
or a well-to-do father. So Reb Feivush became a Talmudic teacher.
As he felt ashamed before his relations, of his occupation, he sought
scenes where he was not known, and wandered from place to place
until he came to Reb Danziger's house, where he was engaged to
instruct the merchant's sons and sons-in-law, and particularly the
youngest son-in-law, whom he wished to make a Rabbi.

And now Reb Feivush, having fled from home, lived in poverty far from his family, whom he only saw on feast days. He hated his pupils, the sons and sons-in-law of the rich man, who were always boasting of their learning; he hated his employer too, who, as Reb Feivush put it, "stank of pride a mile off." The dry scholastic instruction which he had to give to earn his living was not at all to his liking. Far from the community of Kotzk, the center of the Chassid spirit, for which he yearned, he found his sole comfort and refreshment in the Cabbalah and in the teachings of the Chassid Rabbis. They consoled him for the absence of his family, and gave him at least self-respect. When he could bury himself in study, he felt as secure as if he were in a self-built fortress where the arrows of care, his bitter enemy, could not reach him.

His patron Reb Danziger did not like the Cabbalah scriptures, however, and still less the Chassid teaching with its "idolatry." At bottom he was what one would call a freethinker, although he scrupulously observed all the commandments of religion and studied the Scripture almost all day in his room. But his study was more an intellectual game than a religious need, and he pursued it chiefly because it was the right thing to do. For at that time it was the fashionable thing to study the Scriptures. Even in rich and enlightened houses a great deal of reading was done, not so much for its own sake as to make a good impression on society.

Reb Danziger had a weakness for religious philosophy and in the evenings he enjoyed having learned discussions with Reb Feivush. He would take a pinch from his silver snuffbox or sip a glass of Tokay which he had always beside him, and speak of the "efficient reason" of Maimonides, or of Aristotle, and such like themes. Reb Feivush had so to maneuver things that the rich man emerged as victor from these disputations, just as he did from the games of chess which they occasionally played. For apart from the fact that Reb Danziger was the master and so was entitled to win, a defeat at chess or in argument might, God forbid, injure his health, for which he and the whole house were so solicitous. . . .

He was interested also in the movement of "enlightenment," which was still young at that time and just beginning to penetrate into Poland, and in the campaign against Chassidism which the leading writers of the enlightenment were waging. The Chassidim, who in his eyes were fanatics, and a danger and misfortune for the Jewish people, were detested by him from the bottom of his soul.

In the dry rationalistic atmosphere of the rich merchant's house

Reb Feivush would have stifled without the refreshing spring of the
Cabbalah and the Chassid writings. The least opportunity of practic-
ing Chassid customs quickened his soul. He took a ritual bath every
morning with Yechiel before prayer, and acquainted his pupil with the
mystical significance of immersion.

Partly so as to give no offense to Reb Danziger, partly because
he considered himself a sort of wage slave during the day, and so
not master of his time, but especially because the stillness of night
was more suited for the twilit state of mysticism, Reb Feivush spent
the day in teaching the sons and sons-in-law of his employer and in
instructing Yechiel in the Talmud and the commentaries whenever he
had an hour to spare. On the other hand, he studied the Zohar and
the Cabbalah in the hours that were his own—that is at night. Yechiel
learned to turn night into day. After two hours' sleep he awoke Reb
Feivush: this was an arrangement they had come to. He sometimes
felt it very difficult to fulfill his teacher's orders. When he stepped
up to Reb Feivush's bed and examined by the light of the candle
his teacher's birdlike face with the sunken eyes and the long, jutting
nose, and saw the sinews of his neck moving painfully with the labor
of breathing, he could not find it in his heart to waken him. Yet it
had to be. Reb Feivush had been very vexed with him once for not
having wakened him in time. "A man who sleeps more than two hours
a night must be prepared to take the consequences," he had said, and
strictly forbidden Yechiel ever to act against his orders again or
allow him, Reb Feivush, to sleep more than two hours.

For study was the one thing to which Reb Feivush clung. For him
and Yechiel it became a magic island where they sought refuge, a
magic island which was also their real home. Study gave them forgetfulness, protection against the worm of doubt, which softly gnawed
at the teacher's heart. He had actually turned to worldly knowledge
once, had borrowed some of Reb Danziger's "other" books, and
searched them desperately to discover and establish the meaning of
life. But he could get nothing out of them. These books had led him
to a door and left him standing outside; they had not helped him to
penetrate into the innermost secret. He was fond of quoting to Yechiel
a wise pronouncement on knowledge by Rabbi Reb Bunem of Przysucha: "King Solomon says in the Song of Songs, 'We have a little
sister, and she hath no breasts.' What is meant here? Here knowledge
is meant, of which it is written in another passage: 'Say to wisdom,
thou art my sister.' This sister has no breasts, for knowledge has no

refreshing fountains. How far can it get us? We sit in a glass house and beat against the walls. You cannot reach God by knowledge, because knowledge brings us to ignorance. God calls himself 'the infinite'; but there is no word that can embrace the nature of God. The words 'the infinite' did not express God's nature but only our nothingness. There is only *one* way to God, the way of love, as it says in the pious book, 'We must be sick with love for God, as a man is sick with love for a beloved woman.' There is no other way of reaching God."

Yechiel had an open heart for simple ideas which appealed to the goodness within himself. In the complicated labyrinth of Cabbalistic theology with its spheres and graduated emanations he could never find his way about. His heart was barred against all that was complicated or distorted. From his studies he recognized now that he had regarded God too much as a friend and equal, and that the first step in wisdom was the fear of God.

Through his fear of God there awakened in Yechiel a deep reverence for the whole creation. He was no longer afraid to contemplate nature, the glory of the fields, the boundless sky, the flowing streams, though to look upon them was generally considered a temptation diverting one from the study of the Law. He saw in nature itself the greater law, for he contemplated it with deep admiration as God's creation. He felt a longing to kiss every blade of grass, every twig, because God had shaped them so wisely and beautifully. And his heart blessed creation anew and praised its Creator.

He understood, too, the importance which the Holy Scripture gave to the creation of the world. He saw that the world in its immensity was not an inferior creation, but was connected with higher worlds, for it is said: "The spirit does not descend unless it is first awakened and attracted from beneath." He saw that nothing was ever lost, no word, no breath, for everything was a part of the whole. And he came to love the beasts of the field. He remembered a passage that he had once read: "It is wrong to speak evil of God's creation, even if it be only the beasts of the field and the stall." "God's reflection cannot rest on a man who does not love God's creatures."

But the chosen of the whole creation was man, made after God's image. He bore God's lineaments, God's seal. Even his shape was a symbol of the whole creation. He was so great, so noble, that one must bow before the least of human beings as before a miracle. Man was God's reflection, the Shechinah on earth, with whom God had made His covenant. By the creation of man the whole world, the

heavenly one no less than the earthly, was perfected, as it is written:
"God created many worlds, but destroyed them again because man
did not dwell in them."

The service of man formed an important part of the service of
God. No labor was too menial or too humble if one submitted oneself
to it out of love for mankind.

Yechiel learned that the greatest joy, the highest heavenly joy,
could only be attained by communion with God, by vanishing into
Him like a drop into the sea, clinging to Him like a lost child to its
mother's knees. This union with God could only be achieved by
prayer that was freed of all earthly desire, so that it became nothing
but a deep and torturing longing for His presence. Then one's prayers
soared lightly, borne on the pinions of love, to the highest Heaven.

What Yechiel could not achieve by study he strove to achieve
by prayer. And indeed there were moments when he felt a deep
need for union with God. Then there was kindled in his soul an
intense spiritual thirst. In such moments of ecstatic exaltation he
sometimes felt as if he no longer had a body and were lost in the
infinite splendor of God like a drop of water in the ocean.

Naturally in the world of thought in which he now lived the
perfect righteous man, the Zaddik, occupied a very important place,
perhaps the most important place of all. He came immediately after
the Godhead, more, he was in a sense God's representative on earth,
the channel through which divinity flowed down to men. His power
was without limit; it was so great that no other power approached it:
"The Zaddik is the cornerstone of the world; he commands and
God fulfills; God decrees and the Zaddik suspends His decree." The
Zaddik was the incarnation of the highest human perfection. He
united in himself all virtues, and everything about him was of equal
consequence, his studies and his personal attributes, and also his
whole way of life. "I journeyed to the Great Preacher, in Meseritch,
simply to see how he laced his shoes," Rabbi Levi-Yitzchak of Berditchev once related.

Any Jew can become a Zaddik according to the writings. "Any man
can become like Moses, for all have a part in God." To become a
Zaddik one did not require to perform great services; one had simply
to dedicate all one's life and bring it as an offering to God. But one
could not do this by mortification alone, by fasts and lustrations.
God's reflection rests on joy alone, as it is written: "Thou shalt not
hide thyself before thy flesh." Mortification was not the ladder leading

to Heaven. Everything that a man did he must do joyfully, he must always be filled with inner joy: "To trouble is evil."

But by what ladder could one become a Zaddik? By unremitting self-sacrifice.

A Zaddik dared not employ a jot or tittle of the riches of life for himself, dared have no joy of his own, dared breathe no breath, make no motion for his own sake. Everything must be dedicated to one end, God, in the words of the Psalmist: "All my bones shall say, Lord, who is like unto thee... ?" Often the Zaddik went through life poor, unknown, in beggar's garb, like a vagrant. If he was to be recognized as a Zaddik, he must live poorly and wretchedly like the founders of the Chassid faith, who made their wives take in washing, turned their houses into asylums for beggars, laved the feet of vagrants, or went from house to house washing the children's heads.

The lives of these holy men was Yechiel's lesson book, from which he learned to love God, man and the world. And he resolved to live his life after the pattern of the much loved Rabbi of Sassov, who once said: "I have learned three things from a thief. First, he lives in constant fear. Secondly, he does his work unseen and by night. And thirdly, what he gains at great danger to himself he gives away for nothing...."

CHAPTER II

THE INNER LIGHT

YECHIEL arrived one Friday evening at the inn, intending to spend the Sabbath with his wife and parents-in-law. When the learned scholar was at home, the Sabbath in Shloime-Wolf's house was quite different; it was observed more piously and scrupulously. Yechiel stayed in the clean and swept little alcove which he occupied with his wife. Beside the two wooden beds standing side by side in the right-hand corner of the room and separated by a curtain in accordance with tradition, there was a rocking chair—it would later, with God's help, serve as a cradle. In the middle of the room was another chair, and a table on which stood the two candlesticks, over which Reisel now said the Sabbath blessing. But the most important piece of furniture was Yechiel's bookcase. It contained, along with the books which he had himself acquired, a good number added by his father-in-law. These volumes represented a part of the dowry provided for in the marriage contract, and every time that Shloime-Wolf went to the town to buy brandy he brought a book home as a present for Yechiel.

It would have been difficult to recognize the wild ungoverned Reisel of a few years ago in this slender young wife with the boyish shape and the smooth ivory skin gleaming beneath a heavy wig that reached over her very ears. On her hood glittered a brooch or two which she had put on in honor of her husband's homecoming. Though little wisps of reddish-blonde hair always peeped from beneath her mother's wig, Reisel's head was shaven quite clean. Not a single ringlet of her black hair could be seen. Malke's gay dress, as she stood behind the bar, was cut low, exposing her white neck. But the grave black dress of her daughter came up to her very chin. For the mother was only the wife of the Topolye innkeeper, but the daughter was married to a Chassid.

For this reason the mother kept a far stricter eye on her daughter than on herself. When young noblemen visited the inn, she would quickly hide Reisel behind her sumptuous form and whisper to her,

"Reisel, quick, get into the alcove!" And when a drunken peasant became too familiar with the young wife, the mother, in all her ample bulk, would step in front of her and ask threateningly, "What do you want? You can tell me; I'm the woman to deal with—she's no better than a child!" And with a powerful shove she would rid her daughter of the drunkard's presence. In all such situations Malke shielded her Reisel, as for instance when noblemen had to be served in the private room. She always undertook this office herself, for she knew how to deal with such guests. Her daughter had to be protected at any price, for she was a young Chassid wife, not a mere ordinary landlady.

As it was Friday and Reisel's husband was coming, Malke would not allow her daughter over the threshold of the public room. During the week, when Yechiel was away, the meals were got through haphazardly, one ate whatever was at hand from the bare table, often without sitting down and without a grace. But the Sabbath made up in devotion for all the laxity of the week. On Friday the young wife stood by the hearth and prepared the Sabbath dishes. In the five years since her wedding Reisel had become an excellent housewife; she could cook fish to perfection, both carp, cooked with sweet herbs, for the Friday evening, and pickled fish with raisins and grated bread crumbs for the Sabbath supper. She knew also all the rules for baking the Sabbath bread, and cooking game and salting meat in the kosher fashion, so that no drop of blood remained. Naturally she observed with great scrupulousness the other religious commandments for women as well.

"I don't know where she can get her piety from. She might be a Rabbi's daughter instead of mine. Rabbis could eat out of her hand, she keeps the commandments so carefully," Malke would say proudly to the women in the rich timber merchant's house whenever she went there to get the benefit of a ritual bath.

Reisel was in the kitchen busy preparing for the Sabbath. The hard frosts had already begun; the ground was covered with an icy blanket of snow. The air was dry and bitingly cold, and as if filled with ice needles. The vagrants who passed the night in the inn had no blankets. The few who could find a place near the baking oven were warm, but the others froze. During the week nobody troubled about them. But Yechiel's first act when he came home on Friday was always to carry in straw from the shed and spread it round the baking oven, so that the beggars might have a warm bed. The people in the house did not approve of this. From her post behind the bar

Malke had to watch her son-in-law bearing in straw from the shed with his own hands, and chopping wood and flinging it into the stove, and she felt as if she would die of shame.

"In Heaven's name, is there nobody in the house but you to carry in straw for the beggars and stoke the stove? Yadviga! Stepan! Where have you got to?"

But Yechiel would delegate this work to nobody; for him it was a work after God's heart. The poor were God's children, children of the King of Kings, and it was a high honor to wait personally upon a king's son who came to the house.

Today, however, there were no wandering people in the inn; the cold was too keen, the weather too bad. Yechiel was greatly disappointed. Later he learned that a sick man had been lying in the garret since the previous day. The poor creature had managed to drag himself to the village; his feet were frostbitten. Yechiel found him in a lamentable condition; he saw a bundle of rags lying in the straw, but at first could hardly make out a human body among them. Beside the man was standing a loaf and a plate of food, both untouched, just as they had been set there the day before. If Yechiel had not heard a groan coming now and then from the heap, he might have thought he was looking at an ancient tattered quilt. He roused the man.

"What's wrong? Won't you change your clothes and come down for the Sabbath blessing? You'll feel much better after that, I'm sure."

A dark-brown body that looked like tanned leather emerged from the rags. A pair of dull eyes stared stupidly into vacancy.

Yechiel looked more closely at the stranger, the man hadn't a shirt to his back! Evidently he had torn it into strips to wrap round his frostbitten toes.

"This is dreadful. Good heavens, to leave a human being alone in such a state!"

Yechiel rushed downstairs to his wife.

"Reisel, give me a shirt and a belt; I want to change for the Sabbath."

Reisel, who was just lifting the fish out of the pan, raised her flushed face and fixed her great eyes on her husband. There was a puzzled smile on her lips.

"But you put on a clean shirt when you went to the bath."

"I need it for a poor man," Yechiel admitted.

"If mother knows I'm afraid there will be trouble. You've given away already all the shirts she got for you at the Passover."

But Reisel was of one mind with her husband—Yechiel had molded her to his own nature. And so they both fetched a shirt and a belt and stole Shloime-Wolf's best trousers from the wardrobe. Yechiel seized his own summer rep caftan, Reisel filled a jug with warm water, and they bore it together to the garret.

There Yechiel washed the sick man, drew the shirt over his head, rubbed his frostbitten toes with a salve which was used in the house for such emergencies, and bound the man's feet in clean linen bandages. Then he pulled off his white stockings and pulled on the stranger's foot rags instead. He knew that his mother-in-law would give him a new pair of stockings, for she would never let him wear rags round his feet on the Sabbath. The stranger could not pull his boots on his frozen feet, so Yechiel lent him his own shoes and put on an old pair of boots belonging to his father-in-law. Then he helped the man into the caftan, so that he should not feel ashamed of his rags. Finally Yechiel fetched Poor Thaddeus, whom he had noticed about, and along with him led the man, whose frostbitten feet made walking difficult, down into the public room. There they set him down to warm himself at the stove until the Sabbath candles were lit and he had his part of the Sabbath blessing and the supper.

Malke noticed at once that the beggar was wearing Yechiel's best shirt and, worst of all, the new caftan. Her economical heart felt like breaking. She shouted at her husband in exasperation.

"Shloime-Wolf, your son-in-law will bring me to beggary! Every shirt that I get for him he gives away. Now he's given this tramp his summer caftan, his shoes, and his white stockings. In Heaven's name, just see how your son-in-law is dressed. Why, he's exchanged clothes with the tramp!"

"What you give to the poor is never lost. The Lord pays it back a thousandfold. The Psalmist says: 'Cast your bread upon the waters,' and that means, divide it among the poor," replied Yechiel.

"I tell you, Malke, leave me in peace! There's nothing to make a song about. Has Yechiel drunk the things? He knows what he's doing, let me tell you! And he's just as much your son-in-law as mine!"

Shloime-Wolf put his wife in her place with visible satisfaction.

No, Yechiel was no saint, and he was incapable of living like a hermit. He could not control his impulses. The only thing he could do was to purify them by the goodness of his intentions. The faculties that God gave you He gave you for your good; that you might serve Him with them. The Sabbath brings not only spiritual but also earthly joys. Because of that it is called "a day of gladness." Since Reisel had helped him to carry the jug of water up to the garret, Yechiel knew that she was pure for him; otherwise she would not have touched it. And he could not repress that joy that is part of the divinely ordained work of generation. . . .

Outside violet shadows were stealing over the snow. It grew dark. The bare branches of the trees threw long shadows which swallowed up the last vestige of light. In the alcove the Sabbath candles were already lighted, the fish and the Sabbath bread were set out on the table, which was covered with the traditional linen cloth. Behind the gleaming candles the women sat in the splendor of their Sabbath hoods. The men stood by the curtained ark and greeted the Sabbath. Yechiel was absorbed in the Song of Songs, the reading of which was part of the Sabbath Eve ritual. Then fat Yadviga, who served in the public room on the Sabbath, rushed into the room breathless and half dead with terror. Her round face was purple.

"Young noblemen come on horseback . . . making a great noise . . . want something to eat . . . !"

"Conduct them into the private room and give them something to eat," the landlady commanded.

But at that moment the young gentlemen entered in person. They were two country squires in muddy top boots; their clothes were splashed with mud, and they held long muskets in their hands. Their eyes glittered like those of hungry wolves. When they saw the table richly set with fish and brandy they cried joyfully, "This is just what we were looking for!"

"Sirs, this is the innkeeper's room. For noble guests we have a special room. Will you gentlemen have the goodness to go in there for the present; I shall have the table set at once. This is set for my husband's family, it's Shabbos today." The lady of the house accompanied her well-turned phrases with a bow, and finished with a curtsy which not everybody could have brought off. She set herself to put the noblemen in a good humor, and thus keep them from disturbing the Sabbath.

But the gentlemen replied with a laugh that the Jews' Sabbath table was good enough for them; this was just what they had been looking for, Jewish fish and new-baked Sabbath bread.

"Splendid, there's the Jewish Shabbosovka too, the brandy that the Jewesses serve up to give pith to their men...." One of them pointed at the carafe standing on the table.

And before Malke knew what was happening, she was roughly pushed aside. In their muddy top boots the two squires clumped over to the consecrated Sabbath table, filled their glasses with brandy, flung the white cover, with the loaves beneath it, to the floor, and brutally broke the consecrated bread. And one of them, a youth with a short snub nose and restless eyes, spoke jestingly to the other, who was somewhat older, with a dark-skinned, long, melancholy face adorned with side whiskers.

"Here you have the Jews' Sabbath loaves that are cooked with the blood of Christian children. Ho, Jewess, serve the fish!"

Malke stood helplessly, her lips tightly compressed, her hands crossed on her breast, and looked on while her Sabbath was being brutally trodden underfoot. Her throat was dry. As she made no response the youth with the snub nose beat on the table with his riding switch until the candle flames quivered as if in panic.

"Come! Is this how your master in Topolye teaches you to serve Christian gentlemen? You cursed Jews, bring the fish at once!"

Thereupon he raised his rifle and leveled it at the landlady's breast. With trembling hands Malke carried over the plate with the fish.

"The only way one can teach you Jews how to serve Polish gentlemen is with a gun. But your idle master lets you get fat here and has made lazy dogs of you," exclaimed the melancholy one, putting a piece of fish on the plate before him.

Meanwhile the men had ended their silent prayer, which they had not allowed the entrance of the strangers to interrupt. The innkeeper tried persuasion.

"You noblemen can eat to your hearts' content—may it do you good! But will you not have the kindness to use another room? You will be served with the best that I have in my house. I am celebrating the Sabbath in this room."

But that, too, was of no avail. The noblemen were firmly resolved to eat at the Sabbath table by the light of the candles.

"The landlady must bring in the dumplings next. These Sabbath dumplings increase a man's potency, so they say, for the Jewish women put mandragora or some such drug in them," said the melancholy one, smiling at his companion.

"If the dolts insist on eating at the Shabbos table—well and good, we can do nothing, we're in the hands of the goyim," said the innkeeper in Yiddish, so that the strangers might not understand. "Am I to risk my life for such a trifle? When they've eaten and drunk their fill they'll leave us in peace. What can I do? Such things happen. We'll hold our Shabbos later. Serve up the meat to them!"

The landlady did as her husband ordered.

The Shabbos fish tasted excellent; the Shabbosovka which the Jewish women make is strong and inflames the blood. Jewish fish and Shabbosovka rouses a desire for Jewish women....

Malke saw that the eyes of the snub-nosed youth were boring into Reisel's breast like daggers. Trembling violently, Reisel tried to escape from the man's glance like a fish from a net. She stole from behind the table and instinctively made for her mother. Malke saw that she must protect her daughter.

"Slip to your room and bar the door!" she whispered in Reisel's ear, pushing her out.

The melancholy one whispered to his friend with a significant gesture.

"Don't let that nice little morsel slip through your fingers. The Jewess has a good figure. I'll keep the others in check with my gun while you storm the fortress."

The landlady read from their gestures what the noblemen's intentions were. Her heart stopped beating. "Father in Heaven, stand by me!" she murmured and stepped to the door to shield her daughter. But the melancholy one at once put his rifle to his shoulder.

"Jews, into the corner!"

Shloime-Wolf, who was so terrified of his master's dog, rushed forward like a lion. His submissiveness had vanished in a second, for now it was a question of his daughter's honor, which he must shield from unclean hands, even if he had to lose his life a thousand times. With the fury of an enraged bull he ran against the two men, knocked one of them over, and tried to wrest the rifle from the other, crying, "Robbers, murderers that you are!"

A blow with the rifle stock reduced him to silence.

"You dare to attack noblemen, you Jew?" said the long man, presenting his rifle at Shloime-Wolf's breast. "March into the corner, or else I'll shoot you down like a dog!"

"For God's sake, Shloime-Wolf, don't play with your life!" Malke cried in terror.

A second blow with the rifle stock felled him to the ground.

Every eye was turned on Yechiel, who was standing by himself in the corner.

Where is your God, Yechiel? their glances seemed to be asking. Why doesn't He send down an angel with a fiery sword to destroy these blasphemers? Where is your God, Yechiel, on whose help you have always hoped and built? You see your Sabbath destroyed, the angels who came with you into the house rudely ejected—and in their stead two devils! Your sanctities trampled underfoot, the Princess Sabbath driven from the table like a servant maid, beaten with rods and made to serve Satan and his hosts. Where is your God, Yechiel, who does not hasten to your help in His flaming chariot. Show now your power! Your wife, sanctified to you by the law of Moses, is besieged and stormed, the wicked one stands with his gun and beats at her door. And there is none to help her!

But Yechiel, the rescuer to whom all were looking, stood motionless in the corner, and held his hands before his eyes as if in deep meditation, and seemed quite sunk within himself. While it was a question merely of fish and meat, not of a human being, he had refused to let his Sabbath be disturbed. Shut up in his world like a snail in its shell, he took notice of nothing around him. Full of holy ardor he continued to say the Sabbath hymn. And the fact that Satan was pursuing his evil plans so near him only made him lock himself up the more in his inner Sabbath and isolate himself from the malice of the outer world.

But now the young nobleman was beating with his rifle stock on Reisel's door and threatening to burst it in. If Reisel were merely to be alone in the same room with such a stranger she would be desecrated. So Yechiel forsook his Sabbath domain and flew to arms. To rescue a woman's honor or the life of a human being the curtain of the Sabbath may be rent and swept aside like a spider's web. . . .

The weapons of the Jewish heroes are neither cold steel nor hot steel. Does God lack hands with which to carry out His wishes? Yechiel's weapons were the Psalms. Now that all eyes were turned on him he lifted his hands toward Heaven and cried in an almost breaking voice:

"Save me, O God; I sink in deep mire, where there is no standing: I am come into deep waters, where the floods overflow me!"

And when the others heard, they repeated after him in a wailing voice:

"Save me, O God; I sink in deep mire. . . ."

The two noblemen started in alarm at the Jews' words.

The melancholy one had already observed the pale young Jew in the silk caftan and the fur cap, on whom the eyes of the others remained fixed as if in hope.

"That's their Rabbi, no doubt, and the pretty Jewess is his wife," he decided. "Be silent at once, you Jewish lout, or else I'll stop your mouth with a bullet!"

He aimed the rifle at Yechiel.

But, without paying any attention to the threat, Yechiel continued imploringly.

"Deliver me, O my God, out of the hand of the wicked, out of the hand of the unrighteous and cruel man."

The man with the rifle was afraid the Jews' outcry would alarm the village. His mind was charged with rage, his rifle with bullets. But God guided the bullet, and the unbelievable happened—the man's aim which never missed did so now. The bullet merely snuffed out a candle fixed to the wall, brushing in its passage the fur on Yechiel's cap.

The man gazed openmouthed at Yechiel in dumb astonishment. His aim had missed—the Jew must have the devil himself to protect him!

Goaded by fear and fury at once, he aimed at Yechiel's heart. But a strange thing happened. Perhaps it was the terrified outcry of the Jews when they saw him aiming a second time at Yechiel, perhaps it was the calm and confident look in Yechiel's eyes as he said in a loud voice, "I do not fear the wicked, for Thou art with me!"—in any case the man's arm suddenly sank as if paralyzed, he turned pale, foam appeared on his lips, and they all saw the rifle slipping from his hands.

Hastily he dragged his companion away from the door.

"Come, Stepan, they're making too much noise. That Jew has the very devil in him," he stammered, pale as death, shrinking away from Yechiel, who was still praying.

But his companion was by now in the grip of passion. His quivering nostrils could still smell the intoxicating odor of the lovely Jewess who had set fire to his blood. He was already gloating over the pleasures in store for him—such a hard victory appealed to the hunter's instinct and was worthy of a nobleman. And later he would make a great impression by telling his friends and the ladies of his acquaintance all about it. To the end of his days he would be able to relate ... "and the Jewess bit me in the hand, she had sharp teeth, the little devil—you can see the scar still, look...." Absorbed in such fantasies he paid no attention to his friend's request.

"What, show fear before a pack of Jews!"

He had forced the barrel of his rifle between the door and the doorpost and was trying with all his might to push the bar back from outside. Only one more good push was needed to burst the door open.

"You just keep the Jews in check with your rifle; I don't want them to scratch my face. I'll have it open in a minute...."

Yechiel shut his eyes and swayed like a reed in the wind. Now at the hour of need all his powers, summoned by his tense will, streamed into him. And his will was firm and strong as a root; with a hundred suckers it drew strength from newly awakened sources that he had never dreamed of before, sources which till now had slept within him. A burning desire that God's justice should manifest itself, an unshakable trust in God's mercy, a strong faith in the living might of God. All these wakened in him unfamiliar faculties which had the power to influence events and so work by their invisible means that everything should follow the dictates of divine right and justice.

Suddenly he shrank as if he had been touched by an invisible finger. His pale face shone and seemed to become all sight and hearing. What could he be seeing or listening for? Was God's chariot hastening to him through the air? While everybody stood dumb with terror, he could hear steps approaching, stealing round the house, could see hands feeling at the walls. And though the others were still sunk in despair, he started up in joyful alarm, raised his arms and cried, "God is hastening to our help. He is sending messengers to save us. I thank Thee and praise Thy name, Lord!"

The others shrank at his words. Attackers and attacked were united by one fear, shaken by Yechiel's visionary announcement. The Poles daunted by their wicked deed, the Jews rigid with terror; they clung together in their helplessness and remained dumb. Yechiel stood alone, malice on one side of him, terror on the other, burning in ecstasy like a pillar of fire, with eyes that could see through the walls, with arms that were upraised convulsively, his face illumined with supernatural joy, and cried, "I thank thee, Lord! We are saved!"

Before his ecstasy they all started back in pain. They turned their white faces toward him; their eyes confused with fear asked incredulously, "How? How do you know?"

"Who can be coming to help us in the night?" their trembling lips whispered. . . .

Terror now seized the attackers as well, and they glanced at each other fearfully. At last the melancholy man seized the other by the coattails and dragged him away from the door, shouting.

"Stepan, leave off! Come!"

"Are you afraid of a pack of Jews? Stop his mouth!" hissed the snub-nosed man.

Inflamed with fear and lust, he ran against the door with clenched teeth and fists, and it yielded before him. But the room was empty; and the terrified cry of the victim which alone could have broken the unendurable tension was denied him.

The frost-covered window was wide open, letting the cold and darkness stream in unhindered; but the bird had flown.

"How could she have done it!"

The two Poles were seized with impotent fury. They rushed back to the Jews in the other room. Their disappointed hopes, unsatiated lust, bootless labor, demanded a scapegoat. Their eyes gleamed murderously. But before their hands could seize the rifles or commit a crime the village fire bell pealed out.

"Quick, Stepan! People are coming!"

They hurried out. But their horses were gone; some one must have taken them away. Flight on foot was impossible; the snow was yards deep. So nothing was left for them but to try to pass off the whole thing as a jest.

The two men waited confidently for the Count's arrival. They were convinced that he would let them off; after all, he must himself have committed such pranks in his youth. Their only regret was that the lovely Jewess had escaped them.

"A sly little hussy—popped through the window and fled! We'll have to pass off the whole thing as a joke."

Besides, it was not a serious affair; they had not assaulted a lady of quality, but only a Jewess. They felt certain that the Count would invite them to his castle, and there they would crown the adventure with a few bottles of mead.

When the master of Topolye heard how his neighbors, the young noblemen of Sokolna with whom he lived at dagger's drawn, had treated his tenant, his noble blood boiled. He regarded the affair as a personal insult to himself; for it had happened in his village, in the house of his tenant who was under his jurisdiction and protection.

It was an attempt on his own person, an attack on his honor! Certainly only his tenant had been harmed, but he was *his* tenant, *his* Jew: "I whip my Jews myself when I have the inclination. But I won't allow anybody else to touch a hair of their heads!"

With his rifle under his arm, and followed by Titus, he left his castle though it was late at night, a thing which had not happened for many years. He called out the steward, the actuary, and others from the village, and marched at their head to the inn to arrest the interlopers, who were already virtually prisoners.

He began, as if he did not know the two noblemen, "You call yourselves squires of Sokolna, do you? I don't know you! You claim to be noblemen? We'll see about that tomorrow! Tonight you're robbing blackguards. Into the stable with them!"

Then he had them well whipped by candlelight.

"You'll have to answer one day for whipping noblemen!"

"Tomorrow—we'll see about all that tomorrow! We'll be able to see who you are by daylight!"

With that he had the two noblemen bound, and they spent all night in the cold stable. Next morning they were set free and sent home in a four-in-hand.

Such was the last chivalrous act of the master of Topolye.

CHAPTER III

HOW A MIRACLE GROWS

AT the beginning of the next week a great number of guests stopped at the inn. The continuous snowstorms had made the roads impassable, and traveling dangerous. So the passing merchants thought it better to stay at the inn with their wagons, drivers, stands, and wares until the weather improved. The peasants of the village also sought refuge in the warm inn from their cold houses. There was scarcely accommodation for so many people in the long, faintly lit room, which was darkened still more by tobacco smoke and fumes rising from wet clothes.

During these days Poor Thaddeus had a busy time; he kept on repeating with much detail how he had saved the innkeeper's life.

"There was Poor Thaddeus," he began in his circumstantial way, "lying in his little hut, lonely and a dog driven from home, thinking: Well, you're an unhappy fellow, Poor Thaddeus; you haven't even a good buxom wife to keep you warm on a winter night. Yours is consumptive; she coughs and spits the whole night through. It's so cold in the room that the very frost knocks on the door and the window begging you to let it in so as to warm itself for a little. And Poor Thaddeus says to himself: Poor Thaddeus, why are you lying here? You would be wiser to get up and go over to the inn. Perhaps they'll have a glass of brandy to spare there for a poor devil, and even if you get nothing yourself you can watch the others drinking, and warm yourself at the smoke from their pipes. But this is Friday, the Shabbos is beginning, the Jews will be sitting eating their fish. There won't be a single soul in the public room, that's certain. So there's no sense in going, Poor Thaddeus. All the same, there's something tearing at your vitals, don't deny it, as if a hook was tugging at you and saying: 'Get up, go to your door and have a look to see what's going on in God's world!' And I creep out of my straw. When I get to the hill I see the Jews' Sabbath lights shining from the windows. Oh yes, there they are sitting at their table, no doubt of it, enjoying their Shabbos fish. I make to turn back and creep into my hut again.

But then I think of the innkeeper's son-in-law—a pious lad, a pity he isn't a Catholic! He always brings me a piece of white Jewish bread and a bit of fish when he sees me standing at the door on the Shabbos. Well, I go across to see at least what the two horsemen were after that I saw trotting to the inn earlier in the evening. They looked as if they were after no good, and they had guns too. Maybe they're kicking up a row at the Jews' place now, thinks I, eating the fish and courting the women. Oh, a nobleman has a fine time of it! I think to myself. But you have nothing to expect there, Poor Thaddeus, don't you stick your nose in other people's business, go back to your hut, it isn't good for your health to meddle in great folks' affairs. The gentlemen always stick together, and then the peasant has to pocket blows. So I tell myself and turn back to my hut. But when I put my foot on the doorstep something stops me. I look round and then it seems to me I can see the pious little Jew standing there before the inn. He calls to me and waves to me as if he wanted me to come. Something wrong here, thinks I. When the little Jew calls it's best to obey—I knew a long time before that what he had in him! So I set out and plod through the snow as fast as I can. Just as I reach the inn, lo and behold I hear a shot going off! Oh, I tell you I didn't half like it! I creep nearer and see the innkeeper's daughter standing behind a window. She flings herself like a chicken against the panes and tries to raise the window; but it's frozen fast—how could her little hands open it? 'You poor, captive bird,' I says to myself, 'you must be got out of your cage first thing.' I don't consider too long, just take a stone, smash in the window and help the girl out. 'Run across the fields for a bit!' I tell her. But I make straight for the stable. The horses must be got away first, so that the gentlemen mightn't make away. I jump on and gallop like the wind into the village to the fire bell!"

"Jews, you don't know who you have among you here in Topolye," began the Jew with the frostbitten feet. He turned up his eyes in rapture and rocked piously. "I saw it with my own eyes: he only threw the goy one glance, one glance from his holy eyes, and the evil-doer's arm was paralyzed, the gun fell from his hands and he couldn't move a limb..."

Honest admiration shone in the man's somewhat stupid face. His timid eyes almost disappeared beneath their thin slack lids, as if seeking for protection. His short beard quivered as he continued.

"What more do you want? Look at these feet," he pointed to them.

"They were dead, frozen on my way here, I thought I would be a cripple for life. I lay up in the garret like a beast in the slaughterhouse and couldn't move. Then on Friday afternoon he came up to me with a jug of warm water, he bound up my toes in clean linen—and you can see for yourselves, I'm sound again, the scars are quite gone."

Poor Thaddeus, who naturally felt justified in sharing in the general joy, took this auspicious opportunity tó scrounge a glass of brandy, and kindled to pious ardor, "Oh, that's nothing to speak of! I've known for a long time who the Jews have here among them. He saved *her* from certain death," he pointed toward the landlady, who was standing at her usual place behind the counter, but had suddenly taken to wearing her hood very primly over her ears. "I was standing there behind the door waiting for her with the gulley that I stuck my pig with last Whitsun. . . . How did he know that I was standing there behind the door with evil thoughts in my heart?"

It was not the first time that the landlady had heard this story. Poor Thaddeus dished it up whenever he wanted to get a free glass of brandy. Lately the tale had lost something of its drawing power. But now, in this hour of exaltation, the landlady piously raised her eyes to Heaven, dipped her finger in a pool of spilled brandy on the counter, still with the devout air that she had worn for the past few days, rubbed the liquid dry with her hands, as pious women are in the habit of doing, and said with a sigh:

"I am unworthy of the favor that the Lord has shown me in granting me such a holy man as my son-in-law."

Thereupon she poured out a glass of brandy for the little peasant.

"Here! Drink, since God has miraculously saved me from your knife!"

"Yes, you should thank God," said the peasant, turning to the landlady, "and not grudge Poor Thaddeus his little glass. If it weren't for your son-in-law you wouldn't be here tonight, and Poor Thaddeus would have a mortal sin on his soul and be lost forever. That night your son-in-law laid his hand on my shoulder and said, 'Thaddeus,' he said, 'don't burden your soul with a mortal sin!' And the Evil One was gone in a jiffy, as if he had wiped him out with his hand. It's the truth; he drove the devil out of me. I was simply possessed by the devil: that's the only way I can explain it. I had nothing against you. You showed me nothing but kindness." Before the eyes of everybody Poor Thaddeus sank on his knees on the floor, which was covered with the mud of countless boots, crossed himself, struck his breast, murmured a prayer, and tried again and again to clasp the landlady's feet and obtain her pardon.

She struggled to free herself.

"That's enough, Thaddeus, enough!"

But Poor Thaddeus would not be repulsed; he pressed his face into the landlady's skirt.

"I wanted to kill you—the devil drove me on—but *he* saved my soul. He's a saint, as God's my witness! Often and often I've seen him up there praying on the green hill in the early morning, when everything was wet with dew, and a white dove rose up and flew round his head three times—white as snow it was, you can take my word! I could see it whispering something in his ear, and then before you could say snuff it flew up into the sky. Didn't I see him in the early mornings in the forest, with the Pitch Jew? Didn't I see him with the tame deer following him to drink at the pool?"

Shloime-Wolf, with his head bandaged where the young Count had clubbed him, hustled Poor Thaddeus away from the bar, exclaiming, "He's talking nonsense! Pitch Jew indeed! My son-in-law spends all his time in Reb Notte Danziger's House of Study in the forest, studying day and night!"

The snowstorm was still raging outside. To travel farther with the laden sledges would be dangerous—often vehicles had been buried in the snow and their passengers along with them. In the inn one sat warm and secure listening greedily to the most wonderful stories. Brandy and Jewish credulity did their part; they warmed the heart, awoke enthusiasm, kindled fancy. God had once more sent a comforter to the poor, a holy Rabbi who performed miracles, cured the sick, worked wonders. And everybody in the inn had some trouble. Their souls were heavy with care and worry. One had a sick wife who had been bedridden for years. Another had a daughter of marriageable age but could not find a dowry for her. A third had been driven from his village by the landlord because he could not pay his rent. A fourth had seen all his children die when they were young. . . . And here in the public room stood the Jew Ezriel with his frostbitten feet which had been healed by the mere touch of a hand, and he pointed to the door of the alcove where Yechiel had withdrawn to study.

"People, do you want help? There's a young man sitting in there that can help you as he helped me."

The door of the alcove was burst in and Yechiel, who was just reciting his prayers, was surrounded by a piteous crowd.

"Holy Rabbi, help us!"

Yechiel grew pale as death and replied in a tearful voice, blushing red with shame, "What are you saying? I'm not a Rabbi!"

"Yes, you are a Rabbi!" cried the man with the frostbitten feet. "People, do not let him go. He can help you!"

Yechiel replied, trembling with shame, "You're mistaken; I am not a Rabbi."

But the man with the frostbitten feet would not be put off, and turned to the others.

"There! You see how modest he is!"

Luckily Shloime-Wolf hurried up and delivered his son-in-law.

"Give him room to breathe. Don't you see he's in the middle of his prayers?"

So they were pushed to the door. The man with the frostbitten feet at once took on the rôle of attendant, as if Yechiel were a real Wonder Rabbi.

"Out you go, out you go; the Rabbi is praying."

But the Jew who had been driven from his village for not paying his rent refused to budge.

"Who can I turn to?" he cried in despair. "I have nothing but what's on my back. The Poritz has driven me out of my house, my wife and children are lying in the snow! Who can I turn to?" He stretched out his hands imploringly toward Yechiel. "Holy Rabbi, have pity! My wife and children are on the streets."

Yechiel was seized with pity. Without considering the dangerous rôle that was being imposed upon him he said, "Good Heavens—hounded out of the village in this cold!"

"Fifty Polish gulden—where was I to get that when the peasants in the village are starving and none of them will stick his nose into a Jewish shop?"

"Pray to the Lord. He is a God of compassion."

"You pray for me, Rabbi; I have learned nothing."

"We shall pray together," replied Yechiel.

He stepped up to the man and began to recite the Psalms with him.

Then he took out his handkerchief, went out to the public room and began collecting money from the merchants for "the deliverance of the captives," the work which of all works is most pleasing to God. Their hearts had been warmed, their feelings of brotherhood awakened, and they were ready givers.

CHAPTER IV

THE JUDGMENT

REB DANZIGER sat in his big study with the village priest, the provost Sandomierski, as the light from the silver candlesticks played on his bookcases, his heavy iron safe, and the silver dishes, laden with good things, which adorned the table before them. The "daughter-in-law from abroad" who was educated and spoke French, and whom Reb Danziger liked to show off, was also in the study, with her husband, the oldest of the sons, Itche, whom his father was beginning to bring into his business affairs.

Whenever Reb Notte went to a new place, whenever he bought another forest, his first move was to get on good terms with the local authorities and the local priests. He sent them gifts at every festival and contributed to their charities. And the priest often came to visit Reb Notte in the long winter nights, to drink tea with him, and to enjoy the exercise of religious-philosophical discussion. Of course both Reb Notte and the priest keep their discussions within certain limits out of respect for each other, never transgressing the bounds.

At a sign from Reb Notte, the daughter-in-law from abroad and her husband withdrew, leaving him alone with the priest, and they turned to their eternal theme, the Count and his black magic, which was causing the people to stray from the true path. The whole village was talking about the wonderful things the innkeeper's son-in-law was supposed to have performed that Friday night. Such things could lead to no good. Once this magic and miracles business got into the minds of the people, they ceased to respect their own faith.

They mentioned the Pitch Jew whom the Count kept in the forest.

"The innkeeper's son-in-law used to go at night to that mysterious Jew, and that is where he learned his magic. The peasants report that they often saw them both going to the pools to bathe, and deer followed them and doves flew over their heads. No, that stranger is neither Jew nor Christian. He belongs to a secret sect who, they say, indulge in immorality with women and pray to infamous things. And all these miracles which the innkeeper's son-in-law has performed are nothing else but black magic performed by the use of secret Cab-balistic names, by magic spells which he has learned from the Pitch Jew. It is high time to put an end to these ugly doings which are going on in the village."

"Such things are dangerous for the common folk," said the priest. "Whatever differences there are between the accepted faiths are matters for theologians and educated people. But the common folk must walk in the footsteps of their fathers and respect each other's religion, so that the world goes on. Of course, the Count is really to blame. He brought all this magic into the village, and he encourages it and keeps it going. How can things be as they should be if the Count of the village never comes to church and is contemptuous of the accepted religion? Naturally this reflects itself on the people. Last Sunday there was hardly anyone in church.

"They say now," the priest went on, "that the Count has gone mad, that he has terrible plans of burning the whole village, so as to keep it from his heirs. And his heirs are decent people. The young Pan Wydawski, his cousin, is a proper kind of man. He is fighting an action now against the old Count, to take over the estates while he is still alive, on the ground that the Count is neglecting his property, and he is questioning whether the old man is in his right senses at all."

Reb Notte knew all about this. He was in touch with the young Count, was lending him money, was even financing his lawsuit against the old Count. Whatever the result, Reb Notte was sure of his place in Topolye. Besides the forest, he had the mortgages of several farms ly-ing comfortably in his safe. And the agreement for the forest had been signed—for whatever eventuality—by both Counts, the old and the young; Reb Notte liked to walk on an iron bridge. One could deal with the young Count, a sensible man who lived as a Count should live. He spent most of his time in the big city or abroad; he played cards and kept horses and women. In other words, he was always short of money.

The priest also thought well of the young Count. So they sat, on into the night, discussing how to rid Topolye of the devil.

Next morning the snow had stopped, and with the road passable again, the travelers had departed from the inn. After saying his morn-ing prayers Yechiel packed his bundle and prepared to return to his Rabbi, Reb Feivush. His parents-in-law could not understand why he still wanted to learn. Reb Ezriel, the Jew with the frostbitten feet, who was staying on, had told them that Yechiel should be teaching others, and Malke wanted him to stay at home.

"We shall give you two rooms," she promised. "It will be a proper Rabbi's home."

"Leave it to him. He knows what he has to do," said Shloime-Wolf, who believed in his son-in-law and preferred not to meddle in his affairs. "If he wants to go back to Reb Feivush, we must let him. He knows what he is doing better than we do."

"Wait," he added, turning to his son-in-law, "till I have harnessed the sleigh. I'll drive you there."

"Who am I to need a sleigh?" answered Yechiel, taking his bundle and setting out.

"I won't let you go alone. It is not fitting for you to go alone any longer," cried Ezriel, running after him. "You have been chosen and crowned by the Jews."

Yechiel took no notice and trudged on through the snow, soon outdistancing him. But Ezriel followed behind.

Reisel stood with her face pressed to the frost-covered window, breathing on the pane and clearing a space with her fingernails so that she could see Yechiel as he strode off toward the forest.

The two stoves in the big room in Reb Notte's house, which they called the House of Study, had made it very warm. Reb Notte's sons and sons-in-law sat round the long table, which was littered with books, swaying over the big Talmud folios and reading aloud. Each tried to raise his voice above the others, so that Reb Notte and the womenfolk in the adjoining rooms would hear. Reb Feivush, their teacher, sat at the head of the table, next to Reb Notte's place. Reb Notte's armchair was always kept ready for him, at the head of the table, and no one else ever dared to sit in it.

Reb Feivush, the sons-in-law, and the sons all pretended not to see Yechiel as he entered the room. No one made room for him at the table. Only Reb Feivush sighed as he went on explaining a point of the law to Reb Notte's youngest son-in-law, who was studying to be a Rabbi.

Yechiel, sensing the atmosphere, walked sadly to the big bookcase to take a book from the shelves. But from all sides he was assailed by voices, crying, "Don't touch! Don't defile them!"

Yechiel went white and looked round. He saw his teacher, Reb Feivush, his father's friend, rise from his seat at the table, sighing heavily, and start pacing up and down the room, without one glance at Yechiel. All the rest, the sons and the sons-in-law, remained seated at the table.

The one who was really concerned about Yechiel, and who seethed with indignation, was the youngest son-in-law, Moishe, the one whom Reb Feivush was preparing for the Rabbinate. Though the youngest, he was held in high respect, because he was a better scholar than all the others, because he was going to be a Rabbi, because he was the son of a well-known Rabbi and would succeed his father. It was chiefly because of him that Reb Notte had engaged Reb Feivush. So he considered it his privilege and his right to cross-examine Yechiel. After all, he was now something of a Rabbi and a judge; he decided any questions of ritual that arose in Reb Notte's kitchen. He thought himself something of a Cabbalist too. He knew all about "those things." That young man would not be able to dodge round him! He knew all the answers!

And young as he was, he already looked a Rabbi, with his heavy black hair, his long thick side curls, his handsome face and distinguished appearance. His beard, longer and thicker and more imposing than that of any of the others, might have been the beard of an old Assyrian high priest. In this jungle of hair two restless, disagreeable, baleful fires were burning.

He pushed his velvet skullcap over his forehead, tugged at his beard with his fist, and beckoned to Yechiel, who stood by the bookcase bewildered and confused.

"Come over here, young man. Tell us about the miracles you performed among the drunkards in the tavern!"

The big Talmud volumes, the Hoshen Mishpats, the Guides to the Perplexed were left lying open on the table. The sons and the sons-in-law remained seated; only Reb Feivush kept walking up and down the room.

With a broken heart Yechiel approached the table of Judgment.

"What miracles are these that you perform in the tavern?" the young bearded "Rabbi" demanded.

"I perform no miracles," Yechiel answered.

"What did you do on Friday night that you paralyzed the arms of the two Squires only by looking at them?"

"I paralyzed no one."

"What was it you did?"

"I prayed to God to help us in our need."

"How did you pray?"

"I repeated Psalms."

"And you invoked no Names?"

"No."

"If you invoked no names of Angels, perhaps you called upon that Father of Iniquity, may his name be blotted out—Sabbatai Zvi?"

"No, I mentioned no Names."

"How did you know that salvation was near?"

"Because I had trust in God, that He would help us."

"I also trust in God, yet I don't know whether salvation is near."

Yechiel could not answer this.

"And what happened that time in the tavern, at your betrothal party, that you knew the peasant stood behind the door to kill your mother-in-law? How did you know?"

"It seemed to me then that I could . . ."

"Seemed?"

"Yes, I seemed to see him standing there, and I felt that he meant to do her harm."

"So it seemed to you, did it? Why do such things never seem to me? Why don't they ever seem to him?" pointing to one of the others.

This question too Yechiel could not answer.

"Do you often find things seem to you like that?"

"No, not often. Sometimes."

"And you make no use of the invocation of Names for it?"

"No."

"What then?"

"If I feel I am in trouble, or I pity someone, I repeat something from the Psalms."

"What did you do in the forest with that apostate, the Pitch Jew?"

Yechiel went dead white.

"Did you learn from him how to call on the Angels by Name, and other such things, that I must not mention?"

"I never learned any Names from him. Only other things."

"So! What other things?"

"Zohar," Yechiel said shamefacedly.

"And Cabbalistic tricks, how to write charms and amulets, by invoking Names, with spells and oaths that bind you to Satan, the accursed one!"

Yechiel was silent.

"And by the power of Evil, in the name of the demon Lilith, and the demon Ashmedai? What else did you learn?"

"Chassidism."

"Chassidism?" Everybody laughed. "Nice Chassidism! You mean apostasy!"

"No! He did not teach me anything that was not on the Jewish road."

"How do you know what is on the Jewish road or not? Are you so great a scholar?"

Yechiel flushed.

"You have been going to him lately?"

"No, I haven't been going to him for a long time."

"Why did you stop going to him, if he did not teach you anything that is not on the Jewish road?"

Yechiel was silent.

"Didn't he perhaps urge you to apostasy? Is that why you stopped going to him?"

"No."

"What then did he urge you to?"

Yechiel was silent.

"To Sabbatai Zvi tricks perhaps?"

Yechiel was silent.

"Silence is confession!" And the young "Rabbi" lifted up his hand and gave Yechiel the first slap in the face.

Reb Feivush was already out of the room.

The next minute the Talmuds and the Maimonides volumes had been pushed out of the way, Yechiel had been hoisted up on the table, his trousers pulled down, his bare backside exposed, and hands and fingers and nails were digging into his flesh, punching and pommeling him.

"Quiet! Father will hear him! Stuff a handkerchief in his mouth! Gag him!"

But they need not have feared. There was not a sound from Yechiel, not a cry, not a whimper. He accepted the punishment as deserved, as stripes, flagellation, imposed for sins, his expiation in order to be saved from the four kinds of death imposed by the Beth Din, the supreme Court of Judgment, because he had sinned.

Who knows what they might have done to Yechiel, for the young men were only just beginning to enjoy the castigation they were inflicting, had not Reb Feivush come bursting into the room, furious, all his long-suppressed resentment against this presumptuous, conceited family boiling and raging in him.

"Villains! Murderers!" he cried, tearing Yechiel away from them with steel-like grip. He stood still for a moment, eyeing them contemptuously, then he spat.

"Look at them! How their envy maddens them! You are of those who sin like Zimri and want to be rewarded like Phineas!"

Reb Feivush lifted Yechiel to his back and carried him up to his garret, placed him on his bed, and poured water over him until he opened his eyes. He gave him a pair of his own trousers to wear, for Yechiel's were torn and blood-stained.

"Must you blurt out everything you know!" he exclaimed angrily to Yechiel. "Can't you keep what you know to yourself!"

Reb Feivush began packing his bundle; since there was no longer a place for him here in this house of conceit and insolence, he had decided to go to Kotzk, to his Rabbi.

When Yechiel was brought home, Ezriel, the man with the frost-bitten feet, spoke to those in the inn.

"This is their way. No doubt he had to suffer for someone's sins and took the punishment upon himself. Believe me, I don't envy the people who did this! No one has yet seen their end!"

"Of course," said the innkeeper's wife, wiping the tears in her eyes, "they spend a treasure of gold on their children, and they achieve nothing. So they envy the poor man whose child does better. As though riches could buy everything! To God we are equal! Why did he have to go there? Couldn't he sit here and learn?"

Reisel said nothing. She stood at the window and melted the frost-ferns with her tears.

CHAPTER V

IN PURITY

A FEW days later, Yechiel had hardly recovered from the thrashing when people reported in the inn that the Pitch Jew's hut on the edge of the forest had been burned down during the night and the Pitch Jew had disappeared, no one knew where. Shloime-Wolf, having suffered enough because of the Pitch Jew, would not let his name be mentioned, for he feared that Yechiel might be dragged into the affair. He shouted at Poor Thaddeus because he was saying that Reb Notte's woodcutters had done it; after the priest in his sermon had demanded that the Satan of Topolye should be destroyed, the Pitch Jew had been hunted naked, deep into the forest. He must have been frozen to death long ago, said Poor Thaddeus, and was lying in the snow, if the wolves had not already devoured him.

Yechiel said nothing to anyone. But he took Ezriel with him and set out to find the Pitch Jew.

The weather was fine, dry and frosty, the snow hard on the ground. The wind lifted up only the top layer, blowing the soft snow about like diamond dust, but underneath it was like a firm hard road. All the trees of the forest bloomed with glorious snow blossoms, their branches covered with thick clumps of snow which the wind kept blowing off and scattering in the air like silver spray.

They found the Pitch Jew's hut burned to ashes. Only the stove stood black and forbidding in that clean white world. About it were scattered bits of charred wood, the remains of household goods, broken vessels, and half-burned Jewish books and parchment scrolls; but there was no sign of the Pitch Jew himself.

They pushed on into the forest. Soon their feet began to sink into the soft snow, and they saw the trees lifting only their white branches clear of the deep white flood. The air was filled with fine snow dust as the wind sifted it from the branches. The sun was like ice in the sky. They struggled on, knocking against roots and falling into holes that the snow had hidden. But Yechiel knew the way to the hidden stream where the Pitch Jew had taken him for their ritual bath.

And there Ezriel saw a bit of tallith protruding from the snow. When he tried to pick it up, it was frozen fast in the snow. They scraped away the snow and found the body, frozen stiff, as if hewn from a block of ice. He looked like a fallen angel, come down from heaven with the snow.

Since Yechiel had heard the Pitch Jew pronounce the terrible name of Sabbatai Zvi, which had severed like a sharp knife every connection between them, he had never seen him again. Everything he had learned from him seemed to Yechiel unclean and polluted, and he had tried to tear it from his memory. But what the Pitch Jew had taught him had struck such deep roots that he no longer knew whether the fruit growing in him was fertilized by what he learned from this mysterious man, or from his later Rabbi, Reb Feivush. Besides, the Pitch Jew's teachings were so much in the Jewish spirit that Yechiel could not differentiate between them. And though the Pitch Jew had seemed to him since that time alien, incomprehensible, mysterious, his pity was so great that he could feel no anger against him. "Who knows what temptations led him away from the Jewish path?" Often he had had him in his mind while he was saying his prayers, and he had prayed to God to open the Pitch Jew's eyes, so that he might return to the Jewish faith.

Now, seeing the frozen body, the side curls frozen against the face, the snow dropping from the eyebrows, and the beard like a lump of ice, he could feel only compassion. Surely, no matter how great the man's sin, he had atoned for it by his terrible death. And however far the false path may have led him, he was convinced that the Pitch Jew was always bound closely to the Jewish faith. And it would be a good and a charitable deed to give him Jewish burial.

"It is a great privilege," he said to Ezriel, "to fulfill the commandment to bury the dead."

Meanwhile it was growing dark. Blue shadows were already falling on the snow-covered trees. He hesitated to leave the dead body lying where it was, for the wolves to devour; it was a miracle that they had not found him before. To Yechiel this was a sign that the Pitch Jew in spite of his deviations had been considered worthy to be preserved for Jewish burial. There was someone in heaven watching over him, guarding him, for here in the snow were the tracks of wolves, yet they had not found him. Ezriel and Yechiel covered the body with branches and hastened back to the village.

Shloime-Wolf and the other Jews in the inn refused to listen to

Yechiel's plea that they should take the Pitch Jew to the town to bury him in the Jewish cemetery. Yechiel pleaded and stormed and demanded. It was a terrible sin, he said, to shame the dead, since death atones for everything. It was a Jewish duty to bury the dead. He reminded them of the Law: "A Jew, even if he has sinned, is still a Jew." But the Jews were firm in their refusal, and Shloime-Wolf even ventured to rebuke his son-in-law!

"Haven't you had enough trouble because of him? Keep out of it! It's no business of yours! Leave him where he is!"

Before dawn the next day, Yechiel and Ezriel and Poor Thaddeus made their way to the forest. Poor Thaddeus had brought an ax and a spade with him to open up the frozen ground. They had also brought a few boards to make a rough coffin.

Since they found the body untouched, just as they had left it, Yechiel was more convinced than ever that heaven was watching over the Pitch Jew.

When the grave was ready, Poor Thaddeus, exhausted, stood aside while Yechiel and Ezriel attended to the corpse. First they rolled him in the snow, to suffer for his sins in this world. Then they broke open a hole in the frozen stream, and dipped the dead man three times under the ice, saying each time, "You are pure!"

Wrapped in his tallith, in which he said his prayers, the Pitch Jew was then lowered into the frozen earth, with his head toward Jerusalem, as all Jews lie all over the world.

They also lowered into the grave with him what was left of his books and parchment scrolls. Before they had finished filling the open grave with earth a fresh fall of snow covered it over with a white canopy from heaven.

Yechiel stood at the head of the grave and sanctified God's Name.

CHAPTER VI

TITUS GROWS OLD

TITUS the bulldog had grown old. All day he lay beside the stove in the drawing room languidly warming himself in the rare wintry sunbeams that fell through the high windows. His breathing was heavy and laborious, his movements slow; his great round eyes and blunt jaws watered continuously.

Through the short days and the long nights Count Wydawski sat in his top boots and shabby coat in his great armchair gazing at the dog, who lay in his corner breathing heavily and gazing with moist beseeching eyes at his master. Now and then the Count would call him. But Titus's legs had grown feeble, and it took him some time to heave himself up, trot over to his master with lowered head, wagging his tail, and lie down in his new position. The Count seized him by the muzzle; master and dog looked deep into each other's eyes. But Wydawski could not meet that beseeching gaze for long; he stroked the beast's powerful head and said, "You've grown old, Titus."

Then he got up, stretched himself to his full height, passed his hand over his still abundant and thick, but snow-white hair, curled the ends of his gray mustache, and strode up and down the room. He kept murmuring to himself all the time, "You've grown old, Titus."

He was not thinking only of the dog. . . .

Old . . . no! Count Wydawski felt no weakening of his powers. He felt just as healthy, active and enterprising as he had done in his youth. If there were only something worth devoting one's energy and enthusiasm to! Oh, he would soon show them; he would put on his uniform and set himself in the saddle, booted and spurred, as he had done once before when he rode in Poniatowski's regiment behind the Emperor! It was bad, bad, that there was nothing left that was worth one's while to live and to strive for.

No—it was not that he had grown old; it was simply that the world around him had changed. He had stuck to his post, but his whole environment had crumbled, had faded like a Fata Morgana. Poland was lost. The Polish army existed no longer, the Polish eagle dared not

face the light, the double-headed bird of prey of the Czars overshad-
owed the whole land—and yet Poland lived on. The nobility amused
themselves, held balls in their Warsaw palaces, to which they invited
Russian officers. The Russian officers appeared in their gala uniforms,
and the ladies of the Polish aristocracy danced with them. Over in
Galicia they danced with Austrians, over in the west with Prussians.
The living body of Poland was cut in pieces, and the women danced
with its enemies, who still flourished their murderous knives in their
hands. . . .

Wydawski's comrades, the old Napoleonic officers who had taken
part in the uprising of 1831, were in captivity. Some had been par-
doned, others banished to Siberia; all had had their estates confiscated.
They had chosen the better part; for though they could not fight for
Poland's liberation, at least they could suffer for her. But Count
Wydawski had been forgotten; he had not been arrested as he expected; his estates had not been confiscated as he secretly wished in
his heart. He had simply been ignored, as if he had never been one of
Napoleon's old officers whom Grand Duke Konstantin feared and persecuted. No, they left Count Wydawski in peace, they did not fear him,
they had forgotten him. He was only a powerless, half-mad old man,
whose estates his relatives hoped to inherit before his death.

He flew into a rage, remembering the letter which had just arrived
from his Warsaw lawyer, who had informed him that his idle and
good-for-nothing nephew and future heir, who had already mortgaged
Topolye and all the farms to the Jewish timber dealer, in other words
had sold the property that he did not yet own—that this young fool,
being apparently unable to wait for his uncle's death, had appealed to
the court and demanded a share in the administration and revenues
of the estates, on the ground that the present proprietor was suffering
from senile decay and was totally neglecting them.

The Count knew very well who was behind this. It was a plot con-
cocted by the priest and the Jew Danziger. They were supporting the
appeal to get rid of him. They had the power already; they were the
real masters of Topolye, not he. They had set fire to the pitch maker's
hut, a man who was under his protection; they had driven him from
the woods in the middle of the night. The really proper thing would
be to take a rifle, go to the Jew's house, and shoot down the Jews to
the last man, arrest the priest, put him in a dung cart and drive him
from the village!

An inner voice warned Wydawski against attempting such a trial of strength, which would only reveal his impotence. He knew that he was not in a position to carry through his will, that nobody would obey him, nobody take his side either against the priest or against the Jew. Russian law was in force now; they were the masters, not he. . . .

The Count did not want to admit his impotence and took refuge in resignation.

"Why bother? What do I care for a world, for a life, in which there's no spark of honor left?"

This world was no longer his one; his world had been lost along with Poland's freedom. His life was only an illusion now, lived in an environment to which he did not belong.

"But if that is really so, what point is there in my going on living? To see Titus growing older every day, and his eyes watering more and more?"

Hitherto his life had always had some content—the excitement, for instance, of hoodwinking his relatives who were waiting for his death. He would not make things easy for his good-for-nothing nephews in Warsaw: let them go on trying to raise money on their inheritance from the Jew!

This idea had kept Wydawski going hitherto, but, he asked himself, what sense, what value had such a life? At bottom he did not care a straw whether his nephews and nieces had any money or not. What did he care for this life, for this Topolye of his and all its people? It no longer belonged to him, it had slipped through his fingers!

And these awful winter days, too! In summer one could pass the time in hunting the wild birds, and forget everything else. But these long dark winter days, when the sky was hidden behind a frozen pall and the world was contracted into a little space filled with gray mist! Of the only world he cared for, a world that had not yet lost its sense of honor, of that world, where people dealt honorably and were not traitors, nothing remained but his dog; and he was growing older day by day, gazed at you with beseeching, despairingly questioning eyes, and you could not answer him, could not help him. . . .

The Count noticed that Titus was following him with moist, inquiring eyes from his corner. In that glance could be read the beast's unshakable trust in his almighty master, who alone could break the strangling fetters of old age that lay upon him, drive away all the pains and sorrows that assailed him, and dispel the mysterious fear that filled him with the dull premonition which comes to all creatures before their approaching end.

Wydawski did his best to avoid Titus's glance, but at last he was conquered by the beast's dumb, heart-piercing language. He nervously walked over to the dog.

"What can I do if you are old and your stomach is out of order? I can't help you! *Tais-toi!* Down!"

He stamped his foot imperiously.

The dog put his aged nose between his paws and resigned himself to his fate.

Sometimes strange thoughts came to the Count. His conscience pricked him, though he would not admit it. Could *he* be wrong after all; could he have lived wickedly? How narrow was the circle that loneliness drew round a man! It broke one's pride. Perhaps it would have been better not to live at odds with all the world. And from his heart was wrung a cry before which he himself was appalled.

"Oh, God, don't let me die at enmity with mankind!"

In such moments of weakness the Count sometimes resolved to repair of his errors and try to get into touch with his fellow men. He actually nursed the idea of visiting the peasants in their huts, speaking to them as man to man, acquainting himself with their trials and hardships, and helping them by kind words and kind deeds. In his old age he longed for human smiles, for the greeting of a human being, not of a lackey.

But of what use are good intentions! The road of performance is a hard one. It is blocked by all sorts of obstacles, and one has to scale a host of mountains and cross a multitude of abysses, created by life and circumstance, by pride, class consciousness, embitterment. Wydawski recognized that it was beyond his power to carry out his intentions, deeply as he wished it. The self-abnegation demanded of him was too great. And so he kept on postponing his good intentions and let milestone after milestone of his life pass without doing anything.

And the stretch of road that was still left was becoming shorter and shorter. The milestones led inexorably toward the last frontier of all, every step took him nearer to it, and from afar the bottomless night that lay beyond that frontier beckoned to him. And Titus's beseeching gaze, too, perpetually kept him reminded of it.

One day his patience came to an end.

"You can see for yourself that you're an old dog now! I can do nothing for you!" he said between his clenched teeth. "What are you waiting for? For the knacker to put a rope round your neck? Make an end of things yourself, if you still have any honor left in you!"

The Count put on his Napoleonic uniform, set his four-cornered Uhlan cap on his head, and summoned Titus to follow him. He stamped through the soft, dirty snow of the village street in his spurred top boots. Titus laboriously followed him with lowered head.

Wydawski looked at nobody. On the hill at the entrance to the village, beside the inn, he stopped and gazed down at the fields of Topolye in the valley, which lay wrapped in a great warm covering of snow. The white world stretched away endlessly, to the blue horizon and the edge of the forest, which was soft violet in the mist. No beast, no human being was to be seen in that great expanse. The green meadows, the fields sown with winter corn, slept secure beneath the downy blanket of snow. The ice-covered streams, which could be distinguished because of the bushes bordering them, blended into that dazzling whiteness and were lost in it, so that it was as if the whole world were one white plain. Only a few white birches waved to and fro, shaking the snow from their slender branches, and now and then a raven would come flying, descend and leave its delicate track in the snow.

The Count stood for a long time, absorbed in his contemplation of this white Topolye. On some such day long after his death it would look just the same. Just so it had looked many hundred years before him, long before his ancestors came into possession of it, and just so it would look many hundred years hence, when there would be no trace left of the Wydawskis. Men changed their raiment; one man wore this uniform, another that. But the earth's uniform was always the same.

For a long time the Count gazed down at his Topolye, as if he wished to take that scene with him into the unknown world where he would soon have to travel. And strangely enough, now he felt that the impossible was possible, the unthinkable thinkable. It did not seem any longer difficult to him, but rather easy, so easy and so natural that he was amazed how he could ever have thought differently. He loved this Topolye; not the snow-covered fields, not the birds in his lake. His Topolye was these low, little huts half buried in the ground, whose roofs, strewn with fallen leaves, peeped out of the snow; his Topolye was these roofs with the thick cushions of snow lying on them, the soft wreaths of smoke issuing from the black stumpy chimneys; his Topolye was the little paths worn by human feet to the church and the inn; his Topolye was the peasants who lived there. They were children of the village of Topolye, just like himself. A peasant or a cow from Topolye was well known over the whole country. How could it have come about that he, the lord and father of Topolye, he to whom his forefathers had entrusted this patch of earth, was so at variance with his people? There was a grave misunderstanding somewhere, and it must be got rid of at once, now, at the last minute, before it was too late. He dared not carry it to the grave with him.

And the impossible happened. The haughty Pan Wydawski, lord of Topolye, entered the first hut that he came to, wearing the uniform of a Polish Uhlan.

He did so with the best intentions, he wished to be a father to his "children." He wished to ask them what they stood in need of, whether they had enough potatoes, enough fodder for the cattle, enough firewood. He entered with the firm resolve to tell them that there had been a misunderstanding and that henceforth all would be changed and must be changed.

The younger men were in the woods felling trees for the timber dealer. The hut was filled with women and children, and calves and pigs which had been brought into the house because of the cold. A few old crones were pottering over the hearth. The thick, heavy, evil-smelling air in the room and the dense biting smoke from the stove almost took away the Count's breath. He felt as if an invisible hand were at his throat trying to strangle him. . . .

The inmates could scarcely believe their eyes when they saw the terror and nightmare of their lives, their "high and mighty master" himself, standing in the room in full uniform. The blood of many generations of bondslaves awoke, warning them of danger. Their bodies felt the pain of blows that had descended on the flesh of ancestors long since mingled with the dust. And all without exception, young and old, male and female, flung themselves to the ground, beat their faces on the mud floor, and whined.

"Olia boga, have pity!"

For a moment there was a breathless silence. Suddenly the children broke out into a shrill, terrified crying. Even the calves and young pigs crowded together, as animals do when a storm is brewing. A pair of infirm old men sprang out of bed, as if a miracle had suddenly restored them to animation, and supported on their sticks, their free hands outstretched imploringly toward the Count, went down on their knees.

When the Count's eyes at last got used to the dim smoky light, he could see at his feet nothing but backs and hands stretched beseechingly toward him.

"Olia boga, have pity, in the name of God!"

"Get up! I won't harm you . . . I want to be friends with you . . . I want to be kind to you. . . ." This was what both his heart and his head was saying. But his tongue uttered something quite different.

"Oxen! Animals! My horse has more sense than you!"

With a spring he was out of the door and breathed freely again.

"There! You see! What are you waiting for, you fool?" he shouted at his dog, who silently trotted up to him. Then he strode home in furious silence.

As soon as he arrived there he took his hunting rifle from the rack, called Titus, and led him to the bank of the frozen lake where they had lain so often waiting for wild duck.

The dog became uneasy. For the last time in his life he showed signs of liveliness; he sprang round his master as if in youthful high spirits, but at the same time a heart-rending howl broke from his throat, and he tried again and again to catch his master's eye. But the Count stubbornly avoided him. That increased Titus's uneasiness. He made to flee. His master sternly called him back. He came unwillingly; his legs would scarcely support him, but he came straight toward his master. He panted with terror, his gleaming eyes almost started out of his head, and a long-drawn howl came from his chest. A shot echoed over the frozen lake. No wild duck fell this time, but instead Titus the bulldog. . . .

Wydawski commanded his lackey, he who bore the nickname of the Angel of Death, to go to the village and spend the night there with his nephew. The servant hesitated, but meeting his master's imperious glance obeyed as Titus had done.

In the middle of the night the fire bell of Topolye began ringing. The peasants left their warm beds very unwillingly. It was freezing hard outside. When they reluctantly stuck their noses outside they could see great pillars of fire rising toward heaven in the frosty night —the white castle in the park was in flames.

The peasants were afraid to go near. They did not want to have anything to do with the castle. Most of them crept back under their warm blankets again. A few hastened toward the castle to save the Count, but they could not get near the door. Afterward they related that they had seen whole hosts of black devils flying out of the flames, after which they had run away in terror. In reality it was only black clouds of smoke; they came from several barrels of pitch which the Count had sent for a few weeks previously to calk the roof. Now the pitch poured out of the doors of the white drawing room into which Pan Wydawski, still wearing his Uhlan uniform, had shut himself. . .

CHAPTER VII

YECHIEL GOES HIS OWN WAY

TOPOLYE had a new master. Young Pan Wydawski was not carried away by whims and humors. But he was possessed by an uncontrollable passion which nothing could still—an insatiable greed for money. It was simply unbelievable, the huge sums that his noble appetite could devour. Now the whole village, man, beast, and land, had to work their hardest to satisfy their master's hunger for money and stop his greedy maw.

As soon as the first spring wind began to melt the snow in the fields, man and beast set about their labors. The air was filled with the breath of God. From early morning the ground thrilled beneath the firm tread of the powerful oxen, who pulled with such a will that steam soon rose from their backs. Behind the plows strode young lads and sturdy red-cheeked girls. Like their beasts they set down their feet thoughtfully and heavily on the wet soil, just freed from the snow. The keen plow-shares divided the stubborn ground, kneaded it, furrowed it, until all its powers of growth were awakened and summoned to service.

Man and beast suffered equally. All had to give of their best strength to create wealth to feed the invisible Moloch, the insatiable landlord. He was not there himself; he preferred to spend his time in distant cities. His faithful servants, the steward and the overseer, administered his property for him. They were prepared to drain the last drop of blood from man and beast for their master's comfort.

For Shloime-Wolf, too, these were evil days. True, he had peace now from Titus, who, like all the enemies of the Jews since the time of Amalek and Haman, was mere dust, but on the other hand there was no chance either to earn an easy groschen and no Poritz who would let you off a quarter's rent for damaging your trousers. Every groschen had to be paid on the nail. Every quarter the rent was raised, every half year the inn was put up to the highest bidder; one never knew what was going to happen next. The rights of year-long tenancy no longer counted for anything. Every day there were new taxes to pay. Literally everything was taxed—every glass of brandy that one served, every ell of cloth, every candle, every pound of salt that one sold, the malt, the water, the accommodation. And if one refused to pay there were hundreds of people waiting to take the inn over one's head, so that one risked being thrown on the street with all one's belongings overnight. Past were the good times when one could afford to support a learned son-in-law, to feed an apprentice Rabbi, whose studies and good works would earn a golden chair for his patrons in the next world. Now one had to count every bite.

So Shloime-Wolf and his wife were forced to think of an occupation for the young married couple. After the feast of the Passover all Yechiel's possessions, his bedding and his books, were loaded on a wagon and the young couple moved to the town. There was still a little money left, and as the old house adjoining Reb Melech's happened to be free, Rivke's shop was resurrected once more.

Reisel must have been born with the idea in her blood. Although nobody had told her, she seemed to know that she was created to look after the upkeep of the house, so that her husband might pursue undisturbed his study of the Law. Her good neighbor Blimele coached her in certain things and also gave her useful hints in the running of the house. As the young couple were without a mother Blimele took over the post that Rivke would have filled had she been alive.

The Melechs had grown old and shriveled as two poppy heads. Their faces were brown as nuts. Their hair was quite gray, but they were still fresh and lively. Of the two children of Boruch-Moishe whom Blimele had adopted after Rivke's death, only the boy had survived; he was now studying at a Yeshivah. The little girl had died three years before Yechiel's return.

Like his father before him, Yechiel now sat at his studies while his young wife stood behind her booth in the market place. In the slender figure with the girlish neck and the head bowed under the century-old burden of the traditional hood, it would have been difficult to recognize the goosegirl of a few years before, who had splashed about in girlish high spirits with her flock. Soon the yoke of breadearning weighed heavily on her young shoulders, and the cruel actualities of worry piled themselves on her smoothly shorn head. But one trait of her girlhood had survived—her youthful quickness and animation. These excited a strong attraction on her peasant customers, who instinctively discerned that the new market vendor came from one of their villages. Many too, had been at the inn and knew "Shlomko's daughter." Others again could remember Rivke, and bought from Reisel out of old habit.

This excited the jealousy of the other women and they cried out at
such preferential treatment of a newcomer. On market days Yechiel
helped Reisel when help was needed. Actually he only made her work
harder, for he could not bear that his wife's stand should be preferred
by customers to those of the other women.

"Reisel, we're robbing Jewish children and taking away their bread!"

Often he would even advise peasants to try another booth, saying
the goods were cheaper and better. Reisel would reproach him gently.

"What are you doing? You'll bring me to beggary! Do go back to
your House of Study!"

Yechiel once replied, "Reisel, the other women have children to feed,
and we have only ourselves."

Reisel blushed to the roots of her hair and was silent.

In other ways too, Yechiel created unpleasant difficulties for Reisel;
worst of all, he would not suffer a penny to remain in the house overnight. When he returned from the House of Study, the first place he
went to was the money box. He took whatever he found there and distributed it among the poor.

"Money is blood," he said, "and just as the shedding of blood is forbidden because it is life itself, so it is with money; for money means
bread and life itself. And it is a great sin to hoard bread in the house
overnight when other people are starving."

Reisel submitted to her husband in such matters, more, she was
proud of him. She was convinced that her husband was no ordinary
man, that he was destined for higher things, and that she should consider herself fortunate to be his wife. Her heart shrank at the thought
that, because of her sins, Yechiel might not be able to achieve what he
was striving for. She knew that he was striving for some high end,
although he had never spoken to her about it; but she felt that nothing
that her husband did was idle, that he was preparing himself for something. And she did not want to hinder him—God forbid!—she did not
want to stand in his way; on the contrary, she was prepared to do anything to help him to achieve his aim. When she compared herself with
Yechiel, when she thought of her girlish pranks, of the geese, the
stream, the meadow, she would start up in terror and pray from her
very heart, "Lord of the Universe, forgive me my sins!" And every
Sabbath she sent candles to the Psalm Fellowship.

For there was a shadow on the young couple's life: they had no
children. They had been already married for five years, and Heaven

showed no sign of granting them blessing. Blimele, their neighbor, kept asking her, "Well, Reisel?"

And Reisel could only blush and hang her head.

She knew what awaited her, if five more years were to go by without her having a child. Then the saying would be fulfilled: "They shall go together to the Rabbi and return separately." It meant irrevocable divorce.

Reisel felt certain that the fault was hers, and she often wept at night over it. Yechiel would remonstrate with her and take the blame on himself. It was because of his own sin of loving her too much, of coming to her not merely to fulfill the commandment to be fruitful and multiply. So it had been with Jacob in the Bible: "God saw that Jacob loved Rachel, and He closed her womb. And He opened Leah's womb because she was hated."

When she lamented that other women of her age had already a whole brood of children, Yechiel would say comfortingly, "You are dearer to me than seven sons."

To this she would reply, "If you loved me less it might be better for me. Perhaps then God would have pity on me and take away my shame as he did with Rachel."

At the moments when Yechiel's heart was most full, such as Friday evening when Reisel blessed the candles, she became to him a lofty and exalted figure, the Princess Sabbath herself, the mystical embodiment of Divine Grace. His eyes endowed her with the splendors of the divine glory, the Shechinah: "The Shechinah does not descend on any house where a woman is not found...." And Yechiel's shame it must be said that he was unable to think of the highest human rapture merely as a means of propagation. His union with his wife had a deeper meaning for him; it became for him a union in higher worlds, where will and grace embraced each other, leading to that original harmony adumbrated in the Cabbalah when male and female were one, as it is written in the Scripture: "Male and female created He them."

Yechiel fought to dispel the vague cloud of mysticism that obscured his way to God. He had no desire to be anything but a simple, humble, ordinary Jew. But his fight was in vain; against his will and his conviction he found himself forced along the way destined for him by fate, impelled by powers which already ruled him though they were not yet full grown. This alarmed him, and he sought to resist, but against himself he was impotent. Often he would pray to God.

"Lord of the Universe, cleanse my heart that I may serve Thee truly. I am not of Thy chosen sons, I am not strong in Thy spirit, I am not wise, I am not good, and I have not been thought worthy of sitting at the table of the Torah. I am one of the least of Thy creatures; I love Thee and would like to vanish in Thee as a zephyr is lost in the wind, as a blade of grass is lost in the pastures, as a drop is lost in the sea. I pray Thee, remove all the hindrances that lie in the way of my union with Thee. If that hindrance is my body, then break it like a vessel and deliver me from the captivity of this flesh in which Thou hast imprisoned me. If it is my soul, then cleanse it from the alloy with which I have corrupted it, comfort it for all the shame I have brought upon it, and take what belongs to Thee into Thy Heaven again, as pure as when Thou didst send it forth. Cleanse my heart that I may truly serve Thee, God of Abraham, Isaac, and Jacob!"

He turned the pages to find the psalm he had taken as his own, "Blessed are the undefiled," and he burst into tears at the words, "With my whole heart have I sought thee: O let me not wander from thy commandments." After a psalm he always felt comforted and he repeated to himself in humble devotion the words of the singer of Israel: "My soul thirsteth for thee, my flesh longeth for thee." And he began to hum the melody which the Chassidim had brought from Kotzk:

> Where does the Lord God dwell?
> Where they let Him in.
> Where do they let Him in?
> In a dwelling that is clean.
> Which dwelling is clean?
> A man who holds himself lowly.

In order to keep himself in a state of fear, he studied, like all Jews, the stern ethical books. However, he did not study along with the learned, but in the Psalm Fellowship as in his boyhood, when he had gone to the fairs. As then, the Psalm Fellowship still consisted of simple hand workers and carters who clubbed together for a teacher to instruct them in their free hours. Blind Reb Leibush was dead, so Yechiel took the place of his former teacher. He loved to bathe in the simple Jewish piety of these men, when in the faint dawn they filled the low-roofed little room with their warm breath and heart-rending prayers. When he saw them standing round him wrapped in prayer shawls stained with their bitter tears, he felt he was one of them. He read over the Psalms with particular joy to these hawkers, hand workers, and carters. While with them he felt that he had achieved the end of all his strivings—to be a man neither extraordinary nor great, nor higher than anybody else, a blade of grass in the meadow of Jewry, a drop in the ocean of the Jewish spirit.

Just as he loved to be with simple people during the psalm singing, so he sought them out in the street and the market place, at their daily work and in their homes. He was interested in everything that happened in the streets and in the town; he knew all about the trades and wares of the poorer Jews, and knew too where the shoe pinched.

That bowed man over there, with his hand stuffed in the pockets of his rough caftan, was the butcher Chune. He was old and his sons had taken his business away from him. At first they had run it along with him; then they had flung him out. Now he was a beggar and lived in the poorhouse. Usually he was to be found sitting by the stove in the House of Study, his toothless jaws perpetually moving as he tried to chew a dry piece of bread which some kindhearted housewife had given him, while at the same time he recited a few chapters of the Psalms that he knew by heart but did not understand in the least. But, on market days he could not stay in the House of Study; he had to be out in the streets. He would have given his life to buy a plump calf again! And he simply had to be present when a bargain was struck. Perhaps he would be able to skin a gratuity or a glass of brandy off it, by acting as middleman. But those ignoramuses—his sons—wouldn't let him bargain for them. The old butcher looked on enviously while other men bought cattle, and sighed. There he was, trotting along, supported on his old stick, which had served his purposes for half a lifetime. That was Chune, the butcher, a miserable old wreck. Poor man, he had his troubles! thought Yechiel, walking up to him.

"What's wrong, Reb Chune? Why are you hanging your head?"

"Heh? Oh, it's Yechiel! Things are bad, Yechiel, bad! My boys won't let me buy a single bit of livestock—they would like to stuff the whole world into their own sacks."

"But what need have you of livestock, Reb Chune? Your good works and kind actions are ready waiting for you in the next world."

"Ah, you really think so? What, I really have a part in the next world? Why, I don't know even how to pray properly!" the old man muttered with a sigh.

"You've earned your part in the next world in other ways," replied Yechiel comfortingly. "You've given just weight. You've taken poor strangers into your house over the Sabbath."

"Yes, that's right, Yechiel!" the old man's face lighted up. "I've done what I could, with God's help."

"Don't you worry, Reb Chune. All Jews have a part in the next world."

"God bless you, Yechiel, for your kind words . . ."

That was the carter Reb Israel standing over there. Yechiel knew him; he was a member of the Psalm Fellowship. He had a son who studied in the Yeshivah; he was resolved to make a scholar of his only child. The little underset man was very poor. His meager living was earned for him by an emaciated horse and old wagon, in which he conveyed hand workers and their chests to the annual fairs. Occasionally, too, he was commissioned to drive some one to the nearest town. Now he was standing at the corner of the street wondering where he could raise a loan, so as to buy a sack of oats for his horse.

Yet that was not the real body of Reb Israel standing over there, nor were these his real thoughts. Just as there is a lower and a higher Jerusalem, so there was also a lower and a higher Reb Israel. The man standing over there was only the outer husk of Israel, which he wore in humility because God so ordained it, the external mask of a carter waiting for a customer, whip in hand. But there was also a second Israel, corresponding to the higher Jerusalem. If that Israel over there were to fling off his caftan, the king's robes would appear which he wore under it.

"Good morning, Reb Israel."

"Oh, it's Yechiel!"

Israel turned one eye on Yechiel. The whip blows of life had beaten out the other. All that remained was the bloodshot tatters of the eyelids, which protruded slightly. And when Israel spoke to any one he gazed at him, not with his sound eye, but with the reddened, mutilated tatters of the other eyelid—and his lacking eye could probably see further and deeper than his sound one. It was the eye of the higher Israel. What had not that eye seen! God's covenant with Abraham, the tables of the Law on Mount Sinai, perhaps even the coming day of the Messiah. . . .

"Why are you looking so thoughtful, Reb Israel?"

"Oh, maybe you fancy that I'm thinking about heavenly things like you, Yechiel! I'm thinking that if the prophet Elijah were to throw a purse of money at my feet at this moment I would be able to buy a little fodder for my horse; oats are as cheap as dirt in the market today."

For a moment Reb Israel sank very greatly in Yechiel's eyes. God help him, was that all he could think about? But then Yechiel saw that the oats and the horse too had a higher importance and a deeper significance. Reb Israel's horse was part of the creation, and he was in search of food for the creation. For that Reb Israel should merely be worrying about such low things as how to get oats for his horse Yechiel could not believe—everything that Israel did had a deep meaning.

"Wait a minute, Reb Israel! I'll ask my wife," said Yechiel, hurrying over to Reisel's stand.

"Reisel, the Lord of the Universe has blessed us with abundance today; you're having good custom. Lend Reb Israel two gulden from your cashbox; the poor fellow wants to get some cheap fodder for his horse."

What could Reisel reply? No doubt Yechiel knew what he was doing. She gave him the cashbox. He took it and hurried away.

"Here, Reb Israel, I can lend you this. Pay me back when you can."

Once as Yechiel walked across the market square he would hear a forlorn lowing. Several calves were lying bound beneath a peasant's wagon and lowing forlornly to the skies. It was unbearably hot and the poor beasts were thirsty. The peasant was nowhere to be seen; no doubt he had gone to the tavern for a drink. And the bound calves were lowing to heaven for water. Yechiel could hardly bear to listen to them; his heart almost burst with pity for these humble creatures of God. God's creatures were crying for water. So the pious young scholar, who, people were already beginning to say, was destined for great things, hastily went over to a peasant, borrowed a pail, hurried to the well in the middle of the market square, filled the pail, and gave the calves a drink one after another.

Soon a curious crowd gathered to enjoy the spectacle. This young Chassid evidently did not consider it beneath him to water calves in the middle of the market square! Some were touched by the sight; it was a pious thought to show such pity toward God's creatures. Others contemptuously shrugged their shoulders. Reisel, who looked on from her stand, blushed with embarrassment. The other market women chaffed her.

"Your husband is a fine scholar! He waters cattle just like a peasant!"

But Reisel paid no attention. They could jeer and make fun of her if they liked, because Yechiel took away her custom and gave it to other people. If he did that, then she was sure he was acting rightly. For Reisel knew, what the others could not know, that her Yechiel would often get up in the middle of the night, sit down in the corner of the room, on the cold floor, and pray till morning, lamenting over the destruction of Jerusalem, while other young men slept comfortably in their beds. Nobody knew of this, for Yechiel had forbidden her to say a word about it. As, lying in bed, she saw him sitting alone in the corner, often she felt deeply sorry for him. She would have loved to call him to her, but she mastered her impulse. Then sad thoughts would break in upon her, tears would start to her eyes, and with a trembling heart she would pray to God that she might become worthy of being Yechiel's wife. She knew that the road he walked was a stony one climbing to the heights. She prayed that God might help her to follow him, even if it were only at a distance. She would gladly hire herself as a servant to strange people if it were necessary for his work. Oh, that God might make her worthy of being Yechiel's wife!

CHAPTER VIII

YECHIEL PLEDGES GOD'S NAME

POVERTY and hardship are the fertile seeds of faith. Men pant for divine aid as the thirsty for water, and drink from any well that offers itself to them. . . . Yechiel had been born and brought up in the town; everybody knew him, everybody knew that not so very long ago he had trudged round the villages with a pack on his shoulders, and sat in the House of Study at the hand workers' table, that he had married the ignorant daughter of an innkeeper, and had not had any real school training. But neither his humble ancestry, nor the contempt in which he was held by the learned, could dim the halo surrounding his head.

The simple, poor people, the hand workers in the Psalm Fellowship, were devoted to Yechiel; they seemed to feel that the same blood flowed in his veins as in theirs.

Since he was a son of the town, they set great hopes on him. Perhaps they might some day win to prosperity through him! Besides, there was a strange Jew called Ezriel who was always in the House of Study between the midday and the evening services. He would point to his feet, "These same feet that you see now were dead at one time! He only touched them with his hand and they became whole again!"

When Yechiel learned the stories that Ezriel (who stuck faithfully to him and always addressed him as "Rabbi") was spreading, he gave him strict orders to be silent. Ezriel immediately told this to everybody in the synagogue and added, "Perhaps his time has not yet come. But mark my words, Jews: a great light will yet arise in your town!"

And since then Ezriel had been wandering about the whole neighborhood, visiting every House of Study, pointing at his feet and saying, "Do you see these feet, Jews? They were dead once. But he merely touched them with his hand and they became whole again."

And when people asked him eagerly, "Who? Where is this miracle worker?"

Ezriel would answer, "I'm not allowed to tell. His time has not come yet. But I can tell you this much: A great light is about to rise in Israel!"

And good Reb Melech loudly proclaimed Yechiel's fame both in the Psalm Fellowship and the market place.

"Jews, I'm one of the simplest of God's creatures, it isn't for me to mix in such matters; but I firmly believe that great things are in store for us. A few nights ago I went out into the yard; and there the light was, burning in his window. I was properly scared: maybe, thinks I, somebody is ill, God help us! I hurry across to the window and peep in. I'll never tell a living soul what I saw then. But he was always a pious lad. . . ."

And Reb Israel, the half-blind carter, spoke in the House of Study. "These two gulden he lent me out of his wife's takings; they've brought me God's blessing. It doesn't matter how much oats I shake out for my horse, the sack never gets empty."

At this, Chune, the old butcher, grew jealous and interposed, "He never lent me anything, he only said a few words to me, but they are dearer to me than great treasure."

The people read a deeper meaning into everything he did, for the Psalm Fellowship had made him their Rabbi. And Yechiel himself never noticed that he was gradually coming to resemble the image they had formed of him.

The passing of the Sabbath is a tragic moment for Jewish people. When the shadows of evening fall there rises in the soul of the Jew an agonizing conflict between his Sabbath and his workaday emotions. He bids farewell to his royal mother, his dying Sabbath. He clings to the imperial robes of the Sabbath like a child to its mother's apron. With what reluctance he turns again to the torture of the week, where nothing awaits him but shame and contempt and the worries of a hateful existence! So he prolongs the Sabbath as long as he can, and sits up late into the night in the darkness. . . .

At these tragic moments the Chassidim seek comfort at the table of the righteous—of the Zaddik. As they break bread in common they give themselves up to their yearning for the everlasting Sabbath. But the poor people have nobody to give them comfort in these sad hours.

Since Yechiel had come to live in the town, however, the members of the Psalm Fellowship, the carters, tailors, and other hand workers, had gradually begun to gather in his home on the Sabbath evening.

At least once in the week they wanted to rise to higher spheres. They had no name for their desire, did not know in the least how it should be named; all they knew was that for once they did not ask anything for themselves, anything bound up with their livelihood, their health, their wives and children, but yearned for the good of all Israel, more, for the glory of God's holy name. They regarded themselves as soldiers in a great army; they could not march in the first rank, for they had not learned the "art of war" (they had had no opportunity to study the Scripture). But at least they wished to make themselves useful behind the front, and have some share in the great common cause.

Accordingly they met together in Yechiel's home. They did not venture at first to sit down at the table, but stood about in the corners, against the walls, beside the door, so as to be with him and see how he served God at the supper table, how he washed his hands, how he said grace and cut the Sabbath loaf—like a priest worshiping before the altar. They all brought the remnants of their Sabbath meals with them, one a white loaf, another a piece of fish; they piled all these on the table and pulled up their chairs.

Yechiel was powerless. He did not want this; a sure instinct told him that he was playing with fire: "Who are you to dare to play the Rabbi?" But a fellowship had raised him on their shoulders, and he could feel his wings sprouting. To break bread together is a mystical act, which like a flame smelts a company into one. The soul as well as the body finds nourishment at such communal feasts. And as Yechiel sat with the others at these improvised meals, a strange feeling came over him—all the sealed chambers within him flew open, all obstacles were cleared away, his dread of leadership vanished. That inner voice lulled to sleep all his doubts. He saw that these men expected deeds from him, and all his scruples and hesitations melted in the burning flame of faith that environed him. Yearning eyes were fixed on him, greedy for some word of comfort.

Mostly he spoke to them of the portion of the Scriptures read that week in the synagogue, or about the patriarchs. Sometimes he would explain and interpret a psalm. Often he quoted passages in the Zohar which they could understand. "The days of a man are the garments of his soul. After his death, the days of a man come to God, and each day becomes a garment that the man puts on. And whatever garment you prepare for yourself by your actions each day, your soul will wear in the world to come."

He told them the story of the tailor who asked the burial society to construct his coffin from his work table and to place his measure and his tape in the grave with him, so that his tools might bear witness to his just deeds and testify that he had done his work well.

And he taught them how to live, according to the rich didactic literature: to trust in the tried and tested road which leads to bliss; that simple faith redeems in this world and the next; that faith in God is already fulfillment in God. He told them they could come to God by the simplest means; they could be greasing the axles of their carts and reach nearer to God's mercy than through lengthy prayers. And he convinced them that what is important in man's salvation is not seeking, but having, God.

So Yechiel became the burning ring that held these simple men together. And the fact that their Rabbi belonged not to the learned class but to themselves, the ignorant people, brought Yechiel still closer to them. That feeling united the members of the Psalm Fellowship into one great family. At Yechiel's table they did not seek God, they possessed Him. Consequently their prayers to Him were not accompanied by yearning, long drawn out, lugubrious melodies as was customary at the courts of the great Rabbis. Instead they rejoiced in God and gave Him of the best that they had, gave Him a real holiday feast. In the choruses of these simple men could be heard the winds and snowstorms that had howled round them during their journeys, the songs they had heard in the fields which they had passed as they went from village to village, the plashing of the streams and waters in which they had let down their nets or washed their sheepskins. And even when they sighed it was in the confident words of the Psalms; these accompanied them whatever they were doing, whether they were sewing a peasant jacket or cobbling a pair of boots.

Gone was the melancholy sense that the Sabbath was nearing its end. They were no longer afraid of sticking their heads into the devouring jaws of the weekday which lay in ambush for them—for in the Psalms it was said: "Yea, though I walk through the valley of the shadow of death, I will fear no evil: for thou art with me ..."

Soon it was no longer a matter of shame to belong to the hand workers' table; on the contrary, it began to be regarded as a distinction. Admission to the Psalm Fellowship was not easy. When a man married and applied for admission, he had to submit to a very strict examination. He had to prove that he practiced his trade honestly. Two masters of mature age had to testify that he understood his work, that he observed the commandment not to weave wool and cotton together, that he did not keep any scraps of cloth for himself, and that he led a virtuous Jewish life.

For instance: Selig the horse dealer had not yet succeeded in getting into the Psalm Fellowship in spite of all his efforts. Yet he had greatly changed his ways in the course of time. Since his business had begun to go well and he had become the spoiled favorite of all the landowners in the neighborhood, he had done nothing that could be taken exception to, and had done his best to become decent. But the whole town knew about his past; it knew all the wild doings of his young days, and there was always whispering about him. "Luck does not go on foot," says an old proverb. Many a gypsy knew very well the road to Selig's stable; many a lost horse was found there. Not without cause had he been punished by God. He had made his way, and had money to burn, but his wife was childless.

Now, it was true, he had changed his life, gave generous alms, took poor vagrants into his house, supported Talmud scholars, let poor students freely eat at his table; but it was of no use; he remained childless. And as long as he was, it could be assumed with certainty that God had not forgiven him his sins. Accordingly he was not admitted to the Psalm Fellowship, although he would gladly have paid a whole purseful of money for the privilege, or even have presented the society with a Torah roll. But all his efforts were useless, for the Psalm Fellowship had strict regulations regarding admission, which old Reb Mordecai, who for many years had been its rabbi, had once drawn up. Blind Reb Leibush too had constantly impressed on the members to be very cautious in admitting anybody to the fellowship.

Yes, the Psalm Fellowship possessed a tradition! Many of the pious Jews who reposed in the little graveyard of the town had been rabbis, spiritual guides of the fellowship. No, it wasn't an easy matter to get into it! But once you were in it there was no doubt about the fact. Whether rich or poor, the members helped one another in bad times, and lent money to one another whenever it was needed. If a member fell sick, the whole fellowship prayed for his recovery and visited him in a body. And when a member was summoned to meet his great Judge he had nothing to fear, his fellows looked after him, the whole fellowship followed his bier and intoned: "May righteousness lead him!" And psalms were read for him on every anniversary of his death. If you once belonged to the fellowship you would never be let down by it, either in this world or in the next.

One day Yechiel was sitting at his desk, while Reisel was bowed over the hearth, when Reb Melech entered. He was covered with snow from head to foot, for outside a storm was raging and everything was wrapped in white. And little Reb Melech was just as white as the wintry landscape.

"Yechiel!" he cried from the doorway. "I've bad news, very bad news!"

Yechiel's cheeks under his little black beard grew pale with alarm.

"What has happened, Reb Melech?"

"Our Reb Israel of the Fellowship has had an accident," replied Reb Melech with a sigh.

Before he could relate what had happened Reb Israel himself entered with his whip in his hand, and as white as a snowman. The old fellow was weeping bitterly.

"Reb Israel! What's the matter, Reb Israel?"

His sole wage earner, the old horse, had collapsed in a snowstorm on the road to Radom.

"Now I might as well take a sack and go begging!"

"Yechiel, you must help him!"

Although Yechiel was Rabbi of the Psalm Fellowship, little Reb Melech still used the familiar form of address in speaking to him. He himself did not consider it fitting, but Yechiel insisted upon it.

"How can I help him? As soon as I have said my prayers, I'll try to collect money for him in the town."

"No, Yechiel, that's no good," replied Reb Melech. "Who would give you money in these hard times? Nobody has any, this everlasting winter has used up their last penny. How do you expect to raise enough money for a new horse? Why, that would need a fortune!"

"What am I to do, then?" asked Yechiel in desperation.

"If you really want to help him, you can."

"How?"

"Selig the horse dealer is prepared to give him a horse, but on one condition: you must promise him that his wife will have a child."

"How can I promise such a thing?" asked Yechiel, turning pale, "I'm not a Wonder Rabbi, to promise such a thing as that!"

But Reb Melech refused to be put off.

"If you really want to, you can help the man. It says in the Scripture that God fulfills the prayers of the righteous."

"But I'm not a Zaddik."

"Oh yes, you are! Oh yes, you are!" cried Reb Melech. "Help the man; he's in a bad hole, there's no getting around that! Why, what can he do, now he's lost his only support?"

And Reb Israel cried amid his sobs.

"Rabbi, help me! Why does God punish me so cruelly? What crime have I done?"

"Don't say that, Reb Israel!"

"Why shouldn't I say it? God strikes me down, and there's nobody that will take my part!"

"Reb Israel is right!" said Reb Melech.

Two cruel beasts tore at Yechiel's heart; Israel pulled one way, God the other.

"Come, Reb Israel! I'll go to Selig, I'll beg him, I'll implore him, perhaps he'll do it...."

"You can spare yourself the trouble. He's here. He's standing outside the door, for he was afraid to come inside."

"What's he afraid of? Call him in, Reb Melech!"

Immediately Selig appeared in his great top boots.

Yechiel got up and began in a humble and beseeching voice.

"Give Reb Israel a horse. If you do, the Lord of the universe will help you and fulfill your prayers."

No answer. Selig, who was gigantic, and had once been nicknamed "Selig Ganef," looked pale as death. Years of dissipation had left their mark on his face. But since he had married the daughter of a bankrupt grain merchant he had become a respectable man, and had done his best to gain admission into decent middle-class circles. But what did that avail him? He had no children! God knew what He was doing!... Now Selig stood there, his gray eyes moist with emotion, while they gazed pleadingly into Yechiel's face. At last he stammered painfully:

"Holy Rabbi! I know that I am unworthy, God doesn't punish without reason." The huge man bowed his head. "Rabbi, help me to become a decent man again!"

Yechiel's heart was filled with pity for this strong man who stood before him helplessly stretching out his hands for assistance.

"What is troubling you? Tell me frankly," said Yechiel, walking up to him and looking warmly into his eyes. "In what way do you want God to help you?"

"By forgiving me my sins. I've done all I can, Rabbi—these men here can testify to that. My past sins are over now, and forgotten too, so help me God! No bite crosses my lips that I haven't earned honestly by these two hands. If that isn't true, may I choke on the next bite I eat! I'll do anything that you tell me, Rabbi. If you order me to do it, holy Rabbi, I'll even take the road as a beggar. How much longer will this torture last? I'm ashamed to look my wife in the face. Seven years married—and no child yet! Why does God condemn me to live on as lonely as a tree in a field? I can't endure her tears any longer, Rabbi; they break my heart. 'It's because of you,' she always says, 'because of your sins.' I'm ashamed to tell it, but with you I can have no secrets. My wife is always saying: 'A child by you would be certain to turn out a robber.' And she's right, Rabbi! Oh, holy man, give me your promise that God will send me a child! Then I'll know that I am forgiven, and that I'm a decent man like all the others!"

Yechiel gazed at the man, down whose great freckled cheeks tears were streaming. He could sympathize with Selig. For not so very long since he himself had felt crushed to the dust by the selfsame grief. God had taken pity on him: Reisel was at last with child. Yechiel felt like one who, on the point of drowning, finds himself on the bank of the stream; now he could hear another out there crying for help. He was prepared to spring into the stream and save the drowning man, even at the peril of endangering his own life again. And why should God deny His help to this man? Yechiel thought he could see God's sign dawning on the man's face and the marks of the Evil One fading. Did it not say in the Scripture that when a man repented God would help him, for God was a God of compassion? And had He not commanded us to strive to imitate His qualities, and therefore to be compassionate like Him?

"God will help you. I feel certain that God will help you."

Yechiel got up and laid his hand encouragingly on Selig's shoulder.

"Holy Rabbi, I shan't feel reassured unless you give me your word for it. Then I will have firm ground under my feet. Holy Rabbi, please," Selig stretched out his arms imploringly, "give me your word that God will have pity on me!"

"But I've promised you that God will help you!"

"No, no, Rabbi! You know yourself what it is I want! I want to be certain that I'm still worth something, and that God has forgiven me!"

Yechiel was firmly persuaded that God would forgive and help the man, and so he was surprised that Selig himself should not feel it. He became angry.

"What do you want? Am I to pledge God to do what you want?

Very well, I pledge the word of the Lord of the universe, and tell you that you will find comfort and that your wife will have a child! Are you satisfied now?"

Yechiel's words fell like hammer blows. Selig became as pale as death: God's word as a pledge! His mouth opened wide, as if to say something. Suddenly he convulsively seized Reb Israel by the arm.

"Come, Reb Israel! Choose the best horse in my stable!..."

Not till afterward did Yechiel realize what he had done. Horror seized him. He felt he was caught in a snare, from which he would never be able to free himself. He had assumed an obligation in the name of the Most High, had pledged God to fulfill it!

All night he lay on his face on the hard floor, beat his breast, and acknowledged his offense. A dull foreboding told him that all this could not end well. He had dared to tempt God! Now he recognized how perilous was the way into which he had allowed himself to be led.

Then a saving thought came to him: he would go to Kotzk. He had not seen his father for a long time, and could take this opportunity to fulfill the fourth commandment. And also he wanted to beg the great Rabbi Mendele to help him in keeping the obligation which he had assumed in God's name. With a trembling heart he wrote out a petition to the Rabbi from Selig, praying inwardly meanwhile that it might be successful....

Little Reb Melech escorted Yechiel to the sledge which would carry him over the frozen Vistula to Kotzk, and parted from him with the words, "Listen, Yechiel! Don't follow your father's example! Don't stay until we have to send for you! Don't forget that, with God's help, you'll soon be a father yourself."

As an old neighbor and a member of the Psalm Fellowship little Reb Melech arrogated the right to remind Yechiel of his obligations....

Reisel stared dumbly after the sledge, her heart heavy in her breast....

CHAPTER IX

GOD'S ARROWS

FROM his friend, Reb Feivush, Boruch-Moishe had already heard of Yechiel's miracles and other activities, and he was displeased that his son, instead of studying, should employ his time playing the Rabbi to the ignorant members of the Psalm Fellowship.

"I've been hearing fine stories about you!" Thus he greeted his son. "Of course, when ignorant people make you their Rabbi, there's nothing for it but to become a miracle worker! You've got yourself into trouble! The only thing that puzzles me is how anybody can dare to do such things. When one really knows a thing or two one doesn't make such a song about it! We in Kotzk aren't quite without knowledge, but we control our impulses!"

Yechiel stood beside his father like a servant before his master, as is commanded in the Law, and submitted humbly to the paternal rebuke. In the last few years Boruch-Moishe had aged greatly, and was now almost an old man. Of his thick hair little remained; his long, sparse side curls seemed to hang from vacancy. His gray beard had grown thin, and straggling strands of his side curls clung to what was left of his side whiskers; both were damp with the ritual baths that he was constantly taking. His head seemed nothing but hair and bone; it was as if he carried on his shoulders a skull from which hair sprouted. But in spite of all these marks of age he had grown still taller. Growth in old age is often the result of spiritual exaltation, which makes the body strive upward like a Gothic tower. Yechiel, tall himself, had to look up at his father; it seemed to him that his father's head reached the heavens.

Boruch-Moishe's clothes were no longer tattered and torn as they had been in Tomashov. The Rabbi's court in Kotzk had already become the spiritual center of the Chassidim of all Poland. All that was most important in the religious life of the Chassidim was concentrated there. For the more the Rabbi repulsed the people, the more enthusiastically they sought him.

The old men in Tomashov had been right. The Rabbi had not
achieved his aim—the establishment of a fellowship dedicated solely
to God. So he had completely withdrawn into his little secluded house,
and now admitted nobody. His sons and a few men drawn from his
intimate circle ruled in his name. They adopted a policy diametrically
opposed to the Tomashov one, and strove to attract prosperous pilgrims, so as to maintain an imposing court. Now everybody went
about in costly silks and furs. As one of the Rabbi's oldest followers,
Boruch-Moishe naturally enjoyed the advantage of the prosperous
times; he wore a silk caftan and a fur cap even on weekdays. So he
appeared before his son, who with bowed head confessed his guilt in
the matter of the horse dealer.

"Here's a fine story!" the father burst out sternly. "You've promised
a Jew that he'll have children! How could you do such a thing? Who
are you and what are you to have the temerity to pledge the name of
the Lord God?"

"I did it out of pity, father."

"Out of pity?" growled Boruch-Moishe rebukingly.

"Yes, father. I simply couldn't bear to see his sufferings. I'm convinced the Lord of the universe will help him. For He's a God of
compassion."

"Compassion?" Boruch-Moishe repeated the word. "Perhaps you
think that it's all pure pleasure for us here? I can tell you that we're
drowning in an ocean of tears. Come with me and I'll show you what
Jewish tears are. And yet—"

Boruch-Moishe did not finish his sentence. Instead he silently led
his son out of the big, noisy room where they had been talking, into
the courtyard of the Rabbi.

The "courtyard" was a square in which stood a great number of
wooden barracks. They were not set up in accordance with any plan,
but scattered about chaotically. When accommodation was required—a
new one was simply set up somewhere or other. This improvised town
of barracks separated the Rabbi's court from the wide, flat meadows
that stretched away outside. In the rooms lay sacks of straw. These
barracks served as night shelters for poor Chassidim who could find no
accommodation in the town hostels, which were generally full. They
were mainly used for this purpose during the great feast days, which
brought a great number of pilgrims to the court of the Rabbi. The rest
of the time they were occupied by men who were the target of God's
arrows, those of whom the Psalmist says: "Let their way be dark and

slippery: and let the angel of the Lord persecute them." And these men pierced by God's arrows, who still carried the deadly shafts in their breasts, came from every end of Poland to seek help and cure for their spiritual and bodily wounds at that sealed fountain known to the world as the Rabbi of Kotzk.

The winter was nearing its end. The frozen streams and pools were beginning to melt. The snowstorms and frosts which had bound the world in icy fetters all winter now loosened their grip, the hard mail confining the earth burst and dissolved and became a mighty river. That deluge had already swept over the Rabbi's courtyard and as usual had left a thick deposit of wet mud, which made the ground like a soft sponge saturated with water.

Father and son had to wade through mire up to the knees before they reached the wooden huts. Boruch-Moishe told his son to enter the first one. A heavy stifling fog met him in the face, he felt he was choking, and a hundred hammers began to beat in his head, for his entry was greeted by a bestial yelling and howling. When, in the feeble light, he at last managed to take in his surroundings, he was seized with terror. It seemed to him that before his eyes a mound of filth, offal, and rags was slowly piling itself up and falling to pieces. And these pieces of offal could move, were creeping nearer, were making for him. When his eyes were so far accustomed to the half-darkness with its foggy exhalations that he could distinguish separate details, he recognized in the moving lumps and tatters human beings. Only a few of them were actually coming toward him; the others remained lying where they were.

Presently he found himself surrounded by a wall of human bodies, heaped together in every conceivable position on the sacks of straw and the damp floor. And from them rose a dreadful concerted howling, pierced by shrill screams and yells which did not seem to issue from human throats at all. Nor indeed had they anything human in them; human voices could not have produced such cries. For these cries came from men and women whose throats were sealed by the curse of dumbness. Only the throats of the dumb could have produced the helpless and discordant cries that echoed through the room.

The howling and whimpering, on the other hand, came from people who were possessed by evil spirits. Physically quite sound, they were intellectually deformed. Among these unfortunate creatures all the forms of madness and insanity were represented—those poisonous weeds that flourish in the spongy soil of misery and destitution. Most of them, in their madness, imagined that they were possessed by demons and evil spirits who could find no peace in the other world.

It was a popular superstition that the souls of those who went to their graves burdened with sin, and who consequently had to return to earth again, were condemned to dwell in dung heaps and suchlike unclean places—that was the fate of drunkards and other human monsters, but more particularly of informers and apostates. They chose the young bodies of adolescent girls and youths, but sometimes also of pregnant women, and took possession of them. They sought refuge in other people's bodies, so as to escape the torments of hell. Like parasites they lived in bodies that were not their own, and used the senses and feelings of their victims for their own ends. In these bodies they led their own lives, made strange feet dance in their despairing agonies, made strange limbs jerk to their epileptic convulsions.

The innocent victims, bound and fettered, were often brought by their relations to that great redeemer, that lord over life and death, the Rabbi of Kotzk; for by his omnipotent word he could drive the evil spirits out of them and give them peace. He had merely to conjure the devils to leave them and torment them no longer. But if—as sometimes happened—the evil spirit refused to obey, he employed force and with words of excommunication tore it from its lurking place, as one tears a limb from a body.

In numbers the possessed were small, yet their terrible cries drowned the groans of those who were merely physically sick. Among these were many deformed children, who had been brought to Kotzk by their mothers in the hope that they might be cured by touching the Rabbi's robe or obtaining his blessing. Among them crouched blind men and women. They trembled from head to foot every time they heard the unearthly yells and shrieks of the possessed. When one of these "dybbuks," as they were popularly called, lifted his voice, the blind men would raise their sticks in terror, fearing that they were about to be attacked.

The deformed and blind were accompanied by all sorts of questionable figures—whether relatives or strangers, could not be said— who circled round them like vultures round a dead carcass. There were also huge, powerful women with masculine faces and strong arms, wrapped in half-rotten tatters which scarcely covered their nakedness, and men who, though human in form, looked more like gruesome beings from some other world. These were the professional beggars who always gathered where misery was to be found. Mingled with them were consumptives and men who were afflicted with frightful and quite unknown diseases; many of them had gone to all the doctors in the country without finding any help against their mysterious maladies.

In the hut were also men without any physical or mental malady, who simply liked to be with the sick, so as to warm themselves of the fevers of disease and slip under the blanket of pity which is so willingly extended to the suffering. All these wretched, homeless creatures, the really mad and the half-mad, the deformed in body and in mind, were warmed by the sultry exhalations sent out by their own bodies, which at least protected them from the cold striking from the damp sacks of straw on which they lay. They were like a smoldering heap of human refuse, a mound of rotting rags.

And that mound shivered now at the entrance of the two men, as if, suddenly shaken to its foundations, it had cracked and was about to fall into a thousand pieces. Father and son were surrounded by deformed cripples as by a wall of misery; a wall of diseased bodies, of legs cut off at the knee, of naked stumps rose about them. Weeping mothers held up to them, like banners or ensigns, their deformed children. Blind men stumbled up to them, felt their clothes, smelled them, greeted them with despairing cries. And in that howling chorus of human misery there were mingled the bestial yells and choked cries of madmen and souls possessed by the dybbuk.

Suddenly a figure started up before Yechiel's eyes. With the strength of a demon a girl flung herself toward him. From the rents of her tattered dress gleamed the smooth skin of a girlish arm, and a full young bosom shone from out her filthy rags like a rose from the gutter. Her disheveled red hair flowed like a cascade of fire down her face and neck; with her fingers convulsively clinched, she struggled against the gentle force with which her weeping mother and her father were trying to restrain her. But they could not suppress the bestial scream that was torn from her throat, and before the mother had time to stop her mouth she had poured out a torrent of obscene words in a choking voice, and in the language of a prostitute had challenged the two men to glut their lust on her body.

"Aren't you ashamed to speak like that, Surele? Oh, that I should see this day!" cried the mother, beating her head with her fists. "Forgive her, good people. It isn't my daughter who's saying these words! She's innocent. An evil spirit has entered into her, and is crying out of her now!"

Weeping loudly, the mother tried to stop her daughter's mouth with her hands. But the evil spirit was stronger—it cried through the girl's shut mouth as with convulsive fingers she tried to reach Yechiel.

"Silence, you shameless creature! Else the Rabbi will curse you and send you to the lowest circle of hell!" shouted Boruch-Moishe.

"Oh, good people, speak to the Rabbi for me and ask him to admit me! We've been here all winter waiting for the Rabbi to take pity on my daughter. She was betrothed. . . . Eight days before the wedding the evil spirit entered into her. . . . We know the spirit, we know who it is—a scandalous harlot who belonged to our town. . . . She can't find rest in the grave and so she chose my poor child's body to take refuge in. Oh, that I should see this day!" the poor woman wailed.

And her husband, who was trying to control the evil spirit with his powerful arms, cried in desperation, "Jews, have pity!"

With difficulty father and son extricated themselves by violently breaking a path for themselves through the living hedge of imploring outstretched arms. In silence they crossed the muddy courtyard, on which the shadows of the spring evening were falling.

"Now you know something of Jewish misery. But that isn't all. Come, I'll show you something! But see that you don't speak to any one you see; it might bring you disaster," said the father at last to his silent son.

He led Yechiel to the little house of the Rabbi. After Rabbi Mendele had withdrawn himself, the Chassidim had built for him a little low wooden house, which was connected by a long corridor with the House of Study. This passage was used only by distinguished persons belonging to the Rabbi's intimate circle when they wished to see him. He was strictly guarded; nobody was permitted near him but his attendant, Reb Hirsh of Tomashov. The Chassidim did not trust themselves to set foot on the long dark passage, for it was said that all sorts of strange figures were always to be found there.

And right enough, in the uncannily long and gloomy passage, Yechiel could see, moving about or leaning against the walls, strange shapes, supernaturally tall, with waxen faces yellow as parchment, which glimmered out of the half-darkness. In their pale faces their eyes, inflamed with lack of sleep, burned feverishly. These were men burdened with secret sins, some real, some imaginary, which tormented their consciences and filled their minds with pictures of hell;

men who lived in perpetual dread of being sent back after death to this world and condemned to enter the bodies of unclean beasts. People of this kind besieged the doors of all the Wonder Rabbis, hoping to be given some effectual act of penance to perform. The fame of the Rabbi of Kotzk exerted a quite unique attraction on them. For this man who was guarded so strictly behind lock and key had the reputation of possessing great power over spirits. That was the reason why these living corpses pilgrimaged to him and stood at his door, their lips sealed by the curse that rested on them. They stood there like dead men and waited for a faint glimmer of redemption to dawn for them. Nobody spoke to them; everybody avoided their gaze and indeed any communication with them.

"What are they?" asked Yechiel.

"Can't you see? They are people who are afraid they will find no rest in the next world. That's why they're standing before the Rabbi's door waiting for redemption."

When father and son returned to the House of Study the great room was already filled with dense shadows, so that the worshipers were scarcely discernible. Only the singsong of their voices could be heard. Here and there groups of Chassidim were saying their evening prayer. To cut off the lower part of their bodies from the higher, they had tied belts round their waists and rocked to and fro in ecstasy. Other groups sat in the corners listening in the twilight hour to the old men relating legends and miraculous tales. On the long table lay the books of the Law along with volumes of the Talmud, open, but covered with belts, shawls and other objects, for it was the hour of prayer. There was no general service, for the Rabbi was not present; the worshipers prayed singly or in groups as on a day of mourning.

At the top of the table lay an open folio with a shawl covering it. Opposite, against the wall, stood a tall man with black hair and beard shot with gray, his head thrown back. He was praying without moving; his body was as if hewn out of stone. So he stood, like a statue, stretched to his full height in motionless ecstasy. His face with its shut eyes was like an open book turned upward to Heaven. At a little distance stood a group of adoring youths, the disciples of the praying man; they contemplated their master, now rapt up to Heaven, with trembling joy and fear. Boruch-Moishe drew Yechiel's attention to the man by whispering.

"Do you see that man over there? He never moves when he prays. Do you know why? It says in the Bible: 'And Aaron did not move from the place.' So he holds that devotion requires no outward sign, but must burn like a flame in the heart of the faithful. Do you know who he is? He's the famous scholar, Reb Itche Mayer of Warsaw; the most intimate friend of the Rabbi. If he liked, he could cure everybody we saw in the courtyard by lifting his little finger!"

"Oh, why doesn't he do it, then? How can anyone look on the misery of Jews unmoved when he can help it?" asked Yechiel in astonishment.

"That's just what I was about to tell you. Even in such case one must have the strength to control one's impulses. For very often the Evil One assails us through pity. Pity is certainly a good quality, but it must go hand in hand with the Law. If it hasn't justice to support it, it is mere womanish sentimentality."

Yechiel did not venture to contradict this, out of reverence for his father. But his heart was heavy. For he could not understand the ways of these great people. . . .

Misery knocked at the Rabbi's door, but he, who meant help and redemption for the wretched, remained inaccessible.

Like the angel with the flaming sword, Reb Hirsh the attendant guarded the Rabbi's door with his broad chest, and morosely turned away anyone who dared to approach.

But on Friday everybody assembled in the courtyard. Then the Rabbi, escorted by his intimates, was conducted to the ritual bath; that was the only opportunity one had to see him, even from a distance.

Friday. Since early in the morning Yechiel had been standing with his father in the dense crowd, waiting for the Rabbi and his escort. The courtyard was black with Chassidim who were packed so closely together that they formed an almost impenetrable wall.

Suddenly from his place in the crowd Yechiel could see, creeping from the wooden huts and the nooks and corners of the courtyard, the maimed, the halt, the blind, and mothers bearing their deformed children in their arms. From the town, too, sick people were being borne on beds and chairs and set down before the bathing place. It was as if a devouring stream of misery were sweeping onward and was about to deluge the courtyard, the whole earth. The hour when the Rabbi came from the ritual bath was best—then his strength was renewed and all the founts of grace unsealed, then a kind word from his lips, a touch of his hand, even a glance from his pure eyes was sufficient to deliver body and soul from all visible or invisible fetters, to annul every curse, cure every sickness, inspirit the downcast, break every spell. The crowd swept on like a simoom blowing from some curse-laden region and bearing pestilence on its black wings. The sick lay in the gutters and the dirty melting snow, flung themselves down in puddles, and paved with their diseased bodies the way of the redeemer. . . .

Suddenly there broke out an animal-like howling, which sounded as if all the wretchedness of humanity had found speech.

"Holy Rabbi, help us!"

The men and women possessed by the dybbuk began to tear at their fetters and scream at the top of their voices.

Rabbi Mendele had entered the courtyard. He was returning from the bath with his escort. Because of the black-robed attendants who surrounded him on every side, the little man could scarcely be seen. He was almost buried under the long and heavy sable fur cloak which had been flung over him to protect him from the cold. Beneath his reddish fur cap gleamed the white side curls and beard, which framed his tiny face.

Like a tempest blowing from a region of pestilence, the crowd, the women with children in their arms, the blind, the halt, the epileptic, swept toward the approaching Rabbi.

"Holy Rabbi, help us!"

But a hundred-headed throng of Chassidim enveloped him like a thick black cloud, so that his white head seemed to float in the air and move forward along with his escort as if borne by their hands. In front of the black throng strode a gloomy angel with thick hair, beard, and eyebrows, Reb Hirsh the attendant. With a heavy cudgel he clove a way through the sea of misery that broke at the Rabbi's feet, and by merciless blows to right and left cleared a path for the redeemer. Enclosed behind the living wall of his escort, the Rabbi went on, but in spite of that protection the human cry pierced to his ears.

"Holy Rabbi, help us!"

The little old man frowned and muttered in his beard.

"Asses! Beasts! Why do you pester me? What do you want of me?"

That the crowd might not hear these rebukes the Rabbi's escort quickened their pace, and fearing that he might let loose his curse, carried him quickly back to his house.

Yechiel stood with a sore heart in a corner of the House of Study and lamented in the words of the Psalmist: "O my God, I cry in the daytime, but thou hearest not."

CHAPTER X

IN A GOLDEN CAGE

RABBI MENDELE sat alone in his room. It was Sabbath evening. Shadows were already gathering in the corners of the room. On the table the third Sabbath meal was set out: the symbolical twelve little white rolls of bread. The Rabbi was taking his third Sabbath meal quite alone, just as he prayed alone and studied alone. From the House of Study he could hear the yearning melodies which mourned the passing of the Sabbath. The followers were already assembling for the supper which the Rabbi's son and deputy gave to the fellowship of the Chassidim. But the Rabbi of Kotzk sat alone at his table, and troubled thoughts assailed him now at the passing of the Sabbath.

Kotzk was not like Tomashov. Here he was held firmly fettered— by the young wife whom he had married in his old age, by his son, his sons-in-law, his immediate circle, even his attendant Reb Hirsh of Tomashov. In his youth, when he resided in Tomashov and his first wife was alive, he had driven away the rich, kept dealers and merchants at a distance, and compelled his Chassidim to work and to study the Law. Oh, he hadn't tolerated any idlers round him; he would rather have let his whole court starve than accept gifts or allow anything to divert him from his lofty aims. In those days everything had to be done in God's name: prayer, study, even the most menial daily work.

But now everybody accepted gifts. A ceremonial court had arisen, and formed a thick wall round him. Yes, this new life shut him in a barred cage. He had tried to fight, tried to exorcise this abomination. Then they had shut him up in his little house like an idol, had watched over him as if he were a flame, in perpetual fear lest he should set everything on fire and destroy all they had built up. They never let him out of their sight, for he might sometimes let drop a harsh word and ruin the whole business! Finally he himself had wished, more, commanded them to leave him in his seclusion, for he no longer desired to see what they were doing round him, no longer could endure to see them paying court to the rich and giving banquets as if it were the time of King Solomon. No, he had no wish to see it, that hateful outside world. It consisted on the one hand of slaves, who walked the treadmill of daily hardship, worms whose eyes, blinded by poverty, could not see God's light, and on the other of gluttons for whom the whole world was too small, and who tried to beg and wheedle a little share in the next world by a gift, an alms, a Sabbath meal, so as to possess it too. And the Jews danced round these creatures as they had danced once round the golden calf. They were all of them equally beggars—the poor begged for a part in this world, the rich for a part in the next. . . . No, he wanted to have nothing to do with such a life; he preferred to bury himself in his own thoughts, to scratch at the wall of the "infinite" as they did at his door, and like them—to get no answer.

The room in which the Rabbi sat was not like his room in Tomashov. Without his noticing it, they had locked him in a golden cage. Fine mahogany bookcases lined the walls, round the great table were ranged comfortable armchairs, the massive candlesticks were of silver. He had already carried them out to the courtyard several times and given them away to beggars, but his attendant always took them away again and set them back on the table. There was also a Torah roll in the room, in a carved ark with an expensive curtain fashioned by pious women out of their bridal dresses, out of fine Lyons silk and pure gold brocade.

The Rabbi himself wore, instead of the ragged, quilted caftan that he had worn in Tomashov, a thick velvet dressing gown. However, he never noticed how he was clad. A broad prayer shawl, whose sacred fringes trailed on the floor after him, quite hid the dressing gown. The heat which a newfangled Dutch-tiled stove, a gift from a rich Chassid, sent through the room was equally unremarked by him. A costly fur cap of gleaming sable sat on his unkempt gray hair. His eyebrows jutted out over his eyes like penthouses. His short, sparse beard, snow-white except for a yellow patch in the middle caused by a careless use of snuff, rested on his breast. So Rabbi Mendele sat in the darkness before his supper table, with his hands pushed into the wide sleeves of his dressing gown. The attendant Hirsh stood at the door keeping guard on his master and also on the Chassidim, lest someone might dare to disturb the hermit's solitude. And at that holy moment of the Sabbath's passing the Rabbi seemed to be actually sleeping. But no, he was not asleep. The heavy sighs which stirred his white beard as it rested on his breast were not caused by physical weariness, but by disappointed hopes, despondent self-contemplation; for the Rabbi of Kotzk was not satisfied with himself.

What had he achieved in all these years? He had scratched a little at the gate of the "infinite," had stretched out his hand toward Heaven; but in reality what progress had he made? "She has no breasts," Rabbi Reb Bunem had once said of knowledge. How true! Knowledge had no source within itself from which it could draw strength.

Quite near him, in the House of Study, his followers were holding the Princess Sabbath as fast as a prisoned bird, and would not let her go. They did not light the lights, that they might forget the week and its cares, and they greeted the departure of the king's daughter with melancholy songs. The Rabbi could hear these yearning melodies through the wall of his room. And he too was overcome with longing for the Princess Sabbath and her grace, which now—he could feel it— was departing from him and leaving him with nothing but her every-day feelings, with nothing but his righteousness. Soon the gates of Hell would reopen again, in the sky as on the earth. The Rabbi felt no desire to recite grace and begin his Sabbath supper. He sat forlornly at his table. The food before him was still untouched; he too wished to prolong the Sabbath.

Darkness fell in the room, at first slowly, then more and more quickly. Finally veil after veil of darkness settled down, until the Rabbi was enveloped in profound night. He thought of his youth in Przysucha with the Holy Jew. And now he remembered too the words which the Holy Jew had once said to him: "Reflect, Mendele, that there is a test for every being, by means of which one can tell whether it is genuine, just as one can tell gold or silver. The test by which one can tell a Jew is love for Israel. For a Jew is a Jew just in so far as he loves Israel." Had he, Mendele, stood the test that his teacher had imposed on him?

In that hour of tragic conflict between the Sabbath and everyday he remembered his fellow student and teacher, Rabbi Reb Bunem, who so loved his kind that for the sake of another Jew he was prepared even to commit sin; and his friend, the Rabbi of Vorka, who had taken upon himself the noble work of setting free the prisoners, and whose house had been an asylum and place of refuge for the suffering and the persecuted, whose heart had been open to all the sighs and groans of suffering mankind, whose eyes had been dimmed with all the tears he had shed. And what had he himself done, he, the Rabbi of Kotzk?

But the Rabbi of Kotzk refused to capitulate so easily. "I'm no pastry cook; God hasn't given me a tray of honey cakes to distribute! It says in the Psalms: 'Blessed is the man whom thou chastisest, Lord, and teachest by thy law.' Man wasn't created to gorge himself full of good works; he was created to penetrate into the deepest secrets of the higher worlds."

And in the darkness that filled the room Rabbi Mendele once more beheld the vision that had risen before him so often of late, and so clearly mirrored his resignation. He longed for his teachers, and particularly for the Holy Jew, whom he had secretly envied all his life. For the Holy Jew had achieved something which he, the Rabbi of Kotzk, had never regarded or valued sufficiently—love for Israel. Only now, in his old age, did Rabbi Mendele realize what power resided in love of one's fellow men.

On the wings of imagination he soared up to Heaven. He could still do that! Whenever he felt the desire, and concentrated his will upon it, the loftiest heavens opened to him. He wandered from heaven to heaven, higher and higher, ascended to hall after hall where the righteous dwelt. He knew the magic names by which the angels guarding every door of the heavenly halls could be made to obey. Oh, up there they knew who the Rabbi of Kotzk was and admitted him!

The walls were of gold and precious stones. The righteous sat in a long row on golden chairs, and rejoiced in the spectacle of God's glory. Many of them were well known to the Rabbi.

But neither the heavenly halls nor the righteous interested him particularly. He sought his teacher, the Holy Jew. "Isn't the Holy Jew here with you?" he asked. They said no. And suddenly the Rabbi of Kotzk floated in the radiant infinitude of Heaven. He looked round. A fresh green meadow, and in the middle, beside a clear blue river, stood a little bent-backed, white-haired old man, supported on a stick, and gazing pensively into the water. The Rabbi recognized him at once. It was his teacher, the Holy Jew. "Rabbi, is that the fountain of knowledge that you are looking into?" he cried, and tried to float down to him. But a flaming angel barred his way: "That is the fountain of love, but you may not approach it, for the fountain of love is made of tears, and you never shed any!"

Now in his old age, as he sat at his lonely Sabbath meal, the Rabbi of Kotzk felt that the falling of a tear was a thing far more unfathom-

able than the ocean of infinity. For only tears could help him to overcome the star of Edom with whom in his latter years he had taken up
battle in Heaven. Jewish tears were the sole effectual weapon in the
deadly war which, unknown to the whole world, was being waged between the Rabbi of Kotzk and the ruthless Czar of Russia, Nicholas I.

In the year 1842 Nicholas I extended the law of military service,
previously valid only for Russian Jews, to embrace Polish Jews too.
So as to habituate the Polish Jews, who were completely foreign to
Russian ways, to strict military discipline, boys of from ten to twelve
were torn from their mothers and their schools, stuck into uniform,
and put in barracks. To withdraw them from the strict religious way
of life in which they had been brought up, they were sent to remote
provinces of the huge empire and there lodged in seminaries under
strict military supervision, where they were ruthlessly punished for
the slightest violation of discipline. They were forced to infringe the
customs of their religion, made to eat forbidden food, desecrate the
Sabbath, transgress every precept that they had drunk in with their
mother's milk, and break with the holiest axiom of their religious up-
bringing, that which says: Better suffer a thousand deaths than commit such sin. And in truth many of these boys chose death. They
endured indescribable tortures that they might fulfill the command
which their mother gave them on parting: Better die than fall off from
the faith. Thousands upon thousands of children suffered the death of
martyrs at that time.

Lamentation rose in all the Jewish houses of Poland. The synagogues were packed, days of fasting were proclaimed. But it was to
the Rabbis that the people chiefly turned. They were implored to move
Heaven by their prayers until the law was repealed.

In the eyes of the Jewish people, the Rabbi of Kotzk was the greatest man of his age, and on him the eyes of all Israel were fixed. For
this time it was not a matter merely of an individual fate, the ax was
laid to the roots of Jewry; the foundation on which the whole edifice
rested was tottering. Rabbi Mendele regarded the Czar's step as a
declaration of war on the God of Israel. The Jews were, so he argued,
a holy people, owing allegiance to one master only, the Lord of the
universe; they were God's soldiers, the people whom the Lord had
chosen that they might dedicate themselves to Him. To Him alone belonged the Jewish children, whether they were at their mothers'
breasts, or at school where they studied His Law and prepared for His
service, the service of God. And now came a foreign ruler who, having

conquered Poland, wanted to compel the Jews to serve him all their days! No, that must not be!

The Rabbi of Kotzk did not wage his war against the Czar on earth or with earthly weapons, but in the higher worlds. For the Czar had no real say; he was merely the tool of his heavenly star. The source of his power was his heavenly prince. And the heavenly prince of Czar Nicholas was the Prince of Edom, Amalek, the archenemy of the Jews, the original source of all malice. And the Rabbi had resolved on nothing less than the overthrow of the Prince of Edom, the extermination of the root which supported the Czar. When Nicholas's star fell up above, the Czar must fall on earth.

One day the Rabbi had brought to him a soldier's coat such as the Jewish boys wore at the Czar's decree. Then he opened the Torah ark, held up the coat before the sacred roll and in a heart-rending voice repeated the words which Jacob's sons uttered when they brought Joseph's coat to their father: "This have we found: know now whether it be thy son's coat or no." But the Rabbi of Kotzk's despairing cry died away unheard. For the only weapon with which he could fight the Prince of Edom in Heaven was a tear wrung from a Jewish heart, that was the only key which could open the gates of compassion. And tears were denied him.

Yet the Rabbi of Kotzk was not a man who could be dismissed with a wave of the hand. He counted for something in Heaven, and there were his teachers. "If they ban me to Hell I'll take my teachers with me," was one of his sayings. "For it says in the Scripture that if you drive away the pupil you drive away the teacher at the same time." And the Rabbi of Kotzk was resolved not to ask any favor for himself —God forbid—he had never asked anything for himself, for his motto was: "Be a beggar on earth that you might become a lord in Heaven!" Nor did he ask God for any favors for others; he never begged. He *demanded* what the Law sanctioned, keeping to the Law of Moses, which was valid for God Himself. If you were bound to one master you could not serve another at the same time. So the Rabbi demanded his rights in the name of the Law. And when he received no answer, he called his teachers to his assistance. He could not reach them, however, for they were standing up there beside the fountain of tears, which was sealed to him. So he summoned them to his room.

He would sit in judgment on God with his teachers. Yes, he demanded a true verdict in accordance with the Law and justice; for God had delivered His holy people into the hands of strangers. The righteous up there in Heaven sat comfortably in their splendid halls and left all the burden on him. They leaned elegantly on their sticks and contemplated themselves in the fountain of Jewish tears. Was this a time to rejoice in the spectacle of God's glory? "My creatures sink in the flood, and you sing songs of joy?" God had said to the Jews, according to the holy books, when the Egyptians were drowning in the Red Sea.

"I conjure you, my teachers," he cried in the darkness, "you, Holy Jew, you, Rabbi Reb Bunem, and you, Reb Yitzchak, forsake your golden chairs in Paradise, descend to me, and see what is being done to the children of the people whom God chose as His own!"

Out of the dense darkness that filled the room emerged the forms of three old men with snow-white hair. The Rabbi saw their white robes outlined against the dark walls: the little Holy Jew, the tall Reb Bunem, and the bent Reb Yitzchak. The Rabbi of Kotzk rose to greet his teachers, and made to call Hirsh his attendant, so that he might set chairs at the table for his guests. But the three white-haired old men had already seated themselves and the Rabbi thought he could hear them saying, "Rabbi of Kotzk, we have come to share your Third Meal."

The Rabbi interrupted them sharply.

"To share my Third Meal? In the halls up above we'll have time enough for this! Hirsh, light the candles: we must sit in judgment on the Prince of Edom!" he cried, turning toward the door.

But when the attendant entered with the candles, the guests were gone and the Sabbath as well....

Nearby, in the House of Study, the Rabbi's son was sitting with the Chassidim at their Third Meal, the meal of grace. Reb Itche-Mayer of Warsaw, the "guide to new paths," was giving an exposition of the Law. His interpretations were very profound and very hard to understand. In compensation there was much singing. The crowd of men were clenched and smelted into one black mass. And that mass moved to a single rhythm, to the time of a song which came from the single white glimmering patch in the middle of the room, the table. That glimmering white patch was the only remaining vestige of the Sabbath still left uncovered by the drowning waves of darkness. And no one wished to leave the last "Sabbath island." They fought against the rapacious black shadows that flung themselves upon the yearning chorus, the rhythmical motion of that mass of bodies.

The faces of the men were turned toward the door that led to the Rabbi's room. Through that little portal great joy might enter, the holy reflection of divinity, which the Rabbi symbolized on earth. The children of Heaven yearned to behold the shining of that "little light," and the rhythm of their song strove persistently toward the shut door, which led to the "ancient shrine," the Rabbi's room.

"Friend of my soul, Father of compassion, make Thy will manifest in Thy servant. Thy servant would fly to Thee like a doe, to bow down before Thy beauty. Thy friendship is sweeter to him than honey...."

They had not yet given up hope of seeing the Rabbi. Suddenly the door would open and he would appear. As passionately as they yearned for the great Messiah, they waited now for the little Messiah, the Rabbi. Their expectation mounted to more and more ecstatic heights; they wished that every moment of their life might slip by in sweet, rapturous expectation. Longing bears within it the kernel of fulfillment; it is the bud of the blossom, the seed of the fruit. Expectation is the beginning of realization, and intimately bound up with it; through expectation one at last achieves fulfillment.... And so the shadowy crowd rocked in ecstatic time to the rhythm of the song, which mounted and mounted to a burning prayer.

"Beautiful One, Light of the world, my soul is sick for love of Thee. I beseech Thee, O God, heal it. Appear Thou in Thy heavenly glory, and it will grow strong and whole again and joy in Thee for ever...."

A living part of the mass, Yechiel, too, rocked in time to the singing. He felt as though he were a pure longing and nothing else. Now he understood what Kotzk meant. And that was much—a great desire and striving for the holy Light, a resolve not to be content with some scrap of earthly possession. After all, how much could a man possess? How much could he take into himself? Longing and striving were more than possession. For man's thirst was infinite and that with which he could quench it was wretchedly small....

Yechiel rocked in time with the others in a constantly mounting ecstasy, clung desperately like them to the last gleam of the Sabbath, already drowning in the shadows of night, drank in greedily every breath of longing: "O appear, my Beloved, and cover me with Thy wings!"

Yet at the same time Yechiel's heart was elsewhere, with the simple members of the Psalm Fellowship, who gave thanks for their little scrap of worldly goods on the Sabbath evening and sang God's praises with a full heart. These doings here, he thought in a flash, are all very well for the great, who are not afraid to venture into the spaces of loneliness and seek out new paths. But for him, Yechiel, the path of the Psalms, which the simple village Jews had made for themselves, was good enough. . . .

CHAPTER XI

THE CALL

PRAYERS offered up among the sick and wretched are quickly heard, according to the words of the Psalmist: "The Lord is nigh unto them that are of a broken heart." So Yechiel went to one of the huts where the sick were housed, and in a corner near the door softly recited his prayers. The occupants did not notice him. In these rooms, never very light, it was quite dark long before evening fell.

Yechiel already possessed the ability to efface his personal feelings and completely divorce himself from his ego. So he stood for a long time motionless, quite without thought, until he was independent of his body. When he had achieved this neutral depersonalized state, he could enter into any situation which his imagination presented to him. As he now stood sunk in prayer among these unfortunate wretches he pictured to himself that he was one of the sick, that his body was covered with sores, that his flesh was a festering mass, and that he had only enough life to feel the goading spur of pain. He saw himself before God as a trampled worm—who was this wretched man to flatter himself that he was higher than other creatures? A host for passions and lusts, self-deceptions, envies and hatreds that crawled on his flesh like loathsome worms.

Thus Yechiel cut into his own heart that he might be as the wretches round him, and become one of them.

He stood crouching in the darkest corner of the shed and was now one of its occupants, a drop in a sea spewed out by misery. The sick moaned, the sound fought over the scraps of bread which kindhearted housewives had collected and brought to them. All at once uncanny shrieks burst out and some one shouted.

"Hold her! Don't let go! Hold her!"

The shrieks came from the lips of the red-haired girl who was possessed by a dybbuk. They were warning signals of the convulsive outbreaks which the poor girl was subject to; when they came she would fling herself in a mad fury on everybody near her. Her animal-like instinct had divined Yechiel's presence before any of the others. Her unfortunate father and mother had drilled into her a deep fear of the Rabbi, who, they told her, could by force drive the dybbuk out of her. As soon as she discovered Yechiel she felt certain that he was the Rabbi, come to drive the dybbuk out of her by his prayers. This was the reason for her terrible cries, which, convulsively bursting from her strangled throat, produced a sound as if she were being throttled by a hundred demons. She tore her hair, twitched convulsively, and struck at everything round her with her hands and feet, screaming.

"He's whipping me! He's beating me! Oh! Oh! He's tearing me limb from limb!"

"Who, my poor child, who?"

"Him there, in the corner!"

The girl's shrieks set the other mad people going. The blind, who could not see what was happening, raised their arms and sticks in that panic terror which so often seizes people who have lost their sight, and prepared to defend themselves against the unknown danger. The terrified children wept loudly, and such a shrieking and wailing rose in the room that one might have imagined that the occupants were being tortured by invisible demons. At last they discovered Yechiel in his corner; torn out of his absorption by the din, he gazed round him in amazement.

During the whole period of their stay at the Rabbi's court, these sick people had been firmly persuaded that something extraordinary must happen to them. Suddenly the Rabbi would appear in the room like an angel from Heaven and deliver them from their sicknesses by his blessing or his curse. When they heard the mad girl's cry, "He's beating me!" they thought that a holy man must be with them, whose presence was unendurable to the dybbuk.

The dense darkness of the room was faintly lit by the feeble glimmer of a brazier, at which the inmates cooked their meals and warmed themselves. Now they all rushed to the brazier, and snatched from it half-charred brands of wood so as to light up the dark shadow beside the door, toward whom the mad girl was trying to struggle. The uncertain flickering light from these smoldering brands at first only increased the panic among the inmates. The whole room was seized with terror.

"If the dybbuk cries out like that, it's certainly seen something!"

"Don't you see him? There, beside the door!"

"Holy Rabbi, help us!"

In an instant Yechiel was surrounded by outstretched arms, which strove toward him like tongues of fire. A wall of misery rose up before him. Spectral shadows, grotesquely swathed in fluttering rags, whirled in a wild dance round him; he heard uncanny echoing shrieks, saw eyes lit with the clairvoyant fire of madness. It was like a mad dance on the razor edge between damnation and redemption, between despair and hope. The circle of madness surrounded him, helplessly ringed him in. Women pressed deformed children into his arms, blind men desperately fought a path to him, trampling on whoever stood in their way, and felt Yechiel with their hands and fingers, which served them in place of eyes. The mother of the mad girl flung herself upon him with all the strength of her desperate longing for help. Her hands clung to him with iron force.

"Holy man, help my poor child!"

"Holy Rabbi, help my sick mother!... I've been here all winter. ... Holy Rabbi, look on my misery, I can't endure it any longer!" So they assailed Yechiel on every side. They fought for him like wolves for a scrap of flesh flung into their cage.

Their despairing shrieks and wails could be heard in the House of Study and the street. Men, women, and children rushed up from every side. And as so often happens in such cases, strange news presently began to go round about the event of the day.

"If the sick people cried like that, they must have felt something out of the common in him."

Others said, "It was the Rabbi himself that went to the sick people's shed...."

"No, it wasn't the Rabbi, it was a good Jew who's staying with the Rabbi...."

At last some men managed to deliver Yechiel from the raging crowd. Like a lamb delivered from a cage full of wild beasts, he was carried—not very gently, it must be admitted, for the Chassidim were highly indignant at the incident—half-conscious into the House of Study. Boruch-Moishe's son, that ignoramus who played the miracle worker among the yokels in the village, that witless Rabbi (Yechiel's past was already known in Kotzk through Chassidim who had come from his birthplace) who dared to do such things in Kotzk, where men like Rabbi Mendele, Reb Itche-Mayer, and other good Jews of great reputation lived! In Kotzk, where wonder-workers were not considered worth a farthing, where the Rabbi drove away the sick, he dared to play such tricks in Kotzk! All the four death penalties of the Jewish Law would be too mild a punishment for such a crime.

The angry Chassidim laid Yechiel on the long table in the Lesson House and belabored him with their fists. With voluptuous pleasure they unstrapped their belts, tied knots in them, and swung them through the air to test them.... But meanwhile Boruch-Moishe had hurried to the Rabbi, had violently forced his way in, and told everything. And just when the execution upon Yechiel was about to begin, Hirsh the attendant rushed in. With his powerful arms he pushed aside everybody who stood in his way, made a path for himself, and supporting himself on one of the men's shoulders shouted in a loud voice:

"Don't touch him! The Rabbi has summoned him to his room!"

This announcement did not fail of its effect. The men gazed at each other in rigid amazement and a murmuring arose.

"The Rabbi has summoned him to the Holy of Holies. There's certainly something behind this.... Hush.... Hush!"

This last turn of events completely deprived Yechiel of his senses. A jug of cold water was hastily brought; with almost reverential solicitude Yechiel's assailants helped him to a seat, and tried to restore him to consciousness. When he presently came to himself, Hirsh and his father, who had also arrived now, led him, amid the wondering glances of everybody, into the Holy of Holies.

Rabbi Mendele was devoted to his Tomashov Chassidim. They reminded him of his years of power, when he still hoped to reach the higher spheres. For this reason he had a great opinion of Boruch-Moishe, who also had known the Holy Jew. So he was curious to see Boruch-Moishe's son, who had taken upon himself to perform such things.

And now young Yechiel was standing before him; his pale face looked paler because of the young pitch-black beard that framed it. His side curls, lips, and hands were trembling with terror at what he had just passed through and with fear of the Rabbi. Ashamed, he stood looking at the floor.

The Rabbi slowly pushed up with his hand the jutting eyebrows which almost covered his eyes, and regarded Yechiel piercingly.

"Hm, hm!—but the sign of God is very clear here," the Rabbi muttered to himself, rising with an almost kind look. Then he hid his eyes behind his brows again, seized his snuffbox, and took a pinch. For a long time he was silent, as if he wished to deliberate with himself, and then, still sunk in thought, stretched out his hand to Yechiel in greeting, and said, "Sholem aleichem!"

For a long time he held Yechiel's hand in his. He could feel through the skin the violent pulsing of Yechiel's blood, the restless beating of his heart, all his fear of God. And he remembered the years when he too had been young, when he too had been reluctant to learn from the deeds of others, and had striven instead to attempt himself every divinely decreed good work, to make live anew every commandment, to pluck it like a ripe fruit from the tree, to renew the sphere both of prayer and of study. A warm rush of affection for the young man filled the Rabbi's old heart. He recognized in Yechiel himself as he had once been, and he did not want to let go that trembling young hand. He longed for that fresh young life to stream into his own old veins.

Still holding Yechiel's hand, he said, "He's trembling! Hirsh, let him have a chair."

Such a thing had never happened before. The Rabbi had actually asked a Chassid, and a young newcomer at that, to sit in his presence!

As the attendant's amazement could clearly be read in his face, Reb Mendele added in self-justification, "You can see for yourself, he can scarcely stand on his feet."

But in spite of the Rabbi's command, and the imperious sign which his father gave him, Yechiel absolutely refused to sit down.

"When a Rabbi renounces the respect that is due to him, he must not be taken at his word," he quoted, stammeringly.

"Do you hear that, Hirsh? He's no dunce, this lad!" said the Rabbi, with an indulgent smile. "But how does he come to do such silly tricks? Give him a sip of brandy."

Behind the thick curtain of his brows Rabbi Mendele attentively observed Yechiel's behavior; he saw Yechiel's hand trembling so that the brandy almost ran over his fingers, watched him saying the grace, taking a sip at first, then drinking to the company and emptying the glass. The Rabbi followed his every movement. His old heart was made young by the magic of his love for the young man.

Revived somewhat by the brandy, Yechiel became for the first time fully conscious of his surroundings. His heart flamed up with love for the Rabbi. He raised his eyes with such a beseeching and tearful glance that the Rabbi was overcome.

Yechiel stammered, "God is my witness that I went to the place with no other intention than that of observing the words of the Scripture: 'Out of the deeps I cry to thee, O Lord.' What place can lie deeper than that where Jewish tears flow?"

"Jewish tears—" The Rabbi reflectively stretched out his hand for his snuffbox. After a short pause he continued. "It says in the Bible: 'A holy people shall ye be to me.' This means that all humanity shall be holy. Certainly, it is a great thing to help one's fellow men, if one can . . ." the Rabbi concluded, more to himself than to Yechiel.

"Holy Rabbi—" began Yechiel hesitatingly, but fell silent again at once.

Rabbi Mendele gazed at him questioningly.

"What does he want?" he asked, turning to Boruch-Moishe.

"He would like to hand a petition to you, Holy Rabbi. He has done a foolish thing—given a promise to a Jew. Now he is afraid that the promise, God forbid, will not be fulfilled." The father seized the opportunity to bring his son's thoughtless act to the Rabbi's notice.

With a trembling hand Yechiel pulled his psalm book out of the ragged pocket of his caftan, opened it, and took out of it the scrap of parchment on which was written Selig's petition. Rabbi Mendele raised his brows and gazed attentively at the sheet of parchment, as if he were not examining the writing merely but the parchment as well. There were one or two splotches on it; he guessed that these marks were made by Yechiel's tears. For a long time he silently held the sheet in his hand, then he said in a surprised voice, "Why does he bring me a petition that has been granted long ago?"

Son and father started in terror. Yechiel trembled like a leaf; Boruch-Moishe could scarcely trust his ears and did not dare to utter a word. The Rabbi pushed back his chair, rose to his feet, and began to walk up and down the room, muttering to himself, as if in annoyance.

"Incredible! Now they bring me petitions that are already granted!"

These words did not express the thought that profoundly moved him in his heart. Now he understood why the sick people in the shed had flung themselves on Yechiel and begged him to help them; now he saw what the mad girl had divined in him: for the wretched sometimes see further than the upright. They had guessed his power, their broken hearts had felt drawn to him. They had felt that he could help them. But he, the Rabbi of Kotzk, could no longer see clearly; his eyes no longer possessed the power they once had had of recognizing the sign of God. He knew only too well the reason: he was kept in a golden cage, he was not allowed to do what he wanted. The Rabbi's

heart contracted. It was not jealousy, God forbid! The Rabbi of
Kotzk was above jealousy. But the warmth in this strange young man
made him feel his own coldness, and he was filled with dejection.
He remembered his youth, when the instinct of the people had divined
something great in him. A slight trace of irritation was also mixed
with his other feelings: how easy everything came to this young man!
In Przysucha they had had to root in the earth with their noses
before they could bring off such things, they had had to leave wife
and children, spend long years with their Rabbi: first with the Holy
Jew, and then with Rabbi Reb Bunem. And the ages they had to
spend in seclusion, the fights they had to wage with themselves, the
mountains they had to climb and the precipices they had to learn to
avoid! And this young man, who had gone through nothing, who had
remained tied to his wife's apron strings all the time, who possessed
nothing but a little faith—he brought it off at one stroke and arrived
with a petition that was already fulfilled! Still, all this might turn
out to be the Rabbi of Kotzk's advantage yet, he could do with another
henchman! And the young man had the divine fire in him! Rabbi
Mendele turned to the father.

"Boruch-Moishe, why don't you keep him beside you here?"

"I've been telling him that all the time, holy Rabbi," replied
Boruch-Moishe with a pleased smile, now that he could see with his
own eyes how Yechiel stood. "All these scrapes he gets into would
stop if he would listen to me," he added with a sigh in which was
expressed all his paternal pride.

"Good. Leave me now," the Rabbi commanded.

"Come!" The father tugged Yechiel by the arm.

"Let him stay."

Boruch-Moishe and Hirsh stared at the Rabbi openmouthed. When
they grasped the position at last they stole on tiptoe from the room.

The Rabbi led Yechiel to the window and pointed to the crowd in
the courtyard.

"Young man, if you want to help these people, you must be prepared to pay for it with your own flesh and blood."

Yechiel turned pale.

"And if you pledge God's word, you must also be able to redeem
it!"

Yechiel bowed his head in silence.

"You may go."

When Yechiel was at the door, the Rabbi shouted after him, "Per-

haps you think it will be easy for you? We've all set out on the unknown road and returned again pretty battered...."

To his father's great annoyance Yechiel went home again and returned to his Psalm Fellowship. He knew that there was work in
store for him, and he was prepared to do anything, as long as it was
to God's glory.

CHAPTER XII

THE SIGN

REISEL was very ill. Yechiel remained all day in the Psalm Room, his heart filled with dark premonitions. The members of the Psalm Fellowship stood by him; they left their work and recited psalms in the little low room with their Rabbi. For poor Reisel was in great pain. Her groans and shrieks were like whip blows to Yechiel; he knew that she was being punished for his sins, and took all the guilt upon himself. Reisel died after giving birth to a dead child. The skill of the midwife and the surgeon was so primitive that blood poisoning supervened, as very often happened in such cases at that time.

A month after his interview with the Rabbi of Kotzk, Yechiel found himself for a second time bereaved.

He was firmly convinced that he was solely to blame. He had sacrificed his Reisel without desiring it, without guessing that he would have to pay so dearly for the promise he had made to the horse dealer. With dry eyes he gazed up to Heaven and recited in a firm voice the verse of the Psalms: "I am dumb, I open not my mouth; because thou didst it."

And he kept his word. So as to put the Psalmist's precept into practice he resolved in penance for his sins to wander through the country as a poor unknown vagrant.

He would remain in his self-imposed exile until a sign was given him that he was forgiven for the sin of pledging God's name, which had brought such grief upon him. After the week of mourning, Yechiel made preparations to leave the town. He was assailed on every side with petitions to stay. His despairing parents-in-law tried to persuade him.

"We've lost *one* child—must we lose you too?"

Shloime-Wolf simply refused to let him go, for Yechiel was still to him the crown of his existence, the joy and meaning of his life. He clung to him desperately.

"Let me provide you with what you need, at least!"

Boruch-Moishe had come from Kotzk to comfort his son. When he heard of Yechiel's intention, he shrugged his shoulders disapprovingly.

"It's simply a waste of your time: you have better things to do."

Besides, Boruch-Moishe had strict injunctions from Kotzk to bring Yechiel there.

"You must see yourself where your obstinacy is leading you—haven't you learned your lesson yet?" Boruch-Moishe warned his son.

But one morning Yechiel was gone. Of his belongings all that he took with him was a bag containing his prayer shawl and phylacteries. With these he set out on his way. He changed clothes with the first wandering beggar that he met. In a few days he looked so unkempt, so completely changed, that his own mother would not have known him.

He passed his nights on trusses of straw in doss houses, and he never stayed more than one day in the same place. He wandered from town to town, sometimes in the company of beggars, sometimes alone, without ever accepting a lift or indulging himself in any comfort. He chose as his companions the most wretched cripples he could find, so that he might help them on their way.

When asked for his name and birthplace, he gave no reply. Consequently he was taken to be a grievous sinner who had been commanded by his Rabbi to take to a life of wandering as a penance. Such men were not rare at that time, and Yechiel looked upon himself as one of them. It was because of him and his sins—of that he was convinced—that Reisel had had to leave the world so prematurely. He had killed her, he had her death on his conscience. His guilt crushed him. He, Yechiel, had tried in his arrogance and blindness to tempt God. For that he had had to pay with the lives of his wife and child. That had been the meaning of the Rabbi's words: "If you want to help these people, you must be prepared to pay for it with your own flesh and blood." Yes, that was true. The burden which he had taken in God's name from another man's shoulders had been put on his own. And so he waited for a sign announcing that he was forgiven.

For a long time he wandered from town to town in beggar's garb. Presently he forgot that he had ever lived in any other way, had ever looked differently from what he looked now. All the week through he patiently bore his self-imposed wretchedness; but on Friday evening his sufferings ceased; he went to the baths, and begged a pail of hot water from the attendant that he might wash himself. Then he took his station at the door of the House of Study and waited like the other beggars for a ticket to the free table. Yet not till all the others had been given the tickets that assured them their food and their Sabbath did he too venture to ask for one.

In spite of his rags, Yechiel stood out from his companions. The devoutness with which he prayed attracted people's attention, his retiring modesty won their hearts. His readiness to help made friends for him, even among the most wretched of his wandering companions.

Often he grew weary of his wanderings. Then he would stay for a little while at some House of Study and employ his time in studying the Scripture. The little food that he required he earned by relieving the attendant of his more menial work. His honesty and piety raised him out of the ruck of wandering vagrants, and soon people began to say: You can never tell who you may meet in beggar's rags! For people soon saw that this was no ordinary beggar. Goodhearted folk interested themselves in the forlorn figure who sat alone in his corner stubbornly wrapped in silence. They gave him better clothes, and now and then pious women would present him with a shirt.

Once, at a stranger's table where he was sitting as a Sabbath guest, he actually chanced to be the subject of conversation. The people spoke of a young man, the son-in-law of an innkeeper, who had performed all sorts of miracles, and for whom the Rabbi of Kotzk had prophesied a great future. For some time he had disappeared and nobody knew where he was. Another time he was recognized at once, and asked if he were not the famous "Psalm Jew": his name was by then known far and wide.

But as soon as Yechiel saw that the people in any town knew him or guessed who he was, he immediately vanished again. For he was still waiting for a sign that his sins were forgiven him and his prayers answered, but the sign did not come.

This lasted for over a year. Then something happened that caused Yechiel to be sought for through the length and breadth of the land.

Selig the horse dealer's wife was with child. The news spread like wildfire through the town and the neighboring villages. The promise that Yechiel had given the horse dealer had been fulfilled by God!

Selig and his wife had been convinced that if they had no child within a year they would certainly die and be brought to book in the next world because they had not redeemed the pledge that Yechiel had given them in the Lord's name. The consciousness that God had forgiven Selig all his old sins finally cleared away the obstacles between husband and wife and added blessing to their union....

In his wanderings Yechiel had reached a town on the other bank of the Vistula. He was staying at the House of Study, for it was midwinter, and the cold was so great that it seemed inadvisable, and indeed dangerous, to continue on his way. Yechiel's appearance was entirely neglected by now, and nobody would have thought that this man with his tangled beard had ever led any life but that of a tramp. On his thick, matted hair sat a shabby peasant fur cap which someone had once given him. His caftan was full of rents which had been patched by various rags and was bound round his waist by a band of straw. Felt slippers were fastened to his feet by pieces of string. His face and hands were swollen, seamed, and covered with red patches, the result of frostbite.

Yechiel was standing by the stove in the Lesson House, his hairy face turned toward the bookshelves, praying in a low voice. In his absorption he did not seem to know that he was stretching his arms toward Heaven. But the way that he stood with his face upraised and his body rigid attracted the attention of the children and finally of the other worshipers too. A man with a long gray beard, who by his appearance seemed also to be a wandering beggar, stood gazing at him attentively. From the tight lips, staring eyes, and almost awed expression of the stranger, it could be seen that he was nursing some weighty resolution. Yet he did not dare to walk over to Yechiel, but waited patiently for him to turn round. He had already waited like this for an hour. At last Yechiel turned and made for the door. Then the stranger stepped in his way and looked deeply into his eyes for a long time. Suddenly he gave a cry and clapped his hands.

"I knew it, I knew it—it is he! Sholem aleichem, Rabbi!" he cried, stretching out a trembling hand toward Yechiel.

Yechiel looked at him in surprise and turned to go. But the stranger clung to him.

"I won't let you go; I've been searching for you for weeks! You're Reb Yechiel, the Psalm Jew!"

"You're mistaken!" replied Yechiel, trying to get away.

For a brief moment the stranger was filled with doubt, but then he resolutely cast it off.

"No, I'm not mistaken! You're the Psalm Jew, and you're the man I've been looking for! Rabbi, I bring you glad news: the horse dealer's prayer has been heard! His wife has given birth to a girl. They've given it the name of Reisel, after your pious wife, may she rest in peace!"

"Given birth to a girl—how do you know?" cried Yechiel, pale with terror.

"I've been searching for you everywhere to tell you that your prayer has been heard and the hour has come for you to reveal yourself."

"Who are you?" Yechiel had regained his composure again.

"Don't you recognize me, Rabbi? I am Ezriel, the man whose feet you healed."

And now Yechiel was seized with that fear and trembling which comes to every man when, as by a flash of lightning, he sees his fate lying clear before him. A sign from Heaven had been sent to reveal it. He was filled with hesitation and dejection. His heart beat as if it would burst; the blood faded from his cheeks and lips. He lowered his eyes as if he had been caught in sin. His heart thanked God for the grace shown him, but with his lips he still strove to gainsay it.

"I am not the man you are seeking. . . ."

"Rabbi, you needn't try to escape me; you are the man! Jews! Jews, do you know who this man is?" Ezriel made a sign to the others to come near. "Do you know who is living among you? The holy man Reb Yechiel, the Psalm Jew!"

In a moment Yechiel was surrounded by a crowd of men, old and young, who with arms reverently outstretched saluted him.

"Sholem aleichem, Rabbi!"

The Psalm Fellowship came for him, and Yechiel went back to his native town. During the next eighteen years he gathered fame as a Rabbi, being known affectionately to all as the Psalm Jew. Ezriel, the man with the frostbitten feet who had first recognized him, became his attendant.

BOOK FOUR

DUTY

FROM the earliest hours of the morning the waiting room that led into the Rabbi's sanctum was thronged with poor people carrying their petitions written on slips of paper. Old Ezriel guarded the door. After eighteen years of service he had shrunk almost to a skeleton and there was nothing of him but skin, bone, and gray hair. A bent, emaciated figure, he sat at a small table beside the wall and by the light of a wax candle wrote out with a trembling hand the petition slips for the men and women in need. Each newcomer threw a groschen into the plate beside the old man and shouted in his deaf ears his own name, the name of his mother, and the difficulty or illness on behalf of which he desired the Rabbi's intervention.

The waiting room was warm and thick with the sorrowful exhalations from souls in anguish who tried to subdue their tears and sighs out of respect for the Rabbi in the next chamber. Vain effort; for every now and then one of the thickly muffled women would burst out in half-strangled sobbing, crying: "Our Father in Heaven!" and then Ezriel would have to lift a rebuking eyebrow and say: "Hush, be quiet! The Rabbi!"

Behind the door of his room Yechiel was standing, prayer shawl on his head, and his face was pressed to the wood as if he were deep in prayer. He was collecting his forces for the sacred duty of receiving the petitions of the Jews waiting on the other side of the door. Before admitting them he had to concentrate with all his might on his "love to Israel" in order to be strong in giving help. He cried, "Who and what am I, that I should dare to intercede for Israel, God's chosen people?" And he prayed that his heart might be opened wide enough to contain all the sorrow and suffering that waited for him in the other room. He called to mind Rabbi Levi-Yitzchak of Berditschev who took into his heart the sorrow of each and every Jew, and would not let it go again until God had helped the sufferer. He called to mind Rabbi Nachman of Bratzlav, who broke his heart in little pieces before the Lord of the Universe and whose praying shawl was always wet with tears. "These men and others like them," said Yechiel to himself, "were worthy of their sacred functions, for their hearts were consumed by a single flame of love for their people. But who am I and what am I that I should be held worthy of interceding for Israel?" He remembered a verse of the Psalm: "The Lord is nigh unto them that are of a broken heart; and saveth such as be of a contrite spirit." And he labored to break down his heart and be contrite in spirit so that God might be near him.

Suddenly he stretched his arms out and cried in a glad voice, "God has cleansed my heart and raised in me an upright spirit!" Joyfully he lowered himself, kissed the threshold over which the feet of Israel were to pass, and with uplifted hands cried aloud, "Children of Israel, who welcome the arrows of God for the sake of His dear Name—good morning, blessed children of Israel!" Thereupon he drew back the bolt of the door with the words, "May God open to you the gates of mercy, even as I open this door, Israel!" Only then did he fling the door wide and invite the waiting crowd to enter, "Come in, my dear children, come in! God's mercy is open to you."

It was mostly humble people with humble sorrows who came to Yechiel for help and advice. The magnates never called on him, and even after eighteen years he was not very favorably regarded in learned circles. Still, there was a certain respect for him among the learned, since he was known to be a pious Jew with a genuine love for the people. And a reflected glory still surrounded him because the Rabbi of Kotzk, of blessed memory, had once prized him and admitted him to intimacy. The poor people, however, believed in him steadfastly, and in the whole district he was widely renowned for his divinely inspired words and healing hands.

A man came in. He had leased the fruit trees on a nobleman's estate and sunk in the venture all the money he possessed, three hundred gulden, his daughter's dowry. When he took up the lease, shortly after the Passover, everything was in fine trim and his trees were blossoming to delight the heart. But now, at the end of May, unseasonable cold and violent winds had set in. So he had come to the Rabbi to beg him to keep the cold from damaging the young pears and apples or the wind from blowing them off the trees.

This had all been written down by Ezriel on the petition slip, with the full name of the man added, as well as that of his mother, to prevent any misdirection of God's grace. Yechiel had established himself at his table and thrown back the praying shawl muffling his face. In these eighteen years his beard had silvered so that he now looked like an old man. He bent over the slip of paper and long and earnestly rocked himself in meditation. Then he turned to the petitioner.

"My dear son, this is no small matter that you ask of the Lord, no small matter—that He is to keep all the unripe fruit from falling. Unripe fruit!—that can mean much more than you think. Come, take the psalm book and we shall pray together that neither your unripe fruit nor any other shall be torn down by storms."

"I, along with Rabbi? B-but...I've...I've never learned the Psalms," stammered the man in embarrassment.

"That doesn't matter. God listens to the dumb rather than to the eloquent. You can repeat them word for word after me; I'll do a verse and then you'll do it. The Lord sets more store by you than by me"— and Yechiel recited verses of the Psalms together with the Jew.

The next to enter was a villager who kept a dairy. He had quarreled with a peasant about some hens, and so—as he reported—the peasant's wife had bewitched his cows and they were giving no milk.

"What do you want me to do, my dear son?" asked the Rabbi.

"I want the holy Rabbi to curse the goy witch."

"I curse no one," replied Yechiel. "When it is written: 'Let sin be destroyed, root and branch,' it is not the sinners who are to be destroyed, but their sin. Go home, be reconciled with the goy, a few hens are not worth a quarrel. I don't believe in witchcraft. Once your cows have calved they will give more milk."

But he had sometimes graver matters to deal with. The next man who came in was in danger of prison, for he had been accused of selling illicit brandy.

"I don't like to hear of Jews meddling with things that are wicked!" Yechiel put his hand over his eyes to avoid looking at evil. "It is written: 'A holy people shall ye be to me.' "

"Rabbi, I am an innocent man!" The Jew burst into tears. "I have been falsely slandered."

Yechiel lowered his hands and looked into the man's eyes; they were bright and clear. The Rabbi saw the sign of God still undimmed upon the man's face.

"Forgive me, my dear son, for my unjust suspicions."

He read a chapter from the Psalms with the man and sent him away with the comforting assurance: "Without warning misfortune came into your house, and in the same way it will vanish again; be not afraid!"

Yet Yechiel did not always so generously bestow God's mercy with open hands, for while he sat there in his prayer shawl fulfilling the duty laid on him by God, the duty of succoring Israel, he had a more than human power of perception. As soon as his eyes rested on a face he knew for certain whether the sign of God upon it was yet clearly printed or already fading, and he could feel a sweet smell coming from an honorable and pious man and an evil stench from a wicked rogue.

A prosperous cattle dealer now stood before the Rabbi. For years he had been one of Yechiel's regular followers; every time an infant was circumcised in his house he sent the Psalm Jew a pike or a quarter of beef, and he never concluded a business deal without consulting him. He entered with his usual jaunty assurance, for was not this *his* Rabbi? "He fancies he has God in his pocket," thought Yechiel, regarding the beaming face of his visitor.

"What is it, Shloime? I see that all is going well with you, thanks be to God!"

"Holy Rabbi, I want the Lord to make me a wealthy man."

"A wealthy man?" broke in Yechiel with amazement. "Jews don't need wealth; wealth is bad for Jewish behavior."

"Holy Rabbi!" The cattle dealer blenched. "I have daughters of an age to be married, and I want to find learned husbands for them whom I would have to support."

"Our forefather Jacob asked only one thing of God," returned Yechiel, "that he should have bread to eat and a garment to cover him. The Scriptures say nothing about learned sons-in-law. Go in peace, Shloime."

The cattle dealer felt glad to have escaped with a blessing at least instead of a curse.

"I'm going, holy Rabbi, I'm going, and all I ask for is that things shall stay as they are," he stammered, pale as a sheet, and edged his stalwart figure backward through the door.

A frail man with a yellow, waxen face and a long thin nose, who looked as if the angel of death had set his seal upon him, next stood with shaking hands and trembling knees before the Rabbi, fixing him with two glazed eyes from which shone a last, feeble ray of hope.

"Holy Rabbi," he brought out with difficulty, lifting his shaking hand to give Yechiel the petition slip, "holy Rabbi, I have young children to feed."

Yechiel pressed the slip of paper to his forehead, covering his eyes with it, and sank into meditation. He wanted to look into himself rather than at the man, for he had to find some word of comfort, some verse of a psalm that the soul could take with it into eternity, but nothing rose to his lips. For a long time he sat holding the paper and it grew as heavy as if it were a load of sorrow.

"Holy Rabbi," began the man again, "I fear there is evil coming to me. On the way here a peasant called to me from his cart, 'Away, Jew, to Jerusalem!'"

"Did he call out that? 'Away, Jew, to Jerusalem!' Oh, but that was a good sign!" cried Yechiel in relief. "That must have been no ordinary peasant! To Jerusalem—he meant the heavenly Jerusalem. And since that is so, you need have no fear—Paradise is already waiting for you."

"Oh, Rabbi, is that how you understand it?" An extraordinary light shone in the man's eyes. For some time he stood in silent reflection, and his eyes were no longer glazed and fixed; they had come alive as if they had seen something. The little blood that was left in his emaciated frame flushed his yellow sunken cheeks; he stretched out his thin fingers as if to grasp at something, and stammered:

"Rabbi, I am no longer afraid, not even for my little ones, for the Lord is the Father of every orphan!"

Yechiel rose from his chair and clasped the man's hand.

"No, that was not what I meant; to God all things are possible!"

"Rabbi, I am not afraid of anything now. You have given me the good sign, 'Away, Jew, to Jerusalem!'"

Not infrequently Yechiel was consulted by men who were oppressed by fear of the Judgment Day, because of secret sins, and came begging the Rabbi to lay a penance upon them. These men avoided looking him in the face, for the glance of his eye stung them like the burning lash of a whip. Despairing they came to him, and they always went away comforted and reflective.

So Israel filed past Yechiel, and each man left his petition slip on the table. The slips of paper rose into a heap, and to Yechiel it seemed as if the papers before him were heavy sacks laden with sorrow which he had to lift on his shoulders and carry to the gates of mercy.

Now and then a light farm cart rattled up to his door in which some sick woman lay carefully bedded on straw. A peasant with his hat reverently in his hand would step into the house of the Rabbin, and be told by the Jews to put his hat on again while old Ezriel wrote out the petition slip. Then he would be admitted to the Rabbi, and pointing through the window to his sick wife, would hand over the slip of paper. Yechiel, remembering Thaddeus, the poor man in the village, would rise from his chair and look out at the cart. Then, shutting his eyes, he would take the slip of paper and add it to the pile before him.

When the men were gone the Rabbi had the door opened and went into the waiting room to the women, who were interviewed collectively instead of singly. The women had to have their headcloths drawn far over their faces and Yechiel's head was muffled in his prayer shawl. He stood in the doorway and blessed the women with upraised hands. In a voice quivering with emotion he touched upon all the needs and sorrows of their hearts.

"Dear daughters of Israel, ornaments of our race, be ye blessed by our dear Father that you may find favor in the eyes of your husbands and your husbands be pleasant in your sight, that no grief come near you, my dear daughters, that you may have milk enough for your little ones and a sufficiency of daily bread without shame or sorrow. May your pregnancies be easy, and your periods also. And when it is time for you to bring new life into this world, may the fruit of your bodies come easily to birth, sound and flawless. May you have no trouble in the rearing of your children, may you be granted the grace of seeing them grow up in learning and come to the marriage altar and to the doing of good works before God, dear daughters of Israel!"

Then Ezriel collected the women's petitions and added them to the heap on the Rabbi's table.

By the time Yechiel had finished his morning's work his whole body was bathed in sweat as if he had been doing hard manual labor. His shirt was sticking to his skin and beads of sweat were rolling from his forehead to his beard. He shut the door of his room behind him, went up to the small Almemar and took from the Ark of the Torah a common, coarse sack such as Jewish peddlers use for carrying their wares from village to village. Then he gathered up the petition slips that lay on his table, Jewish and Christian together, and poured them into the sack.

All at once the sack grew heavy, as if the human suffering poured into it weighed it down like lead. And as he had once been used to do in his youth Yechiel shouldered the sack and started on a journey. A laborious and dangerous journey. Cold snow thickened the air and icy blasts shook Yechiel's frame. And as once on the snow-covered fields unsuspected rifts flowing with water had suddenly opened up before his feet, so now gaps yawned in front of him and destroying angels barred his way with threatening, fiery swords; impenetrable walls stood blank before him, and whirlwinds snatched at him with clawing fingers. But Yechiel wrestled with the evil demons as Jacob once wrestled with the angel; he waded through lakes of fire, razed walls, evaded mountains and crevasses, burst open locked doors and struggled across menacing frontiers. No storm, no danger could make him stagger or fail.

"Away, begone! I am carrying human sorrows on my shoulders. Out of my way! Prayers and laments and tears make up my load."

The weight of it bowed his back and loosened his knees. But now he was within sight of his goal—the gate of flame was already shining in the blue. One more step, the last, and a Hand would be stretched out to him, a Face must show itself, for the grace of God stands waiting at the gate of mercy. He would lay down the heavy sack, and grace would empty it before God's throne. One more step, one last step! Yechiel drew a long breath and with all his strength carried the sack right up to the Ark and buried his face in the curtain—soon, soon he would have reached the goal.

There was a loud knocking at the door, a violent knocking that roused him from his trance. No, he had no more strength to spare; his heart was full to overflowing and could not hold another drop of human sorrow. "The load I have is not yet warmed enough at my heart, I can't take any more, my sack is full," he thought. But the knocking at the door went on. Something important must have happened, he suddenly realized, something that was calling him back. Was it decreed that his sack would not be accepted on this day, and that he must therefore go back before accomplishing the last step of all? Reluctantly and anxiously he opened the door. A broad-shouldered man with a beaming face stood there, holding out a silver dish with an enormous honey cake on it.

"Holy Rabbi, I have come to invite you to my daughter's wedding!"

"Your daughter's wedding? Who are you?"

"Don't you recognize me, Rabbi? But I'm Selig the horse dealer, and tomorrow, if God wills, I am giving my daughter Reisel in marriage."

"Reisel?"

"Yes, the child you begged for us from God; she's called Reisel after your late wife, the peace of God upon her."

"Ah, Reisel. The peace of God upon her. Yes, yes." Little by little the Rabbi came down to earth again. "That's a good omen!" He drew a breath of relief. "A bride means grace. . . . Ezriel, bring a drop of brandy!"

Yechiel sank in his chair to master his exhaustion. His eyes grew bright as if he saw a vision. Reisel's image rose before him, and he knew with certainty that it was a vision sent by Heaven, a sign that his prayers were heard.

He pledged Selig, ate a small piece of the honey cake, and sent out the rest to the poor in the courtyard.

CHAPTER II

REISEL'S WEDDING DAY

I N Selig the horse dealer's house the last preparations were being made for the wedding of his daughter Reisel. Mountains of honey cake, tarts, almond and sugar cakes in the form of rings, hearts, and birds, gigantic pancakes and pastries all stood ready. For a fortnight the two cooks and the proprietor of the local cookshop, who officiated at all weddings and circumcisions, had not moved out of the house.

The rich horse dealer Selig was marrying off his only child, and that was no mean occasion! For the whole of the past week free meals had been served out continuously to the poor; enormous bubbling pots hung over a fire in the courtyard, replenished all the time with joints of meat. Dinner was served at long tables in the courtyard, in the various rooms and storerooms, wherever there was a free corner in the house, and Selig himself watched over the feast, standing there in the new clothes he had got for the wedding with a heavy gold chain dangling on his flowered silk waistcoat and his hands thrust into his trouser pockets. Again and again he ordered, "Bring out a whole pike for each of them! Don't give any man less than a pound of meat! Let them understand that Selig is marrying off his only daughter!"

The bride, too, was in attendance at these meals, the bride Reisel who was born under a lucky star and had a special pleader for her in Heaven. No other conclusion was possible; some holy patriarch in person must have interceded for her since she had been found worthy to get such a fine husband. He was the best scholar in the Yeshivah; he was said to have a Rabbi's certificate already in his pocket. A great brain, a man that would be heard of in the world! Reisel wore a wide crinoline frock decked with fringes, all of the finest silk, and her bridal jewelry, the golden brooch and the long gold chain her father had given her on her betrothal, while a fine lace scarf covered her dark hair. Modestly she went from table to table and handed a Polish gulden out of a silk handkerchief to each of the guests. Selig had insisted that his daughter should put on her wedding finery to distribute the alms. The

old women with their greasy fingers felt the silk of her frock, the lace
scarf, the fine handkerchief, and whispered to each other.

"A kosher maid, she might be a Rabbi's daughter! How on earth
did Selig come to have such a child?"

"Rich men have all the luck. He's led an evil life; there's no end to
the scandal about him; and yet he's been granted the luck of marrying
his daughter well and leading her under the marriage canopy himself!"

"The Rabbi must have done it for him."

"That's what the holy man had to pay for with his own wife and
child."

From the whispered mouthings and meaning looks Reisel gathered
that she was the subject of discussion. A delicate flush rose in her
cheeks. She had long known that she had come in answer to the Rabbi's
prayers to Heaven, and that he had paid the price with his own wife
and child. She hung her head and flitted away to the men's table, where
the last fragments of meat were being gnawed from the bones and the
strong brandy was mounting into heated heads. One man, blind of an
eye and with matted hair sticking to his sweaty forehead, seized in his
thick fingers the heavy black plaits that swung over the girl's shoulders,
and clicking his tongue weighed them as if they were of shining gold,
his lustful eyes twinkling greedily.

Twice every day Reisel had to run the gauntlet in this fashion. Every
beggar to whom she handed a Polish gulden during his meal took an
appreciative sip from the cup of her bridal charms. Desirous looks and
evil eyes stripped her naked. Fingers poked at her, and stroked her
clothes, her hair, her throat. And each time she had to dance with the
beggars, in accordance with old tradition, the so-called Mitzve dance;
one partner snatched her from another, she whirled from arm to arm,
until, exhausted and overcome by shame, she ran for refuge to her
room with an aching head.

"It is a good thing to do," insisted her father. "Since God has fa-
vored us and given us such happiness it is your duty to dance with the
poor."

"You're not merely our child; we got you from God in answer to
prayer," said her mother to comfort her as she lay limp and weary on
her bed.

Selig was a man who wanted all his possessions to make a brave
show, and he had only the one child, after all. So in the bright spacious kitchen the copper pans shone in all their glory; polished for
Reisel's wedding. On the wooden tables a countless row of roasting

pans was ranged, in which ducks and chickens lay cushioned in fat sauce, flanked by stewpots containing boiled chicken, liver, and enormous chunks of meat—was not the whole town to be royally entertained? Lord over all these pots and pans was the cookshop proprietor, who with a white cap on his head hectored the two female cooks, while Rachel-Leah, the pastry expert, floury and sweating, drew from the oven her last detachments of tarts and pancakes. From the bakery, enormous baskets came in full of confectionery, whole sacks of bread, great pans of biscuits, enough to feed the wedding guests for a week. Onions and radishes in large bundles rose mountain-high in the kitchen, and in a corner two maidservants were slicing carrots for the sweet, rich dish that was called Tsimess, a dish for which old Aunt Sara, scarlet with heat and zeal, was melting the fat on the glowing stove. The pike and carp which the fishermen had caught in the Linsk ponds for their friend Selig were still at ease in their watery element; they were swimming about unsuspecting in great tubs of water. They were not cooked until the very last minute as they had to come fresh to table.

In the large living room, where meals were taken and business deals put through, Selig's wife, Zlotte, was now inspecting the last installment of the bride's outfit, which had kept Hindel the seamstress busy for years. An ample apron was tied about her and round her head a damp towel with slices of lemon in it as a compress to cure the headache caused by all the hurly-burly in the house. She was examining one by one, with proper pride, the linen sheets, the pillow slips, and bedcovers which Hindel had just brought from her workshop. All through the winter six girls had sat by the light of sooty pine torches ruining their eyesight to make the tiny rosettes, leaflets, hearts, and eyelets in the snowy linen; every stitch that they made had drained another drop of blood from their cheeks. There had been so much to stitch that Hindel's face had gone quite yellow. Bent by long stooping over her work table, she passed the crackling linen through her thin, needle-scarred fingers and pointed out with pride the fineness of the work, the tiny rosettes, the delicately cut leaves. She handed over every piece with the humble wish that the bride might have health and joy and happiness in the using of it. And every time she uttered the wish she uttered a sigh of envy; her own lot was none too happy, for she had married an old widower.

One of Zlotte's neighbors, who had been summoned to pass on expert opinion on the trousseau, stood by to investigate each item with an experienced eye.

"No, it isn't worth all that. A whole gulden for a pillow slip! I never heard the like!"

"This wedding will bring me to ruin and beggary; I've spent far too much on it already," groaned Zlotte.

In a corner of the room the horse dealer himself was trying on the silk caftan which the tailor had just brought him; when it came to leading the bridegroom up for the ceremony he had to be every whit as grand as his partner, the father of the bridegroom, who was a learned Talmudist.

Selig called out to his wife, "This isn't a time for haggling! Pay her what she asks and give her something over. You haven't ten daughters to marry off! And I want everybody to be happy today; nobody is to feel wronged on my daughter's wedding eve."

With a sigh of resignation Zlotte answered, "Well, if you say so. . . ."

In the bedroom Reisel's lavish outfit of clothes was all laid out in orderly array. The red, white, and blue flowered silk dress in which she was to be married had cost a fine round sum of money; a special journey had been made to the city to procure that particular pattern. Beside it were ranged her bridal shoes with the silver buckles and the white stockings with their gay garters. A hand-embroidered shawl, trimmed with real lace, went with the dress and would be worn each year in the Temple on the Day of Atonement. And what a wealth of other garments there was! A "morning frock" of spun wool with padded sleeves and innumerable fringes; a frock for going to synagogue in, of the heaviest silk edged with gold brocade; a mantilla and a pelerine of fine velvet; a countless array of bonnets glittering with spangles and bright ribbons; endless pairs of shoes! It was really impossible to enumerate the articles in the famous trousseau that the rich horse dealer had bestowed upon his daughter.

The bride had locked herself into her own room, the smallest room in the house, where was also lodged the iron chest in which Selig kept the dowry money and the valuable wedding presents. The bride, it was said, had a headache and wanted to lie down for a little. That was not to be wondered at, for these last days had been very trying. And tomorrow would be still more of a strain for her, with the long fasts and the standing about she would have to endure. She still had to take her ritual bath under the eye of the bathwoman, and for the moment she was hardly able to stand up on her feet; she had always been delicate, poor girl, ever since the Rabbi had wrestled with God to let her be born.

"Have a good sleep, my love, and that will soon cure your head-ache," her mother had called after her. And now all the people in the house were going on tiptoe and holding their breath, "Hush, the bride's trying to get a little sleep."

But Rachel-Leah the old cakemaker and Genendel the bathwoman, with the great haircutting scissors dangling at her apron, rather frowned on this proceeding, since a bride should never be left alone on the eve of her wedding. For that was the time when evil spirits and demons—God defend the house from them!—were lying in wait for her; when clawing devils—God avaunt them!—were reaching out after her from all sides, and chief among them Lilith herself, who had sworn to Asmodeus, her lord and master, to bring him all brides before they were safely wedded. And so a bride had to be specially guarded and watched on her wedding eve—not left alone.

"Oh, leave me in peace and don't bring bad luck into the house with your talk! The girl has no evil in her, and she's only resting a little in her room after all the excitement, and there are plenty of good angels watching over her!" retorted her mother sharply.

The bride was alone in her room, certainly, but she was not asleep nor even resting on her bed. She was standing by the tall window from which she could see far across the fields. Her father's handsome horses were feeding below her in the meadows running down to the stream which wound its lazy way beside the forest that veiled the horizon in blue. It was an evening in May, the loveliest season of the year. And tomorrow, on the day of the Jewish school fête, she was to be married. A fine haze of rain filled the air as if it were dew that had risen in a mist. Twilight was falling and the sky was dappled with little clouds chasing each other like cherubs across the azure bowl of the sky. Here and there a ray of sunlight peeped out for a moment before vanishing again. The meadows were richly green; every blade of grass looked fresh and radiant, and the level stretches of pasture ran far into the distance.

But the bride saw neither the green pastures nor the shimmering clouds nor the delicate foliage of the birch trees. With her firm young cheeks resting on her round arms she was fixing a wide dreamy gaze on the fringe of the forest across the stream, and her eyes were dim with unshed tears of longing. By that verge of the forest ran a long meandering road lined with poplars and as she gazed at it her small ears reddened to the very tips, while her shoulders twitched nervously below the nape of her downy neck.

"What will they say tomorrow?" Whenever she thought of her father and mother it gave her a stab of pain. She was much less concerned about her betrothed, whom she had encountered only on one occasion when he was staying in her parents' house for the Feast of Purim; she had first peeped at him through a crack in the door and then sat opposite him at table. All she could remember of him was a head shorn almost bald, two large projecting ears partly concealed by side curls, a very long nose that looked as if it had strayed from some other face and an enormous Adam's apple that wobbled up and down beneath the skin. She could not help comparing him with another young man, the young man for whom she was now watching and who might emerge on horseback at any moment from the verge of the forest, the son of the estate agent at Lonkyshin, young Dombrowski, her own Stepan—a youth with bright yellow hair, gray eyes, and closely shaven side whiskers. She trembled like a young pine tree in a gust of spring wind, shaken as she was by pain and love together. She was so happy —and yet so miserable.

The first time she saw him he was sitting magnificently on a horse; his gray eyes and yellow hair gleamed through the thick cloud of dust that had settled on him during his ride. Holding his riding switch negligently in his hand, spurs clinking at his heels, he was talking to her father about horses, about the lord of the estate, about markets and stables, and yet not for one moment did he shift his gaze from her; she was standing then as now at the window leaning on her arms, her beribboned black plaits of hair drawn forward over her shoulders to cover her throat, and his eyes were fixed as if spellbound on these black braids. Her heart fluttered in panic. But she too stood as if rooted to the spot, tranced by the magic of his eyes, his hair, his fair lithe body. Dumbly, with her eyes only, she implored him, begged, cajoled, resisted him, wrestled with him until of her own accord she gave up the struggle and surrendered—like a little bird that beats feebly with its wings and legs as it is put into a cage, but finally resigns itself to its fate. Her eyes were still imploring, still begging to be let go, and yet of her own free will she had delivered herself to him.

Since that day he had ridden every evening past the house. She listened for the tread of his horse and every hoofbeat was a jubilation to her. Hidden behind the curtains she watched him long after he had passed. . . . And one day in the heat of summer as she went to bathe in the stream she stole away from the rest of the girls and crossed over to the other side by the footbridge leading to the mill. A narrow path wound there toward the forest, little used because it was overgrown with raspberry canes. "Oh, what a lot of raspberries!" Reisel quickly picked herself a basketful. "Father will like these for his breakfast!" But at the fork in the path, beneath an oak tree on which hung a carved figure of Christ, the handsome Stepan stood waiting beside his horse. That was how it began. . . .

In the winter the evenings were long. And so Reisel would set off, escorted by a maidservant with a lantern, to visit the sisters Chojnacki who lived at the far end of the town near the windmill. These were two elderly spinsters, pious Catholics who appeared at every Church festival in bridal white and wreath of forget-me-nots in their hair. They took part in the Corpus Christi procession and held the white ribbons of the canopy. Their profession was vague—they were teachers, midwives, dressmakers, milliners, nobody quite knew which—but they belonged to the best Christian society in the town. Selig regarded these visits with suspicion. "What's Reisel got to do with these goy old maids?" But his wife smoothed him down, "She's a grown girl now and could help you in lots of ways. She can at least learn how to write a Polish letter and how to speak to the gentry and carry herself properly."

In the town the Chojnacki sisters enjoyed the highest esteem. They belonged to a respectable though impoverished, landed family and had been educated in boarding schools and elegant establishments. Both, or at least one of them—nobody quite knew which—had almost entered a convent, and they were honored as ardent Catholics who were ready to go through fire for their beliefs. Their visitors included His Reverence the Provost of the local chapter, the Mayor, the Town Clerk, Pan Grabowski with his long mustache, and the Assessor, who had once fought for the liberation of Poland and boasted a round dozen of military decorations, which he had of course to wear in his pocket because the Muscovites were now masters in the land. Two ladies from the town completed the circle, members of the Order of the Sacred Heart of Jesus. At the Chojnackis' social evenings the prevalent topics were convents and churches, chapels and cathedrals, shrines for sacred relics such as fragments of the True Cross or the handkerchief that wiped the face of Jesus. But when the doors were locked and the shutters were fastened there was also much talk of armed revolt and campaigns in the forest that bode no good to the Russians. A dash of local gossip spiced the whole, and now and then a game at cards or dominoes, which was played, of course, not for money but merely for amusement.

The Town Clerk usually arrived with a bag of warm doughnuts fried in lard, the Assessor with half a pound of sugar or a packet of real China tea, while the ecclesiastical dignitary brought his blessing. And so they spent many a profitable evening in pious talk or harmless play.

But during the long winter evenings there were usually two young people sitting in the adjoining alcove, young Stepan, the estate agent's son, with the yellow head and gray eyes, and the black-haired daughter of the rich Jewish horse dealer Selig, sitting there with burning cheeks and ears.

As zealous Catholics the sisters Chojnacki ardently desired to bring new souls to Christ. And so with the utmost enthusiasm they had set themselves to the pious work of making Selig's daughter into a convert, thus at one blow winning a Jewish soul for Jesus and a wife for their young friend Stepan.

The chaste walls of the little alcove were covered with sacred pictures—Jesus with a short, fair beard and a bleeding heart on His breast, the Holy Virgin with her child. And the air smelled faintly of incense and lavender from the old clothes chests, withered garlands, branches from the Corpus Christi procession sprinkled with holy water and innumerable little representations of the Crucifixion. On the table stood a figure of the Czentochau Madonna in Byzantine black and gold, her mournful eyes gazing sorrowfully at the Jewish girl.

Uneasy among all these sacred images and oppressed by the smell of the incense Reisel turned for help and protection to the bright eyes of the young man beside her. He took her white fingers in his great firm hand and comforted her tenderly, "My lovely Jewess, you have bewitched me!" . . . Her fingers caressed his yellow hair, "Oh, Stepan, I'll do whatever you want me to."

In Stepan's strong arms she sought a refuge from the fears that rose in her own bosom, "Oh, God, what a step to take!" And an uncertain smile wavered round her mouth even while her warm red lips were whispering close to his, "I have no father and no mother except you!"

In that alcove the decision was taken, confirmed and translated into a detailed plan of action. "On the very eve of your wedding, when your things are all ready and your dowry and jewels are wrapped in a package, when everybody's worn out with labor and sleeping sound in bed, I'll come on my horse and swing you up behind me and then— hurrah, we'll be off! For a day or two the Chojnackis will hide you here and then you'll be taken to the Convent of St. Catherine nearby. The nuns will teach you your catechism, the priest will sprinkle you with holy water, you'll be received into the Catholic faith, and then— you'll be mine. . . ."

So there she was standing at the window, Reisel the bride, the horse dealer's only daughter, whom Yechiel the Rabbi had once won from God by prayer and at a great price. On this very night, the eve of her wedding, her heart should have been filled with fear of her Judgment Day, but there she stood gazing eagerly toward the verge of the forest. All was still over there; of Stepan and his horse there was no trace.

The little clouds sank lower and lay in wreaths on the green grass. It was growing late, night would soon be coming on—and not a sign of Stepan! The girl's heart contracted with a spasm, her cheeks burned, and her eyes glistened and a tear hung in each of them, "O Father in Heaven, what am I thinking of? To desert my faith for another . . . on the very night before my wedding! To bring such a shame on my parents . . . ! I should never be able to see them again. I should be dead to them. Oh, Stepan, my darling, don't be angry with me, but I can't do it. We must part, Stepan! My father and mother would never be able to bear it if I left them. . . ."

But all these good resolutions vanished like spindrift as soon as she saw a rider on a magnificent horse careering at full speed through the white mist that couched on the bed of the stream. "Oh, Stepan, my darling!" Nearer he came, with his yellow tuft of hair gleaming, his firm hands pulling at the reins, his eyes shining in the darkness, her handsome lover. "Oh, I'll do everything you ask! Father, mother, forgive me, but I love him!" Hastily she brushed the tears from her eyes and a happy smile banished the droop from her mouth. Hastily she undid a red ribbon from her hair and waved it out at the window, the signal they had agreed on to show that all was going well, the signal that meant, "True unto death!" Joyously Stepan waved back and his riding switch whistled through the air, "Tonight, my darling!" and he was already spurring his horse; clods of earth rose in a shower from his hoofs; steed and rider had vanished again in the mist.

Reisel passed her fine silk handkerchief over her eyes, tidied her hair, and caressed the shining plaits; how lovely to think that they would not be cut off tomorrow, they belonged to Stepan, and he would play with them! She lifted a braid to her lips and kissed it, thinking of Stepan. Then she left the window. With shy, bridelike steps she flitted across the room; her knees felt weak. Still walking softly and gracefully she traversed one after another the many rooms of the house; in each one of them there was bustling and activity. In spite of the hurly-burly around her Reisel's mother perceived that something was troubling her daughter, "Have you still got a headache? Oh, dear; Selig, just see how pale the poor child is!" Her mother kissed the rising tears from her eyes, her father's large hand slid caressingly over her hair.

"What's the trouble, my dear? Wouldn't you like something to eat? Poor thing, you've eaten next to nothing today and tomorrow will be a hard day for you."

The old serving maid came scurrying up with a cup of freshly made chicken broth, while Rachel-Leah with a piece of apple tart in her right hand and a slice of almond cake in her left cried, "Try some of my baking so that a blessing rests on it!"

The cookshop man in his cap added his jest, "There's an old saying: what the bride swallows makes the bridegroom hungry!"

Reisel escaped from their attentions and turned to her mother.

"Mother, dear, I'd like to go to bed early, I'm dreadfully tired."

A blessing from her mother and looks of pride from her father accompanied the answer. "Sleep well, child, and may holy angels watch over you this night!"

With a burst of sobbing Reisel fell on her mother's neck. "Forgive me, darling mother, do not curse me and wish me dead, I'm so young, so young!" was what a voice cried within her.

"What's the matter, love? Are you afraid to sleep alone?"

"It's the last night she'll be lonely," said her father jocularly.

The horses were being yoked four-in-hand to bring the bridegroom. "It's you I'm most sorry for, my dearest father," thought the bride, as she clasped his hand and pressed her last good-night kiss upon it. "What will you say tomorrow? Will you lament me as if I were dead? Whatever may happen, fare you well!"

Next morning as Yechiel was stretching out his hand to admit the Jews waiting in the anteroom the door was violently dashed open and a bellow like that of a wounded animal resounded through the house.

"Holy Rabbi, give me back my daughter!"

It was incredible to see the change that one night had wrought in the horse dealer Selig. The man's strong, powerful, energetic body seemed to have been shattered by some frightful blow. In one night he had aged twenty, no, a hundred years. His hair had turned gray and hung matted and staring like the hair of a corpse; his body had shrunk to a smaller size and looked like a flabby carcass without any life in it. His eyes were wild and bulged from under his eyelids as if they would fall out. His mouth was distorted in a maniac grin showing all his teeth and the point of his tongue. His enormous hands pawed convulsively at the air as if they were clawing at something evanescent which they sought to throttle in helpless fury—helpless, for it was only the empty air they clutched. With tottering knees Selig stumbled toward the Rabbi, clutched at the fringes of his prayer shawl and tugged at them, helplessly, crying.

"Holy Rabbi, give me back my daughter!"

CHAPTER III

WEEPING IN THE NIGHT

LIKE a log Selig lay at the Rabbi's feet, dumb, unheeding, and it was a hard task to get him removed.

Half the population of the town besieged the Rabbi, men and women together. For this misfortune was theirs as well as Selig's; Reisel had never been regarded merely as the horse dealer's daughter, she was the pride of the whole community. Since the day of her birth she had been as the apple of their eye to all the Jews, for of course everybody knew that her very existence was a miracle. And when she was betrothed to the cleverest student of the Yeshivah, the son of a Rabbi, the whole street in which she lived rose in status—it was *their* Selig who had scored such a triumph! And for weeks every inhabitant of the street had been getting ready for the wedding.

And now this disgrace! This shame! It was a blow not only for Selig but for the whole Street of the Butchers, even for the whole town; it was a stain on the honor of every Jew.

So the Rabbi's hut was besieged by people, with the Psalm Fellowship in the van, the butcher's apprentices, the carters and carriers, all Selig's friends. Some Christians were there, too, mostly men who were employed by Selig to take his horses to the annual market. As for those Christians who lived in the Street of the Butchers, they also took Selig's part, even   though it was their own faith that came in question. They could not stomach the affront to Selig; "No, that's a bit too much!" they said. "Religion's all very well, but human feeling is human feeling. Besides, everybody should die in the faith in which he has been born. And a father's a father, even if he is a Jew. It's a sin to do a thing like that to one's parents!"

Partisanship ran high even among people who had long been considered outcasts not only from the Jewish community but from human society at large. Oyserl the thief, for instance, one of whose ears had been bitten off in a gambling den—so it was alleged—Oyserl the thief turned up among the others at the Rabbi's. His appearance caused the utmost astonishment, for Oyserl was supposed to be the epitome of wickedness—he publicly desecrated the Sabbath, he ate forbidden food, he was actually an informer. Only recently he had threatened the town Rabbi that he was going to get himself baptized, so all in all he was a sure target for some evil dybbuk. And now here he was among the others, clamoring against the dishonor done to Selig, and through Selig to all Jews. He came escorted by his pal, one Nussen Bastard, by profession a smuggler who swathed rolls of silk around his huge body and ran them over the Prussian frontier. At the Rabbi's Nussen remained inarticulate as usual, but the ferocious twist of his mouth and the fire in his small, half-hooded eyes proclaimed that he too was furious and ready to whip out a knife, if need be, in order to wrest the girl from the goys and drag her back by her hair to her father.

The wrong done to Selig had goaded all these people to assemble on Yechiel's doorstep. Awe and reverence kept them quiet and restrained their excitement, yet it was easy to see what mood they were in; lowering brows and clenched fists made their silence menacing, like the lull before a storm.

"Does anybody know where she is?" Yechiel addressed his question to the crowd in general, not to the prone Selig.

A murmur arose and everybody began to speak and to close in on the Rabbi. But the cattle dealer Notte, whose huge paws and thick stick were feared, shouldered the rabble back and yelled at them, "Keep your distance!" After quiet was restored he ventured to speak in the name of all.

"Holy Rabbi, they told us that the goy had taken her to the house of the Chojnackis, and we broke in there and hunted all through the place but we didn't find her. . . . They're supposed to have taken her by night to the convent of Grochov, but we don't know for certain."

Yechiel remained silent. A faint flicker of red showed in his face, the sunken hollows of his bearded cheeks were inflated and his breathing was labored. His large and somewhat projecting eyes were hooded and glimmered like frosty black cherries between the blanched, blue-veined eyelids. The Rabbi's gaze was turned inward. Slowly his fingers combed the straggling long beard that reached to his chest, and without moving from the spot he began slowly to rock his lean, sinewy body like a boat rocking on water. With a shudder of awe the people watched his movements, cowering against the wall and holding their breath. Then Yechiel gave a start, as if he had awakened from a long sleep, and gazed at the waiting throng with the bewildered look of one who did not know what was expected of him. After a long pause he said, "Go home for the present and pray God to help us. . . ."

When some of the men took hold of Selig to lift him up and bear him away he turned his glazed eyes on the Rabbi and stared at him dumbly. Suddenly his tongue was loosened and to the horror of the bystanders he cried.

"Holy Rabbi, this is all I ask; let her rather die than desert the Jewish faith!"

"That's a thing no Jew must ask; God forbid! It is written: let sin perish, not, God forbid, the sinner!" returned Yechiel.

"I don't care. Rabbi—I won't be able to lie quiet in my grave because her children will be born goyim!"

The inhabitants of the Street of the Butchers who had accompanied Selig murmured and nodded their heads in agreement. They understood the horse dealer and were of the same mind: "Let her rather die . . . !"

That morning Yechiel felt incapable of fulfilling his usual duties. He sent away all his waiting petitioners. For the first time he felt inadequate—he could not help them.

When night came he got up from his couch earlier than usual, refusing the indulgence of even a brief sleep. At about midnight he awoke Ezriel, who was guarding his door, and bade him open the bathhouse. He then descended the fifteen steps and fulfilled the ritual with passionate devotion; sitting afterward on the ground in tunic and prayer shawl, in his stocking feet, by the light of a candle end. His body glowed like a fiery coal. The ritual bath and the self-castigation had brought beads of sweat to his brow.

He had confessed his sins, dwelling long and earnestly upon them. He had stripped himself naked before God, had humbled his heart, had suffered in imagination the four modes of death and embraced them all in love. He lingered long on the passage: "By the rivers of Babylon, there we sat down, yea, we wept . . ." and over the words: "The heathen are come into thine inheritance . . ." he wept bitterly, weeping for the exile of God's majesty and finding no consolation. When he came to the verse: "Rachel weeping for her children refused to be comforted for her children, because they were not" he paused, shut the book, and sat without stirring, gazing into the darkness. No, he would read no further, he would not let himself be comforted by the marvelous verse that summoned up the future Zion: "Awake, awake, shake thyself from the dust; arise and sit down, O Jerusalem; loose thyself from the bands of thy neck. ..." He would not abandon himself to the longing for God in which he was usually absorbed for hours, roaming through infinity, remote from this world. On this occasion Yechiel was to be deaf and blind to everything but the one great need, all the powers of his soul were to sleep except for that directed to the one end: to save a Jewish soul from the abyss.

"To save one soul is as much as to save the whole world," says the Scripture. But this one soul was strangely involved with his, and he felt as if it were his own soul he had to save from plunging into the abyss.

He sat brooding silently for a long time. One by one he cut off his perceptions of the outer world and freed his senses from the external influences that hampered them; he became a mere point of waking life that hovered in space, shaping itself unconsciously to one purpose, one mission; to fly, as an arrow flies to the target, straight toward the soul it was seeking.

No easy task. The regions in which that soul now dwelt had never harbored him, nor had he ever felt impelled even to explore them. He had his own province in the Kingdom of God; his sphere of action was Israel. He was at home there, he knew every corner of it; he knew where it was strong and where weak, what methods he had to employ, what rights he could claim and on what merits he might rely. In the province of Israel he could offer battle to anyone, overcome any obstacles, stand up to any opposition. One single verse of a psalm could open all doors to him. But in the unfamiliar region to which he was now beating his way he felt uncertain and met with hostility. He had not suspected that the others had also rights in Heaven, that powerful spirits were on their side also.

It was amazing—their forces were not the forces of evil and impurity. The Others had merits of their own, unknown to him. They too had their pleaders, their partisans in Heaven—and he could find no admission to their realm. But Yechiel did not give up; he went on hammering, he went on boring, like a red-hot iron that ultimately splits the hardest rock. For how could he lose from sight one child of Israel? The child might have fallen into the very pit, which God forbid! No, let the Others rely on whom they might, he demanded admittance; the gates must be opened to him! "Help me, O God, for the sake of Thine honor! Why should the Others cry, 'Where is your God?'"

He refused to yield, to move from the spot; he went on forcing his way in. And all at once he found himself in a small vaulted chamber with a window let in one side and a crucifix on the opposite wall. He shut his eyes to avoid looking at the crucifix. Beneath it was a bench on which "she" was sitting. He had not seen her before, and yet her appearance was strangely familiar. He sat down beside her and spoke to her with the yearning of a father over his child. He could hear her soul weeping and his own heart overflowed in sympathy.

Next morning the Rabbi sent for the unhappy parents and instructed them as follows:

The mother was to go to Grochov where the convent stood. There she was to pace seven times round the convent wall, repeating continuously: "Lord of the Universe, as Thou didst open my womb to bear this child, do Thou open now her heart to believe in Thee!" Then she was to stand over against the convent windows, from sunrise to sunset. Even if they sought to drive her away she was to persist in standing where she could be seen from the windows. He turned then to Selig and said, "And in your house meanwhile a deadlight must be kept burning day and night for the soul of your daughter. Also, take ten Jews into your house and pay them to sing psalms for the girl's soul day and night, as if she were sick unto death. Let them repeat three times the chapter: 'Blessed are the undefiled in the way, who walk in the law of the Lord.' Perhaps the Lord will then have mercy on your child."

CHAPTER IV

IN THE CONVENT

DURING the selfsame night in which the horse dealer's daughter fled with the handsome young Stepan, she was received into the convent of Grochov where she was to be prepared for her baptism into the Roman Catholic faith.

The convent lay about two versts beyond the town in the middle of an old park surrounded by a high spiked wall. Reisel was received by two sisters with kindly, welcoming faces under their enormous white-starched coifs. She had been well instructed by the Chojnackis and knew what to do; she knelt and kissed the nuns' hands, saying that she wanted to be admitted into the fold of the true and only blessed Faith. Thereupon she was led to a spotlessly clean, ascetic-looking cell, furnished only with a bed above which hung a great wooden crucifix, a table, a chair, and a tiny oil lamp burning before the Holy Virgin. Reisel was tired and shy, so exhausted by the struggle between her love for her parents and her love for Stepan that she was incapable of seeing or feeling. She sank on the bed and fell asleep at once.

In the morning she was awakened early by the bright sunshine that streamed into the cell through the window. Dismayed and bewildered she gazed at her new surroundings and remembered that this was her wedding day. Her imagination began to paint in the strongest colors all the misery reigning at home; her father would be sitting in her room with his face in his hands, ashamed to look any one in the face. The whole town would be cursing the renegade. Horses were being yoked to tell the bridegroom's friends not to come, since there was to be no wedding. "Oh, father, what have I done! Don't curse me!"

But Stepan's kisses were still burning on her lips. She could still feel his fresh young cheeks, his eyes, his yellow hair; on the way to the convent he had caressed and embraced her, leaned his head against her cheek, and sworn by the Holy Mother of God that he would never forget what she had done for him, that he would love her forever and ever and set her on high and worship her like a Madonna. "My lovely Jewess!" his warm lips had whispered in her ear.

And how firmly and strongly had his arm enfolded her! She had shed tears, but he had kissed the tears away, murmured tender, consoling words and strengthened her courage. Truly, if she had ten fathers and ten mothers she must have left them all for Stepan—and, of course, for the new religion. Yes, she loved the new religion because it was Stepan's. No, she was not at all afraid of the new God—He was kind, He would protect her and make Stepan and herself the happiest pair on earth!

She went to the window. The springtime outside was so lovely! A long alley of acacias ran through the garden, and white tassels of blossom were hanging on the trees and the ground was covered with drifts of snowy petals. She opened the window and looked down into the garden. The window was high up and the garden lay far below; the blossoming tops of the acacia trees were level with her feet. The chestnut trees had kindled all their red candles. Down there, among the green trees, black figures went to and fro; the nuns were working in the garden, and some were pacing two by two in the alleys with small books in their hands. It seemed to Reisel that she had been transported into a different world. But the wall of the garden gave her a feeling of being in prison.

Her eye fell on the white road beyond the wall. One or two small farmhouses lay there, and behind them the common with the well-trodden footpath and the small track leading over the stream. A little behind that were the pastures where her father's horses were feeding, and in the far distance she could make out the houses of the town. How often she had traversed that common! She needed only to open the door of her cell, go downstairs into the garden, lift the latch of the postern gate, and in a trice she would be on the common, very nearly home! For a moment she felt as if nothing had happened, as if things were the same as ever; this was her wedding day, she had to fast, the wagons were already gone to bring the bridegroom. But suddenly she became conscious of where she was. There was no going back. She must tread to the very end the path on which she had set her feet. "Fare you well, father and mother! I'm dead for you and you for me." . . . No, she could not say that; in some corner of her soul she was still joined to her parents.

Hastily she wiped the tears from her eyes like a child afraid to be caught in wrongdoing. For she had heard steps outside in the corridor. Someone was coming, someone was already at the door! It opened and a sister came in with a bowl of warm milk and a freshly baked roll.

Reisel bent over the nun's hand to kiss it, but the sister would not permit her. Reisel ate and drank, washed herself and carefully combed out her black plaits. The sister helped her silently and silently led her downstairs into a large, dimly lit hall.

The Mother Superior sat in a high armchair. She was not one of the nuns who had received Reisel but an old woman with a great iron crucifix on her breast. Beside her Reisel saw the familiar face of the priest, with its kindly, encouraging smile—even the famous silver snuffbox was in evidence. That made the dim, unfamiliar room at once homely and friendly to the girl; she knelt before the priest as she had been taught to do, and kissed his hand. The old Mother Superior also presented her hand to kiss. They spoke kindly to her and made the sign of the cross over her. Then some of the nuns came in, and they all smiled upon her. They were so friendly, so pleasant, and were so glad to see her there—no, there was no going back!

The whole of that day was spent by Reisel in the park with Sister Helene, who taught her first the "Ave Maria." She already knew her Pater Noster and could cross herself, for the Chojnackis had coached her in that. She learned eagerly, since she wanted to be received into the new faith as quickly as possible in order to be united to Stepan, and so after reading the prayer through several times she knew it by heart. Then she walked up and down in the lovely acacia alley memorizing the Apostolic Creed: "I believe in God the Father Almighty, Maker of Heaven and Earth. . . ." She was so intent upon her task that the nun's prematurely withered pale face and large, watery blue eyes beamed with satisfaction—Sister Helene was pleased. At the midday meal Reisel sat among the nuns at a long table in the dim refectory where a large wooden image of Christ hung on the end wall. A sister stood up on the dais reading extracts from a holy book. Since no one else spoke during the meal, Reisel too remained silent. At vespers she was taken into the chapel, and at supper there were more readings from the holy book and the nuns sang hymns in chorus. They were all so friendly, so amiable, so kind—no, there was no going back at all.

In this fashion passed the first day.

But, during the night, while Reisel lay alone in her cell, fears came crowding upon her and she could not sleep. The little room lay in darkness made only more uncanny by the red glimmer before the Virgin in the corner. Reisel shut her eyes and tried to think of Stepan: where would he be now? He was certainly thinking of her as she was thinking of him. But her thoughts would not settle, they kept returning to her parents' house: "O God, this is my wedding night, this is the night when my fate is decided in Heaven—that's what my mother told me. This is my Day of Judgment, my Yom Kippur, this is the day when the verdict on me is passed in Heaven!"

"Try to think that I'm dead," she implored her parents in a whisper, "think that I never was born!"

On this conclusion she sought to compose herself and fall asleep. Her lips moved as she murmured the newly learned prayer which should have been her refuge, but like mill water in spate her thoughts went rushing through her brain—she *had* to think, whether she would or not. And the subject the waters kept turning was one she had obstinately tried to avoid, because she was afraid of it—the holy Rabbi.

From childhood she had been persuaded that this holy and uncanny man, for whose sake so many Jews came to the town, who performed incredible miracles, who read everybody's thoughts, who was transported each night to Heaven—that this holy Rabbi, Reb Yechiel, was the person to whom she owed her existence. He had begged her in prayer from Heaven, he had promised her to her father in the Name of God, and in order to let her come into the world, entirely on her account, the Rabbi's wife had died in childbed.

And so from her earliest days the girl had cherished a belief that there was a mysterious bond between herself and the awesome holy man. She had no clear conception of the relationship between them; she had merely an inarticulate but vívid feeling that she was a part of him. And for that reason—this was Reisel's firm conviction—he knew all her thoughts; whatever occurred in her mind was immediately transferred to his; he ruled over her destiny, but at the same time he was her patron, her protector, the man who would not let her come to harm and who took her part as if she were his own child. . . .

She felt a deep and grateful love toward him, such as a favorite child might feel toward a benevolent father, who yields to it in everything, and shields it in all circumstances. But at the same time she had a quite incomprehensible fear of him. She did her utmost to avoid meeting him, whenever she passed his house her heart palpitated with terror. Only at the annual Torah Festival, when the Rabbi danced in the court of the synagogue with the sacred scrolls, did she ever see him; she was sent on that day to the Rabbi with all the other children and stood among them beside the women, a flag in her hand, to watch the Rabbi and his Chassidim dancing with the scrolls of the Torah.

The last time she had seen him had been stamped with special clearness on her memory. He was walking in a white silk caftan under a canopy. He was very tall; to Reisel he seemed supernaturally tall. He was carrying a Torah scroll in his hand and dancing, or rather rocking to and fro with a rhythmic movement. His face was very long and very pale, and the look in his half-hooded eyes was so sad, so profoundly sad, that it almost made her cry. And as he advanced, so tall and all in white, under the canopy, she was as proud of him as if he had been her father, yes, more than a father.

On this night, then, the Rabbi appeared to her in a dream. He was clad in white and his face was still paler and sadder than it had been at the Torah Festival. But curiously enough she was not now afraid of him. Nor was she surprised to see him in her cell; it seemed quite natural that he should know the way to it and that all doors should be opened to him as to the Holy Ghost of whom Sister Helene had told her. The Rabbi uttered no word, he merely gazed at her yearningly with his great eyes.

The silent sadness of his eyes stabbed her to the heart. So much pain lay in that narrow, white face, round those thin, blanched lips, that it was more than she could bear. She burst into wild sobbing and was ready to renounce everything, even the handsome Stepan, if only the Rabbi would not look at her so sadly and would forgive her!

Reisel woke up in a hysterical fit of weeping.

CHAPTER V

THE PRIEST

THE town priest Wisniecki was greatly troubled by the Jewish religion, and strove unceasingly to combat it. With the Jews themselves he had no quarrel; indeed, he had a great affection for them and their simple piety, and more than once had intervened to protect them from the hatred and fury stirred up against them by agitators. From the bottom of his heart he was sorry for the Jewish people because they were denied the light of the Christian faith, and all his scorn was reserved for their spiritual leaders, the Rabbis, whom he regarded as the direct descendants of the Pharisees who had had Jesus put to death. He never referred to a Rabbi except as "the Pharisee." As for the Jews themselves, the Bible told him that they were "the chosen people," the race who had produced the Messiah. And the humiliations they had to endure were only a penalty for their stiff-neckedness, which was also mentioned in the Bible. They had rejected the Son of God who appeared among them for their salvation. Strangers had acknowledged Him and won redemption, but His own people had cast Him out, as Christ Himself said: "Many shall come from the east and west and shall sit down with Abraham and Isaac and Jacob in the Kingdom of Heaven. But the children of the Kingdom shall be cast out into outer darkness; there shall be weeping and gnashing of teeth."

Yet although banished from the King's table they were still King's children, and the world could not come to its perfection until the King's children were admitted again. All would have been well, the Kingdom of Heaven on earth would have been long established, Christ would have been by now sole ruler of the world if only the Jews had let themselves be redeemed. But they were a perverse generation, they turned away from the Word of God. And yet they were the people to whom the Messiah was sent, and the King would count it for righteousness to all who treated his rebel children kindly.

So when the priest saw in the market place the huckstering little Jews of the town his heart bled for them; what a fate for the descendants of Abraham, Isaac, and Jacob! His sympathy moved him to lend the poor wretches a helping hand whenever he could. He had his own special Jews for whom he could not do too much, such as Yekel the ferryman, Isaac the peddler, the widow Hannah, whom he called in Biblical language "Hannah with the seven sons," for her husband had dowered her well with children before removing himself to Paradise and leaving her to bear the heat and burden of the day. Hannah was a "basket woman"; she carried the heavy market baskets to the various houses and so earned a few groschen. And whenever the Jewish fishermen had a good catch and secured a salmon, or a dozen crayfish, which they themselves never ate, the widow Hannah would carry these delicacies to the priest.

He knew very well where the shoe pinched his pensioners, and he would send them a sack of potatoes for the winter or a small load of firewood that he had begged from some landowner for the poor of the town. Sometimes he gave them money as well, to get medicine for a sick relative, for instance, but he usually handed that over in person. And whenever any one abused the Jews, the priest felt it laid on his conscience to defend them.

He was actually jealous, however, of the Jews' feast days, of their piety and fidelity to God. Because the Jews all shut their shops on the Sabbath, and had candles gleaming festively from their windows, the priest would hold them up as an example to his own erring flock, "Look at the Jews," he would thunder in his deep voice; "they keep their Sabbath so piously that not a drop of brandy can be bought anywhere! But you, you cultivate your fields on the Sabbath, you violate the day of rest, you hardly even come to church!"

But most of all he grudged the Jews their great festivals, the prep- arations for the Passover, the New Year's Eve celebrations and, above all, the Day of Atonement, when, all clad in white, men and women alike, holding candles in memory of the dead, they proceeded to the synagogue and into the Chassidic prayer rooms. That always excited the priest and roused his most secret feelings. No, this was no worship of an alien God, no heathen rite with which he had no concern and to which he could remain indifferent—this was a literal assault on Heaven, a war between spirits and angels on the highest plane of all. The Jews were attempting to take Heaven by storm and humiliate Jesus forever! Wisniecki's blood ran hot. He had the church bells rung more loudly and insistently than usual to call true believers to vespers —it was like a cry for help. And he recited the Latin prayers with

double intensity and bowed himself before the altar in a frenzy of
devotion.

His highest and most sacred ambition was to be found worthy to
bring one soul from the ranks of the chosen people to the feet of
Christ; that was an ambition for which he would cheerfully have laid
down his life. He was an ascetic, but this was his secret passion and
he did all he could to further it. To the poor Jews who needed his help
he would suggest—of course, in guarded terms—that a terrible fate
awaited them in the next world, that they were doomed to eternal Hell,
not because of their own sins but because, smitten with blindness, they
had refused their sole redemption, the faith of the Catholic Church.

The Jews, however, as soon as they observed the tendency of his
remarks, faded away as if from the face of the earth. A sack of potatoes, a load of wood, a few coins for their sick, they would not hesitate
to accept, but as soon as the priest touched on "these things," they
made themselves scarce with embarrassed shrugs and head shakings.
They never let themselves be drawn into argument; they simply vanished.

Many a time had he spent the night prone before the Cross, his
forehead on the ground, imploring God to open the eyes and hearts
of the Jews so that they could see and experience their true salvation,
the redemption they so obstinately rejected. How often had he fasted
and mortified his flesh for the Jews' sake! He believed with all his
heart that the Catholic Church was the sole instrument of grace and
salvation, that the Lord of the Universe had endowed it with a portion
of his Majesty and committed to its care the Holy Ghost. He was
firmly convinced that all who remained outside the Church would die
in sin and burn in Hell forever. And those to whom God had first
revealed Himself, among whom Christ had appeared, in whose land
He had lived and preached, were the very people who had rejected
Him right up to the present! Was it not time that the whole world
was redeemed from sin and the Kingdom of God perfected? Humanity
was sufficiently burdened with sin and evil. And the Jews were the
obstacle; their stiff-neckedness was the sole hindrance to the redemption of the world. In the priest's eyes the Rabbis were responsible for
everything, these Pharisees who had once condemned Jesus to death
and had sat in judgment on Him ever since. They it was who kept the
Children of Israel from coming to Christ, and they cheated the brethren of Christ from a share in His Kingdom. How were the poor blind
victims to be rescued from the ravening jaws of the Rabbis?

Like everybody else in the town the priest had, of course, heard the strange rumors about the birth of Selig's daughter. And of course he believed that the so-called miracle was a piece of devil's work which that Pharisee, the Rabbi, had brought off by means of his "secret Cabbalistic arts and Talmudic ingenuity." For that reason he felt embarrassed at the sight of the girl and regarded her with suspicion. He was convinced that this product of black magic would bring evil in her train and prove a misfortune to the whole town. Even her looks betrayed her diabolical origin, in his opinion, for she was dowered with an infernal beauty. Her eyes were like black coals and she always wore red ribbons in her heavy black plaits. How could the horse dealer have begotten such a lovely daughter, with her noble bearing and proud gait, her refined and well-bred manners? The very way she dressed herself had something of the devil in it; she wore such bright-hued frocks and scarves. It seemed advisable to have as little to do with her as possible.

It can be imagined into what agitation the honest priest was thrown when the pious Chojnacki sisters informed him that the horse dealer's daughter wanted to be admitted into the Roman Catholic Church. His first thought was that this was a trick of Satan's. He counseled caution, since the consequences of such a step were impossible to foresee. The two old maids, however, insisted that the child had a pious soul and that God had worked upon her heart; besides, she was in love with a good Christian, young Stepan, the estate agent's son, who wanted her to become a Catholic so that he could marry her. And so the priest decided to probe into the matter himself and to speak face to face with the unfortunate creature. . . .

The "she-devil" proved to be a shy, trembling girl with a pale face and quivering lips; he could hear her teeth chattering as she stood before him. A poor little Jewish girl who had fallen in love with all the ardor of her passionate temperament and was ready to do anything for her handsome Christian sweetheart. She crossed herself reverently and recited the Pater Noster which she had learned from the Chojnackis and knew by heart.

No, this was no instrument of the devil! The old priest was convinced that God's hand was at work. This girl whom the Jews regarded as a miracle wrought by the Rabbi had been chosen by God to be a shining light of the true faith. And he himself in his old age had been granted the grace he had prayed for all his life, the joy of bringing a Jewish soul to the feet of Christ.

When Reisel was found in the morning, hysterical in her cell, she kept on crying that she had seen the Rabbi in a dream and that she must go home. The nuns, at their wits' end, sent for the priest, and told him that Reisel had repented her intention to enter the Church and was crying to go back to her parents. Wisniecki blamed the Rabbi for this change of front on the part of the pious girl; the Pharisee was entirely responsible, and his power must be broken first of all.

So he bade the nuns send the girl down to him in the garden. And, as usual, his presence had a calming effect on Reisel, chiefly because of the respect bordering on fear that he evoked from her. All his words were grave and deliberate, and she believed in him almost as much as in the Rabbi. Like the Rabbi he radiated moral force, but she was not awed by the priest, she had confidence in him.

His appearance alone had made a deep impression on her. He was tall and strong and the long soutane made him look taller than any ordinary man. He seemed to be cast in one piece, and his hands, his feet, his head were all enormous. The great square skull was made more imposing by the sharp projection of his forehead, the bones of which looked as if they were cutting the skin. His hair was dove-gray, as were his thick eyebrows and his eyes, which were like deep pools between dark-veined eyelids. His voice was resonant, and seemed to come from unimaginable depths, from remote distances. It was as if he knew everything and saw everything, for his speech was firm and clear, and every word rang out like a bell. In his presence one felt as if in a church. Wherever he stood was holy ground, even here in the bright, sun-dappled acacia alley, and Reisel scarcely dared to lift her eyes to him.

The mere sound of his voice reduced her to insignificance. And yet she had no uncanny feelings about the priest; on the contrary, his presence was a shield to her, an assurance of safety. While she was with him everything looked clear and right; she felt quite calm and entirely resolved to embrace the new life. She was no longer afraid of any one, neither of her parents nor even of the holy Rabbi himself. Beside the tall, strong priest, Reisel not only felt secure from all harm, she desired to please him and to do whatever he required of her. She had a personal affection for him, a childlike trust somewhat like her trust in the Rabbi.

For tenderly as the nuns treated her—and Sister Helene above all —friendly as were their words and kindly their manner, Reisel was quick enough and intelligent enough to divine the limits of their kind-

liness, the sense of duty that dominated all they did. She knew very
well that they were her friends but only as far as their vocation required it. In their attentions she could feel the anxious effort of those
performing a pious duty. Not so with the priest. From her very first
encounter with him Reisel felt a bond of intimacy between them. He
showed a personal interest in her approaching marriage to Stepan; he
was as glad about it as if Stepan were his own son. She took pains
to please him, therefore, just as she tried to please Stepan's relatives,
so that she might be thought worthy of being received into the bosom
of the Church and of marrying her beloved.

Being a woman, Reisel soon knew that the reverend gentleman was
very pleased with her, that she had quite won him over, that he was
willing to help her wholeheartedly in her intended plans. He was not
so cool and distant as the nuns where her love for Stepan was concerned. In sheer self-defense she had kept silent before the nuns about
her feelings for Stepan, since she had a vague instinct that they would
attribute her conversion to this entirely selfish motive. But she had no
need to hide her feelings from the priest; indeed, he himself had
opened the subject. When he had come the day before to see her at the
convent he had brought a message from Stepan, and he never failed to
indicate by some jesting remark how much he approved of their relationship. And so a personal note of intimacy was added to Reisel's faith
in the priest.

She now advanced trembling and with burning cheeks toward the
bench on which he sat under the blossoming acacias and kissed his
hand, while he spoke in jesting reproach.

"I hear that the Rabbi came into your dreams last night and gave
you a fright. I should have thought that you would have dreamed
about somebody else. A pretty girl that's just going to be married
usually dreams of her bridegroom, not of an old Jew. . . ."

Reisel blushed. The good man was delighted, both with his own
joke and the effect of it.

"Am I to tell Stepan that you're dreaming of the Rabbi instead of
him?" he asked, letting his eyes rest paternally on the girl. "He comes
to me every day for news of you."

Reisel plucked up courage. She knelt down and groped for the
priest's hand. "Reverend Father . . . the Rabbi . . . I'm terrified of
him. He looked at me with such sorrowful eyes! He can do miracles.
All the Jews are afraid of him; he can walk through the thickest walls.
They say too that he begged me from God. I'm afraid that he'll do

me some harm." She bent her head and hid her lovely face in the priest's hands.

"Don't come to me with tales of what the Jews say!"—the priest was all at once in earnest. "My dear child, you must put these things out of your head once and for all if you want to join our Church. Will you promise me that?" He spoke severely and took a pinch from his silver snuffbox.

"Yes, Reverend Father," Reisel nodded.

"Listen to me, then, my child. God has been specially gracious to you. From among all your brothers and sisters who were born in unbelief and sin He has chosen you and lodged in your heart the wish to embrace the true faith, so that you may be redeemed by the Holy Ghost and may rise up on the Resurrection Day and not sink into Hell forever like all your brothers and sisters. Therefore you must be grateful to Jesus and with all your heart love Him and the Holy Mother of God, and the Church, the Apostles and the Christian saints. You should thank Christ a thousand times daily for the divine grace that He has shown you, and cast out of yourself all the foolish superstitions that were given you at home. Let them all be dead and buried together with your past life! You have died and been born again in the true redeeming faith of the Catholic Church. Have you understood what I have been saying to you, my child?"

"Yes, Reverend Father."

"And will you promise me to act upon it?"

"Yes, Reverend Father."

"Are you learning your catechism zealously?"

"Yes, Reverend Father."

"Well, tell me: can we do any good work of ourselves toward our salvation?"

"We can do no good work of ourselves toward our salvation; we need the help of God's grace."

"Good, my child, very good. You have a good Jewish head," he added in the Yiddish which he liked to quote when speaking to Jews and could not now refrain from using. "Do you see now that you cannot be redeemed but by the grace of God? Pray to God that His grace does not depart from you." Once more the reverend father held out his hand for the girl to kiss. "Here is a blessed talisman for you, and if the Rabbi ever appears to you again take it in your hand and make the sign of the cross and that will send him packing in a hurry!"

With these words he hung a medallion of the Virgin Mary round her neck. She thanked him, tears rising into her eyes.

"What are you going to do now?"

"I'm going to pick some flowers for the Holy Madonna."

"Good, my child, that's an excellent thing to do, a Christian task. Go and God be with you."

The priest sat later in the Mother Superior's room and said, "A clever race, those Jews! Our convert isn't baptized yet, but she has already a fine sense for the spirit of our religion. They're our superiors in everything, even in Christianity! It's a good thing that they don't all come over to us or we should have nothing but Jewish bishops!"

Reisel in a white frock with her braids carefully combed out went through the convent garden and picked half-blown dark pansies and bright blue forget-me-nots to make a wreath. Then she ran to her room to hang the wreath round the picture of the Madonna. The day was bright and clear, the windows of her cell were open and she could see the main road and the green meadows beyond the garden wall. That was the only view of the world which the convent walls permitted.

Reisel was feeling resolved and assured that she was doing the right thing. Her former life, her old associations, meant nothing to her now. She was acquiring new parents, a new family life. The whole world was open to her. She felt free and as if newborn—everything and everybody waited for her alone. In triumph she clasped the priest's medallion to her bosom, and it was as if she were embracing her new fate, her new family, in which Stepan would take first place by general consent. Reverently and lovingly she bedecked the picture of the Madonna with the garland and for the first time pressed a kiss on it of her own accord.

No hesitation now, no fear, come what might! Her eyes shone with courage and determination as she walked to the open window and gazed out at the wide world spread out so bravely before her beyond the convent walls. It was a world she had conquered for herself through the new faith she had adopted.

All at once her throat contracted and a stab of pain went through her heart. Oh, God, who was that standing there?

She drew back hastily from the window and covered her eyes with her hand like a small child unwilling to look at a horrible sight. But her heart was already moved, and she returned stealthily to the window and peeped round the edge of the white curtain. Yes, that was her mother! There she stood, wrapped in a shawl, right in front of the smithy, moving her lips as if she were calling out something!

"Mother, don't curse me! I can't help myself. For you I'm already dead."

But her peace of mind was shattered. Wherever she was she saw her mother's face gazing at her from the other side of the wall, peering at her from beneath the dark head shawl. When she lay at night on the bed in her cell she fancied that she could hear in the silence the stealthy footsteps of her mother prowling by the convent wall. She told no one that her mother was posted outside, but her peace of mind was gone.

CHAPTER VI

WAR OF THE GODS

THE gods were at war and had chosen as their field of battle the heart of one poor little girl.

Reisel's curtains were tightly drawn; never again would she gaze freely out of the open window. The world outside was as if poisoned. But the eyes in her mother's face had a magic power and could pierce through stone walls. Reisel could not help taking a stealthy peep now and then to see if her mother was still at her post. Now she stood before the carpenter's new house, which lay exactly opposite her cell. She saw the carpenter coming out of his door to drive her mother away. His gestures made it plain that he was ordering her to clear out from the spot where she had been planted since the dawn of day. The carpenter must have said something very insulting, for her mother was crying. Reisel could see her putting her black shawl to her eyes and walking away a little, her shoulders shaking. Then she stood still again, but the Christian took a stick to her and set his dog upon her. "Get out of this, Jewess!" The dog sprang on her mother and tore at her dress. Reisel could not bear it any longer; she put her head out of the window and called.

"Mother, I'm here!"

From the other side of the wall, arms, lips, and eyes yearned up toward her. Shouts for help arose. Then all grew black around Reisel and she saw nothing more.

The nuns came running in and found her lying senseless on the floor.

Like wildfire rumors of this incident spread through the whole district. In the synagogues and praying rooms, in the market places, at the selling pitches, in the shops and butchers' booths, wherever Jewish men and women congregated, the story ran: "The nuns are keeping Selig's daughter by force in the convent"; she called out to her mother, "Mother, save me!" Some claimed to have heard that Reisel threw her mother a note on which was written that she would commit suicide if she were not rescued. Others added that she tried to jump out of the window when she saw her mother, but that the nuns had forcibly

pulled her back. Heads began to grow heated, religious zeal found vent
in threatening looks and gestures. There was no damping down the
ardor; everybody fanned it to a hotter glow. None of the Christians
now sympathized with the horse dealer; the line of cleavage was
sharply defined, Catholics on one side, Jews on the other. The gods
were at war and human souls were drawn into the lists. The Jews
summoned up all their resources—any action was justified in a religious struggle. They turned to the local authorities for help and laid
a charge of theft against Reisel for having robbed her father and gone
off with both dowry and jewels. That would have brought her to jail,
but anything was better than the convent! Where tears failed to make
any impression they had recourse to other shifts for winning partisans
—there was a golden key that never failed to unlock all doors—or so
one would have imagined. On this occasion, however, gold proved of
as little avail as tears. Blood is thicker than water and no man will
lightly betray his faith. Besides, as the Jews were exiles the Christians
had the advantage, and they stood their ground firmly.

In default of law and justice the only remedy is one's own right
hand, especially when feelings run high and prudence is cast to the
winds. Both sides were preparing for battle and answering the call of
their blood. "The Jews have insulted the Catholic religion," cried one
party, and "They have kidnaped a Jewish girl, a bride, into a convent
and are trying to baptize her by force," cried the other. The atmosphere was tense with impending storm. The Christians walked on one
side of the street, the Jews on the other. On every Christian face a
triumphant smile announced that the Jews were getting what they
deserved. The Jews shrank into themselves but their eyes gleamed
dangerously. In the Street of the Butchers itself things were quiet,
but the butchers and fishermen and carters who lived in it, all friends
of Selig's, whispered together in corners.

No Christian entered any Jewish shop. The peasants refused to sell
calves to the Jewish butchers. The Jewish village peddler, Leiser, was
brought home with his head broken. And at the annual fair at Tomashov there was almost a set-to with knives, and some Jewish hatmakers and furriers went home swathed in bandages. On Corpus
Christi Day, the rumor ran, accounts were to be definitely settled, and
all the peasants were beginning to sharpen their scythes.

With helpless rage the Jews now saw the Christians radiating triumph. Preparations were begun for the baptismal ceremony which was
to take place with great pomp in a day or two. It was rumored that

the Bishop himself was to attend it. The country people from all round about were getting ready to come to town to assist at the christening of the rich horse dealer's daughter whom the Rabbi had brought down from heaven. The young peasants of Lonkyshin, the native village of the bridegroom, were to escort the bride; they were already flaunting long white ribbons on their sleeves to the great chagrin of the Jews. In the Street of the Butchers they were nicknamed "Selig's sons-in-law." As was only to be expected all the Christians in town were in high feather. The two Chojnacki sisters, who were to be bridesmaids, were already wearing their white frocks and making themselves long veils for the wedding. The dress and the wreath which the bride was to wear at her christening were purposely set out on show in a shop window and all the young girls were already trying on their white ribbons for the bridal procession. The carpenter even got a new frock coat made, for he was the bridegroom's cousin and was to be one of the witnesses at the wedding. The Christian baker stood all day in the door of his shop boasting that he was baking a wedding cake as tall as a church tower and that he would set it in his window. The Christian butcher chaffed his Jewish colleagues unceasingly and called out to every passing Jew, "You're invited to the christening along with the others!"

The local gentry had engaged to send their equipages to the town. The bride was to drive to church in the four-in-hand coach of the owner of Lonkyshin, right past her parents' house and the Rabbi's house, just to let the Jews see what was what.

Reisel's father and mother were utterly cast down. The very town in which they lived, in which their daughter should have been married, was to be the setting of her baptism! Had the girl only gone into some other part of the country, so that they might have been spared the sight of her! But everybody averred that the young couple were going to settle down in a neighboring village, and at every annual fair she would be flaunting herself in the town—the disgrace, the shame did not bear thinking of!

Selig, who had fancied that he was going to get a Rabbi for a son-in-law and thus purchase himself honor in the next world, was now lying prostrate in his house, gray with despair, roaring like a wounded animal, "It's goyim she'll bring into the world!"

In bed he had dreadful nightmares. He was lying dead in his grave and long evil snakes came crawling upon him and coiled round his arms and legs and strangled him round the throat. Every child that *she* was to bear in the Christian faith engendered a demon which spitted Selig on a long fork and threw him into a furnace, so that he shrieked in his sleep like a madman and his wife had to throw cold water on him to wake him up. Then he would sob his heart out, big strong man as he was; he would never survive the shame of it! Memories of bygone days haunted his mind, rising from remote recesses like adders, steaming up like unhallowed vapors from the pit, wreathing round him, pecking at him, seizing him by misty tentacles and seeking to drag him down into the abyss. He screamed and yelled for help.

As for the mother, she stood daily like an outcast in her black shawl before the convent wall. The Christian inhabitants of the locality, led by the carpenter and the smith, hunted her from pillar to post. Dogs were set upon her and pails of garbage emptied over her. But since the Rabbi had ordered her to stand there all day she obeyed the order. When she was driven from one place she took up her post at another. The street boys threw stones at her, the passing carters jeered at her —one peasant actually slashed her across the face with his whip— but she obeyed the Rabbi's order. Like a wandering shadow her black figure strayed round the convent, face muffled in shawl, murmuring unceasingly the one sentence: "Lord of the Universe, Thou didst open my womb to bear this child, do Thou open her heart to believe on Thee!"

CHAPTER VII

THE LAST NIGHT

THE night before the baptismal ceremony was black and still. The close thick spring darkness lay heavy on the little town. The crooked houses looked like gnomes in pointed caps; weary with age they slept as they stood. All living creatures were mute, stamped by the night's black seal of silence. Wreaths of vapor were drenched in the scent of the blossoming shrubs and acacia trees behind the garden fences, but the prevailing scent was that of the springtime itself, rising from the green meadows behind the little houses. From the young grass a heavy, fragrant mist steamed up and veiled the sleeping earth. In the black stillness only two points of light kept watch, one at either end of the town; two lighted windows illumined the wreathing mists of the night; two human beings could find no sleep. Ruthlessly and obdurately they were concentrating their energies on some end that they viewed by the light of the candles shining through their windows. These two men were the Rabbi and Father Wisniecki, the priest.

In his dim room where the candle glimmered but feebly before the "Light of the World" Yechiel stood in a white robe, motionless, tense as a wire, his head thrown back and his arms outspread. He was praying, but not according to the Book; he was not even reciting the midnight lament, but was speaking in his own words.

"As the smith his iron, so hast Thou beaten us thin with Thy hammer; as the brass founder his molten metal, so hast Thou poured us into ten forms a day and yet we remain the same. God of Israel, our Father, what are we without Thee? Stray sheep, a prey to wolves, the mockery and laughingstock of the world, defenseless victims for every hunter. Thou alone givest a meaning to our distress and our suffering. Thou dost illumine our darkness, Thou dost lift up our agony until it becomes a martyrdom in love for the sake of Thy Holy Name, and only for Thy Name's sake; whosoever thinketh of Thee must desire ten times a day to lay down his life for Thee, as it is written: 'Unless thy law had been my delight, I should have perished in mine affliction.'

Only through Thy law and Thy statutes which we observe can we embrace the sorrows which we endure for Thy sake, can we rejoice in
the tears which we shed for Thy sake."

Yechiel was speaking as if to himself, yet it was not himself he was
addressing but One before whom he humbled himself as a servant
before a beloved master. Like a lover wrapped in dreams of his beloved
Yechiel wept tears of joy and in a full voice vibrant with longing
abased himself before God's radiant majesty and cried:

"Lay upon our shoulders all the sorrows of the world, for the children of Israel rejoice in the suffering they take upon themselves for
Thy dear Name's sake !"

He fell silent and lost himself in his thoughts. In what regions was
he straying, what heights did he reach, what visions, what words of
comfort were vouchsafed to him? Above the white robe the shadowed
face suddenly beamed with great joy and Yechiel all at once grew
young again and bloomed in strength and beauty. In a transport of
ecstasy he threw himself on the ground and stretched out his arms
toward an invisible Someone, imploring: "God of Israel, bring back
the lost lamb to the fold! Beasts of prey are lying in wait to devour
it, but the poor creature is smitten with blindness and does not know
its danger. Do Thou, who seest all the dangers that threaten Thy flock,
make haste to rescue it, O God of Abraham!"

He waited long for an answer but no answer came. Then he sat
up, took the candle from the reading desk and set it beside him on
the floor, opened the psalter and read with hot tears in his eyes:

"A prayer of the afflicted, when he is overwhelmed, and poureth
out his complaint before the Lord.

"Hear my prayer, O Lord, and let my cry come unto thee.

"Hide not thy face from me in the day when I am in trouble; incline
thine ear unto me; in the day when I call answer me speedily.

"For my days are consumed like smoke, and my bones are burned
as an hearth.

"My heart is smitten, and withered like grass; so that I forget to
eat my bread.

"By reason of the voice of my groaning my bones cleave to my
skin. . . ."

So he lamented heartbreakingly, until he achieved his desire and
reached the goal he sought. At last he saw the man, the Satan, who
had crossed his path and destroyed his handiwork and seduced the
wandering sheep from the fold. Yechiel sprang to his feet and, aban-

doning the words of humility, began to cry in a loud voice a mighty appeal to the highest of all authorities, the law of God in whose name and with whose weapons he was fighting against the devil:

"Blessed are the undefiled in the way, who walk in the law of the Lord.

"Blessed are they that keep his testimonies and that seek him with the whole heart.

"They also do no iniquity: they walk in his ways.

"Thou hast commanded us to keep thy precepts diligently.

"Oh that my ways were directed to keep thy statutes!

"Then I shall not be ashamed, when I have respect unto all thy commandments...."

And in the name of the erring soul he begged:

"Remove from me the way of lying: and grant me thy law graciously.

"I have chosen the way of truth: thy judgments have I laid before me.

"I have cleaved unto thy testimonies: O Lord, put me not to shame...."

In the middle of the psalm he broke off, covered his head with his prayer shawl and cried aloud as if his heart were bursting:

"Salvation is far from the wicked; for they seek not thy statutes...."

At the other end of the little town, where the other ray of light pierced the darkness, the priest too was awake and arming himself for the final struggle.

He knew very well that he had no sure grasp of the soul he had caught for his God. In the last few days Satan had insinuated himself into Reisel's heart and was gaining power over her; she had quite lost her happy delight in the grace of God. She was always melancholy now, growing thinner and paler day by day. She refused to eat or listen to the Word of God; she was shut in upon herself and at night tormented by demons. The nuns reported that she sobbed in her sleep and screamed for help. Ever since that accursed Jewish witch had taken up her stand before the convent the poor child had had no peace. All efforts to drive the woman away had failed. Reisel had been given another cell on the opposite side of the convent, looking out on fields, but her mother had turned up even there. The priest was convinced that this was a machination of the Rabbi's. At first he had thought of going to see the Rabbi and begging him to stop torturing the poor child who was knocking at Jesus's door, to stop snaring her in Cabbalistic spells, but at the last moment, in this final, decisive crisis, he was unwilling to come into any personal contact with the "devil" and turned instead to Christ and the saints. This very night—he knew—would be the worst; Satan would deploy all the powers of darkness to hound the fleeing soul in the last hours before its redemption.

So, all night through, he knelt before the Cross on which Jesus had hung suffering with the despairing cry on his lips: "My God, my God, why hast thou forsaken me?" All through the night the priest prayed to Christ, and like the Rabbi he prayed in his own words.

"Almighty Christ, open Thy door and take under Thy wing the poor soul that comes fluttering like a stray bird through storm and rain and darkness to seek refuge with Thee. Lo, the hounds are baying at her heels, black crows are setting upon her to devour her utterly, and the poor creature with her last remaining strength beats her frail wings against Thy door. Open to her, give her shelter; spread the wings of Thy faith to cover the trembling creature that shivers in outer cold and darkness; shower Thy grace upon her like a loving mother, O Christ!"

The priest too took up a firm stand on God's Word and God's Law. He too in a confident voice appealed in the name of his Church to the eternal verities entrusted by God to her keeping. He too pleaded the cause of the erring soul, and in the name of his religion quoted the selfsame verses as the Rabbi. In his metallic, sonorous voice he recited from the Latin text:

"Blessed are the undefiled in the way, who walk in the law of the Lord.

"Blessed are they that keep his testimonies and that seek him with the whole heart.

"They also do no iniquity: they walk in his ways.

"Thou hast commanded us to keep thy precepts diligently.

"Oh that my ways were directed to keep thy statutes!

"Then shall I not be ashamed, when I have respect unto all thy commandments. . . .

"With my whole heart have I sought thee. . . ."

His words came thundering out, for they were designed to rout the devil who persisted in waylaying the girl's soul. He faced toward the Jewish quarter, the source of all the trouble, and cried in a ringing voice, to confound Yechiel, the Pharisee:

"Rebuke the proud that are cursed, which do err from thy commandments."

Then in the name of the tormented girl he proclaimed with assurance:

"Remove from me the way of lying: and grant me thy law graciously.

"I have chosen the way of truth: thy judgments have I laid before me.

"I have cleaved unto thy testimonies: O Lord, put me not to shame."

And, just as Yechiel was doing, he cried in an access of passion:

"Salvation is far from the wicked, for they seek not thy statutes."

Reisel too was lying awake in her cell. The nuns had warned her that in this last night before the decisive step was taken she might expect to have a terrible struggle with Satan, who would torment her and wrestle with her to induce her to leave the way of salvation. But for Reisel the struggle had begun days ago, from the moment when she saw her mother standing outside the convent. The gods were waging war for a human soul, and all the thunders and lightnings they loosed against each other passed through the quivering nerves of the girl and shot their bolts in her heart.

Reisel set herself to make the preparations for the sacred ceremonies of the ensuing day, when before God and men she was to be first baptized and then married to Stepan. The white frock she was to wear in the procession lay carefully spread out on a chair together with her bridal veil, her myrtle wreath, her white stockings and shoes. All these had been procured for her by the two Chojnackis and her bridegroom. Reisel knew that her baptism was to be made the occasion for a great ceremony attended by the gentry and the peasantry of the whole neighborhood. She knew also that for the past week none of the Jews had ventured to show themselves in the streets. According to the nuns, the Jews were all shut in the synagogues praying by candlelight for Satan to use his power upon her; but the Lord Jesus and the Holy Mother of God would guard her, if she only prayed urgently to the Madonna in her own room for help against the wiles of Satan.

Before it was dark she had taken a last peep through the window

and bidden a silent farewell to her mother. It was very strange, but
on this day her mother's face looked remarkably like the sorrowing
face of the Madonna. Reisel had recognized on her mother's countenance the same tokens of tears and suffering. But all that was now
over, she could not alter anything; tomorrow she was to be baptized
and married and everything was made ready. She had ceased to feel
any joy in the prospect, she had ceased to be capable of feeling.
The torments she had endured in her soul these last few days had
blunted her capacity for emotion of any kind. It did not matter what
happened to her; she only wanted it to happen as soon as possible so
that there might be an end and she might have peace. She was so
tired, so tired!

And now she lay awake on this last night before her baptism.
The ghostly white raiment on the chair scared her a little, for it
looked like something that was alive. She was weary and she needed
sleep, but sleep would not come. If only the night were over! The
time dragged on so slowly. Reisel longed for sleep, yet she was afraid
to fall asleep, for the Jews were shut in the synagogues and were
praying by candlelight with their prayer shawls wrapped round them
as they did on New Year's Day. Oh, if the night were only at an end!

Once more the thought of the Rabbi haunted her. They said that
he could drive out evil spirits—he could drive out even a dybbuk.
Reisel could remember how he had driven out a dybbuk that had taken
possession of a girl like herself who was brought to the Rabbi bound
with ropes and a strange voice shrieking out of her; it was dreadful!
But the Rabbi could work miracles. Father Wisniecki said it was only
black magic conjured up by Cabbalistic spells. What were Cabbalistic
spells? She did not know, for she had never been properly instructed;
she was only a girl. The young man her parents had chosen for her
would certainly know what the spells were; they must be rather
terrible since they could drive out even a dybbuk. What was a dybbuk?
It was the spirit of some one who had been baptized a Christian or
committed some other great sin and so could find no peace in the
next world and had to come back to earth and seek a habitation in
some human being. Dreadful—and that was what would happen to
herself! She was going to be baptized, and when she died she would
turn into a dybbuk and haunt human beings! She would be bound
with ropes, like the dybbuk in that other girl who was brought to the
Rabbi! A cold sweat broke out on her forehead and her hair was
damp although her cheeks were fevered. She stared wildly round

her—the white frock that she was to wear on the morrow for her baptism had suddenly come alive and was walking on feet of its own across the room!...

No, they couldn't do anything to her, for she was already under the protection of Jesus. The priest was praying for her. She remembered the nun's admonitions: if Satan should come by night to tempt her she was to kneel down before the Madonna and pray. She started up from her couch, tottered toward the small red lamp glowing above the Madonna, threw herself down on her knees and with outstretched arms began the "Hail Mary."

Her eye fell on the Madonna's face. It looked old and drawn with pain; she was gazing at the body of her Son which had been taken from the cross and laid at her feet; she was weeping; from her reddened eyes tears—tears of blood—were running down her cheeks. These reddened eyes were like the eyes of Reisel's own mother; the face was like the face Reisel had glimpsed at a distance that very day, yes, that was just how her mother had gazed at her, with the same tears flowing from reddened eyelids—and indeed they were tears of blood!

"Oh, my dear mother, what am I to do?"

She needed help, she felt as if she were suffocating. She must pray, pray to Jesus. She crossed herself before the picture of Christ. That helped her a little and she grew calmer. Tomorrow it would all be over, and now she should go to bed. No, better not fall asleep; she might dream again. But how suffocatingly hot the room was!

Reisel went to open the window. Down in the garden there was still thick darkness but across the wall and over the fields pale wreaths of mist were rising.... Oh, God, who was that standing there? Her mother, wrapped in a shawl! Her mother, out in the night alone!

Reisel recoiled as if stricken from the window and cast herself on her couch, her hands over her face. But as she lay there a vision suddenly projected itself on the blank darkness before her eyes, an infinite plain, an Elysian field. On one side stood Jesus and Mary upon a small hill, together with the priest and a great crowd of peasants and other people, Stepan among them. On the other side clustered another group, the Rabbi, her mother and father and a whole synagogue of Jews in their white robes and prayer shawls. And between them she saw herself standing, quite alone. To her great amazement she saw herself, standing barefoot in a little white frock, quite small, still a child, alone and forlorn looking between the two groups.

This image of herself terrified her and she snatched her hands from before her eyes. The vision had vanished; she was alone in her cell. What, oh, what was she to do? She was too terrified to stay in bed, for she did not want to see herself again in a vision. And outside there was her mother! Reisel paced restlessly up and down her cell, and in the darkness struck against something. She started in affright —perhaps she was already a dybbuk.

"No!" she cried, sobbing loudly. "I belong to another faith already; Christ and His Blessed Mother are watching over me!"

To reassure herself she put on the dress in which she was to be baptized, throwing it hastily over her nightgown. And so, barefoot, in her white frock, she roamed around the cell, trying to persuade herself that her parents would come to her wedding next day. Why shouldn't they? She wanted to forget all that had happened in the meantime. And in imagination she saw them all at her wedding, the Rabbi, the priest, Stepan, and her parents, all together.

Pale light was stealing in through the window. Reisel was no longer afraid to look outside, and she threw the casements open. The glimmering wreaths of mist that rose from the fields were now curling into the garden, and the chestnut candles and acacia clusters gleamed palely among them. It looked as if everything were floating in the air. The soft white vapor rolled over the earth like a sea and the sky came down to meet it. The sky must have lowered itself right down to earth, and it should be easy now to peep into heaven and see who were there: the angels, Jesus, the Mother of God. . . . And indeed she could see them! And they were reconciled! Jews and Christians were walking on the white cloud together! There was the Rabbi hand in hand with the priest, and over yonder was Stepan standing beside her parents and smiling to her! The Rabbi was smiling, too, and the priest; they were all smiling and friendly, and so glad to see her! How had it happened, that they were all reconciled?

"Oh, Mother, how lovely!" whispered Reisel, weeping tears of joy, and spread out her arms to fly toward them, to be at one with all of them. . . .

Next morning the nuns found her lying in her white frock like a stricken dove on the stone pavement beside the steps, her black braids clotted with the blood that had oozed out of her shattered skull.

CHAPTER VIII

REPROACH

ALL that night farm carts went rumbling into the town. Through the thin walls of the Jewish huts the rattling of wheels, the jingling of harness, the clop-clop of hoofs on the badly paved roads could be heard with dreadful distinctness. And husbands and wives whispered to each other in bed, "They're coming to Selig's funeral." That was just what they were doing, for they were all rumbling in to attend the baptism and Christian marriage of Selig's only daughter. The whole village of Strzelec was there with gay, flower-bedecked carts and horses: all the "long fellows" from the village of Chmiel were there, and enormous loads of country girls adorned with strings of coral and bright ribbons. The tall men from the estates of Count Dombrowski were there in their harlequin woolen garb, although they really belonged to the next district. For people were coming long distances, even from faraway districts, folk who were only to be seen at the great fairs: the news of Reisel's conversion had spread far and wide and everybody wanted to attend the baptism, partly out of pious sympathy and partly from mere curiosity. It was said that the Bishop himself was to perform the ceremony, assisted by six dignitaries of the Church, and that ladies of the highest nobility were to escort the rich horse dealer's daughter on her journey into the bosom of the Catholic Church.

The whole of the Jewish community, however, was assembled in the synagogues. Rabbi Yechiel had ordained a day of general fasting and repentance for every one, young and old alike, as if (which God forbid!) a roll of the Torah had fallen on the ground. He himself stood at the head of his congregation, close up to the east wall, completely muffled in his large prayer shawl, motionless, stiff, and rigid as death. It looked as if the prayer shawl were swathed round a corpse. The schoolboys gazed at his figure from the distance with awe and amazement, as if it were something extraordinary and incomprehensible. The whole congregation was reciting psalms, for not a Jew present but was oppressed by fear. Every one of them felt the disgrace and

311

the sorrow laid upon the community as if it concerned his own child. And all eyes were turned to the corner beside the Ark of the Torah where the Rabbi was posted. That was the corner from which help must come. Would he achieve it? Would he succeed at the last minute in averting the impending evil by some stroke in Heaven, where his spirit was now sojourning? No man let his heart sink utterly, no man quite gave up hope. And all the time every bell was ringing in all the town belfries, calling the Christians to solemn triumph in their Church.

At the far end, by the water cask near the door, Selig the horse dealer, father of the renegade, lay prone on the floor, a ruin, the wreck of a man. His enormous body filled the whole breadth of the entrance. There he had flung himself to be trodden on and spurned by every pious member of the congregation. No Rabbi had laid this penance on him; he had adopted it of his own free will to rescue the soul of his daughter from the bonds of sin.

The renegade's mother in the women's room was in much the same case as the father among the men. She was left to sit alone on a bench, save for a neighbor on whose shoulder her hooded head was leaning. The half-crazed woman beat upon her bosom increasingly and cried, "O Lord, rend to pieces this bosom that has given suck to a renegade!"

Waxen tears ran from the great death candles that were burning for Reisel's soul all over the synagogue in brass pots filled with sand. Waxen tears ran from the candles in the seven-branched candlesticks before the cantor's desk, in the hand-wrought lanterns hanging from the roof and set against the wall. In frenzied ecstasy the psalm verses mounted up to God, and still all eyes were fixed on the white, silver-bordered prayer shawl swathing the motionless figure that stood with its face to the wall.

Suddenly something happened. No one knew exactly what caused the abrupt change in the atmosphere, but a peculiar uneasiness had suddenly seized on the whole assembly, and the voices reciting the psalms faltered of their own accord. Heads peered out from prayer shawls and glanced at the door as if expecting somebody. The interruption was so clearly perceptible that the Temple server found it needful to beat on the desk and cry, "Silence there!"

And still nobody knew what had happened. Eyes were fixed intently on the white figure by the wall, the Rabbi Yechiel, but he was still and silent as ever; not a breath, not a movement could be discerned; it was as if a mummy stood there. Yet everybody was convinced that whatever caused the uneasiness had emanated from that corner, from that white figure by the eastern wall. The whole assembly was waiting breathlessly for something else to happen in that corner where the Rabbi stood, but there was nothing for any one to see. The uneasiness increased, even the candle flames wavered and the waxen tears ran more thickly and rapidly down the brass candlesticks. A whisper ran from mouth to mouth, "What is it? What's happened?"

"Haven't you noticed—the bells have stopped ringing!"

It was true. The congregation only now became aware that a silence had fallen outside. A terrifying, suffocating silence that pressed in through doors and windows: the bells had stopped ringing in the very middle of a peal.

The next occurrence came like a thunderclap. Oyserl the thief appeared suddenly in the door of the synagogue, breathless, with foam on his lips, and deathly pale as if he had risen from the grave. His coat and shirt were flying open and an uncertain gleam wavered in his dark eyes. He could not speak at first for exhaustion and the press of the crowd thronging around him; he merely rolled wild eyes at the panic-stricken mob. But then he fell upon the prone figure of Selig and shook him and jerked him with demoniac strength into a sitting position. "Selig, get up, there's to be no baptism, there's to be no wedding!"

The horse dealer glared at him dumbly with bewildered eyes.

"She's dead, Selig!"

A short high shriek of lamentation rose and died away immediately, followed by wild cries from the women's room and shouts of "Water, water!"

But the psalm chanting did not stop; it gathered strength and all at once rang out more powerfully than ever, sweeping up to heaven in a frenzy of enthusiasm that sounded almost like a triumphal march.

Reisel's young life, cut short so cruelly, was still, as it were, bleeding like a felled pine tree, and yet people were already accepting her fate. With a tear and a sigh her mother thought, "It was the best way out!" Her father growled a curse between clenched teeth, and the mother soothed him with the words, "She's standing now at the judgment seat of God." The whole town inclined to the opinion that it had all happened for the best. There was already a growing belief that Reisel had committed suicide as a last desperate resort to save herself from being baptized by force. "In that case she's sure of eternal bliss," people said, "and not one of us is worthy to stand beside her."

But there was one man who could not accept this conclusion. One man there was who struggled against the unjust fate that made his heart bleed—and it was the man who more than any other was responsible for Reisel's death. Reb Yechiel the Rabbi. He was asking himself: "Am not I to blame for everything? Shall I not have to account for it at the bar of God's judgment that I helped in the untimely destruction of a young life, even though it was the best fate for her? How much evil may a man be allowed to do in order to save a soul? Where is the line to be drawn?" And while the others saw in the tragic event merely the righteous hand of God, or even vaunted it as a miracle wrought by the Rabbi, Yechiel was telling himself, "The works of my hands are swept away in the flood, and you sing songs of joy. . . ." He fell into a state of dejection, not the grief that rends a man's heart and humbles his spirit and brings him in due time contrite before the Lord, but the black melancholy that destroys all joy in life. Day after day passed over the Rabbi without his feeling the glory of God shining on his head. He felt rather that God had forsaken him, that His eye had waxed dim. This was no doubt a trick of the Evil One, who had long been lying in wait for Yechiel, but had not hitherto been able to trip him up.

Yes, Yechiel's melancholy was certainly prompted by the Evil One. For, after all, what happened to the girl had had to happen, was bound to happen. Yechiel had himself desired it and had prayed God that she should die rather than betray the Jewish religion, that she might be permitted to leave the world in purity and holiness. She had been given the same name as his own blessed Reisel—might she rest in peace!—and there must have been a spark of the divine fire in her soul, and for that reason heaven had succored her so that she repented before dying and was saved from crossing the threshold of the underworld. In that case she was a martyr for her faith, and was assured of bliss everlasting. Then why such melancholy? Because she had missed some portion of our miserable life on earth?

These admirable arguments had no effect on Yechiel. Hundreds of times he tried his conscience to discover whether he had been justified in praying for Reisel's death. Was that following the way of God, Who should be his pattern in all things? The Scripture said: "The Lord is righteous in all his ways," but had *he* been righteous in all his ways? "One hour of repentance and the doing of a good deed on earth is better than an eternity in Heaven," it was written, and further: "Even when Israel sins it remains Israel." The gates of mercy and repentance stood open to Israel at all times. How could

Yechiel have lifted a finger to bring a young life to an untimely end?

His condition grew even worse; in the middle of a prayer evil thoughts would trouble him and break the tie that bound him to the upper regions. He observed that his prayers and entreaties came dropping back from heaven like wounded birds; nothing that he said found admittance any longer into that kingdom. The light went out of his eyes and wisdom departed from his heart; he no longer could read the sign of God on men's faces, and he was terrified at himself.

Yechiel's was no speculative mind. He had always avoided whatever searched into God's ways, following the precept: "Seek not to discover what is hidden from thee." Consequently he held all speculative thinkers for men of little faith. Such researches were alien to his nature; his own strength lay in his faith, a deep, inward blind faith in God's goodness, which mankind, he thought, should emulate. And so whenever he came up against the age-old question why the wicked should prosper on earth and the righteous be afflicted, he simply evaded it. He believed with his whole heart that there was no evil either in God or in His creation, because of the Scripture which said: "And God saw everything that he had made, and, behold, it was very good."

But in this battle for Reisel's soul tempests had shaken Yechiel and shattered the foundations of his world. Worse than that, they had cast veils of dust before his eyes so that he was being seduced along hitherto untrodden paths. Until now he had followed the prevailing tradition among the Jews which accounted for the existence of non-Jewish races by supposing them to be merely God's instrument of oppression, a rod for the back of Israel when it fell into sin; he knew that they had their own part in God's grace and their own pleaders in Heaven whose influence waxed when Israel went astray, but he had never regarded them as existing independently and for their own sakes; to his mind they lived only for the sake of the Jews dispersed among them. Nations who harbored Jews thereby earned a high place in creation and were also made in God's image and belonged to the righteous peoples of the earth who were sure of a life hereafter. But further than that Yechiel had never gone. He lived as it were on a small chosen island, the Kingdom of the Jews, the children of Abraham, while around him the non-Jews existed in a foreign country, on alien plains and deserts and unharvested seas. Doubtless God's attributes reigned there too as in the whole of creation, but Yechiel had no concern with that; it was not his world.

And now he was troubled by new thoughts which had arisen from his contact with that other world during his struggle for Reisel's soul. He began to ask himself: "What are these nations of the Gentiles? There is no creature breathing that is not made by God, and so they are also a part of God's creation. Why do they not all acknowledge His name? Why do we not see the fulfillment of our New Year's prayer that all might make a covenant together to do His will wholeheartedly?"

He saw now in anguish that he had always put these things far from him; he had been too busy giving himself away piecemeal and had done nothing for himself . . . he had not cultivated his own garden.

Nothing availed to counter these painful broodings; not even the knowledge that he was one of the chosen by whom alone God desired to be acknowledged. Doubt was tearing at Yechiel's soul like a beast of prey, and his heart was tormented by the divisions among mankind. His simple mind could not grasp the double game which the Godhead seemed to be playing with humanity; on the one hand, an omnipresent Providence and, on the other, mankind's privilege to choose for itself between good and evil. That seemed to Yechiel an irresponsible, even a wicked arrangement, exactly as if a father were to let his ignorant child play with fire. "What then is man that Thou hast raised him so high and bestowed so much of Thy care upon him? Can any man stand up against Thee? The Scripture says: 'How should man be just with God? If he will contend with him he cannot answer him one of a thousand.' . . ."

It looked almost as if Satan had wormed his way into the simple and credulous heart of the Rabbi in order to snare him completely. Yechiel went on to ask wherein the powers of these Others resided, and what their merits might be. He had failed to rescue alive a Jewish maiden who had fallen into their clutches and had had to be content with saving the child's soul. But it said in the Psalms: "The dead praise not the Lord." It could not have been merely the power of Satan or of evil spirits that had so stoutly resisted him! He himself could oppose holiness to impiety—one chapter of the Psalms opened the most tightly sealed doors of Heaven and made him capable even of striding through flames that barred his path. This time, however, it had been equal powers that were ranged against him, forces that brought up their own values and covenants, their own divine advocates, with celestial fires shooting from some Heaven of

their own. During that battle he had felt that these Others had their
roots in regions from which he was excluded.

"If that is so, wherein lies their assurance? Their power cannot
derive solely from the fact that the Jews are sinful!" And yet he
simply could not admit any other basis on which to rest their claims,
for that would mean that the Godhead possessed more than one face,
that would mean admitting Evil not only as a temporary cause but
as a primal cause, eternal and inexhaustible as Good!

Yechiel flinched. "O God in heaven, what am I coming to?" He
felt suffocated, as if a cord had been tightened around his neck. And
as a man of heroic temper cuts out of his body any flesh that has
mortified and casts it far from him, so Yechiel with his last strength
excised the poisonous thought from his soul and hurled it away.
Shaken as if by an ague he cried in an ecstasy of devotion: "He is
the One and Only, and there is no other Oneness but His, He is
hidden from our eyes and his Oneness is infinite, He is the First
of all things which He created, He is the First and there is no beginning to his Firstness!"

No, it was out of the question to think otherwise. The sole value
of the Others consisted in the fact that the Jews were perverse, that
they had rejected their privilege of being God's chosen, that they
refused to be a dedicated race. "O Lord, what have we become?"
Yechiel wailed, and beat his head on the wooden Ark of the Torah.
"Are we not yet punished sufficiently? Thou hast sold Thy people,
and not even at a price; Thou hast rated them low indeed! We are
become a shame and a mockery to our neighbors, a byword and a
laughingstock to the world. The nations hold us up to derision and
shake their heads over us. All day long the dishonor of the Jews
stands before my eyes, and I am ashamed because of the curses and
reproaches of our enemies, Thy avengers. Our sufferings are great,
indeed, and yet we have not forgotten Thee, we have not denied Thy
covenant. . . ."

At these words his heart almost burst in torment, remembering
the misery and shame that Israel had to endure. The poor Jews of
the town were cowering in their houses, afraid to peddle their wares
through the country, for the fate of Reisel had made the peasantry
hostile and angry. This hatred had already cost a few human lives,
and to go trading in the villages was to risk one's neck. In the town
itself things were almost as bad. And the poor Jews endured it all
for the sake of God's dear Name! And yet they were denounced as

evil, they were delivered into the hands of strangers and oppressed by aliens; God's chosen people had become a butt for the nations of the world! The thought of this injustice made Yechiel's heart overflow with pain and resentment. He forgot before Whom he was standing and poured out a stream of reproaches and accusations against the Lord of the Universe:

"How long, O Lord, how long shall Thy quarrel with Thy people endure? Would it not be better for Thee to live at peace with them? I will say as Job once said: 'Why dost thou not pardon my transgression and take away mine iniquity?' Why canst Thou not forgive us? Thou art said to be a God of mercy and compassion and we are to learn to be like Thee, and yet Thou dost deliver helpless men and women and children into the power of savage beasts who know not Thy Name and have none of Thy compassion in their hearts! What is Thy quarrel with us? Why dost Thou persist in making us the target for Thy arrows? Why has it pleased Thee to make *us* Thy chosen people? We can bear it no longer—go to the Others, let *them* be Thy servants! We are weary of suffering and injustice Thou dost lay upon us, we can no longer bear it! Take back Thy charge, release us from being Thy chosen, for we are so weary, so weary!"—Yechiel sank to the floor in a swoon.

Old Ezriel, waiting behind the door, felt that something strange was occurring in the room, but he did not dare to enter, he merely stood trembling and listening. He had great difficulty in keeping back the impatient throng of petitioners; his whole attention was concentrated on the door and he could hear the faintest movement in the Rabbi's chamber. His heart was uneasy and he was too agitated to bring out any articulate words—his toothless jaws merely mumbled.

When he heard the noise of the Rabbi's collapse he burst the bolt, pushed his way in, and found Yechiel lying on the floor. Stooping hurriedly he lifted up the emaciated body, exerting unexpected strength, and muttered almost inaudibly, "The Rabbi! The Rabbi!"

The crowd pressed in after him. They brought water and laved Yechiel's brow and temples. Slowly his eyes opened and looked around him in bewilderment; little by little he came to his senses and began to remember all that happened. Ezriel set him in the armchair and with senile trembling hands tried to fend off the crowd that threatened to overwhelm the Rabbi. The old man actually succeeded in getting the petitioners into the anteroom and in shutting the door on them.

But Yechiel, suddenly recollecting something, was staring in terror at the floor as if an abyss had yawned before his feet. Horror-stricken, he gestured with his hand as if to ward off something that was stretching tentacles toward him. His pale face went gray as if the flesh had been consumed to ash beneath the skin. He shut his eyes and sat like a rigid pillar.

Old Ezriel, trembling like an aspen leaf, wrung his hands and stammered, "Holy Rabbi! Holy Rabbi! The people have been waiting for three days!"

In a wailing voice the Rabbi answered, "Send them home! It is written in the Psalms: 'Unto the wicked God saith, What hast thou to do to declare my statutes, or that thou shouldst take my covenant in thy mouth?' And I am wicked, for I have blasphemed and insulted God."

Old Ezriel wept bitterly.

CHAPTER IX

RECONCILIATION

OLD EZRIEL was standing at the door, twisted and bowed by
old age, grief, and incomprehension. His whole life spoke out
of his bewildered gray eyes with their inflamed lids which
seemed to be weeping tears of blood. Imploringly he stretched his
gnarled and thick-veined old hands toward the Rabbi.

Yechiel was sitting mute in his armchair at the head of the table,
his face buried in his hands and his emaciated body rocking like a
stripped bough in a gale. As he gazed at his Rabbi old Ezriel was
torn between sympathy and ecstatic devotion; his face puckered, his
whole body trembled and his legs seemed to be on the point of re-
nouncing their office; his gouty fingers plucked at his short white
beard, and he stood there apparently incapable of uttering a word,
weakly twitching his toothless gums. And yet his weeping eyes were
eloquent enough. All at once, however, his agony found vent in an
incomprehensible mumbling and stammering which, when translated
into human language, meant, "What's to happen now?"

Yechiel made no answer. He had not heard the mumbling, and
only went on rocking himself to and fro with his head propped on
his hands. His thoughts must have been infinitely far away, for his
eyes were glazed and dim like rain-swept windowpanes.

Old Ezriel tottered forward step by step till he reached the chair,
and ran his knotted fingers caressingly over Yechiel's caftan until
he touched his master's hand, on which he pressed a despairing kiss.

The Rabbi awoke from his trance, rose to his feet and stood rigid.
His body looked longer and leaner than ever as if it had been
stretched. His voice seemed to issue from his beard.

"What can I do? My eyes are blind, my strength is gone."

"R-r-r-r," mouthed the old man, which, being interpreted, meant,
"Holy Rabbi!"

"I am no longer that, Ezriel," said Yechiel to his servant in a
beseeching voice, as if he were begging his life from a bandit. "A
Rabbi is one who binds the hearts of men to the Lord of the Universe.

But how can I do that, when I am myself severed from all connection with Him, like a leaf blown from a tree?"

"R-r-r-r," protested Ezriel. His eyelids, looking as if they had been chiseled, seemed to form the words his lips refused. He never stopped stroking the sleeve of Yechiel's ancient caftan, which was green with age.

"What can I do?" Yechiel looked into the old man's eyes as if they were the eyes of a dumb animal, and felt a spasm of sorrow both for Ezriel and himself.

"What do you want me to do? You can see for yourself. . . ."

Ezriel muttered "R-r-r-r" and indicated the door, from behind which came the muffled voices and movements of the waiting petitioners, who had filled the house for days expecting to see the Rabbi.

"Send them home!" implored Yechiel.

Ezriel's toothless gums mumbled some syllables which meant, "They won't go."

The Rabbi strode hastily to the door, hearing the movement of the crowd as the murmur of many waters. But at the door he stopped, pressed his face to the wood and clutched with both hands at the lintel; he stood like that motionless for a long time. With reverent awe Ezriel kept his distance, his knees shaking, in a frenzy of fear and hope: he covered his eyes as best he could with his knotty and recalcitrant fingers; his small figure shrank visibly.

At long last Yechiel opened the door. Imploring arms and faces stretched toward him, and the warmth of the throng waiting in the anteroom steamed up to him like a vapor. For a moment there was a breathless silence in which every noise died away, but the sighs and groans soon began to rise again and there were cries of "Holy Rabbi!" A few voices bade the others hush, and presently a silence fell that was like a hush in the synagogue.

"My dear children, I cannot help you. Go home in peace, and may our dear Father in Heaven succor you in your need."

"Holy Rabbi!"

Yechiel was engulfed in a wave of clutching arms: an iron wall of human bodies, an impassable barrier of men's beards and women's headcloths ringed him round. Men, women, faces, beseeching lips, imploring eyes, despairing voices: "Holy Rabbi! Holy Rabbi!"

Sorrow and pity gnawed at Yechiel's heart. He felt that he too was one of the despairing, crying "Holy Rabbi!" His white face glimmered above the surrounding black mass and he stretched out his own arms toward the others. But they flung themselves on his hands as if on a healing spring; they struggled with each other to touch him. And suddenly the Rabbi was overcome by a desire to escape from this press of people. With fists and elbows he tried to make a breach in the living wall around him, but in vain.

"Holy Rabbi, help us!"

"I can't, I can't do it...." he cried.

The throng of people flinched, horror stricken, and for a moment or two stood in amazed silence, exchanging furtive glances. Yechiel tried to exploit the sudden stillness by forcing a way through to the door, but all at once the mob recovered from its shock of dismay and began to storm the Rabbi again. Once more a wave of bodies broke upon him.

"Holy Rabbi! What do you mean? You *can't* help us? Alas for us!"

"Ezriel! Ezriel!" cried Yechiel helplessly.

The servant's wizened little figure cut through the living wall like a sword of tempered steel; his gnarled fingers clawed at the sturdy bodies and jerked them aside, forcibly clearing a path toward his helpless master. And as a mother drags her child out of reach of the fire, so the old man dragged his Rabbi, belaboring the people right and left with his hands, his feet and his head. "Leave the Rabbi in peace!" he gasped, and the mumbled growling had its effect; he managed to get Yechiel into his room. Then he locked the door, leaned against it, and closed his crooked fingers round the bolt. So he kept watch over Yechiel, mumbling continuously, "Oh, Rabbi, Rabbi!"

The crowd fell silent, and the silence became heavier and more oppressive, bearing down on the people like a black cloud. A subdued whisper went rustling round the room, as one asked the other, "What has happened? What's the matter?"

No words were uttered in answer: a helpless gesture sufficed.

Yechiel remained locked in his room. He could hear the souls that were beating at his door—the soul of Ezriel, fluttering like a tired bird, the souls of the men and women that flocked around him like doves, sighing faintly and imploring help. But he admitted no one....

Yechiel's soul had been shaken in panic terror ever since the wicked thoughts of disbelief had settled on it like vultures. Without God Yechiel could not live, and he felt the ground giving way beneath his feet; it was as if he were hanging between heaven and earth without any air to breathe.

With all his strength, with nails and teeth he clung to his belief, as a little bird clings teetering to a twig when a storm has blown it out of its nest. In desperation he fluttered, trying to get back to the nest, but he could not find the way in. . . .

And so he stood for hours beside the Ark of the Torah, his slim hands clutching at the curtain, his emaciated and still youthful figure pressed close to it. He stretched his neck as if he were trying to reach upward and labored in his breathing as if he were climbing a steep mountainside: his eyes, covered by their tenuous eyelids, looked like two dark hollows deeply indented in the angular skull whose bones seemed to be cutting the skin: his cheeks too were hollow, like fallen-in ruins. He stood there as if turned to stone, unmoving. And his mouth was open as if flaming words were issuing from it—unheard, uncomprehended.

But what the words meant and said was expressed in his deathly pale blind face, drenched with cold sweat, and in his white hair trembling against the curtain of the Ark of the Law.

"Cast me not out from before Thy face, take not from me the spirit of Thy Holiness."

He could not even find relief in tears. Yechiel by this time was dried up with grief and longing for God. His hard fingers worked convulsively in the curtain, and in an access of devotion he buried his face in the brocade. So he would stand for hours at a time.

Every now and then a convulsive shudder ran through his whole body and a dull groan burst from his laboring breast, "I am forgotten as a dead man out of mind: I am like a broken vessel. . . ."

Then he would relapse into his tranced rigidity, as if he had fallen asleep, drowned in a sea of silence.

All at once a light of pure ecstasy shone on his countenance and he raised his arms high, standing on tiptoe, as if to grasp at something beyond his reach. The lines on his face were wreathed in an expression that was half-smiling and half-tearful, such as is evoked by an access of great joy. The whole of man's existence on earth, stripped of irrelevances, lay before him in all its littleness, like a child's map; he could examine it and comprehend it at a glance. He could see all the ramifications of its paths, the windings of its labyrinths. And it was in a mere blind corner, overgrown with brushwood, that he had been trapped for a moment into thinking that eternity went no farther! During the brief span of his earthly life, man, the child of Heaven, gets lost too often in the maze of the labyrinth, and forgets who he is, and refers all his thoughts and feelings to the temporary environment in which he is caught. Because his whole existence on earth is made up of needs and imperfections he attributes petty meanness and imperfection to everything that happens. But if he can throw his earthly ballast aside like an old sack, if he can begin like a spider to spin gossamer threads from the great Selfhood within him and climb upward by means of them, he perceives the greatness of Being, of perfect and flawless Being. Step by step he is led upward, from fear to love and from love to oneness. And when he has achieved that height he finds himself lifted into eternal joy, the joy that springs from completion.

When Yechiel felt himself in contact with the affirmations of Being, when he mounted into the realm of infinite joy, the whole of life became clear and comprehensible to him, and even earthly existence took on its own value, becoming a link in the chain, a bridge leading from one eternity to another.

In earthly existence the soul remains invisible. And yet we apprehend a man's soul in his deeds, which make visible the content of his soul. Thus a man can also ennoble his soul by the deeds he does; he can enrich it through his personality and bring it to a higher development. That is the true purpose of man's life on earth, to enrich his soul and bring it back to the throne of God's Majesty more noble and beautiful than when he received it. And therefore the Lord of the Universe had endowed man with the gift of free will, as it is written: "All things come from God saving only the fear of God." For the fear of God is the beginning of love for God. Man is to come of his own free will to God, so that he may become a personality and radiate a nobility of his own.

"What is man, that thou art mindful of him?... Thou hast made him a little lower than the angels," says the Scripture. For by his own will, the gift of God, every man can reach the highest rung of the ladder. And Thou, O God, hast granted him a powerful helper in this life; Thou hast planted in him a part of Thyself, his soul, which is forever joined to Thee. Thou hast made him in Thine own image so that he may never forget his divine origin. Thou hast given him a heart and a mind so that he may feel and discriminate between good and evil. And Thou hast created evil in order that man may combat it. For that is why he is set on earth, to redeem what is evil; to perfect what is imperfect...."

In this hour of grace Yechiel's eyes were opened and he saw his error.

"Who am I and what am I that I should dare to think of understanding the ways of the Lord?" he cried in horror. "That was to shake myself free from the yoke of God's sovereignty! Have I made terms with God that He should bring his works within the compass of my understanding? And what if He does not? God is to be feared, not understood!"

Yechiel recognized that he had fallen into great error. He had not been far from desiring to pry into the works of God. Fear of himself seized upon him; he called a halt and began to reflect on what he had done. In the hour of grace God had opened his eyes and he saw his way clear.

Hesitatingly he approached the Ark and with a deep reverence prayed.

"Lord of the World, my eyes are troubled, my heart is hardened, because I stood before Thee in pride and conceit of myself. Have mercy on me, for I have no one beside Thee. My roots are loosened from this world and I am bound to Thee alone. I am full of sin as a grave is full of worms. Open my eyes and my heart that I may repair my faults and venture once more to look on Thy face—for without Thee I can no longer live. . . ."

Trembling he stood before the Ark. Soul and body were now united in oneness and filled with a single yearning desire: to perceive a sign that his words had been heard. He sank wholly into himself, concentrating all his newly awakened forces on the one task. And he heard a voice within him that spoke clearly:

"Since thou didst show no mercy and didst send one of My creatures naked and unprepared from the world, without time to repent, thus robbing her of both this world and the world to come—"

"Then I am nothing but a murderer, who sent a living soul from the world! Let Thy Law be fulfilled: a life for a life!"

At that moment he felt as if he were standing stripped with nothing but his soul in his hand, for he had given up his life to God.

Once more his heart perceived the voice:

"That is too little! The Courts of Heaven have decreed that since thou hast forced a Jewish soul unprepared out of this world thy lot and portion in the world to come shall be taken from thee and given to her."

These words struck him down almost to the ground. He bowed his head and spoke:

"Thou art just, and Thy verdict is just."

But his heart was filled with joy.

"Even that is good! From this day, O Lord, I shall serve Thee without hope of reward, for Thy Name's sake alone!"

He was still lost in amazement over the great happiness that filled his heart because of this sacrifice, when the inner voice made itself heard again:

"Thou hast won Me over, my son, thy portion in the world to come is restored to thee. Thy sacrifice is accepted as an expiation. The young creature shall have her share in the next world as a return for her life!"

In exultation Yechiel cried:

"Thy grace hath raised me up, it is the comfort of my poverty!" and he wept tears of joy.

The next day he set aside as a day of repentance from the morning hours, and neither ate nor drank. In order to impress the fear of God rightly on himself he spent many hours reading moral books such as simple people read, in which Hell is described in all its frightfulness with every detail of the torments it contains.

In the evening, before prayer, he sent for Reb Nachman, the attendant of the large synagogue in the town, a sturdy man whose office it was on the eve of the Day of Atonement to chastise every Jew in the congregation with the prescribed nine-and-thirty lashes. Reb Nachman paused in the doorway and gazed sympathetically at Yechiel's white face which bore all the marks of suffering.

"Why has the Rabbi sent for me?"

"Have you a stout belt, Reb Nachman? There's a servant needing castigation for having insulted his master and run away from him."

Reb Nachman divined what the words implied and turned pale. He replied deprecatingly, "The Scripture forbids us to deliver any servant into the hand of his master."

But Yechiel smiled and returned, "This is a servant who once told his master: 'I will not go out free, I love my master and his house.' "

The attendant, now as pale as the Rabbi himself, sighed and said, "Where is the man? I see no servant here."

"I am the man, Reb Nachman; take your belt."

Reb Yechiel the Rabbi laid himself prone along the threshold, according to the custom on the Day of Atonement, and the Temple attendant flicked him lightly on the back nine-and-thirty times, while he made confession of his sins and beat himself on the breast. The Reb Nachman helped him up, set him comfortably in the armchair and quitted the room hastily to hide his tears.

It was with a lighter heart that the Rabbi performed his evening devotions. He felt that God had literally renewed his spirit. And when Ezriel arrived with the bowl of hot milk to break his fast, Yechiel was sitting wiping his eyes with his handkerchief, exactly like a child who has been comforted after a beating. The old man took the liberty of mumbling in his beard a few syllables which stood for: "There's been enough of this!"

"Ezriel, it's good to be a sinner if only for the joy of repenting!" said the Rabbi with a disarming smile.

CHAPTER X

SNOW-WHITE GEESE

THE Rabbi Reb Yechiel longed to return to the source of his being. Intensely he longed to be free of the flesh in which life had caged him, to enter into eternal rest, stripped of all passion and desire, beneath the sheltering wings of God's majesty.

It was not death he feared but life. What man can go surety for himself? And Reb Yechiel the Rabbi was by no means sure of himself.

True, it is written that one hour of this life spent in doing good works is better than an eternity in the next world, and yet the Rabbi could not deny that recently a great longing for the next world had overcome him.

In vain he asked himself, "What makes you so certain, Yechiel, that Heaven is waiting for you? Have you forgotten that there is first a Day of Judgment? Aren't you likely to shrivel up before the judgment seat of God?" He could not affright himself even by thoughts of Hell.

From childhood he had been accustomed to regard this world as a temporary habitation in which man is only provisionally lodged while he prepares himself for his eternal home. Heaven to Yechiel was not only the seat of eternal bliss and truth, it was also the home of all that had made his life on earth sweet, all that was dear and good and beautiful; it was the dwelling place of his mother, of his wife Reisel, for whom he longed with constant solicitude, of the teachers who had guided him on his way, and of his father. And so Heaven was not only a spiritual home for Yechiel; it had become the home of his personal self.

He felt himself ripe to fall from the tree. In these last days he had disciplined his body severely, fasting almost continuously, taking ritual immersions and praying from morning till night. And more and more frequently he was haunted by visions and tranced in illimitable joy. Over and over again he meditated on the verses: "My soul longeth, yea, even fainteth for the courts of the Lord: my heart and my flesh crieth out for the living God. Yea, the sparrow hath found an house, and the swallow a nest for herself, where she may lay her young, even thine altars, O Lord of hosts, my King, and my God."

"Why are you so insatiable?" he asked himself in gentle reproach. "Here you are, ready to gobble up world after world, like a ravening beast of prey! Is it not enough for you to be a plain Jew and to be assured of God's eternal rest? What else are you craving for? Are there any bounds to your greed, Yechiel?"

One morning he was taking his customary walk in the open with his old servant Ezriel, and he saw the world spread out before his eyes, broad fields rolling far into the distance. It was autumn and the grain had been carried home and the fruits picked from the orchards. Exhausted by labor the fallow fields were lying like weary cattle after a hard day's work, all their energy spent in the service of their masters, desiring nothing but rest. Great troughs could be seen in the ground where the potatoes had been lifted that had been bedded in the soil for the winter: stacks of turnips were piled high in other fields. And the weary earth was furrowed and wrinkled like an old mother that had wrung from her withered breasts the last drop of nourishment for her children. The sight of the earth made the Rabbi feel humble and he said to Ezriel, "See how the earth fulfills God's commandment to nourish mankind! How tired and exhausted she is, poor thing! She serves the Lord dumbly, asking for no reward, for no share in Heaven! And I, sinner that I am, spend my time in thinking of nothing but the rewards I am to get in Heaven!"

He turned to the fields and cried, "Good morning, dear earth! How good you are, how lovely in the zeal with which you serve the Lord's will! If only Yechiel were half so good a servant of God as you are!"

Ever since Yechiel had been without a wife—which the higher authorities cast up to him as a reproach—he had begged God for the same boon that his own father had desired: the boon of being turned into an old man. And God had granted his desire; he was now really an old man.

The Cabbalah tells us that Woman is related to the visible glory of God. For the righteous man is irradiated by God's glory only when he is rightly mated. Without a wife no man is a complete person; the complete person is not a mere individual but a married couple, as the Scripture says: "Male *and* female created he them." Yet when the righteous man lives alone, without a woman, then the glory of God, the Shechinah, is joined to him and abides with him to keep him from loneliness and the persecution of evil thoughts.

Yechiel felt the Holy Spirit descending upon him to comfort him whenever he felt forlorn. Many a time he fancied he could hear the soft beating of doves' wings over his head, or sweet strains of music. By night, at the time of the midnight prayer, in the hours of grace when the soul pours out its yearning for the holiness of Israel, he was often seized by a rapture so sweet and thrilling that his senses reeled, while an exquisite fragrance pervaded the air, and all the odors of Paradise seemed to have descended upon him. These were the moments when he heard the rustling of pinions and caught a fleeting glimpse of a shy, delicate Presence robed in dark veils which seemed to take him lovingly under its wings.

Recently the Presence had visited him more and more often, and was become curiously familiar. And he thought it was trying to tell him something, to make some announcement. He knew what the message was: it had come to take him home to his Father. . . .

Yechiel felt himself growing feebler from day to day. He could depend upon his body, which was subject to its master, the soul, but he could depend on it only up to a point, for in spite of all submissiveness the body had maintained a certain independence. However severely Yechiel mortified it by long fasting, night watching, the coarse sackcloth he wore next his skin, he could not wholly subdue it. He was already so lean that all his bones could be counted, and when he ate or drank his bite and sup was visible beneath the skin as it went down his throat. And yet his sinewy limbs were strong enough for any effort, and he had still a youthful elasticity and was an excellent walker; he remained unwearied even after miles of wandering on foot. His arms, too, were strong, and he had every opportunity to display their strength when he carried heavy bundles of wood by night to the huts of the poor.

This physical toughness was the result of his earlier hard life, when he had to carry packs round the villages and spent whole days in the open air. Yet the many ritual immersions which he had prescribed for himself had begun to undermine his physical strength in these cold autumn nights, and were to undo him at the last.

From the far-off times of the Essenes, from the hot sandbanks of the river Jordan and the warm waters of Gennesaret, the Jews by the cold northern Vistula had taken over a ritual of ceremonial immersion. The idea of impurity crops up in countless forms among the ceremonies with which pious custom surrounds the individual, not only the idea of actual uncleanness, but even more strongly that of impurity in the spiritual realm. Every prayer, every act of service to God must always be preceded by the ceremony of purification by water. But in the Jewish communities of Yechiel's country the clear blue waters of Gennesaret were replaced by a deep trench filled with water, called the Mikvah. Into this trench Yechiel prepared to dip himself.

He roused his faithful servant who was keeping watch before the door and stealing forty winks over the book open on his knee. Old Reb Ezriel lit the lantern and escorted his master to the Mikvah. Fifteen steps led down to the surface of the water. The gray-headed servant began to descend together with the Rabbi, but in the middle of the steps Yechiel halted and announced that he needed no company, it disturbed him in his worship if Ezriel were standing by with the lantern, he preferred to be left alone so that he could the better concentrate his thoughts. And then in the cold of that September night he went down into the water up to his neck. Twenty-six times he dipped himself under, the numerical sum of the letters making up Jehovah's name, and at every immersion he meditated upon the magic name of some angel.

Suddenly he felt his head spin. A succession of pictures went racing over his field of vision: he was no longer in the Mikvah, he was standing in a green meadow at the height of summer with tall green dewy grass around him.

He could see a far, far distance—it was marvelous that the human eye should have so wide a range! And in the background a little stream was babbling along, with water as blue and clear as if it consisted of tears wept by grieving people everywhere. But who was that standing beside the brook? It was indeed Reisel! She was actually standing in the water behind the tall willow bushes, surrounded by her geese, which were of a dazzling white such as Yechiel had never seen: he never knew that such a white color could exist. The Biblical metaphor "white as new-washed wool" came into his mind.

He wanted to start forward, to reach Reisel and her snowy geese, but he could not manage a step. In sudden terror he feared that he was drowning; the world reeled before his eyes. He called out "Ezriel! Ezriel!"

He need not have called, for Ezriel was still close at hand, in disobedience to his master's strict command. He had not left the steps at all, but had merely concealed himself behind a projection of the masonry and hidden his lantern under his cloak; he had never taken his eyes off his master in the water, for he knew well enough that the Rabbi was not feeling strong. Although he was much older than Yechiel he took a flying leap into the water like a youngster, caftan and all, lifted up his master and carried him bodily out of the Mikvah. Once at the top of the steps he rapidly dressed the shivering man.

The Rabbi was breathing deeply; his face glowed, his eyes wide open and radiant—at least, so it seemed to Ezriel—with ineffable joy for which there was no evident reason.

Only later, after Ezriel had got him back home, did he say, "Ezriel, God willing, we'll be granted a good year when the Day of Atonement comes, and all our sins will be forgiven us—I've had a certain sign from God."

In that same night Yechiel fell seriously ill.

CHAPTER XI

DANCE OF DEATH

THROUGH the length and breadth of the country the news ran that the Psalm Jew had suddenly fallen ill, and that both worlds were fighting for him. On the next Sabbath, the Sabbath of repentance between New Year's Day and the Day of Atonement, a very strange company of men from a distant region came to visit the invalid.

It was quite usual for wandering strangers to foregather over the Sabbath at the Psalm Jew's house, and not a few of them were queer figures about whom all kinds of tales were told.

The tailor of Zachlin came often, a short, bent little man, about whom little was known, yet who was held in high esteem. When he had first appeared at the Rabbi's door, the Rabbi had sent for him, seated him at the table by his side, and shown him great honor. And whenever he returned the Rabbi shut himself in a room with him and talked with him for hours at a time. It was said of the little tailor that he was one of the Thirty-Six Righteous Men by whose merit the whole world stands. In his house in Zachlin a light burned in his window all night long; Elijah the Prophet came to him in the thick of night and they studied together the mysteries of the Torah. But by day he was an ordinary tailor who made over clothes for poor Jewish children.

There was one man who had appeared only once, but the manner of his arrival was so extraordinary that it had struck the imagination of the Chassidim with peculiar force. On a certain day the Rabbi had asked for his Sabbath caftan and summoned Ezriel to accompany him on a walk along the main road. As Ezriel later told the story, they were proceeding along the highway when they saw a cloud of dust approaching in which moved a one-legged man on a wooden pin, a man with a powerful lionlike head and a great coal-black beard. Both his eyes and his beard reminded one of dark flames.

"I never saw such eyes in my life," said Ezriel, "and his eyebrows hung over them like thunderclouds. Although he had a wooden leg he was coming along at a great pace, striding as fast as if he had wings or as if a stormwind were behind him. When the Rabbi saw him striding along in the distance he bade me wait behind and went on alone to meet him. And then with my own eyes I saw our holy Rabbi saluting the man with reverence and bowing down before him. I trembled all over, for I knew at once that this could be no ordinary meeting. Then the three of us came back to the town, but the man with the wooden leg was always ahead of us, we could hardly keep up with him. The Rabbi put him up in his own house, but the stranger stayed only for one night. At supper the Rabbi made me light all the candles as if it were Sabbath, and ordered Sabbath dishes for the table, although it was only Wednesday. And with these eyes I saw the Rabbi waiting on the stranger at the table, the Rabbi himself! And while he did so his eyes and his face were shining with joy. But the stranger with the lion head and the wooden leg came only that one time and never again."

Most of the Rabbi's guests and dependents were from the poorest classes: he had always been a good friend of wandering strangers and nobody was much surprised to find the Psalm Jew's hut crammed with poor wretches. But on this Sabbath great amazement prevailed in the town, for never had such an array of strange people been seen. Some were familiar, like the tailor of Zachlin; a few others had been there before; most of them, whom no one knew, appeared for the first time.

Just before the third Sabbath meal, to the astonishment of the whole congregation, the Rabbi took a decided turn for the better. He called Ezriel and had himself dressed in his white satin caftan, insisting that he was going to preside over the Third Meal in person, sitting at table with his guests.

The synagogue on this day was packed to bursting. The whole town was there. Everybody was downcast and fearful. Nobody knew what might happen, and all felt as if they were orphaned already; the anxious question ran from one to the other: "Who is to look after us if he leaves us?" Besides, there was such a remarkable array of strangers, obviously no ordinary men: one could suppose that they belonged to the Secret Council of the Thirty-Six Righteous; at any rate their presence was certainly no accident, and gave rise to forebodings.

So all through that Sabbath of Repentance psalms had been chanted continuously for the Rabbi's welfare, and the women pressed up to the windows weeping, although they had been warned that it was a sin to sorrow on the Sabbath and that the Rabbi was vexed at their behavior.

No warning had any effect, for all were convinced that the Psalm Jew had only a few more hours to live.

In the middle of this dejection the news spread like wildfire that the Rabbi was preparing to come out and be present at the Third Meal. The amazement was great—what was going to happen next? The tables, so it was reported, were to be spread in the synagogue, as on high feast days, not in the Rabbi's room as usual. And there was not enough food to go round the whole congregation. So the inhabitants of the town hastily brought out all they had left of their Sabbath dishes, the pious women routed out whatever eatables they could find, for the congregation was enormously augmented.

It was already dusk and everybody was sitting down at the tables when the sick Rabbi was borne into the synagogue by two men. He was laid among cushions on his own armchair; his face was shining so that it could be seen from the farthest corner of the dark room, and his white Sabbath caftan looked dazzling in the dimness. The Rabbi ordered the remarkable strangers to be placed beside him, together with the tailor of Zachlin, and some cripples and poor hand workers, then he bade his people find and set at his right hand a humble little cobbler who was a familiar figure at the annual fairs and had come into the synagogue unremarked by any one until this moment.

The general amazement grew when the Rabbi, after the white bread and the fish had been distributed, commanded Mottye the bath attendant to sing the Sabbath grace, "Sanctify our meal...." When the song had died away some one beat his hand on the table and an uncanny silence of expectancy fell on the congregation. The Rabbi then began to expound the Law. That roused more astonishment, for everybody knew how frail he was and had not thought ever to hear him speak again. And this time his exposition was not brief and concise as usual; he gave a long and continuous sermon, though sheer weakness made him pause now and then. And feeble as his voice was from illness, it could be heard through the whole synagogue, for it had a touching purity of tone. A solemn hush reigned like the hush at the New Year's Feast as the Rabbi began.

"In his holy Psalms King David, may he rest in peace, says: 'I will abide in thy tabernacle for ever: I will trust in the covert of thy wings.' What meaning does this convey? Man, who was sent down to this world to sanctify and exalt it by the power and greatness of his soul— man must make the whole world a tabernacle for God, he must feel always that he is in the covert of God's wings. And how can man make the world a tabernacle for God? Through his works, and by following God's example, which he must imitate. Even as God sanctifies Heaven by His purity and His Oneness, so must man sanctify the earth by his purity and singleness of heart. For he is set on earth as God's representative, to exalt it and bring it nearer to Heaven.

"And how are you to exalt this earth? Through living holy lives upon it. Thus your table is transformed into an altar, your meal into a sacrifice, your bed into Jacob's ladder.

"Let your first commandment be: 'Love thy neighbor as thyself'; so that you can pray for one another. For prayers are only acceptable when one prays for others, not for oneself.

"Avoid evilspeaking and scandal; abuse nobody, abuse no human being nor the smallest of God's creatures, not even a blade of grass or a twig! For when you abuse God's creatures you abuse their Creator Himself.

"Know that each thing, even the smallest in creation, possesses a soul—that is the intention of the Lord of the Universe Who made it. And do not imagine that each thing is unaware of its soul! Oh, it knows well enough! When a thing is employed by man for a good purpose it rejoices, but when it is used to further a sinful act it is pained and sorrowful. Is it not written that there are plants which shrink and feel pain whenever they are touched by an impure hand?

"Seek not to pry into God's ways. King David himself, may he rest in peace, said: 'The heaven, even the heavens, are the Lord's: but the earth hath he given to the children of men.' Man has enough to do on earth without trying to interfere in Heaven. God is not to be inquired into but to be loved; we should be consumed by our love for Him; and it is not by inquiring into His way that we shall be joined to Him, but only by love, by humbling our hearts before Him and leading a serene and holy life.

"Let the Lord bear your burdens, and He will help you in your need. Cast your bread upon the waters, and be not men of little faith.

"Be humble in your spirit, our teachers tell us. And yet you must not misprize yourselves; self-contempt is a device of the devil, a path as slippery as a snake. To despise oneself is to despise the world. Let your guiding principle be the words of that holy man, Hillel: 'Without me there is nothing.' Say to yourselves that the fate of the world hangs in the balance and that you and the deeds you do may turn the scale.

"God has expressly commanded us to love each individual not only mankind in general, for in the words, Love thy neighbor as thyself, it is each single human being that is meant.

"Do not pray for afflictions, but when they come do not evade them. Endure them quietly so that no one remarks your suffering—afflictions are a private concern between God and yourself and should not be published abroad.

"Many ways lead to God, but the shortest and nearest way lies through His children. For when one cannot gain access to the King one tries to win the ear of the King's son. And God's majesty dwells in all mankind, in every man who seeks Him. Therefore you must be careful to respect mankind. Every man who seeks God should be your brother, according to the words of the holy Rabbi Mair: 'A non-Jew who devotes his life to seeking God should be revered as if he were a high priest!'

"Give no helping hand to evil, not even if you think to achieve good thereby. For know that good never comes of evil.

"Overthrow nothing, that you may not yourselves be overthrown. For he that overthrows anything falls with it.

"Keep the Sabbath day and sanctify it, for it is the day of your soul, of your eternal life; and as your Sabbath is on earth so will your eternal Sabbath be with your Father in Heaven.

"Humble your hearts before the Lord! Fear Him in love, not in terror. May your eyes remain clear and your hearts open so that you recognize how righteous He is in all His ways. Then you will see and understand clearly, for only those who cling to God can see the clear path that runs from earth to Heaven, only those who humble their wills to His, who order their purposes to His. Remember the words of King David: 'O send out thy light and thy truth: let them lead me: let them bring me unto thy holy hill and to thy tabernacles.'"

Deep darkness now filled the synagogue: everything was swallowed up in night, except that in the impenetrable blackness a wavering, formless mass was perceptible, looming around a point of dim whiteness that sent a vibration of light through the gloom. Suddenly a voice rang through the darkness, singing in short, beseeching and yet hopeful phrases.

"The Lord is my shepherd: I shall not want. . . ."

Again silence fell, and the gloom seemed to have become more palpable. The walls and windows were no longer visible; nothing was perceptible save the black formless mass that closed in more and more on the slowly fading white gleam. Once more in the darkness the Rabbi's voice was heard.

"My soul thirsteth for God, for the living God: when shall I come and appear before God?"

His words were echoed by sighs from every side. But in the middle of the anxious silence a triumphant song arose, with a rhythm more like a military marching song than a religious chant, and soon it was ringing through the room like a fanfare of trumpets. The queer company of strangers had started it, and they kept it mounting and exulting in spite of all attempts to hush it by the rest of the congregation, who had no idea what was happening and in their bewilderment called for silence. The next occurrence was a noise of benches being pushed aside, and some men, taking each other by the shoulders, began to dance in time to the rhythm and to stamp on the floor with their feet. Among them there must have been a man with a wooden leg, for the sound of his wooden pin striking the stone flags was clearly to be heard.

And then a strange thing happened. The Rabbi, sunk in his cushions, looking like a corpse in his white caftan and being held up by a guard of Chassidim, was suddenly seized upon by the dancing strangers, pulled to his feet and drawn into their circle. Screams arose, shrieks of "Don't touch him! What are you doing?" and Ezriel rushed up to protect his master, but was flung ruthlessly aside by a powerful hand. Yechiel was lolling helplessly on the shoulders of two of the men who bore him round with them. The tempo of the song and of the dance now slowed down, and the strains were beseeching rather than triumphant. The Rabbi, held up by the linked arms of the dancers, looked like a mummy with his white robe and deathly white countenance; his eyes were shut and their dark hollows looked more cavernous than ever in the gloom. His parchment-white face was set like a mask, only the great fur cap on his head nodded to and fro. And so the strange dancers dragged the Rabbi, hanging strengthlessly on their arms, little by little, almost imperceptibly, from the table right up to the Ark of the Torah. There the swaying dance stopped, the song swelled louder and the voices literally yelled:

"A song of degrees of David: I was glad when they said unto me, Let us go into the house of the Lord."

The Rabbi was seen to bow three times before the Ark, and his lips opened to join in the singing but no sound escaped them.

Half-suppressed cries and wails arose from the congregation: "Holy Rabbi, who is to look after us if you leave us?"

That brought the dazed crowd to its senses. Some men ventured to call out, "Let him go! Let him go!"

Ezriel once more pushed to the front, mumbling curses and heaving out of his way all who hindered him; he seemed to have superhuman strength and reached the Rabbi at last. Quickly he took his master in his arms and bore him back to his sickbed.

CHAPTER XII

REACHING THE GOAL

THE Day of Atonement had arrived. Yechiel lay in bed in his tunic and prayer shawl, with the door leading into the synagogue standing open so that he might listen to the service. His strength was so far gone that he could no longer sit up; whenever he made the attempt he collapsed among the pillows. But when it was time for the prayer to begin which the High Priest once made in the Holy of Holies in the Temple at Jerusalem on the Day of Atonement, Yechiel raised himself up with superhuman strength, called Ezriel and had himself washed and robed. As if by a miracle his strength seemed to be renewed.

He sent a message to the cantor that the prayer was not to begin until he, Yechiel, gave the sign that he was ready. Thereupon he bade Ezriel bring out the sack in which he had so often carried the Jews' petitions to the mercy seat. And then, begging everybody, including Ezriel, to leave the room, he gave the sign for the prayer to begin.

The fever was burning up fiercely, fed by the last flicker of his conscious energy. The heat in his frail body could be felt even through his clothing, and the soles of his feet were scorching, so that he was not aware of treading the floor. But the great longing he had to serve the Lord for the last time and to be in contact with Him through prayer gave him the strength to cling to the praying desk and stand upright. Soon, however, the praying desk became a soaring tongue of flame that carried him through the air: the fever burning in him had fused away his conscious mind. Only one thought remained clear, that he must not let go the sack; it was a precious burden that had been entrusted to him and for which he was responsible. So awareness and blankness contended in him like summer and winter in an autumn storm; and the curious thing was that in spite of the heat consuming him he was shivering with cold as if he were in an icy wind.

Suddenly he found himself crossing a wide plain of snow. He was carrying a pack on his shoulders; his mother was lying ill at home and he was returning to her with a pack laden with food. The blizzard was piercing him to the marrow and blowing the very clothes from his body; his cap had already gone. Fighting against the wind he struggled on, plowing his way through snow and squalls. But the snow turned into enormous bits of sky beneath his feet, and from these came terrible blasts and hurricanes with a wild piping and howling. The illimitable reserves of snow laid up in the sky were laid bare before his eyes—he actually saw them, and they looked like great tongues of frozen fire; the snow was scorching to the touch like fire.

"But how can fire be frozen?" the question darted through his mind, and with that he woke from his stupor. Through the open door he heard the cantor's voice intoning:

"... and the priests and the children of Israel stood in the court of the Temple. And when they heard the ineffable Name of God uttered in purity and holiness from the mouth of the High Priest they bowed themselves with their faces to the ground and blessed the Lord, saying, 'Praised be the honor of His kingdom forever and ever.'"

Not until then did Yechiel fully realize where he was; of course he was worshiping God in the Temple at Jerusalem! That was the High Priest in his white robes—and his robes were made of fragments of sky, of frozen fire, of eternal snow! And in this array he was advancing towards the Holy of Holies.

"But I must bow down too and cast myself on the ground!" thought Yechiel. He did so, but the earth was so far beneath him that he could not reach it. At length he managed to fall on his face upon the bits of broken sky, he sank down on the cold fire, the eternal snow—and it was the forecourt of the Temple, thronged with innumerable souls, just as if it were Mount Sinai where the children of Israel received the Law. "That's a good omen!" it occurred to Yechiel. "Our sins will surely be forgiven, for I can see so much snow!" And he rejoiced in his heart for the last time.

But soon the icy blasts began to pierce once more through his frame, searing him like red-hot iron. Yechiel no longer felt his limbs; he was already loosed from his physical self and soaring far and wide on the wings of thought. Yet at the same time he was still on the plain of snow, alone and forlorn; the chanting from the Temple was receding; from an enormous distance he heard the faint echo of a voice saying "... and the priests and the people...." Now he was utterly alone. And again he was worried about his pack. "Where's the sack? How can I go home to my mother without it? For it's filled with the petitions of the Jews; they entrusted it to me to take home to my mother...."

He was determined not to let the tempests rend it from his grasp, he was resolved to fight to the last and to spend all his strength in bringing his burden to its appointed goal.

The blasts redoubled their violence. A mighty whirlwind of snow came billowing to engulf him, and his strength was ebbing. Unable to stir he lay prone in the snow. The storms howled round him like a pack of wolves, ready to devour him—and he had such a long way to go! "O Lord, where is my help to come from?" Yechiel turned despairing eyes this way and that. A figure was looming through the raging snowstorm; some one was coming nearer. Who was it? His eyes were dim; he could not distinguish.... A shape, veiled in black, was gliding toward him over the white surface, so lightly that its feet barely touched the snow. A familiar shape; he had seen it before: "Is it not Matronitha, of whom the Zohar says that she leads the souls of the righteous home to the Father? I must bow down before her!" and with that he sank down and down....

Someone took him by the hand, raised him up, and led him away.

They found him lying on his face before the Ark, his hand convulsively clutching the sack. His soul had not yet left the body, and he was exerting all his strength to keep from dying before the final prayer of the Day of Atonement should be pronounced, for he wanted to take the petitions of his people with him.

They laid him down on his couch. His face was tranquil and radiant, his great eyes were wide open. An unearthly serenity clothed him; there were no signs of a death struggle; he seemed to be gazing into a distant heaven. Neither sorrow nor joy could be read on his countenance, nothing but great purity and wondering seriousness. So he lay until the final prayer was spoken.

Then at last his death struggle began. At once some of the strangers made a close ring round his couch and kept everybody off. In their tunics and prayer shawls they joined with the cantor in the next room in summoning to the remembrance of the dying man the Oneness of God: "He is one and incomprehensible. He is endless, and there is no end to his end. He is the first of all created things, and there is no beginning to His beginning."

As darkness began to fall they cried once: "Hear, O Israel, Adonai our God, Adonai is One." Then they cried three times: "Praised be the honor of His kingdom forever and ever"; then seven times, "Adonai is God"; finally, once only, "Adonai is King, Adonai was King, Adonai shall be King forevermore."

When the first star was visible in the sky the great flourish was blown on a ram's horn as a sign and a memorial that Abraham, Isaac, and Jacob had been shepherds, as a sign and a memorial that Abraham had brought his only son Isaac as a sacrifice to God, as a sign and a memorial of that great Day when the anointed of the Lord, the Messiah, should arise to redeem the world and the dead should be resurrected into eternal life.

The Day of Atonement was over and Reb Yechiel the Psalm Jew was no more. And he was spoken of as men once spoke of Enoch: "He was not, for God took him."